A Very Merry Christmas

LORI FOSTER
GEMMA BRUCE
JANICE MAYNARD

BRAVA

KENSINGTON PUBLISHING CORP.
http://www.kensingtonbooks.com

BRAVA BOOKS are published by

Kensington Publishing Corp.
850 Third Avenue
New York, NY 10022

All Kensington titles, imprints and distributed lines are available at special quantity discounts for bulk purchases for sales
promotion, premiums, fund-raising, educational or institutional
use.

Special book excerpts or customized printings can also be created to fit specific needs. For details, write or phone the office
of the Kensington Special Sales Manager: Kensington Publishing
Corp., 850 Third Avenue, New York, NY 10022. Attn. Special
Sales Department. Phone: 1-800-221-2647.

Brava and the B logo Reg. U.S. Pat. & TM Off.

ISBN-13: 978-0-7582-1541-3
ISBN-10: 0-7582-1541-X

First Trade Paperback Printing: October 2006
First Mass Market Paperback Printing: October 2007
10 9 8 7 6 5 4 3 2

Printed in the United States of America

CONTENTS

Do You Hear What I Hear

Lori Foster

One

Osbourne Decker had no sooner pulled his truck into the frozen, snow-covered parking lot to start his night shift than his pager went off. Typical SWAT team biz—a barricade with three subjects holding two hostages. He'd grabbed his gear, run into the station to change so he could respond directly to the scene, and from that point on, the night had been nonstop. Being SWAT meant when the pager went off, so did the team.

After a lot of hours in the blustery cold that stretched his patience thin, they resolved the hostage situation without a single casualty. And just in time for his shift to end. He couldn't wait to get home and grab some sleep.

He'd just changed back into his jeans, T-shirt, and flannel shirt when Lucius Ryder, a friend and sergeant with the team, strolled up to him. Osbourne saw the way Lucius eyed him, like a lamb for the slaughter, and he wanted to groan.

He fastened his duty firearm in a concealed holster,

attached his pager and cell, grabbed his coat, and tried to slip away.

Lucius stopped him. "Got a minute, Ozzie?"

Shit, shit, *shit.* He already knew what was coming. Lucius would be on vacation for ten days—the longest vacation he'd ever taken. He'd be back in time for Christmas, but laying low until then, soaking up some private time with his new wife in Gatlinburg. But the wife was concerned about her loony toons twin sister.

And that's where Lucius wanted to involve him.

"Actually," Ozzie said, hoping to escape, "I was just about to—"

"This won't take long."

Ozzie thought about making a run for it, but Lucius would probably just chase him down, so he gave up. He dropped his duffel bag and propped a shoulder on the wall. "Okay. Shoot."

"You think Marci is hot?"

Ozzie did a double take. "Is that a trick question?"

"No, I'm serious."

Serious, and apparently not thinking straight. Marci and Lucius's wife, Bethany, were *identical* twins. No way in hell would Ozzie comment on her appearance. Hell, if he admitted he thought Marci was beyond hot to the point of scorching, well, that'd be like admitting that Lucius's wife was scorching, and his friend sure as hell wouldn't like that.

If he said no, it'd be a direct cut to Bethany.

"She's a replica of your wife, Lucius, all the way down to her toes." Ozzie shook his head. "You really want to know what I think of her?"

Struck by that observance, Lucius said, "*No.* Hell no." He glared at Ozzie in accusation, then slashed a hand in the air. "Forget I asked. I already know you're attracted to her because you went out with her a few times."

"No way, Lucius."

Lucius warmed to his subject. "I thought you two had something going on for a while there."

"No."

"You were chasing her pretty hot and heavy—"

Ozzie forgot discretion. "She's a fruitcake. Totally nuts. Hell, Lucius, she stops to talk to every squirrel in the trees."

"She does not." But Lucius didn't look certain.

"She even chats with birds." Ozzie nodded his head to convince Lucius of what he'd seen. "She gives greetings to dogs as if they greet her back."

"She's not that bad," Lucius denied, but without much conviction.

"Not that bad? I've heard her carry on complete conversations with your dog!"

Lucius shook his head. "It's not like that. Hero doesn't talk back to her. She just . . . She's an animal nut, okay? She's real empathetic to them, so she likes chatting with them."

"No shit. But she doesn't chat the way most of us do. She chats as if she knows exactly what they're saying, when anyone sane knows that they're not saying a damn thing."

Lucius paced away, but came right back. "It's an endearing trait, that's all."

Because Ozzie loved animals, he might have been inclined to agree. But crazy women turned into insane bitches when things didn't go their way, and he'd had enough of that to last him a lifetime. There was nothing more malicious, or more determined on destruction, than a woman who ignored logic. "No thanks."

"Okay, look, I'm not asking you to marry the girl."

"I'm not marrying anyone!" Just the sound of the "M" word struck terror in Ozzie's heart.

"That's what I said, damn it, and keep your voice down."

Ozzie glanced around and saw that the others were watching them, their ears perked with interest. Dicks. Oh, yeah, they all wanted to know more about Marci. None of them would hesitate to go chasing after her. In the three months that they'd all known her, more than one guy on the team had tried to get with her.

Course, none of them had yet discovered her whacky eccentricities. Then again, maybe none of them would mind.

In a more subdued tone, now infused with annoyance, Ozzie said, "Any one of them would be thrilled to do . . . whatever it is you want me to do."

"Bullshit. This is my sister-in-law we're talking about. Any of *them* would be working hard to get in her pants."

True. And it pissed Ozzie off big time, but rather than say so, he pointed out the obvious. "And you think I wouldn't be?"

Lucius's eyes narrowed. "Not if you know what's good for you."

Ozzie threw up his hands. "Great. Just friggin' great. So what the hell am I supposed to do with her, if not enjoy her?"

Disgruntled, Lucius growled, "You talk about her like she's a pinball machine."

"Right." Ozzie rolled his eyes. "With a few lights missing."

Lucius drew a deep breath to regain his aplomb.

Ozzie watched him. He really didn't want to get on his buddy's bad side. Lucius stood six feet four inches tall, and though he was a good friend with a sense of style that leaned toward raunchy T-shirts, he also took anything that had anything to do with his wife very seriously.

"Nice shirt," Ozzie commented, hoping to help Lucius along in his efforts to be calm. The shirt read: "World's Greatest" and beneath that sat a proud-looking rooster.

"Forget the shirt." Lucius glanced at his watch. "I need to get going. Bethany's waiting for me. So do we have a deal or what?"

He had to be kidding.

On an exhalation, Lucius barked, "I only want you to keep an eye on her. There've been a few strange things happening—"

"Like her talking to turtles or something?"

"Your sarcasm isn't helping," Lucius warned him. "I meant something more threatening. Marci feels like someone's been following her. She's not a woman given to melodrama—"

"That's a joke, right?"

"So her concerns also concern me," Lucius finished through gritted teeth. "And they concern my wife, who won't be able to enjoy our belated honeymoon unless we both know someone is keeping an eye on Marci. Someone I can trust not to hurt her."

"I don't hurt women."

"Exactly." Lucius glanced away. "But I was talking about her feelings, actually."

Seeing no way out, Ozzie crossed his arms over his chest and conceded. "So what's in it for me?"

"What do you want?"

"I very recently inherited a farmhouse from my granny. It needs some work—"

"Done." Lucius stuck out his hand.

Whoa. That was way too easy. "Understand, Lucius.

This is an old house. I don't want to just slap up drywall and cheap paint. I want to maintain the original design and—"

"Shake on it, damn it, so I can go."

Ozzie shook and, he had to admit, anticipation stirred within him. So he'd be seeing Marci again. Huh. He had very mixed feelings about that, but mostly he felt challenged.

Rather than release his hand, Lucius tugged him closer to whisper, "Put on your coat. You're advertising a stiffy. And, you know, I think maybe you should be wearing my shirt." Then the bastard walked away laughing.

Ozzie glanced down at the rise in his jeans. Cursing his overactive libido, especially where it concerned Marci Churchill, he turned his back so no one else in the room would notice.

He didn't have a full boner, but rather a semiboner. Though for a man of his endowments, it showed about the same.

And just because they'd discussed Marci.

How the hell was he supposed to watch over her, be close to her, and *not* touch her?

Working night shift meant that Ozzie seldom saw daylight during the winter. It was dark when he went to bed and dark when he got up. He missed the sunlight. But at least the bitter cold of December helped him keep a clear head while he pondered the ramifications of getting close to Marci again.

Oh, he saw her often enough. Bethany dragged her around all the time, and Bethany and Lucius were nauseating in their marital ecstasy. That meant whenever the team got together after work, the twins were there.

And given what the twins looked like, no doubt more than one fantasy took place in their honor. But for Ozzie, he only fantasized over one twin: the cracked one.

He saw her at picnics, at a local bar where they all hung out, at parties, and sometimes in the station, waiting for Lucius to get off work.

Marci fit right in, laughing with the men, joking, and turning down offers. Sometimes she watched him, and sometimes she pretended he wasn't in the room.

But no matter what she did, the chemistry between them was enough to choke a bear.

As Ozzie's truck cut through the snow and sludge clogging the streets, he absently took in the multitude of lights decorating houses and businesses. He liked this time of year. It was pretty. But this would be his first Christmas without Granny Decker and he already missed her so much it was nearly unbearable.

He was thinking of warm Christmas cookies, songs on the piano, and strings of popcorn, when he spotted the confusion in front of the funeral home. Lights from a police car flashed blue and red and an elderly couple, bundled in coats over pajamas, gestured with excitement.

Ozzie pulled up behind the cruiser and parked. It took him only moments to identify himself to the officer and to find out that someone had stolen a donkey from the Nativity scene erected on the funeral home's lawn.

Marci. Somehow, he just knew she was behind this. She'd probably claim the damned donkey was shy, or that he didn't like the colored lights, or God-knew-what. But Ozzie's instincts screamed, and so with a few more words to the officer, he gave up on the idea of sleep and instead headed to Marci's apartment.

Lucius used to live in the apartment across from

Marci but, thankfully, he'd recently moved out—so Ozzie didn't have to worry about Lucius finding him at Marci's door. He and Bethany had purchased a home of their own. Lucius still owned the apartment building, but he left Marci in charge of it.

Not a good idea, in Ozzie's opinion, given that Marci was a kook. But far be it for him to tell Lucius how to run his business.

When he parked out front of the building, Ozzie looked toward Marci's porch window and, sure enough, her inside lights were on. Okay, so it was seven-thirty and she was maybe getting ready for work.

Or hiding a donkey.

Ozzie slammed his truck door, trudged through the crunchy snow and ice, and went up the walk, inside, and up to Marci's door. He knocked twice.

Breathless, Marci yelled, "Just a moment!"

His body twitched. More specifically, his cock sat up and took notice of her proximity. *Damn it.*

A full minute later, Marci opened the door. A look of pleasure replaced her formal politeness. "Osbourne. What a surprise."

He stared down at her and thought, if she'd just not talk about animals, if she'd just smile at him like that, he'd be happy to ravish her for, oh . . . a few hours maybe.

When he said nothing, her smile widened, affecting him like a hot lick. She wore a soft pink chenille robe, belted tight around her tiny waist. Her small feet were bare, crossed one over the other to ward off the chill. Her baby-fine, straight brown hair had the mussed look of a woman fresh out of bed—or fresh inside from the blustery outdoors.

Shaking out of his stupor, Ozzie looked beyond her.

He saw nothing out of the ordinary in her tiny apartment, but that didn't clear her.

She took a step closer to him, staring up in what seemed like provocation to him, a heated come-on, a . . .

She tilted her head and said, "Osbourne?"

Lust tied knots in his muscles. He cleared his throat. "Busy?"

Big blue eyes blinked at him, eyes so soft, and with such thick, long lashes she didn't need makeup. "I just got out of the shower, actually." She patted back a delicate yawn. "It's early. Would you like some coffee?"

He'd like her.

Flat on her back.

Buck-naked.

His nostrils flared, but not from the scent of brewing coffee. "All right." Yet he stood there. He knew that once he stepped over the threshold, he wouldn't be able to keep his hands off her. Damn Lucius for putting him in this torturous position. And damn his weakness for wanting her. He knew, absolutely knew, that off-kilter broads not based in reality were a complete and total pain in the ass.

Yet he trembled with the need to gather her near and devour her. Marci got to him in a big way and he hated it. With most women, he enjoyed himself, and he made sure they got enjoyment, too. Mutual enjoyment, yeah, that's what he liked.

Not this insane torment and out-of-control craving. Not this trembling lust and gut-twisting need.

Fuck it.

He stepped in and demanded, "Where's the donkey?"

She twittered a laugh. "Donkey?" Giving him her

back, she sashayed into the tiny kitchenette and got out two mugs.

Spellbound, Ozzie stared at her ass. Through the chenille, he could see the perfect heart shape of that fine behind, the softness of it, the slightest jiggle. When Marci wasn't tormenting him or conversing with critters, she taught an aerobics class, and it showed in the graceful muscle tone, the feminine strength of her willowy . . .

"What donkey, Osbourne?"

Lost in fantasies, he stared at her, confused.

Her lips curved, and she prompted, "You asked me about a donkey?"

Oh, yeah. He took an aggressive stance. "There's a donkey missing from the funeral home's Nativity scene."

She raised her brows at him, then lowered them in thought. As she came back to him, carrying the coffee, she asked, "And you assume I stole him?"

"Did you?"

She offered him a mug, and he accepted. Their fingers touched, and it struck him like a jolt of red-hot electricity. The old John Henry jumped up with a hearty, *"Hello!"*

"Why would you think I did?"

The pounding of his heartbeat almost drowned out her question. "Did what?"

This time she laughed. As if speaking to a slow-witted fool, she repeated, "I'm curious, Osbourne. Why would you think I stole a donkey? I have no record for thievery. In fact, I have no criminal record at all."

He couldn't think while drowning in lust. He had to get a grip or run like a scared rabbit, and running had never appealed to him. He dragged his gaze from her and strode to the couch, seating himself in the middle.

Rather than look at her again—because that'd do him in—he sipped his coffee, then set the mug on the end table. "I think you took the donkey because you have some weird thing going on with animals."

"It's not weird."

He smelled her approach. Like a starving man, he inhaled the scent of woman, of sex, of pure, ripe temptation.

"It's a gift." Marci sat beside him, and the instant her hip brushed his, he bounded up as if she'd goosed him.

From several *safer* feet away, Ozzie turned on her. "Do you have the stubborn ass or not?"

Again, she seemed to ponder it. "What type of donkey are we talking about?"

"What *type?*" He frowned at her. "What the hell does that—"

Her eyes locked with his, she set aside her own coffee and rose from the sofa. As she stalked toward him, he went mute.

Horny and mute.

No one stalked like Marci Churchill, with that particular enticing gait.

"Marci," he warned, and he really, really meant it.

"Is it a miniature Mediterranean, a standard, large standard, or—"

"I have no friggin' idea. There really are different types?" He shook his head. "Who cares?" She drew nearer, and he felt himself sinking deep. "The important thing is that the donkey is missing."

"Donkeys aren't really stubborn, you know. They're just more laid-back and self-preserving in nature than many animals."

Self-preserving? Why did she always say the most peculiar things? "What does that mean?"

Her gaze drifted over his body, from his booted feet to his drawn eyebrows. "They prefer to do what is good for the donkey, which isn't always what the human thinks is best, especially when it comes to getting wet feet."

Aha. Eyes narrowing, Ozzie asked, "Wet, as in standing in snow?" Is that why she stole the donkey? She thought it wanted dry feet? Er, hooves. Whatever.

With a shrug, Marci touched his chest. "Stay awhile. Get comfortable." And with that, she began unbuttoning his coat.

Ozzie was so rigid with excitement that she'd undone the last button before he thought to move. But if she got the coat off him, she'd see he had a lethal hardon and then she'd take advantage of his weakened state.

Survival instincts kicking in, Ozzie caught her hands. But rather than remove them, he just held them still. Near his belt.

Oh, God.

Her voice lowered and she stared at his sternum. "Donkeys are friendly, Osbourne, did you know that?"

He shook his head. Hell, at the moment, he didn't even know his own name.

"They're excellent with children, too. And they make wonderful guard animals."

A guard donkey? The absurdity of that cut through the lust and he almost laughed. "You're making that up."

She smiled and pulled her hands free to slip inside his coat. His breath caught. Okay, so he still wore a flannel shirt and a T-shirt, but he wished he didn't. He wished her hot little hands were on his bare skin.

"The right donkey will take care of an entire herd of cattle, sheep, or goats." Her fingers spread out, and she pushed the coat off his shoulders. "Their natural aversion to predators inspires them to severely discourage any canine attacks on the herd. Dogs and donkeys don't mix well, but a donkey can be trained to leave the house dog or farm dog alone."

Her hands were small and soft, and warm, and like any red-blooded male, he knew when to give up graciously. "Marci?"

"Hmmm?" She started on the buttons of his shirt.

He lowered his head and inhaled the sweetness of her silky hair. "I don't think I care about the damned donkey anymore."

"Do you care about me?"

Shit. What kind of tricky question was that? Somehow, he knew no matter what he said, she'd take it the wrong way and he'd end up—

"I didn't ask you an algebra problem, Osbourne. You don't need to do equations in your head. Just tell me, yes or no."

He locked his jaw, and almost got lost in her beautiful eyes. "If I say no, are you going to make me leave?"

She looked at his mouth, and her gaze warmed. "Do you want to stay?"

Damn it, he hated getting a question answered with another question. "I want what I've always wanted."

"Sex?" She moved closer, until her breasts brushed his chest, her thighs nudged his.

"Yeah." Hell yeah. Hot, sweaty, no-holds-barred sex. Naked, gritty sex. Wet, slippery, prolonged—

"Me, too."

Ozzie almost swallowed his tongue. He forgot the donkey. He also forgot Lucius's instructions to merely watch over Marci, *not* enjoy her. He forgot her featherbrained relationships with animals and her propensity to make him nuts.

Before he even knew what he was doing, he had her backed up to a wall, his mouth sealed over hers, his tongue past her teeth, tasting her deeply. And he didn't want to stop this time, not until he was in her, not until she wrung him out, not until she screamed out a mind-blowing climax.

Maybe not . . . ever.

Marci clutched at him. Finally, finally he wanted her again. She'd never met a man who both infuriated her and made her frenzied with need. But Osbourne Decker did just that.

Why him? she wondered, even as she struggled to get closer to him, as close as two people could be. She sucked his tongue deeper into her mouth and lifted one leg up to wrap around his hip.

He ridiculed her psychic ability with animals.

He made his desire for an emotion-free, no-ties relationship clear.

He epitomized everything she disdained in a man: pigheadedness, macho control, an overflow of confidence.

But he looked at her, and her stomach did flip-flops. He touched her and flash fires burned everywhere. He kissed her, and she wanted to be the most flagrant hoochie imaginable.

Before Osbourne, she'd been circumspect and withdrawn, and maybe even inhibited. But with him, she wanted everything, including wild, unrestrained sex.

Bracing one hand on the wall beside her head, Osbourne levered away enough to reach the front of her robe. His mouth continued to devour hers, and Marci loved every second of it—the musky taste of him, the rasp of his beard shadow on her face, the heat and strength of his big body against hers.

If Osbourne wanted her naked, fine. Then maybe he'd get naked, too, and she could finally satisfy her hunger to touch and taste him everywhere.

But he didn't reach for her belt. Instead, his rough hand clasped the leg she had twined around his hip. His fingers slid around her bare knee, then up her thigh, and onto her bottom. He froze.

"Holy Mother of God," he breathed. "You're naked under there."

Never had a man sounded so profoundly grateful. Smiling, Marci nodded. "Yes, I am. I told you I'd just gotten out of the shower."

"Bless your heart." And then he was eating at her mouth again while his hand explored, touching every inch of her backside, squeezing, cuddling, before coming around to her belly.

Muscles bulged on his body, making him seem even bigger, stronger. His hot breath fanned her face. His teeth and tongue played with her, feeding her hunger, and further inciting it at the same time.

So many sensations overwhelmed her at once that she stalled.

"Osbourne?" She could barely breathe and her limbs were starting to tremble. His fingers angled downward on the sensitive skin of her belly.

He all but panted. "Yeah?"

"It's too much too fast."

Breathing hard, his fingertips just touching her pubic hair, he considered that. Slowly and deeply, he inhaled, then carefully withdrew his hand. He cupped her chin and turned her face up.

She thought he had the most incredible eyes. Blue like hers, but darker, a midnight blue. His black lashes were thick and, on a lesser man, they would have seemed girlish. But with blatant lust showing in his gaze, Osbourne looked all male.

And at the same time, very tender.

After a gentle kiss to her lips, he slowly licked his way to her throat. Lazily, he sucked at her skin there, maybe marking her, but who cared? Marci didn't.

She turned her head to make it easier for him. His mouth was so hot, his tongue so silky, and being this close to him let her familiarize herself again with his delicious scent. Osbourne always smelled so good. Not like cologne but like a man, earthy and a little warm and raw.

As he continued to kiss her, he nudged aside the neckline of her robe.

Against her skin, he growled low, "Better?"

"Yes." Her heartbeat thundered. "Please." And Marci herself tugged the robe open so he could get to her breasts. She shuddered, waiting impatiently.

He seemed content to look at her.

"Osbourne?"

He never wavered from his perusal of her breasts, his dark blue eyes burning and bright. "I feel like a kid in a candy store." He bent his bracing arm to bring himself closer to her. So close that she could feel his breath on her nipple when he whispered again, "Beautiful."

Twining her fingers in his silky hair, Marci tried to urge him forward. But he was a muscled lug, especially thick through the shoulders and chest, and he didn't budge an inch.

He said, "Shhh," and cupped her breast in his palm.

With the side of his thumb, he taunted her nipple, gently rolling over it, around it.

Months ago, they'd gone out and indulged in fevered petting, yet never consummated their attraction. But since then she had not even been kissed by another man. She couldn't take it. She needed him, now. "Enough."

In reply, he closed his thumb and finger around her, holding her gently, tugging, applying just the right amount of pressure.

Marci knotted her hands in his hair and forced him to her while arching her back. With a rough laugh, Osbourne obliged, and his mouth closed around her.

Heaven.

He began a wet, hot sucking, and she melted.

The sensation was so acute, so wonderful, she squeezed her eyes shut and couldn't stop moaning.

After treating her other breast to the same teasing torment, he whispered, "Now?" and she again felt his hand under her robe, resting lightly on her belly.

More than ready for him, she breathed, "Yes, please." She needed his touch, was anxious for it.

He wasn't subtle. He cupped his hand over her mound, searched and, separating her labia, worked one thick finger into her.

In sheer, shocking pleasure, Marci stiffened and pressed back, but Osbourne didn't let up. He stroked his finger deep, until the heel of his hand pressed flush against her, giving her even more pleasure. Her muscles clamped down in reaction.

"Yeah," he whispered, "you're nice and wet now. You won't have any problem taking me, will you, honey?"

Unsure of his meaning, Marci moved against him. "I'm not a virgin, Osbourne."

"Virginity is overrated."

"Then, what?"

He pulled his hand away and scooped both hands under her behind to lift her. "Hold onto me."

She wrapped her arms around his neck, her legs around his waist. He lifted her, and something big and hard pressed against her. "Osbourne?"

"Hmmm?"

"Your gun is in the way. It's prodding at me."

"That's not my gun, sweets." With a wicked grin, he turned them both away from the wall.

Not his . . . Well, what then?

He started toward her bedroom, and her thoughts scattered. Uh-oh. "Osbourne?"

"Yeah, babe?"

His long legs quickly traversed the limited space of her apartment. "We're going to make love now?"

"You betcha."

She bit her lip, then offered, "The couch might work better."

"No way." He kissed her hard and fast, his eyes glittering. "I need plenty of room for what I want to do to you."

Wow, that sounded . . . *enticing*. She glanced at her closed bedroom door. "But . . ."

"Don't pull back on me now, Marci. I need you."

Her heart expanded. He *needed* her. She cupped a hand to his jaw and smiled. "Okay."

"Thank God." He reached for her bedroom door.

Marci rushed to say, "If you insist on the bed, though, we'll need to do one thing first."

"Yeah?" He opened the door. "What's that?"

He no sooner asked the question than the donkey rushed him, screaming, *"Aw-ee, aw-ee, aw-ee."*

Shocked, Osbourne stumbled back, tripped over his

own feet, and they both went down in a tangle. "What the hell!"

The donkey loomed over them.

Full of apology, Marci winced. "You'll need to help me get the donkey back to his rightful owners."

Two

Slowly, his gaze ripe with accusation, Osbourne turned to stare at her. Never before had Marci seen anyone so red-faced, so enraged, or so disappointed.

"You had to take the damned donkey, didn't you?"

Because Osbourne lay over her, pinning down her legs, she had to stretch to reach the donkey. She patted his soft nose and said, "He doesn't mean it, honey. You're not damned."

"Oh, God." Groaning as if in horrible pain, Osbourne collapsed back against the wall. Still tangled with her, he scrubbed both hands over his face, then scrubbed again, this time growling like a wild beast. "I'm going to kill Lucius. It doesn't matter that he's the team leader. He got me into this—"

"Did you see the donkey's flank?"

Through his fingers, Osbourne peeked at her. Just that one eye, but it looked pretty incredulous.

"His flank?"

"Yes, you see . . ." But it was difficult to talk in that

particular position. "Osbourne, could you please let me up?"

He didn't look like he wanted to. That one eye glared at her, and finally he dropped his hands and started to rise.

Her robe gaped open—all the way to her navel—and he went deaf and dumb, but apparently not blind. His gaze burned her, leaving her scorched.

He closed his mouth. Swallowed. Licked his lips.

"Stop that, Osbourne."

"All right."

But he didn't. As hot as flames, his midnight eyes examined every inch of her until Marci flushed hot with embarrassment and shoved at his shoulder. "*Osbourne.* You're pinning down me *and* my housecoat. I can't make myself decent until you move so I can rearrange things."

"Okay." He nudged aside a mere inch.

Painfully aware of her exposed nudity, Marci groaned. "Snap out of it, Osbourne." And to help him, she covered herself with both hands, but that just made him suck in a breath and lean closer again—until the donkey took exception and began its brassy, raspy braying.

"Good God." That got Osbourne moving, and quickly, too.

He stumbled to his feet, which put his crotch at eye level for her.

She stared. No, that couldn't be, but . . .

He grabbed her arms and hauled her upward. "Shut that donkey up before the whole apartment complex knows he's here."

Distracted, Marci readjusted her robe and then stroked the donkey's long ears until it quieted. "It's okay, baby. We'll get you back where you belong."

Like a man bent on murder, Osbourne growled, "To the Nativity scene."

She didn't bother to look at him. "No, to Kentucky."

"Marci," he warned.

"Osbourne," she said right back. "Let me show you. Do you see this marking here on his flank? Well, it's a discriminating mark, so I'm sure when he was stolen, it was included in his description to help identify him."

Osbourne frowned. "I see it."

"When he was a baby, he got caught in a fence and cut himself. The wound left a scar. If you'll just go check"—she shooed him toward the living room—"with whoever lists stolen donkeys, I'm sure you'll find out who his real family is, and then we can return him."

Nodding, Osbourne went to the living room but then, realizing what he'd done, he stopped. Marci almost ran into his broad back.

He turned to glare at her. "There is no damn 'stolen donkey' list."

Ignoring that, she smiled. "The phone's right over there." Again, she shooed him.

He pushed her hands back down. "Stop doing that."

"Osbourne, be reasonable. I can't keep a donkey here. It's not like he's housebroken. We need to return him."

Teeth locked, Osbourne leaned down and said, "To the Nativity—"

Marci kissed him.

He jerked back so fast he almost fell.

"I'm sorry." She couldn't hold back her long, dreamy sigh. They'd been moments away from making love, and her body still sizzled with need, and she just knew when they did finally get around to being intimate, it'd be too wonderful for words. "When you're that close, I just can't help myself."

"Oh, no." He covered his ears and fled to the other side of the room. "No, you don't. Not again." And then, finger pointing and voice harsh with accusation, he growled, "You used me!"

Confused, Marci shook her head. "No, I didn't."

"You were going to have sex with me—"

"Oh, yes I was." She nodded. "Because you're irresistible."

"For the love of—"

"And, yes, if you had agreed to the couch instead of insisting on the bedroom, you'd have been used. For sex. For satisfaction. My satisfaction." She shrugged in apology. "Again, I'm sorry, but it's been a very long time for me, and you're a terrible temptation."

His eyes crossed. "Be quiet. I mean it, Marci. You're doing that on purpose."

"Doing what?"

"Making me hard."

Scoffing, she felt compelled to point out the obvious. "You were hard about two seconds after you got here."

He covered his face again and dropped onto her sofa with a deep groan. "No," he said without looking at her. "I was semihard. There's a difference."

"Semihard?" Intrigued by that idea, she inched toward him.

But he must have heard her approach because he snarled, "Stay. Away."

"Why?"

"Because you can't be trusted. Hell, I can't be trusted. You're like a damned lodestone. You get close and my hands are all over you."

"But I like that."

"Not. Another. Word."

She sighed. "Will you quit hiding long enough to call whoever keeps track of stolen donkeys?"

His hands fell to his sides. "Surely, even you can't really think there is such a list?"

"No?"

He shook his head.

"So . . . Donkeys are just listed with the thefts of material things? But that's terrible. He's a living, breathing, sensitive creature. Why, just look at him."

In disgust, Osbourne peered at the donkey.

Lowering his ears, his big brown eyes going soulful, the donkey peered back, and then he brayed again.

"Shhh." Marci patted him while frowning at Osbourne. "You need to reassure him."

He stared at her, blank-faced, then, very forlorn, he muttered, "If only you weren't so hot."

Joy blossomed inside her. "Why, thank you." Marci beamed at him. "You're hot, too. And, I agree, it would be so much easier if you weren't."

His blank look continued.

In explanation, Marci said, "I don't particularly care for wanting a man who thinks I'm daft."

"I never said—"

"Oh, please. You look at me like I need to be committed." She rolled her eyes. "See, you're doing it right now."

He tried to wipe all expression from his face, but it only made him look ridiculous.

"Osbourne, would you please just call whoever you need to call, check to find out about a stolen donkey with a scar on his flank and collar buttons, and that'll prove his ownership."

"Collar buttons?"

Marci stroked the donkey's throatlatch. "Yes, these small dark spots right here. They're called collar buttons."

For a moment there, Marci thought Osbourne would refuse, and she didn't know what she would do without his help. It was difficult enough stealing the donkey from the Nativity scene. Getting him back to his home would be nearly impossible on her own.

Osbourne's eyes sort of glazed over, then he shook his head as if to clear it. "Fine. I'll call and check on it. But while I do that, will you go put on some clothes?"

"If you want."

"I don't. Not really. I'd much rather you strip down to your birthday suit and that we . . . Well, forget that. If I don't find any information on a stolen donkey, I'll have to return him to the Nativity scene. You do understand that, right?"

She licked her lips, thinking it through. What if he couldn't find what he needed to be convinced? That didn't mean the donkey was wrong about his situation, only that Osbourne hadn't uncovered the proper information.

The donkey trusted her, and she supposed she'd have to trust Osbourne. What else could she do?

"If you're sincere, and you actually do all you can, follow every lead to find out if he's been stolen, then yes, I suppose we can take him back there."

"All right, then." He chewed his upper lip and, with blatant regret, dragged his gaze off her. He went to her phone.

Marci patted the donkey. "Wait here, darling. I'll be right back."

Ozzie gripped the phone a little tighter. "Come again?" Surely he hadn't heard Sanderson right.

"It was reported a few weeks ago. Actually, the owners have hired people to find him. He was a beloved family pet or something." Sanderson added, voice low, "If you've got him, there's a reward of five grand."

Five *thousand* dollars? "Un-fucking-believable."

"Yeah, but that's what the bulletin says."

From behind him, Marci replied, "Told you so."

He whirled around, and though she had covered herself from neck to toes in a pair of skinny faded jeans, thick white socks, and an oversized hooded white sweatshirt, she still turned his crank in the most sizzling way.

Remembering the taste and texture of her nipples caused his jaw to tighten. He thought of her smooth belly, and his heart thundered. He recalled her gasp as he'd pushed his finger into her, and his palms went damp.

He had to have her, no matter what. Just once. Maybe. Or twice. But not enough to get involved. Not enough to make her think she had claims. He never, ever wanted to deal with another irrational broad bent on revenge.

First, though, before anything else, he had to deal with a pilfered donkey.

Oblivious to his suffering, Marci smiled brightly. "Your truck is full of SWAT gear, I know, but I still have the truck I rented to steal him from those unscrupulous donkey thieves."

Lord help him. Giving Marci his back, Ozzie said into the phone, "What's the address? I'll take him back to the owners right now."

After reciting the directions, Sanderson asked, "You want me to run this through the legal channels?"

"Not yet." If it turned out to be the wrong donkey, he didn't want Marci arrested for stealing the beast. He'd rather just return it quietly, and hope no one would be the wiser. "Keep this to yourself for now, will ya?"

"You got it, Oz. No problem. But I'm curious now, so let me know how it turns out."

"Will do."

After hanging up, Ozzie turned and found Marci seated on the couch, snow boots on her feet, with her coat, mittens, and scarf beside her. "Are you ready?"

Don't ask. Don't ask. Do not—"What made you think he was stolen and that he lived in Kentucky?"

"He told me."

Eyes closing, Ozzie cursed himself. He knew better, damn it. But oh, no, he had to go and quiz her.

"I'm not bonkers, you know." Marci tipped her head, sending that long, baby-fine brown hair tumbling over her shoulder and curling around a breast. "It's just, well . . . I'm a pet psychic."

No. He'd just keep looking at her chest, the way it filled out the front of that thick sweatshirt, and he'd pretend she hadn't just said that.

"Did you hear me, Osbourne?" She stood and started toward him and Ozzie wanted to jump her, to drag her to the ground and pick up where they'd left off. Although maybe he'd be smarter to get the hell out of Dodge. But if he made a run for it, would Lucius find out and tell everyone else on the team that a slip of a woman had chased him off? Would the other guys volunteer to finish what he'd started, would—

The donkey nibbled on his butt.

"What the hell!" Leaping a foot, Ozzie jerked around. The donkey was right *there*, not two inches from him, his ears laid back and his big brown eyes soulful.

How had the damned thing moved so silently?

"He's just being friendly." Marci shared that special smile that felt like a caress. "He likes you."

Appalled, Ozzie said, "He likes my ass." And he backed out of the donkey's reach.

"I do, too."

No, no, *no*. He wasn't about to touch that one. "It'd help if you'd just be quiet, Marci."

Unaffected by his dark mood, she laughed. "Lighten up, Osbourne. It's not my fault, or the donkey's, that you have such an irresistible bod."

"Can we talk about something else, damn it?"

"Okay." Her lips curled. "What would you like to talk about?"

Ozzie shook his head. With her again so close, he noticed that she was just the right height to tuck in close. And built just right to align all her female parts with his male parts, if he bent his knees the tiniest bit. And she smelled good enough to eat. *Whoa*. Totally bad image to get in his head. Bad. Bad.

He started to back away again, but the donkey didn't budge. Hemmed in by a donkey and a doll-face, both of them hazardous to his health.

"Tell me about this pet psychic business."

"All right." Oblivious to his internal struggle concerning sexual positions that made him sweat, Marci said, "For as long as I can remember, I've had a special ability with animals."

"An ability, huh?" Ozzie edged out from between the two of them.

"I'm sorry that it makes you uncomfortable. I'm sorrier that you think I'm a flake."

His head shot up and he looked at her face. She appeared so earnest, and so wounded, that he frowned.

Damn it, he did not want to hurt her. And he had promised Lucius that he wouldn't.

But she patted his chest as if forgiving him, then went on with her explanation. "It's okay. Most people think I'm unhinged. Back when you first asked me out, I had hoped you'd be different, but . . . you're not." Her narrow shoulders lifted. "And that's okay. I understand. I'd have a hard time believing it, too."

Maybe if she explained, it wouldn't be as bad as he thought. "What exactly is it that you do, Marci?"

"I know when animals are upset and why. I understand them. I hear their thoughts and fears and worries."

"Oh-kay."

"It's easy, really." She caught his hand and pressed it beneath her breast, over her lightly bumping heartbeat. "When you bother to listen with your heart. But few people do. They arrogantly go around as if being human makes us supreme."

Ozzie snatched his hand back, but he still felt burned.

She sighed. "What other creatures feel doesn't concern most people, or at least not enough to be bothered with it."

"So . . ." What the hell was he supposed to say to all that? "The donkey asked for your help?"

"It doesn't really work like that. Obviously, he's not a talking donkey."

Well, thank God for small favors.

"But when I passed the funeral home, I felt his unhappiness."

"His unhappiness? Huh. Imagine that."

"Yes. The other animals are content. They like the attention, if not the exposure to the cold. But the donkey was so miserable, and so lonesome, I got a lump in my throat and a pain in my chest. I felt everything he felt and it nearly broke my heart. So I stopped."

He couldn't bear to think of her that upset, so he focused on something else she'd said. "Lonesome? But didn't you just say there were other animals there with him?"

"He wasn't *alone*, Osbourne, he was *lonely*. There's a difference."

His guts cramped. Maybe that was the crux of her problems. "You're alone," he pointed out. And then softly, with caution, "Are you lonely?"

For once, she seemed evasive, waving away his question. "I stroked the donkey, petted him, and I opened myself to him—"

"Opened yourself to him?"

Propping her hands on her hips, Marci huffed. "Are you going to repeat everything I say? Because if you are, we should sit down and get comfortable. But if that's the case, I'm going to take the donkey out first so he can, uh, take his constitutional in the snow instead of on my floors."

Ozzie sighed. There'd be no help for it. He put his coat back on. "Let's talk in the truck on the way. Give me the keys. I'll drive."

She frowned in disapproval. "Didn't you just get off work?"

"Yeah, but I'm fine."

"You haven't been to bed yet. You must be tired."

Tired, no. Exasperated, yes. Confused, yes. Horny as hell, yes, yes, *yes*. But he'd manage. "The keys?"

"Fine." She lifted them off a peg on the wall and handed them over to him. "But don't make any sudden or jarring turns or anything. I don't want the donkey to fall down."

Ozzie ran his hand over his head. He pictured the donkey toppling sideways and had to roll his eyes.

But he didn't want the donkey to fall down, either.

Marci pulled on a down-filled coat, wrapped a scarf around her neck, put on her hat and mittens, and then she leashed the donkey.

"Don't be nervous, darling." She briefly pressed her

cheek to the donkey's head. "I'm taking you home. You'll see. It'll be okay."

And like a contented puppy, the beast followed her out the apartment door and out the building, into the snow, to take his constitutional.

And like the bigger ass, Ozzie trailed along.

As if the foot of snow they'd already gotten wasn't enough, the sky softened with flurries. As the sun struggled to peek above the horizon, an awful glare reflected off the white landscape.

"We're in for a two-hour drive." Ozzie watched as Marci opened the back of the big truck. The bottom half of the door unfolded like a loading hatch. "Will he need water or anything along the way?"

Smiling at him over her shoulder, she said, "No, he'll be okay. Before I swiped him, I put some hay inside. It's still there. Generally, donkeys need to eat less than a horse does of the same size. Two hours will be like nothing to him. But it's very sweet of you to be concerned."

Ozzie felt like a jerk. "It's not sweet. It's just that I don't want him . . . suffering."

"Or unhappy?"

A sharp quip concerning sensitive donkey-feelings tripped to the end of Ozzie's tongue, but before he could give them voice, the donkey rushed up the ramp and into the truck.

And damn if he didn't look anxious to be on his way.

Surely, the animal didn't realize . . . No, of course he didn't. Odds were, he'd been trained to get into a truck. Ozzie couldn't let Marci's cockeyed perceptions affect him.

Disgruntled, he stepped around her and closed up the truck bed securely. "Come on." Taking Marci's arm, he led her to the passenger's side door. Their feet crunched through frozen snow, wind whistled against them, ice crystals formed on their faces—and Marci kept smiling.

He'd noticed that about her early on, the way she took whatever life threw at her and stayed happy. She had the most optimistic outlook he'd ever known. Maybe because he was such a pessimist, he liked that about her.

The smile was enticement enough, but Ozzie also noticed how it nudged a little dimple in her rosy cheek. Snowflakes clung to her thick lashes and settled on the tip of her cute little nose. Now that she'd gotten her way and the donkey was ready for its journey, she positively glowed with pleasure.

He couldn't help himself. He bent and pressed a soft, gentle kiss to her cold lips. He could feel that smile of hers, and it fed something in his soul.

And that scared him.

He drew back and frowned at her.

Puzzled, she asked, "What?"

"Nothing." Catching her around the waist, Ozzie hoisted her up into her seat, then, without thinking about it, he fastened her seatbelt. With her gaze glued to his face, Marci kept that crooked, endearing smile in place the entire time.

Their eyes met, and Ozzie couldn't look away.

Would she wear that sweet smile while coming? Or would she clench her teeth and groan and . . .

When he realized he still loomed over her for no good reason at all, he cursed and stepped away, then slammed her door. On his way to his own seat, he lectured himself on the impropriety of lusting after a woman not based in reality. He knew the consequences and he knew, if he was smart, he'd satisfy his lust with a staid, no-nonsense woman.

Problem was, he'd never wanted another woman the way he wanted Marci.

He climbed into his own seat and Marci said, "That was a nice kiss."

"Forget about it."

"I don't think so. I think I'll cherish it, and remember it always."

"Oh, for the love of—"

"You're sure you're okay to drive?"

A safer topic. He grasped it like a lifeline. "Don't worry about it. I've worked fourteen hours straight and still gotten myself home."

"Fourteen hours?"

Ignoring the sexy, totally kooky broad beside him, Ozzie started the truck and eased it from the apartment parking lot out onto the road. "Sometimes standoffs take a hell of a long time. You don't just up and leave in the middle of it."

"I'd never be able to do that. I was up most of the night staking out the funeral home so I could sneak off with the donkey without anyone knowing."

Ozzie refused to ask, but that didn't stop her.

"I parked the rental truck in the empty grocery lot and walked down that way, then hid in the bushes. It was so cold and I got so sleepy, and my feet and behind were wet from sitting in the snow."

Do. Not. Ask.

"It wasn't until this morning that the road quieted down enough for me to slip away with the donkey. I was so cold and stiff, and tired, I could barely move. I'd planned to sleep in this morning, then you showed up. But at least by then I'd showered and thawed out all my body parts."

He couldn't think about her thawing. "What would you have done with him if I hadn't showed up?"

Marci shrugged. "I was going to try some sleuthing on my own, but I realize now that I probably wouldn't have gotten very far with that." She pulled off her hat and put it in her lap, then, staring down at her hands, said, "I'm glad you did show up. Thank you." And with that, she turned on the static-riddled radio and found a station playing Christmas music.

Ozzie was glad he'd shown up, too. What if someone in her apartment building had called about the noise, and Marci had gotten arrested? Worse, what if someone had found her on that dark, cold road and . . .

That thought was so disturbing, he cut it short. Holidays or not, there were still bums and creeps hanging on every street corner.

Out of the blue, taking Ozzie by surprise, Marci said, "I'm used to ridicule and disbelief, you know."

He did a double take. "What?"

"Everyone thinks what you think. That's why I don't let many people know about my gift. In fact, I moved here to hide it. I don't tell anyone now, and when I help an animal, I do it anonymously, to avoid some of the mockery." She turned to look out the window. "When I was younger, I used to talk about it. But I quickly learned that it's not a good thing to admit being different. I got called names by the meanest people, and the others just kept their distance."

The way he'd kept his distance.

What kind of childhood must she have had? Hell, what kind of adulthood was she having? He knew for a fact that she didn't date much, and other than her sister, she didn't seem close to anyone.

To give himself a moment to think, Ozzie adjusted the heater and defroster. Being SWAT required that he know how to deal with all types of people and their problems. He didn't consider Marci delusional, just fanciful. She wasn't a risk, except to his sanity. But she definitely had some ideas that needed special care.

When he said nothing, she sighed. "Bethany is really protective toward me. She loves animals as much as I do, but she doesn't share my intuition. When I tell her something about animals, what they feel and need, she believes me a hundred percent, and she'll do whatever she can to help. But it's harder for her than it is for me."

Never before had Marci conversed so casually with him. Their few attempts at dating had focused on the sexual chemistry between them, not on feelings. He enjoyed seeing Marci this way: relaxed, open, trusting.

Trusting? Well, yeah.

Giving it some thought, Ozzie supposed he had to consider her actions based in trust. Hadn't she just said that she didn't tell many people about her . . . gift?

But she'd told him.

And then he'd done the expected and avoided her. Stupid ass.

Okay, so he now knew enough about women to know not to get overly involved with the . . . unique ones. But that didn't mean he had to steer clear of Marci altogether. He didn't have to shun her.

He just wouldn't entangle himself with her romantically. He'd keep things casual. Sexual, maybe, but casual all the same.

It amazed him, but Ozzie wanted to learn more about her and her strange predilections toward animals. "Since you and Bethany look identical, it's surprising that she doesn't share your gift."

Resting her head back on the seat, Marci closed her eyes. "Lucius has always been able to tell us apart."

Oh, ho. That sounded like a challenge. "And you think I can't?"

She opened her eyes again and surveyed him. "But you just said we look identical."

"Outwardly, sure. But you smile differently. You walk differently and laugh at different things. You're usually off in your own little world, while Bethany is always on the attack."

That had her laughing. "No, she is not. Well, except maybe with Lucius, before they got things ironed out." Then, more quietly, "Or when she's defending me."

And that probably explained why Bethany didn't seem to like him. From jump, she'd been prickly with him, always watching him as if she expected him to sprout horns. Or maybe . . . hurt her sister's feelings.

Shit. He hated being predictable.

Marci touched his arm, causing him to stiffen. "I've noticed that people do different things in order to protect themselves. Bethany was afraid of her growing feelings for Lucius, so she picked arguments with him, forcing an emotional distance."

The way she said that, with ripe anticipation while watching him so closely, raised Ozzie's suspicions. He scowled. "Is that some kind of dig toward me?"

"Not a dig, but an observation. If you'll be honest, you'll admit that you use sarcasm and negativity to shield your feelings for me."

Whoa. Hold the farm. *His feelings?*

Ozzie glanced toward her, but the snow flurries were thick enough now to require that he return his attention to the road. "What the hell is that supposed to mean?"

"You like me."

Despite the cold, he broke out in a sweat. "I *want* you, Marci. It's not at all the same thing."

Taunting him, she leaned closer. "But you like me, too. Admit it."

Get a grip, Ozzie. Don't let her rile you. He clutched the steering wheel and formulated a plan of response. "Okay." Forcing himself to relax, he feigned mere curiosity. "What gives you the impression I like you?"

"You watch me all the time."

True. But easily explained. "You're hot. Great ass. Stellar legs. More than a handful up top."

Hell, he was turning himself on.

In a gruffer tone, he stated, "*All* the guys watch you."

"You also glare at the other guys watching me."

He snorted, but had to wonder . . . did he? Sure, he hated seeing any man disrespect a woman. But he had no claim on Marci. Just because he'd gone out with her a few times, and hadn't yet had her, even though he wanted her bad . . .

No claim at all, damn it.

He'd refute her. He'd tell her he didn't give a rat's ass who looked at her, then she'd understand he wasn't the one smitten.

He glanced at her. "Are you saying you like the other men eyeballing you?" Appalled at himself, Ozzie snapped his mouth shut. Had that aggressive, barked question reeking of jealousy actually come from him?

Marci's smile spread slow and easy. "Not really."

He was so lost in self-recriminations, he didn't know what she was talking about. "Not really *what?*"

"If it wasn't for you," she assured him, "I probably wouldn't have noticed anyone else looking at me. But because I'm always looking at you, I've seen when you get that murderous glint in your eyes."

So he'd just clued her in? Great. Just friggin' great. He could hardly deny the truth of her observations, so he just kept quiet.

"And your reaction has to mean something, right?"

"It means I don't want anyone else jumping your

bones before me." Actually, he didn't want anyone touching her. Ever. Period.

"Because you like me?"

Ozzie had never been the type to abuse anyone, but especially not a woman. At the same time, he didn't want to give her false impressions. "Look, Marci, I like you fine. Really." How could he not? She was sweet and cheerful and . . . "But I don't *like* you, if you know what I mean."

"No, I don't."

He groaned. "You're a nice-enough woman. You seem kind. And usually smart."

"Usually?"

He would not belabor her weirdness with animals. "The thing is, I enjoy being single."

"I didn't ask to marry you."

That made *twice* he'd heard that cursed word today, and both times in relationship to Marci. Driven by desperation, he squeezed the steering wheel and scowled. "I'm not looking to get involved beyond anything sexual."

Marci tilted her head, as if trying to understand him. "Why did you come to see me this morning?"

Shew. An easy enough subject, one he could discuss without caution. "Lucius says someone's been maybe bothering you." At least that was the bona fide truth. "He wanted me to keep an eye on things."

"Oh." Disappointment had her crossing her arms. "And that's why you're helping me return the donkey? Because Lucius is your friend and he told you to babysit me?"

Not exactly, but it sounded good to him. "That's about it."

Silence reigned. He could actually feel her regret as she stared at him. For the longest time she said nothing, and Ozzie was starting to squirm. What if she cried? What if he'd just broken her little screwball heart?

"Okay then."

He tucked in his chin and spared another glimpse in her direction. "Okay, what?"

"Okay, I believe you don't like me."

But . . . "Look, Marci, I don't *dislike* you. Didn't I just say that overall you're a nice, sweet woman?"

"But you only want sex?"

The Inquisition couldn't have been this tough.

Be noble, Oz.

Be strong.

Do not pull over to the side of the road to show her the exceptions you'd make for sex.

He cleared his throat and attempted to be as blunt as possible. "I want you, but then, we've already acknowledged that. The thing is, I'm sure you don't want to get involved in a purely sexual encounter."

"I don't?"

Ozzie concentrated on not getting a Jones. Again. "No, you don't." And then, because he couldn't help himself: "Do you?"

She took her own sweet time thinking about it, probably to further torment him.

"I don't know," she finally said. "I want you an awful lot, too, and I'm not sure I want to go my whole life wondering how you would have been."

Of all the dirty, rotten . . . ! Ozzie could feel himself hardening. And she'd probably done that on purpose, just to get even with him for being surly. He shifted in his seat, trying to get comfortable, and considered apologizing for his less-than-sterling mood.

He tapped his fingers on the steering wheel, figured out what to say, and cleared his throat again. "Look, Marci, I guess I'm just tired and in a bad mood."

"And our aborted lovemaking this morning has us both edgy."

He locked his teeth. "Right. But I shouldn't take that out on you. Just forget everything I've said, okay?"

"No, I won't do that." She looked out the window at the passing scenery. "Don't you just love this time of year? Look at the Christmas lights. I especially like the blue ones. They're so pretty."

Oh, no, he wouldn't let her switch topics on him that easily! "What do you mean, no?"

"I'm sorry, but I can't forget that sweet kiss earlier, or everything you've said. It'd be impossible. I'm used to people not liking me, but it bothers me more with you."

It bothered him that she was bothered. "Marci—"

"And you should know, there *is* someone following me. I realize Lucius doesn't believe it, he just asked you to look out for me to appease Bethany. He hates to disappoint her."

Lucius was whipped big time.

"But if you look in the rearview mirror, you'll see a van. It's been there since we got on the main road. Watch and see if it stays with us."

Startled by that, Ozzie glanced in the mirror and saw the van she meant. He grunted. "Could be anyone." But there weren't many cars out and about on that early snowy morning.

"Want to make a bet?" Marci twisted toward him as much as the confines of the seatbelt would allow. "A real bet, not just a verbal one."

Everything male in him went on the alert. "What are we wagering?"

She didn't even take a second to consider it. "In a few minutes, you can pull over for gas or a drink or something. If the van pulls over, too, that'll be proof enough, okay?"

"I suppose." He looked again in the rearview mirror, and felt his instincts kick in. They *were* being tailed, and he hadn't even noticed. He didn't like slacking. He didn't like being so distracted by a woman that he missed something that major.

"If he is following us, I win the bet."

"Not yet, woman." He wouldn't agree to anything blindly. "What are we betting?"

"That you'll spend Christmas with me."

Huh. Had he really thought she'd ask for sex?

In his dreams.

"I just inherited a house, and I'd planned to work on it over the holidays."

"Then I'll spend Christmas with you. Either way, you'll give me some time, okay?"

That didn't sound too heinous. But it brought up a new question. "So if he's not following us, what do I get?"

The dimple showed in her cheek. "What do you want?"

Such a loaded question. Ozzie firmed his jaw, flipped on his turn signal to switch lanes, and headed for the nearest exit.

The damn van followed.

"I don't think it matters," he muttered. "The bastard is following us—and I want to know why."

Three

"I haven't eaten," Osbourne said. "I'm going to pull in and get a breakfast sandwich. You want one?"

It fascinated Marci to see Osbourne go into SWAT mode. Oh, he spoke casually enough, but a new alertness straightened his spine and firmed his jaw. He looked everywhere, at everything, as he eased the truck to the right and took an exit.

The few times she'd dated him, he'd been charming at first, then wary, then finally distant. All because she'd tried to be herself with him.

When he'd shown back up today, primed and in sexual overdrive, her hope had renewed. But so far he'd been churlish and sarcastic and she didn't like it. His attitude hurt her feelings when she'd thought herself long immune to the criticism of others.

Seeing that the van had also switched lanes and taken the same exit, Marci sighed. "I'll take a donut and orange juice. Thank you."

When Osbourne got in the drive-thru lane, the van

went past, but pulled into a gas station nearby. No one left the van to pump gas.

Only someone familiar with Osbourne would note the growing tension in him. Not sexual tension this time, but an angry tension that bunched his impressive muscles and put an anticipatory glint into his blue eyes. It didn't bode well for somebody.

He put in their orders without an obvious care, paid, accepted their food, and then handed her the bag.

"Get that out for me, will you?" He steered the truck out of the parking lot and onto the main road, heading for the exit that'd take them back onto the highway.

Marci unwrapped his sandwich and handed it to him. He balanced it on his knee while driving.

"Osbourne? The van is following again."

"I know. Normally I'd make a few sharp turns, but I don't want to alarm the donkey."

So considerate. So why didn't he give her the same consideration? Surely it was as she suspected—that he did care for her but wanted to protect himself.

The questions uppermost in her mind were: Why? And who had hurt him?

"In fact," he said, as much to himself as her, "I'll just let the idiot follow us all the way to the donkey's home. Once I don't have to worry about the animal, it'll be easier for me to take care of this."

After a bite of her donut, Marci licked her fingers free of glaze. "Take care of it how?"

"Don't push me, Marci."

"It was a simple question."

"Yeah, well keep your fingers out of your mouth and your tongue where I can't see it."

Oh. So that's what he meant by pushing him. Feeling a little devilish, Marci took another bite of her donut.

"So . . . Do I spend Christmas with you? Will you honor the bet?"

"We never actually shook on it or anything."

She wouldn't let his reluctance bother her. One way or another, she'd wear him down. "So is it that you like being alone during the holidays?"

"Usually I wouldn't be." He bit into his breakfast sandwich with gusto.

Jealousy prickled up her spine, and Marci said, "Yes, of course. I'm sure you have your pick of women to celebrate with."

He laughed without humor, and then, in somber tones, he explained, "I've spent every Christmas since my sixth birthday with my grandmother. It's always been just the two of us. But she recently passed, so this year I'll be solo for the holidays."

Oh, God. "Osbourne, I'm so sorry. I didn't realize."

"Granny was a hoot. And she'd have loved you, because she loved animals and anyone who had anything to do with them."

"Even kooks?"

"Especially kooks, being as she was a little nutty herself. But in a loveable way. When my mom died and my dad took off, she gathered me up and said she'd finally have me to herself, as if it was something she'd always wanted."

"What do you mean he took off?"

"He was young, unwilling to be burdened with a kid. Granny said I reminded him too much of her. But I think that was bullshit, just her way of softening things."

"I bet you must have missed them a lot."

"With Granny around? Hell, no. She made growing up fun."

Fascinated, Marci smiled at him. "How so?"

"Granny didn't believe in rules. If I wanted dessert instead of dinner, we'd eat it in the yard, in the rain, while listening to coyotes howl. During my rowdier teens, when I wanted long hair, she offered to dye it blue for me."

Marci laughed. "She does sound fun."

"Yeah, but she was wily. I always thought she should have been a shrink, because she sure knew how to play mind games."

"What do you mean?"

"When I was eighteen, I wanted a tattoo. You know, something gnarly and macho around my biceps. Granny thought that sounded cool, and she wanted to go along to get one, too."

They both laughed.

Shaking his head, Osbourne added, "Hell, I was afraid that if I slipped off to get it, she'd find out where, and she'd show up there to get her ass tatted or something, and I'd never be able to live it down. For sure, she'd have told the tattoo artist she was my granny, and word would have spread like wildfire."

"Pretty ingenious on her part."

"No kidding. I failed a test once because I hadn't studied. She sat down with it, looked over the answers, and damned if she didn't know them all! Made me feel like an idiot, all the while telling me how smart I am and that obviously the test was messed up because, hell, what old lady could pass it when a sharp young man couldn't? From then on, I aced everything, and she'd beam, telling me how much smarter I was than her." His voice softened. "But I never believed that. She was the wisest, most incredible woman I've ever known."

Marci touched his thigh. "I'm glad you had her in your life."

"Yeah, me, too." His hand briefly covered hers and gave it a squeeze. "Having Christmas without her just doesn't feel right."

When he retreated again, she felt the loss, both physical and emotional, deep inside herself. "Maybe it'd be easier if you had someone around to . . . you know, maybe deflect the memories." Marci knew she lacked subtlety, but she couldn't bear the thought of him spending Christmas alone.

Osbourne grunted. "Sharing holidays with women gives them the wrong idea. It puts too personal a slant to things. Women start thinking you're committed to them, whether you are or not."

"Committed?"

He worked his jaw a minute, then shrugged one heavy shoulder, as if deciding it didn't matter what he shared. "I had one friggin' holiday with a woman, and she thought we'd get married or something. I told her nothing had changed, that I liked her but I wasn't in love with her."

"I take it she reacted badly?"

His hands tightened on the steering wheel. "I'd always known Ainsley was a little screwy, but after that, I realized she was certifiable. She did everything she could to harass me. She kept calling me at home and at work. She dropped in unannounced. She stalked me, hoping to catch me with another woman. When I told her to back off, she . . ."

"What?"

"Claimed she was pregnant."

"Oh." Dread settled in Marci's belly. "You're a father?"

"No." After a deep breath, he said, "It's a long story, and I won't go into details, but for months, she put me through hell. She was pregnant, she wasn't pregnant.

She'd had an abortion, she hadn't had an abortion. It was mine, it wasn't mine. I had no idea what to think. When I considered being a father . . . I dunno. I took to the idea. And then she'd say she'd aborted the baby, just to see my reaction. And the next day she'd tell me she lied, that she was still pregnant, but not by me. She ranted and raved and drove me nuts."

"How did it finally get resolved?"

"After a few months, when she would have started showing if she was in fact pregnant, she found some new schmuck to torment." He shook his head. "She wanted to make sure I didn't ruin things for her, so she confessed that she'd made it all up."

"Dear God." Marci now understood, but she almost wished she didn't.

He thought she was another Ainsley.

"Since then, I've kept things simple. Limited dating—with very rational women."

"And no holidays?"

His frown eased away. "Most of the women I know aren't the type to enjoy a quiet Christmas at home."

Forget subtlety. "I would enjoy it."

Mouth quirking in a half-smile, he said, "Yeah, you made that clear."

Still, he didn't invite her to join him, and she slouched back in her seat, disgruntled. "But I'm a vindictive flake, right? Way too cruel to have hanging around."

His frown took the chill out of the air. "Don't put words in my mouth."

"Why not? Kooky is kooky, right? You've seen one, you've seen 'em all."

"I didn't—" Osbourne huffed, glanced in the rearview mirror, then at his directions. He switched lanes. "Look, let's start this debacle over, okay?"

Now he called their time together a debacle? Worse and worse. "Start over how?"

"Forget the past. From this second on, we'll just play it by ear. One thing at a time."

She supposed she could do that. "The donkey first?"

"Right. Hopefully this is where he belongs and we can be heroes by returning him, then we'll head home."

Marci wondered whose home he meant, but she decided not to push her luck. "Deal."

"Great." From one minute to the next, the snow turned to frozen sleet, hammering the windshield and making travel more treacherous. Osbourne eased off the highway on the next exit. "Help me look for Riley Road."

The wipers could barely keep the ice off the windshield, even with the defroster going full blast. They'd slowed to a crawl with visibility limited.

A crooked road indicator came into view. "There it is." Marci pointed, and Osbourne pulled down a narrower gravel drive.

The van stayed behind them, but held back when they drove down a dirt road leading to an old, stately farmhouse fenced in and surrounded by towering trees. Osbourne parked in front but left the truck running.

Back in SWAT mode, he ordered, "Wait here."

Orders had never gone over big with her. "Why should I?"

"I don't know these people, and I don't like taking chances with you."

Well, the order sounded much nicer put that way.

"Lock the doors and I'll be right back."

"Okay."

Her quick agreement earned her a double take. Osbourne's gaze was fraught with suspicion, but he said nothing.

Marci watched as he trod through the now ankle-deep snow, up the hidden walk to the front porch. He knocked on the door and seconds later a middle-aged woman, wearing jeans and a flannel shirt, answered. As she dried her hands on a kitchen towel, Osbourne spoke, gestured toward the truck, and the woman screamed.

Even through the thick sleet and snow, Marci could see that he jumped.

The woman shoved Osbourne aside and went slipping and sliding down the walkway to the truck. Shocked, Osbourne hurried after her. The woman was still yelling excitedly, which brought a tall, portly man charging out the doorway to join her at the truck.

Over the truck's idling engine and the blasting defroster, their words were indecipherable. But their expressions were clear enough: naked, tearful, overwhelming joy.

Grinning ear to ear, Marci opened her door and stepped shin-deep into the drifting snow and ice.

Struggling against the surging wind, she reached the back of the truck just as Osbourne lowered the hatch. There was a single moment of speechless expectation, then the donkey brayed, the man and woman gave a robust shout, and within seconds, the truck bed was filled.

The man, overcome with joy, cried, "Magnus! Finally, you're home!"

The woman threw herself around the donkey and hugged him tight.

Wide-eyed and mute with incredulity, Osbourne looked at Marci. Grinning through her tears, she mouthed the words "Thank you."

And slowly, Osbourne's smile came in return.

*   *   *

An hour later, Osbourne continued to smile, and said again, "I can't believe it."

Marci sipped the hot chocolate that River and Chloe Parson had insisted on fixing for them. They'd also tried to give them a hefty reward, but Osbourne and Marci had refused the money at almost the same time.

Osbourne told the Parsons that seeing their happiness, especially at Christmas, was more than enough reward.

It thrilled Marci that he looked at their efforts the same way she did: as simply the right thing to do, not something done for financial gain. After their repeated refusals, the Parson couple gave up.

After a time, she and Osbourne got on their way with warm hugs, hot chocolate, and a lot of gratitude.

"It's a wonderful feeling, isn't it?" Marci asked him.

"Yeah. That donkey is like a member of their family."

"Magnus is a fine creature. I can see why they love him so much."

Osbourne laughed. "Yeah, I figured you would feel that way."

Toying with the lid on her cup, Marci asked, "So now do you believe me?"

"That we're being followed? Damn right." They'd just reached the gravel road and there sat the van, nearly snowed in, but with the engine running. As they passed, it pulled out behind them.

Well, shoot. That wasn't what she'd meant at all, but Marci really didn't feel like having her ability with animals questioned yet again. Osbourne would either believe her or not, and she wouldn't try to convince him.

"Hang on to that cup," Osbourne told her.

"Why?"

"Because I'm going to find out what the hell he

wants." And with that, Osbourne turned the truck sharply, stopping it crossways in the road, blocking both narrow lanes.

Face set and brows down, he put the truck in PARK, again ordered Marci to lock the doors after him, and got out to stalk toward the van.

Marci sighed. Releasing her seatbelt so she could climb to Osbourne's side of the truck for an unhindered view, she watched him.

The van sat idling, the driver confused. But with Osbourne's stomping, hostile approach, clear alarm showed on his face. The driver looked to be in his early thirties, average in build and appearance with straight brown hair and shifty eyes.

To hear their verbal exchange, Marci quickly rolled down the window.

With one hand braced on the roof of the van, Osbourne leaned down to the driver's door and ordered, "Open up."

The man pressed back in his seat and shook his head. "What do you want?"

Rolling his eyes, Osbourne reached inside his coat and produced a badge that he held against the window. "Open it *now.*"

The man gulped. His window lowered a mere five inches. "What's going on here? Why are you harassing me?"

"You're following me. I want to know why."

"But . . . I'm not!"

Osbourne leaned closer, and the man screeched. "Don't you dare touch me! I'm warning you, I'll call the cops!"

"I am a cop, you ass." Straightening again, Osbourne put away the badge and bundled up his coat against the whistling wind and sleet. "Stop that noise and tell me why you were following me, or we can talk at the station after I have you arrested."

The man didn't ask on what charge, which Marci thought would have been a good question, especially since Osbourne was an Ohio police officer, and they were currently in Kentucky.

The man glared toward the truck—*toward her*—and said, "I'm not following you. I'm following her."

Rather than appeasing Osbourne, that seemed to annoy him more. *"Why?"*

Gaining confidence, the man lowered his window more and offered his hand. "Vaughn Wayland."

Osbourne ignored the conciliatory gesture.

"Right." Mr. Wayland retreated. "I'm working on a story, actually. I'm a freelance reporter and she's hot news."

"What the hell are you talking about?"

"You don't know?" Wayland stared toward her with anticipation. "She's a psychic."

Huffing, Osbourne said, "Don't be an idiot."

Well, Marci thought, so much for him believing her.

"But it's true!" Wayland insisted. "I'd heard about her for a few years, but I didn't believe it any more than you do. Then my neighbor's cat went missing for months. Everyone sort of figured the mangy thing had gotten run over or eaten by a dog when, out of the blue, Ms. Churchill brought it back to her."

"So she found a lost cat. Big deal."

"I located another woman who claims Miss Churchill helped cure her dog of nightmares."

This time, Osbourne turned to glare at her in clear accusation.

Marci glared right back. She remembered that poor dog. A neighborhood kid would torment it while hiding in bushes so that the dog's owner didn't know. The dog was a frazzled mess because of that rotten kid. But Marci had ratted out the boy, and not only had the dog owner given him hell but his parents also.

"I have a file folder full of pet owners she's helped. They've all been more than willing to sing her praises. All I need to finish my piece is an interview with her."

"I don't believe this."

"She's the kind of human interest story that appeals to readers, especially this time of year."

"You're fucking with me, right?"

Wayland sniffed. "No, I am not. And you have no right to interfere with my research."

"Stalking her is *not* research."

Affronted, he squared his shoulders. "I'm not stalking her. I just need her to share some of her background and history."

"Have you asked her?"

"Yes. Twice."

Marci didn't recognize the fellow at all. She yelled out the window, "He could be telling the truth, Osbourne, although I don't remember meeting him."

"I asked over the phone," the man yelled back.

"Oh." Marci thought about it, and then nodded. "I always turn down that stuff, and then I change my phone number again."

Osbourne rubbed his face. "Look, she doesn't want to be interviewed, so leave her alone."

"But . . ." the man sputtered, "I can't do that. I've already promised the story to a magazine and I'm behind on my deadline as it is."

Once again, Osbourne leaned down close, and though Marci couldn't hear what he said, she saw the driver's face, and knew that Osbourne wasn't being polite.

The man cowered back as far as he could, nodded agreement several times, but still, he looked far from resigned to failure.

Maybe Osbourne realized it, too, because he took the time to write down Vaughn Wayland's name and license plate number.

When he returned to the truck, he still looked very put out.

Marci rolled up the window, unlocked the door, and slid back to her own seat. Without a word, Osbourne got behind the wheel, turned the truck, and headed for the highway.

For several minutes, they rode in utter silence. Then Osbourne asked, "Does that happen often?"

"What?"

"Jerks following you around, pressing you for answers?"

She shrugged. "Usually it's people who don't believe me, who want to expose me as a fake. They think that I extort money from people, or that I prey on their emotions."

He shook his head. "You'd never do that."

Marci blinked at him. Aha. Maybe he didn't consider her an Ainsley after all. "No, I wouldn't. I try to keep people from finding out who I am, and what I know. But it's not always possible, not if I want to help—and I do."

"If you didn't, Magnus would still be at the funeral home instead of where he belongs."

Was that an admission of her ability? A warm glow spread inside her. "True. When an animal has a problem, I can't ignore it. It hurts me too much. But whenever possible, I help anonymously."

"How does that work?"

"I'll contact the owners—maybe by a note, or phone if I can figure out their number. Most take my advice or at least listen enough to check into what I tell them. I don't have to expose myself or leave myself open to more ridicule."

"*More* ridicule?"

She flattened her mouth and looked out the window. "Trust me, it's never been easy. From the time I was a little girl, I could sense things. And any time a kid is different . . ."

Very quietly, he said, "I'm sorry."

Marci turned toward him again, wanting to explain. "It hasn't been a picnic for Bethany, either. All through school, she got teased about having a loony sister."

He winced, probably remembering the times he'd thought similar things. The difference was that Osbourne had never been deliberately cruel. Quite a distinction.

He'd dodged her, but he hadn't ridiculed her.

As if offering another apology, he reached for her knee, settled his big hand there, and stroked her with his thumb. It was a casual touch, yet at the same time intimate enough to feel special.

And to raise her temperature a few degrees.

While deciding how much to tell him, Marci finished her hot chocolate. She didn't open herself to too many people, but right now, in the quiet and cold, with Osbourne, it felt right.

She laid her hand over his. Despite the weather, his fingers were warm. She loved touching him, and even a simple touch on the hand let her feel his strength. "For as long as I can remember, guys have tried to use Bethany to get close to me."

She waited for his disbelief, or his humor. After all,

they were identical twins. Most people would wonder why one twin would be preferable to another.

Osbourne considered her statement. "It's because you come across softer, less independent."

Startled that he'd hit the nail on the head, Marci barely noticed when he turned his hand to clasp hers, then tugged her closer to him on the bench seat, as close as the seatbelts would allow. "That's it exactly. Men see me as an airhead, and maybe easy."

The corners of his mouth lifted, and he returned both hands to the wheel. "I'd say they don't know you very well."

"No, they don't." Her spine stiffened. "I'm not an airhead."

"Don't confuse me with any other idiots you've known, Marci. Hell, you're more complicated than any ten women combined. And I know firsthand that there's nothing easy about you. But you're definitely smart."

"You really believe that?"

"Hell yes. You're smart enough to figure out that a donkey is unhappy, to steal him without getting caught, and to get him back home safely."

A blush of pleasure colored her cheeks. "I couldn't have done it without you," she pointed out.

He ignored that little fact to say, "You're also kind and funny and . . . caring."

The warmth spread, melting her heart. "Thank you."

"You're welcome. Now tell me more about these idiots you've known."

It wasn't easy to admit, but she forced the words out. "With Bethany and me being identical twins, a lot of men consider us interchangeable."

"Lucius doesn't."

She laughed. "True enough. Almost from jump, Lucius treated me like a little sister and Bethany like a sex goddess."

"That must've been a change for you." Some new inflection entered his tone. "I imagine you have men hot on your heels all the time."

"No. At least, not the way you mean." Her pleasure faded. "Too many times in the past, men have shown an interest only because of my ability. Like the clown following us, they want to interview me, or maybe expose me or use my talent in a way I'd never condone. When I turn them down, they go to Bethany, hoping that they can get closer to me through her."

"That's why you don't date much, huh?"

She could feel his heat, and his caring. "I have great intuition with animals, but I'm not that good at figuring out which men to trust." And after meeting Osbourne, she hadn't wanted any other men.

Two heartbeats of silence passed before Osbourne said, "I don't work tonight, but then I won't have another day off for a week."

She tipped her head, unsure where he was going with that disclosure, but hopeful all the same.

"What about you?"

"Like Lucius, I'm on vacation. This close to Christmas, women aren't that interested in exercise. They're too busy shopping and baking and fitting in all the holiday craziness. I have the next seven days free."

"Good." He glanced at her, then away. "Will you spend Christmas with me?"

Her heart soared, her face warmed. But suspicion niggled. "Because you want to spend time with me, or because you're worried about the guy following us?"

"Both."

At least he was honest. She looked at his mouth—and wanted to melt. "And because you want to have sex?"

"Definitely."

Her toes curled inside her shoes. She gave it quick thought, but really, the way she saw it, it was a win-win situation. She smiled, and said, "Okay."

Four

They returned the rental truck first, then went back to Marci's apartment so she could throw some clothes and other things into an overnight bag. He should have been exhausted, Ozzie thought, but instead, anticipation sizzled inside him.

While he waited impatiently, his mind abuzz with what would soon happen, he called the station and explained that the donkey was now at his rightful home. Someone else would take over, to figure out how the funeral home came into possession of the donkey in the first place.

When he finished that, Ozzie roamed the living room and kitchen of Marci's tiny apartment. Everywhere he looked, he saw surprising little clues to her personality. Tidy surfaces. Organized drawers. Light, feminine touches.

Even her bathroom was devoid of the clutter typical to women. Everything had a place, and was in it.

It seemed his sentimental, whimsical little elf was a

neat freak. He'd honestly expected her to be scattered and somewhat disorganized. Ainsley had been so chaotic all the time, in her emotions and in her surroundings.

But then most of what he'd learned of Marci today had proved she was not only different from Ainsley but from most other women he'd known.

Her incredible vulnerability, combined with her compassionate tears when Magnus finally reunited with his family, had pushed Ozzie right over the edge. Marci was one of a kind.

He'd have her today, and to hell with what Lucius had said.

To hell with his own misgivings, too. Getting too involved with her might be a bad idea, but he couldn't resist the sexual lure any longer.

As he left the bathroom, he thought he heard her muffled chatter. Cocking a brow, he called out, "Marci?"

"Be right there."

Curious now, Ozzie wandered to her bedroom door and silently pressed it open. He found Marci on her knees beside the bed, looking under it.

The position elevated her sexy backside and put thoughts of sex on the fast track in his brain. "Damn, I love your ass."

Laughing, she looked over her shoulder at him. She balanced herself on one hand, and with the other she held a phone to her ear. "Sorry. I can't find my car keys. They're here somewhere. The donkey sort of bumped things around so I think they must've fallen off the nightstand—"

"Who are you talking to?"

"My sister."

"So your sister *knew* you'd stolen a donkey? Does that mean Lucius knew?"

Suddenly Marci blushed and whispered into the phone, "No, Bethany. No, that's *not* what he said."

She cast an uncomfortable look at Ozzie, but he wasn't about to budge.

In an even lower tone, her face red-hot, she said, "Not *me*, my ass."

Ozzie grinned. So, Bethany had heard his comment about Marci's backside.

"It's not at all the same thing," Marci argued while turning her back on him. "I have to go. Yes, I know. You, too." When Marci faced him again, she wouldn't meet his gaze, and that bothered Ozzie enough that he decided not to tease her.

"You don't need your keys. I'll drive."

She shook her head. "No, thanks. You'll be at work at night and I don't want to be stranded."

That made sense, so he let it go. "Then let's find the keys and get out of here before the roads get any worse."

As he started to bend down to help her look, she straightened with the keys in her hand. "Got 'em." Still flustered, she started to close her overnight bag, and Ozzie noticed the thermal pajamas she'd included.

"You won't need those."

She nudged him aside and shoved the bag shut. "Maybe not tonight, but after that . . . Um. I *am* staying more than one night, right?"

Damn, but her uncertainty got to him. Catching her shoulders, Ozzie drew her toward him and kissed her soft mouth. "Through Christmas, if you like."

"I like," she whispered back.

She tried to kiss him again, but he leaned out of reach. "If we start that, we'll never get out of here."

Her tongue came out to slick over her lips. Her big

blue eyes darkened. She laid one hand lightly on his chest. "Well, my bed is right—"

"No." She'd be the death of him. From one second to the next, he got so primed he hurt. "I don't want to start anything here, because I haven't been to bed yet. Let's get to my place so I can sleep afterward." If she objected to his third-shift lifestyle, better to find out now.

Her touch went from seducing to soothing. "I bet you're pretty exhausted, huh? You've been up so long now."

He was horny, not sleepy, but he didn't say so. "If it'd been a normal day, I could just stay up and sleep tonight. But it's been nonstop since I got to work."

"How come?"

He shrugged. "We had a barricade/hostage situation with lots of gunfire. Everything worked out, but that kind of situation gets the adrenaline pumping. When it fades, so does the energy level."

"And then I dragged you into my donkey adventure." She looked up at him with apologetic eyes. "I'm sorry."

"Actually, returning Magnus to his rightful owners was nice." The highlight of the day—if he discounted the intimacy he'd shared with her.

He kissed her again, quick and hard, then hauled up her bag. "Let's go."

On their way out of the bedroom, she said, "I just need to let the others know where I'll be."

That stalled him. Telling her sister was one thing, but, damn Lucius, the apartment building overflowed with busybody women. He didn't want them all privy to his business. "You're going to advertise what we're doing?"

She looked up at him, saw his discomfort, and laughed. Catching him by the front of his shirt, she towed him along.

"I won't shout it from the rooftops, but all the tenants are close and I don't want anyone to worry when they don't see me around."

"Why would they worry?"

"We're all single women, so we look out for each other. Now, come on, quit dragging your feet."

A minute later, Ozzie stood still in the hallway, surrounded by curious female gazes. After the first knock on her next-door neighbor's door, every other door opened.

Marci said, "I'm going to spend Christmas with Osbourne," and that started a barrage of questions, accompanied by several skeptical glares in his direction.

A lesser man would have withered under such scrutiny, but Ozzie held tough. When the babbling finally calmed, he said, "Ladies," and he took Marci's arm to lead her outside.

It was like walking the gauntlet.

Women of various ages and professions watched them every step of the way, some of them whispering, some laughing, one whistling, and overall acting bawdy and suggestive.

When they were out of sight of prying eyes, he allowed himself to grin. It pleased him that Marci had such close friends. She often seemed so dreamy, that he'd worried about her. But she was obviously very well liked.

"I'll follow you," she said, breaking into his thoughts, "since I don't know where you live."

"All right, but stay close. And keep your cell phone on. The road crews might not have gotten out yet and the streets could be bad."

She put a wool-covered finger to his mouth. "I know how to drive in the snow, Osbourne. Don't worry. I'll be careful."

Snowflakes gathered on her nose and lashes again. He shook his head, opened the driver's door to her blue Dodge Neon, and set her overnight bag on the passenger seat.

Marci got behind the wheel to start the engine and turn on the heat. Ozzie went to his truck, got a windshield scraper, and came back to clean away the ice and snow so she'd have a clear view.

Rather than sit in the car as it warmed, Marci got out with her own scraper and helped. It was a good ten minutes before her car was drivable.

The roads weren't as bad as he'd feared. They made decent time, all things considered. He drove cautiously, constantly checking on her and at the same time watching for that idiotic reporter. He thought he spotted the van once, but with so much blustering wind and drifting snow, he couldn't be sure.

The house his grandma had left him sat on an isolated twelve acres, surrounded by woods and overgrown fields. Not since her early days had she done any farming, but she'd been too content with her privacy to sell the land. She hadn't been rich, except in spirit and love, but she'd never really wanted for anything, either.

When they reached the long driveway, Ozzie pulled over and instructed Marci to precede him. He wanted to make sure no one followed them. She looked at him curiously through the frosty window, but did as he asked. No other cars came into view, so after a few minutes, Ozzie joined her under the sloping carport roof.

In the gray light, the house showed its age. All along the foundation and walkway, dead, brittle weeds and wild shrubs poked up from the snow. Stark, multipaned windows were in desperate need of cleaning. Ancient patio furniture had all been moved to one side of the porch, giving the appearance of a salvage yard.

He'd have to explain to Marci, to make her understand that he'd wanted to update his grandmother's house, but she'd refused to let him spend a dime of his own money. As he stepped out of his truck, she got out, too, and she looked around with awe.

"Osbourne," she breathed, "it's incredible."

Explanations died on his tongue. He retrieved her bag, saying, "It needs some work."

"It's charming. And look at all that land. How much of it is yours?"

The temperature hung in the twenties, and Marci had her arms around herself. Yet she still stood staring out at the vast expanse of snow-covered acreage.

"All of it. In front of us, it goes all the way to the road. To the sides, it includes the woods, and some into the clearing, up to the fence line. Behind us it runs to the creek. Twelve acres in all."

"A creek." She whirled to face him. "Maybe tomorrow you can show me?"

His mouth, half-frozen, lifted into a smile. She was the charming one, so delighted with everything, so nonjudgmental. "Sure. We'll make a snowman. Come on. It'll be a lot warmer inside." He led her to a door on the other side of the carport. "I usually park in the barn, but this is closer."

She stared down at the bottom half of the door. "Is that a doggie entrance?"

"Yeah. Grimshaw uses it. He was Granny's dog, but now he's mine."

The carport opened into a heated mudroom, so that when Ozzie worked, Grimshaw could get into the warmth of the house or outside to run, as his mood led him. Another doggie door opened into the main house, and when Ozzie was home, he kept it unlatched. But for reasons of safety, he secured it whenever he was away from the house. He'd had everything from raccoons to skunks try to enter and root around.

Expecting Grimshaw to come greet him as he usually did, Ozzie unlatched the door. But there wasn't a single sign of the dog.

"He must be out playing. He does that. And with me being late, he probably got tired of waiting for me. The area is all fenced, but even if it wasn't, he knows his perimeters. He's safe enough. And I've found out that he loves the snow."

Stepping from the mudroom into the kitchen, Marci asked, "What kind of dog is he?"

"I don't know. A mixed breed. That was the only kind Granny ever had. I grew up with all kinds of animals, but now there's only Grimshaw."

Marci turned a circle to take in the spacious country kitchen with lots of wood trim. As she tugged off her boots to leave by the door, she said, "Wow."

"When I find the time, I plan to refinish all the wood trim, replace the cabinets and countertops, and install new appliances." Never taking his eyes off her, he removed his snow-covered boots, too.

"It's amazing."

At the end of his tether, Ozzie relocked the main door, set her bag on the table, and put his arms around her from behind. "My restraint has been amazing. But no more." While kissing the nape of her neck, he deftly began opening her coat.

At first, she melted, but she quickly rallied. "Osbourne, wait."

"Can't." He pushed his groin against her bottom and wanted to groan. "I need you."

"I'd like to shower first."

"I hope you're joking." He got her coat free and stripped it off her.

She turned to face him, her cheeks rosy, her eyes bright. "But . . . I smell like a donkey."

Anticipation growing in leaps and bounds, Ozzie looked her over. "Trust me, Marci, you could smell like the donkey's . . ."

"Osbourne!"

"Foot." He smiled at her. "And I wouldn't care." She giggled, and that was enough to send him into a frenzy of lust. Scooping her up and over his shoulder, he said, "I'll shower with you. After."

He bounded up the winding stairway two steps at a time, his hand on her behind, caressing her. Thank God, Grimshaw was out playing somewhere, otherwise he'd need to spend a few minutes greeting the dog and he just didn't have the patience right now. Poor Grimshaw had become especially needy since Granny's passing, and Ozzie never ignored his feelings.

But right now, he had only one thing on his mind.

After moving into Granny's house, he'd taken his old bedroom, the first at the top of the landing. That's where he went now to dump Marci on the big brass bed.

She surprised him again by withholding all arguments. Instead, she began stripping away her clothes with the same frenzied need he felt.

Perfect.

Watching Marci as she twisted and turned on the bed in her efforts to get rid of her sweatshirt, Ozzie reached over his shoulder, grabbed a fistful of his shirt, and yanked it off.

With her sweatshirt bunched above her breasts, Marci paused to watch him.

"No, don't stop." Putting one knee on the bed, he hauled her into a sitting position and easily removed the roomy top, leaving her in low-slung jeans and a sexy white lace bra.

To Ozzie, she looked like an advertisement. She looked like raw temptation. She looked . . . like a fantasy about to happen.

A small, feminine smile tilted up the corners of her mouth and her eyes grew smoky as she watched him through lowered lashes. Baby-fine hair hung over her naked shoulders and her breasts quivered with her deepened breathing.

He could see her nipples, stiff and rosy, against the thin bra cups. His chest expanded, his erection grew. Blindly, his gaze glued to her breasts, he popped open the front closure of her bra and at the same time, bent to take one nipple into his mouth.

On a soft gasp, Marci arched her back. Her fingers sank into his hair and together they went down onto the mattress. He wished they were already naked, but he couldn't seem to give up this pleasure to advance his position. She tasted better than perfect, and the small sounds she made, the way she squirmed, burned him.

He switched to her other breast, then stroked one hand down her narrow rib cage, to the waistband of her jeans, then onto the denim to stroke that fine behind.

"Osbourne?"

He didn't answer. He couldn't.

"I've waited long enough," she whispered. "Let's get naked." Her hands roamed his shoulders before going to his neck and back into his hair. "I want to touch all of you."

A shock of electricity couldn't have jolted him more. In a nanosecond, Ozzie was off the bed. Their hands tangled as they both tried to attack the fastenings to her jeans. Ozzie gripped her wrists, pressed them upward to lie beside her head, and said, "Let me."

With another contented smile, she settled into the

covers and let him take over. Impatience had her squirming as he opened her jeans, got them down as far as her knees, and paused to look her over again.

"Osbourne . . ."

He stripped away the jeans.

Her panties matched the now-open bra. His gaze scorched her; his hand followed in the same path. From the inside of her left knee, up her thigh, over her belly and to a plump breast. She felt silky and warm, and so damn soft.

He actually trembled.

Forcing himself to a modicum of patience, Ozzie cupped his hand over the crotch of her panties.

Hot.

His guts clenched, and he accepted the inevitable. "I'm sorry, babe, but this is going to be fast and hard."

"Good."

Her agreement nearly laid him low. "I'll make it better later." And with that, he skimmed off her panties, and knew he wouldn't last more than a minute.

Marci edged her arms out of her bra straps while he finished undressing. He placed his pager, cell, and gun on the nightstand. When he dropped his jeans and boxers he heard her sharp inhalation, but he didn't look at her. Not yet.

Women always got giddy over his size; he'd learned to take it in stride. In fact, sometimes their enthusiasm almost seemed demeaning. Dumb as it sounded, and he'd *never* admit it to another guy, he wanted to be seen as more than a well-hung stud.

Doing his best to ignore Marci's stare, he pulled out a condom from the dresser drawer and ripped open the foil packet with his teeth.

"Um . . . Osbourne?"

"Hmmm?" Please don't let her start fawning on his proportions.

"Are you sure this'll work?"

His head snapped up in surprise. Marci sounded more than a little apprehensive, and she was staring at his cock—but not with excitement.

Well, damn.

Her gaze lifted to meet his, and he couldn't help but smile at her reservation. "Don't worry. It'll work."

"You think?"

"I guarantee it." Given her wary look, he probably should spend a little more time reassuring her. But he wanted her too much to waste time with conversation. Instead of telling her, he'd just show her how great it'd be.

She pushed up to one elbow. "I had no idea . . ." Her words trailed off into nothingness.

"You'll like it, Marci, trust me."

"Somehow I'm not as sure as you."

Moving closer to the bed, Ozzie clasped her ankle and said, "I've never hurt a woman."

"I know you wouldn't on purpose, but . . ." She raised a brow at his erection.

Half-laughing, Ozzie used his hold on her ankle to open her legs a little, then he stretched out over her. He cupped her face and looked into eyes round with uncertainty. "We'll be a perfect fit." His voice turned gruff with need. "I swear."

She nodded, but said, "It doesn't seem . . ." Rather than finish that thought, she cleared her throat.

"Seem what?"

A frown marred her brow. "Why didn't you tell me that you. . . ?"

She wasn't finishing her sentences, and Ozzie managed another laugh. "That I wear a magnum extra large condom?" Her skin was so soft, he couldn't stop stroking her cheeks. "Yeah, that'd be a conversation topic, wouldn't it?"

"Magnum extra large? That big?" She nodded. "I rest my case."

Done with the chitchat, Ozzie kissed her gently on the lips and said, "Open your legs more, Marci."

As if preparing for the unthinkable, she slowly sucked in a deep breath, and her legs parted more so that he naturally settled closer. His chest pressed her soft breasts, his erection nudged against the notch of her open legs.

It wasn't close enough.

Watching her, Ozzie reached down between them and parted her soft sex. He didn't enter her yet, he just rested against her. "Okay?"

With his weight on her, she squirmed, and said, *"Oh."*

He pressed firmly against her little clitoris, and every movement she made stroked her along the ridge of his erection.

Softly, he asked, "Feel good?"

She licked her lips, and nodded.

"How about this?" Shifting the smallest bit, he rocked forward and back, and was rewarded with a groan and the bite of her nails on his shoulders.

"That's what I thought." Cupping her breasts in his hands, Ozzie kissed the corner of her mouth. "I'll fill you up, honey. And you'll hold me so snug. But I won't hurt you. You're almost ready for me. Can you feel how wet you're getting?" He continued to move gently, holding himself in check to keep from rushing her. "Wet enough that I'll go right in. And you'll like it."

"Osbourne . . ." Showing blatant need, she held his face and kissed him deeply.

From the very first time he'd seen Marci Churchill, Ozzie had felt drawn to her. Deep down, he'd known how perfect it'd be with her.

Now he also knew that he loved the taste of her, her scent, the feel of her skin and hair. Her openness and sexual honesty.

Marci *was* a little nuts, but not in a mean-spirited way. She'd focused on his size, but without lascivious glee. How could he keep himself distant from her, when on every level, she touched his heart?

Marci was special, and he needed their time to be special, too. While Ozzie let her control the kiss, he teased her erect nipples with his thumbs and continued that subtle body friction, back and forth, wetter and hotter with each stroke.

It seemed he'd been denying himself for a lifetime, and if she didn't accept him soon, he'd embarrass himself. That thought no sooner entered his brain than she hooked her legs over his hips, wrapping herself around him.

Out of desperation, Ozzie took that as an invitation to proceed.

He drew back, and this time when he came forward, he sank into that wet heat.

She broke the kiss with a gasp, her eyes closed, her lips parted. Watching her, gauging her every reaction, he pressed in farther. Her nails scored his shoulders, but he didn't mind.

"Easy," he whispered, feeling her clench tight around him as he worked beyond the natural resistance of her body. He kissed her again, stifling her groan, holding her still as he squeezed in deeper and deeper. He wanted all of her. He wanted to bury himself in her.

When her legs dropped to the side of him, her heels bracing against the mattress, he raised his head to look at her. She appeared dazed and excited, and very accepting.

"A little more," he encouraged.

Her breathing turned ragged, and her slender frame went taut.

He slipped one hand beneath her hips, tilted her up, and her body welcomed the rest of him.

Marci arched into him.

Ozzie held perfectly still.

Sweat dampened his shoulders, and he felt his muscles quivering with the restraint. His cock throbbed and pulsed with the need for release.

Through clenched teeth, he whispered, "Talk to me, Marci."

Instead, she moaned, not a moan of pain, but one of acute pleasure. Her arms went around his neck, her legs wound tight around his hips. She opened smoky blue eyes, and murmured low, *"Osbourne . . ."*

He was a goner.

Sealing his mouth over hers in a voracious kiss, he began thrusting, hard and fast, just as he'd warned her it would be.

Unfortunately, she liked it enough that her internal muscles clamped around him, and she made small sounds of rising satisfaction that sent him right over the edge.

He left her mouth to growl, "Sorry, so *damn sorry . . ."* and he came in a blinding rush that wiped all coherent thought from his mind.

Marci held him, caressed him, moaned with him, and when the storm finally passed, she hugged him and put small, sweet kisses on his shoulder.

Lethargy held him for long minutes. In Marci's embrace, he basked in the afterglow of release, the complete elimination of tension and the relaxation of every muscle. It had been a long night and a frustrating morning. The day had passed into afternoon and he was suddenly so tired he couldn't see straight.

He was just about to doze off when Marci let out a shuddering, soft sigh. Ozzie returned to the here and now with startling speed.

Oh, shit. *Talk about blowing it.*

With much effort, he rolled to the side of her and tried to gather his wits. After that disappointing performance, he didn't want to look at her. And with the way his legs still trembled, he wouldn't even be able to make it up to her until he got some sleep.

But he wouldn't be a coward. He'd apologize. He'd man-up and promise to do better next time. Soon. Like in a few hours.

Raising himself on one bent arm, he looked down at her, and was surprised to see her smiling at him.

What the hell did she have to smile about?

Ozzie frowned. "You okay?"

The smile widened. "I'm terrific."

He glanced down over her naked body. Her legs were still parted, and one of her socks had fallen off, leaving a small foot bare. Her silky skin looked rosy. The light brown curls between her thighs were damp.

Hell, maybe he didn't need to sleep after all.

He reached for her, and a distant bark carried over the wind.

Groaning, he flopped back on the bed.

"What's wrong?"

"The dog must have finally seen my car. He's on his way in."

She crawled over the top of him and propped her pointy elbows on his chest. "That's a problem?"

"It's just that he likes a lot of attention when I first get home." Ozzie put both hands on her bottom and patted. Damn, but being this close to her felt nice. Talking with her was nice.

Having sex with her had blown his mind.

"You don't like to give him attention?"

"I do." Her disgruntled frown eased. "But a sexy broad has pretty much taken all my steam. I'm beat."

"Oh." Her lips curled again. "I can take care of him."

That smile was starting to get to him. "Let me up, woman, or we'll be taking part in naked wrestling with a wet dog."

She moved off the bed, stood before him beautifully nude, and stretched. Without a speck of modesty, she bent and picked up her sweatshirt, then shrugged into it. "It's chilly in here."

Ozzie still felt like a furnace, but he said, "I'll adjust the heat." He scooped up his jeans and then caught her arm. "Bathroom is this way."

Leading her out of the bedroom and a little way down the hall, he said, "Wait here. I'll be right out." He closed the bathroom door on her, rid himself of the condom, and splashed his face.

God, he wanted to sleep for a week, but it'd seem pretty crass to bring a woman in, do a wham-bam-thank-you-ma'am, and then leave her to her own devices.

He was such an ass.

He pulled on his jeans and when he stepped out, Marci was peeking into the next room down.

"That's a guestroom. Granny's room is at the end of the hall, with a sewing room in between. When I get to renovating, I plan to connect the bathroom and my bedroom, and turn the sewing room into a guest bath."

She trailed her fingers along a ragged piece of flocked wallpaper in the hall. "This place is huge."

"And run-down. Granny didn't take much to change." He gestured for her to use the bathroom. "Make yourself at home. I'll go down to greet Grimshaw. Join us when you're ready."

"Wait for me! I'll only be a second." And sure enough, she was in and out of the bathroom in a flash. Bare-assed and beautiful, she darted into his bedroom to retrieve her panties and jeans.

They were halfway down the stairs when he heard the clicking of Grimshaw's nails as he raced over the kitchen floor.

Ozzie stepped in front of Marci. "Brace yourself."

A second later, tongue hanging out one side of his mouth, eyes wild with excitement, Grimshaw skidded around the corner. He saw Ozzie, and he howled with berserk rapture before pounding up the stairs in a blur of black fur.

"Oh, Osbourne, he's beautiful."

Ozzie sat on a step so the dog couldn't knock him over and then Grimshaw was in his lap, wiggling and licking to the point that Ozzie couldn't help but chuckle. He tried to get around Ozzie to inspect the newcomer, but his paws were frosty with snow and he was slobbering, so Ozzie played defense for Marci.

He should have known it wasn't necessary. With no hesitation at all, she sat down beside him and let Grimshaw shower her with affection.

Turning her face, she avoided a doggy lick on the lips, and laughed. "You're a wild one, aren't you?"

"He's always like this," Ozzie told Marci.

"He's relieved that you came back." She stroked the dog as he moved back to Ozzie's lap. "With the way your grandmother passed so suddenly, he's never certain if you'll leave him, too."

Ozzie froze at that awful thought. He hugged Grimshaw close and frowned at Marci. "What the hell are you talking about?"

She smiled at the way Grimshaw rested his head on Ozzie's shoulder. "Losing your grandmother has been really hard on him, and adjusting to your schedule isn't easy, either. She didn't work, did she?"

"No. She didn't have to. She owned the house and had enough in the bank to live off the interest."

"So she spent most of her time here with him." With Grimshaw quieter now, Marci studied him. "She died in her sleep?"

"Yeah." How the hell had she known that?

Ozzie had the weird suspicion that she was reading the dog's mind. He shook his head at himself.

"Granny wasn't sick or anything. I spoke with her every day. One day she told me she was feeling tired, so she planned to go to bed early. She was always so full of energy, it worried me, so I told her I'd come out after work. When I got here that next morning, she was gone."

"Whenever she went into town to shop, or whenever she had an appointment, she took Grimshaw with her. He wasn't left alone very often. That's why he runs the property, to keep busy, to try to find someone to keep him company." She scooted closer and held Grimshaw's face up to hers. "Poor baby, you're lonely, aren't you?"

Fury, fueled by guilt, rushed through Ozzie. "I have to work and I have to sleep."

"Oh, I know that. But he doesn't. He's just a dog. All he knows is that his days are suddenly long and empty."

"So what the hell would you have me do?"

She put her arms around Grimshaw and hugged him tight. "You need to get him some permanent company."

Ozzie stiffened. "Uh . . . permanent company?"

Did she mean herself?

Was it such a repugnant idea?

Marci nodded. "A friend to be here when you're

not." Looking up at Ozzie, she stared him in the eyes. "I could make a really good suggestion, that is, if you're interested."

And then she started smiling again.

Five

Osbourne looked like he'd swallowed his tongue. Why, she didn't know. He obviously loved animals, and he had a big heart, so why would he be so stunned at her suggestion?

"I don't know about this, Marci. To be honest, after our discussion, I hadn't expected you to push like this. I mean, why would you even want to, after that less-than-perfect performance of mine?"

What in the world was he talking about? "Your performance?"

"Well . . . yeah. I pretty much molested you."

Realization dawned. "Oh." She grinned as pleasurable memories swirled through her, then she sat up away from the dog. "Your, er, performance seemed pretty perfect to me."

"*Perfect?*" If anything, he went more rigid. "You're kidding, right?"

"Not at all. I liked it that you were all wild and out of control and turned on. It was exciting. You're exciting." Then in a whisper, "I'm sorry if I was a little precipitous in my reactions. But there were . . . sensations I've never felt before. And I've wanted you a very long time."

Heat shot into his face and he shoved to his feet. Hands on his hips, brows down in a hot glare, he stared at her for what felt like an eternity. "Are you telling me you came?"

"Osbourne!" Marci covered the dog's ears, but then thought better of that and stood to face him. In a quiet rush, she said, "We should discuss this in *private.*"

"Oh, for heaven's sake. The dog doesn't understand us, so answer me."

She tucked in her chin. "You don't know?"

He brought his nose close to hers. "I was a little pre-occupied—and don't you dare start smiling again."

Puckering her lips to keep the smile at bay, Marci stared at his sternum. She absolutely, positively, could not look him in the eyes while discussing this. "Yes."

"Yes what?"

A glance at the dog proved they had his undivided attention. She went on tiptoe and breathed into Osbourne's ear, "Yes, I climaxed." And she thought to add, "You were wonderful. Thank you."

He clasped her shoulders and brought her into his chest. "You came?"

She still couldn't look at him. "Of course I did."

Then her feet left the floor and his mouth covered hers, and the dog started barking in glee. By the time Osbourne ended the kiss, she hung limp in his arms.

His now-damp mouth lifted in a cocky grin. "All right."

Marci shook her head at him, totally confused.

His tone gruff and indulgent, he said, "I suppose you can move in."

That brought her gaze to his. "*What?*"

"You can keep Grimshaw company." He lowered her

feet to the floor and patted her butt. "We both welcome you."

Marci wasn't at all sure she understood him. Hoping to clarify, she asked carefully, "You want me to move in with you?"

Now he looked uncertain. "You said you wanted to."

"I did?"

"Didn't you?"

She hadn't. But she loved that idea. Surely, Osbourne wouldn't make such an offer unless he cared for her beyond the sexual.

"Marci?"

She gave a firm nod. "Okay."

He groaned in grievous confusion. "Okay *what?*"

"Okay, I'll move in." So that he couldn't change his mind, she patted his chest and then hurried down the stairs. "Show me the rest of your house, then you can go on to bed and get some sleep."

Both he and Grimshaw were hot on her heels.

"Damn it, Marci—"

"You shouldn't swear in front of the dog. You're stressing him."

"He doesn't understand me."

"Maybe not your words, but he feels your tension."

She was almost to the kitchen when Osbourne caught her elbow and spun her around. She landed in his arms, hugged up to his massive chest. "Enough, woman."

Loving the way he put things, Marci smiled.

"And no more of that sappy smiling. It confuses me even more."

That made her laugh. "I smile when I'm happy. Forgive me."

"You said you had an idea of who should keep Grimshaw company. I assumed you meant—"

"Myself? Oh, no, I would never be so presumptuous. But that is an excellent idea, and naturally I'd be thrilled to stay here and be his companion." Even more, she'd love being Osbourne's companion. However, she still wanted to fulfill her other plan. "The thing is, I also know a dog at a shelter that no one wants, but she's wonderful and she'd fit right in here. She's about Grimshaw's age, and she's very passive, so Grimshaw could remain the dominant male—much like his owner. She's used to being kept outside, so all this land will be a joy to her."

If anything, Osbourne looked more furious. She worried about that, until he demanded, "What do you mean, she's used to being outside?"

Such a wonderful man. He was already worrying for the dog when he didn't even know her. "Her previous owners kept her chained to an old car in the backyard. When they decided to move, they dropped her off at the shelter."

"Bastards."

"Yes." Remembering the dog's desolation put a very real pain in Marci's heart. She pressed a hand there and her voice lowered. "She's not the prettiest dog, Osbourne, but she has beautiful brown eyes and a gentle heart and she wants so badly to find a loving home. All she's really known before now is neglect."

Osbourne's hand covered hers. "How about you call the shelter and tell them we'll take her? If the snow doesn't get too thick, we can go pick her up tonight."

Well. If she hadn't already loved him, that would have done it. "Really?"

"Yeah." When she launched herself at him, he caught her and swung her around. Grimshaw went nuts again, barking and running circles around them.

Catering to the dog's excitement, Osbourne lifted

Marci into his arms and then sat on the floor. Both she and Grimshaw shared his lap.

They ended up playing for a good fifteen minutes before Marci recalled that Osbourne really did need to get some sleep.

She put a hand to his jaw. "You're exhausted. Go on up to bed and Grimshaw will show me around."

Reluctant, Osbourne glanced at his watch and winced. "Yeah, I suppose I could use a few hours." He yawned and stretched. "You're sure you don't mind?"

She patted Grimshaw. "We'll be fine."

"Don't leave the house."

Another order? "Excuse me?"

"Your reporter buddy might still be poking around. I don't trust him. I'll feel better if I know you're safe inside."

"Oh." His concern pleased her. "Okay, then. Now go." She shooed him away.

Rather than leave, he bent to give her a sound smooch on the lips. "Make yourself at home." Then, to Grimshaw: "Keep an eye on her, boy, and as soon as we can, we'll go get you a woman friend."

Whether or not Grimshaw understood, he yapped at that promise.

Later, when Ozzie awoke from a sound sleep, he noticed several things at once.

First was the time. He'd planned to sleep only a couple of hours to refresh him, and instead he'd conked out for five hours. It was nearing Marci's bedtime now. Shit.

Next, he heard the barking, and not just Grimshaw's bark. Another dog? He sat up, wondering if she'd gone out without telling him. He didn't like that idea at all, and if they were going to make this work, they'd have to set up a few ground rules.

Then he inhaled the delicious scent that filled the air. Marci had cooked for him? His stomach rumbled, reminding him that he hadn't eaten anything since that breakfast sandwich early in the morning.

As he left the bed, he also heard the chatter and laughter. Did she have company? Had that damned reporter come back?

In his boxers, he left the bedroom and went to the top of the stairs. He could hear music playing and Marci speaking, but she didn't sound alarmed. Curious, he went to investigate.

The kitchen was empty, but a big pot of soup simmered on the stove, filling the air with fragrant steam. His stomach rumbled again.

Stepping back into the foyer, he listened, and realized the music came from the family room. One glimpse into the room, and he froze.

There in front of the television, with music videos turned on, wearing only a T-shirt, panties, and socks, Marci was doing aerobics. While she moved to the beat of the music, she talked to the dogs. Plural.

Grimshaw paid no attention to Marci's prattle. He was too focused on a big, loose-skinned female dog sprawled on the floor. From Ozzie's quick glimpse of the animal, she appeared to be a Labrador–Beagle mix. A few scars marred her beige fur, and she was missing the tip of one drooping ear. She lay flat on the floor, her head on her front paws. Her eyes—big, beautiful eyes, just as Marci had claimed—took in everything at once: Marci, the television, and Grimshaw.

Whenever Grimshaw got near her face, the dog half-cowered, and licked him.

Ozzie's heart turned over.

He started to speak, and Marci bent from the waist, causing the words to strangle in his throat.

"Don't worry, Grimshaw. I'll explain to Osbourne when he awakens, and we'll see what we can do. I'm sure he'll agree, and it might even be a comfort to him, too. But I have to be careful. He thinks I'm a kook and I don't want to do anything to encourage those sentiments."

Guilt roiled inside him. She was a kook, but now he considered it cute. And sweet. She used her kookiness to help animals, even when it earned her disdain from others.

"It's a miracle I'm here in the first place. Most guys are really freaked out by me. Do you know one young man I dated was so certain I'd flipped my lid that he went to Bethany and offered to help her get me committed!"

Torn between the luxury of watching Marci's sensual, fluid movements in a state of undress, and hearing the painful reminder of how hurt she'd been, Ozzie didn't know if he should speak up or slip away unannounced.

"Deep down," she continued, "I think he cares as much about me as I do him. From the beginning I've felt connected to him."

He'd felt that connection, too. And sometimes it spooked him, because Marci was so unlike other women. Not just unique but gifted in a way that defied all reason.

"It didn't matter that I scared off other men, but I don't want to scare off Ozzie. I want to try to make this work. It's just that with him—I suppose because I trust him and care for him—I sometimes blurt things out, and then everything is ruined."

Because he couldn't tear himself away, Ozzie cleared his throat and asked, "So this is my new dog?"

Screeching, Marci straightened upright and pushed sweaty hair away from her face. Eyes watchful, she tried an uncertain smile and said, "How long have you been there?"

"Not long." He eyed her up and down. "You look great, by the way."

Both animals had jumped at the intrusion. As usual, Grimshaw went berserk, more so now that he had something to show Ozzie, meaning a new friend. Running between Ozzie and the other dog, he barked and pranced and acted much like an excited puppy.

The new dog stood, but she tucked in her tail and lowered her head, and basically tried to make herself as small as possible.

Then she peed on his hardwood floor.

Marci said, "Oops. Sorry about that. She's still nervous. I'll clean it up."

"No. It's okay. I'll get it in a minute." Doing his best to ignore Marci's exposed legs and the way he could see her nipples through the tee, Ozzie went to one knee and held his hand out to the dog. "It's okay, girl. Don't be afraid." Then to Marci, "Does she have a name?"

"Lakeisha."

He smiled. "Did you name her that?"

She shrugged. "Her previous owners just called her dog, but Lakeisha suits her, and it goes well with Grimshaw."

"I agree." The dog watched him, then crept forward with hope bright in her big eyes. "You're a beauty, aren't you? It's okay. I won't bite, even if you do. C'mon. That's it."

She finally inched close enough for Ozzie to stroke under her chin.

Relying on Marci's talent, he asked, "Am I winning her over?"

Marci eased over to sit beside him. "Yes. She's more worried than afraid. This is all so new to her."

Grimshaw plopped down by Marci and tipped his head at Lakeisha.

"Is he jealous?"

Laughing softly, Marci said, "No. He's just trying to figure her out. He really wants to get to know her, but she's shying away from him. Grimshaw is a very gentle dog. He doesn't want to spook her, either."

Lakeisha got near enough to sit by Ozzie. She kept her head low, her ears down, but the more he petted her, the closer she got.

"She likes you, Osbourne. Isn't that wonderful?"

"Yeah." He rested his right hand on Lakeisha's neck, and gave Grimshaw a few pats with his left. "How'd she get here?"

"When I called the owner of the shelter to say we'd take her, he offered to drop her off. He's a friend and I think he was afraid we'd change our minds."

Ozzie acknowledged that with a nod. "What is it you want to tell me?"

She pokered up and stared at him. "You said you hadn't been there long."

"I wasn't. Just long enough to hear you tell the dogs that you'd talk to me about something. I'm starving and that soup smells awesome, but I want to hear what you have to say first."

It wasn't easy for Ozzie, because she sat beside him cross-legged, smelling of warm woman and wearing very little. But he sensed this was important and, like her, he didn't want to blow things.

"Your grandmother always decorated for the holidays."

Of all the things she might have said, he hadn't expected that. "Yeah, so?"

"Grimshaw misses it. He wants to see the decorated tree and the lights, and he wants to hear the music. Did you know your grandmother always had a real tree and Grimshaw had a terrible time resisting the urge to mark it?"

Ozzie stared at her. "How do you know that?"

Her expression went blank.

"Did you see photos of the house during the holidays?" He didn't know of any photos left lying around, but he wanted to be sure.

"No."

Lakeisha rolled to her back, and Ozzie absently scratched her belly. "So, tell me, Marci. How did you know?"

Staring down at her twined hands, she whispered, "Grimshaw has those memories."

"And you're a pet psychic."

Her shoulders sank. "I won't apologize for who I am."

"Of course not."

She frowned at him. "I know you don't believe me, but it's true. Grimshaw knew your grandmother as well as you did. He knows that she was very proud of you, and that she made special cookies for you at Christmas."

"She always sent a batch home with me."

"He has memories of playing in the snow with you. You've always been good to him and—"

Ozzie bent and took her mouth in a gentle kiss that sufficiently hushed her. "I like who you are, Marci Churchill."

"You do?"

"Yeah." Rather than belabor that point, he added, "And you're sexy as hell when you're sweaty."

"Sweaty?" Her brows pinched together, then shot upward. "Oh, I forgot!" She jumped to her feet and plucked the damp shirt away from her breasts. Fidgeting, she said, "I think I'll go shower while you eat."

He pushed to his feet, too, then stared down at her. "Tomorrow we can put up the lights. Maybe not all of them, since it's so close to Christmas already, but enough to make Grimshaw happy. And we can go find a tree. Granny always took one from the property. Not the best, you know. But a scraggly one that looked like it wouldn't have made it anyway. With the right decorations, even a half-dead tree looks nice."

Her smile lit up the room. "I'd love that."

"I'll clean up Lakeisha's mess. Go get your shower."

"You don't mind?"

"She's my dog now, right? I know she needs time to adjust. It's not a big deal."

She looked at him with naked adoration, then touched her fingers to his chest. Shyly, she asked, "What about you? Do you want to shower?"

An invitation? "Will the soup keep for another hour or so?"

Her eyes darkened. "I'll turn it on low."

Marci knew she should feel a little timid. After all, her sexual experiences were limited, and she'd never been with a man like Osbourne. But all she felt at that moment was anticipation. She wanted them both naked, now. She wanted his body against hers, she wanted to taste him—she wanted to feel him inside her.

He wore only snug boxers, and she loved looking at his broad chest, his strong shoulders. And his abdomen. The man had an impressive six-pack that begged to be stroked.

Locking her fingers together, Marci cautioned herself not to rush him. Earlier, when they'd made love, she'd been such a twit. First, his size had startled her, but Lord have mercy, she'd known only average men, and there was nothing average about Osbourne.

Then, within minutes of him touching her, she'd forgotten her worries and had been ready to climax. She'd tried to hold back, without much success. Luckily, he'd been just as aroused, and in his own release he hadn't even realized how uncontrolled she'd become.

She wasn't a wild woman. Sex for her had been pleasant, but not overwhelming. With Osbourne it was . . . explosive. Mind-blowing. So very, very special.

"You're okay?" Osbourne asked.

She nodded, cleared her throat, and said the first thing that came to her mind. "That tub doesn't look big enough for both of us."

He smiled. "We'll have to stay close, won't we?" He bent to turn on the shower, and the small room began to fill with steam.

Old-fashioned black and pink ceramic tiles surrounded the narrow tub. Osbourne parted the clear shower curtain, and when he straightened and faced her, his expression was hard and dark with desire. A quick glimpse down proved he was already hard, and it was all she could do not to reach for him.

He stood within inches of her. She'd pinned up her hair to keep it from getting wet, and Osbourne smoothed back a wayward curl. "The dogs are outside playing, so we shouldn't be interrupted."

Marci cleared her throat. "Do you have a condom in here?"

He shook his head. "We'll start here, but finish up in the bedroom. I'm not going to be rushed this time."

"Oh. Okay."

"You're not still nervous?"

"Nervous?" She wanted to jump him.

"You know, most women who comment on my . . . proportions, do so with excitement. I wasn't expecting it to worry you."

Marci licked her lips and gave him a dose of honesty. "I was startled, that's all."

His big hand cupped her face. "But now you like it?"

Her smile came easily. "Don't be silly. I want *you*, Osbourne Decker. It doesn't matter if you're big or small, or somewhere in between. You're still you."

For the longest time, Osbourne just stared at her. He had an odd, arrested look on his face. Then he gave a wry smile. "Well, I prefer big, but thank you for the sentiment."

Without her realizing it, he'd caught the hem of her T-shirt, and before she could think to say anything he whisked it off over her head. For only a moment, he admired her breasts, saying, "You are so beautiful." Then he bent to tug down her panties.

While on his knees, he cuddled her bare behind, drew her forward for a sizzling kiss to her navel and a slow lick down . . .

"Osbourne." Stumbling, Marci stepped out of reach and climbed into the shower. The warm water trickled down her body, doing little to help compose her. From the inside out, she trembled.

Wearing a sexy half-smile, Osbourne stood again. "Shy?"

She shook her head. "Sweaty. From my workout. Perhaps we should shower first—"

He laughed. "You taste good, Marci." After shoving down his boxers, he joined her in the shower. "But I want a better taste."

She'd never survive this. "Okay." Marci put her arms

around him and kissed his mouth. But Osbourne allowed that for only so long. The man seemed intent on devastating her.

Using the fragrant bar of soap, he lathered his hands and washed her all over, taking his time on her breasts, her belly, her behind. The soap made his fingers slippery, adding to the sensations.

This time when he knelt, Marci braced her back against the cool tile wall and planted her feet apart. Anticipation built, but Osbourne only looked at her, stroked her belly with the backs of his knuckles, trailed his fingertips through her pubic hair.

Her heart threatened to punch through her ribs. She couldn't take much more of this. She was about to encourage him to hurry things along when, after gently parting her, he leaned forward and closed his mouth over her.

"Oh, God."

There was no prelude, no easing into things. His hot tongue moved over her, in her, and his teeth nibbled on her most delicate flesh. Marci squeezed her eyes shut and moaned.

To keep her close and still, Osbourne opened one hand over her backside. With the other, he touched her and teased her. It was enough. It was too much.

Slowly, with infinite care, Osbourne concentrated his efforts on her clitoris while working his fingers deep inside her.

Somehow, he kept her upright through the orgasm, even though her legs felt useless and her bones were like noodles. When the sensations began to fade, Osbourne stood with her and cradled her close.

Marci had no idea what to say. "Thank you" didn't seem appropriate. "Wow" would be an understatement. "Your turn" was a given.

"Let's dry off and head to the bed."

Marci nodded, but she couldn't quite stand on her own.

Chuckling, Osbourne reached for the towel and did all the work for her. By the time he finished, she'd recovered enough to walk to the bedroom under her own steam. As they went down the hall, they heard the dogs back in the kitchen, and it sounded like they were playing.

Marci felt good. Really good. Things were coming together nicely.

And when Osbourne put on his condom and stretched out over her, it was even better. Now, she thought, if only it lasts.

Six

It was nearing midnight, and Ozzie couldn't keep his thoughts—or his hands—off her. Marci curled into his side, her naked thigh over his, her head in the crook of his shoulder. Cuddling with her left him with a deep sense of inner peace, and a physical sense of desperate need.

She was quiet, but she wasn't asleep, not with her hot breath brushing his skin and her inquisitive fingers busy on his chest.

He kissed the top of her head and said, "I feel like a horny high school kid."

With a purr, Marci trailed her hands down to his abdomen, perilously close to his groin. "You feel like a very sexy man to me."

After making love, they'd eaten soup, talked quietly, and then played with the dogs for a while before getting them settled in the hallway.

Ozzie should have been sated, but already he wanted her again.

Given the way she toyed with him, she felt the same.

His second effort at making love to her had been an improvement, but it hadn't abated the urgency he felt. He was starting to worry that he'd always feel that way with Marci—on edge, anxious, soft and hard at the same time.

She left him so confused, he didn't know what he wanted, or for how long, or when. Sex, definitely. Time with her, sure. A future? He'd never thought so, not with lessons learned from Ainsley.

But were there any real similarities between the two women? It nettled him to think he'd allowed Ainsley's machinations to affect him so deeply. So she'd lied, and tormented, and—

Marci slid atop him and put her mouth to his chin in a gentle kiss, then his brow, each cheekbone—and Ozzie was a goner. Her touch obliterated all thoughts of other women. Concerns drifted away, replaced by arousal.

He cupped her face, kissed her hungrily, and Marci kept pace with him every step of the way.

Very early the next morning, bright sunshine, reflecting off the snow-covered landscape, flowed in through the windows and stirred Ozzie awake. Automatically, he reached for Marci but found her side of the bed empty. He opened one eye. Huh. He'd need to talk to her about sneaking out on him, and he knew she had sneaked, because he was a light sleeper. She should have awakened him.

He glanced at the clock. Seven-thirty. Still early enough to put in a full day. He stretched, and grinned.

Today they would put up lights and a tree . . . things he hadn't considered doing because the loss of his grandmother had taken him out of the holiday mood.

Marci had gotten him right back into it, in a big way.

He wanted to make her happy. He wanted to make Grimshaw and Lakeisha happy.

And he knew that pleasing them would have pleased his grandmother also. She had no patience for melancholy and she'd loved him enough that she never wanted to see him in a funk.

He couldn't wait to go pick out a few gifts for Marci, and maybe a few things for the dogs. Because he often took walks with Grimshaw around the property, he already knew the perfect tree to cut. He could envision the house lit up with twinkle lights after he cleared the walkways and porch. This Christmas would be a special one, a tribute to his grandmother, and a chance to get closer to Marci.

Sudden, furious barking brought him out of his revelry and upright in the bed. Grimshaw sounded outraged. The dog was so friendly that Ozzie wasn't accustomed to hearing that particular sound.

Seconds later, as he was leaving the bed and searching for his jeans, Grimshaw's paws hit the closed door and he demanded immediate entrance. Forgoing the jeans, Ozzie opened the door and Grimshaw, overly anxious, immediately turned to go back downstairs.

Ozzie didn't need to be a pet psychic to know that Grimshaw wanted him to follow. Something was wrong.

Buck-naked, Ozzie raced down the steps. He could hear Lakeisha snarling and his heart shot into his throat. He rounded the corner of the kitchen—and came to a stunned stop.

Marci had her hands full holding Lakeisha back. Lakeisha fought her, but with good reason.

That damned annoying reporter, Vaughn Wayland, had wedged himself in the doggy door, apparently trying to break in. From all appearances, he was stuck. Grimshaw joined Lakeisha with a lot of threatening bluster and a growl that sounded feral and deadly.

Vaughn whimpered and choked in fear.

Marci spoke to the dogs, saying, "It's okay, guys. He's an idiot, but we don't want him to be a mangled idiot. Now, please calm down. Osbourne will take care of him. You don't have to do a thing."

Neither dog appeared to be listening to her.

Ozzie shouted, *"Just what the hell is going on here?"*

Silence dropped like a lead weight.

Everyone turned to look at him—Vaughn and Grimshaw with relief, Lakeisha with uncertainty, and Marci with wide-eyed shock.

"Osbourne!" Her face went red-hot. "You're *naked.*"

He slashed a hand in the air over that. "How long has he been there?"

"Not long," she choked, then she ran to get a dish-cloth to try to cover him. He took it from her and tossed it aside. The dogs sat back to watch.

"Vaughn, you've got some explaining to do."

The idiot started whimpering again. He had his head, right shoulder, and arm through the opening. But the rest of him remained in the mudroom.

Ozzie took two steps to stand over him.

Marci covered her eyes, but Vaughn stared up at him in fear.

Crossing his arms over his chest, Ozzie said, "You know I'm going to have your sorry ass arrested, don't you?"

In a pathetic whine, Vaughn cried, "I just needed an interview, that's all."

"There'll be an interview, all right. With the authorities. You can explain to them why you broke into my house."

Vaughn turned pleading eyes on Marci. "Just a few confirmations, that's all I need."

She joined Ozzie's side. "You're lucky I didn't turn the dogs loose on you. Lakeisha really doesn't like you at all, and that makes Grimshaw, who's usually such a friendly fellow, despise you as well."

Vaughn's head dropped and nearly hit the floor. "I'll do the article anyway."

Shaking her head, Marci said, "Go ahead. It won't be the first time. But people will call you a fool. Trust me, Mr. Wayland, no one will believe you."

His head lifted again. "But it's true, isn't it?"

Marci sniffed. "I have no idea what you're talking about." She turned on her heel and strode away.

"Where are you going?" Ozzie asked.

Over her shoulder, she called back, "To get you some pants. If you're going to call your police friends, I don't want them to see you like this."

He grinned—until he looked back at Vaughn Wayland. The bastard looked utterly defeated. How must Marci feel? She'd said it wasn't the first time someone had done an article on her. She also said no one ever believed in her ability.

Yet that didn't stop her from helping animals. Her heart was too big for her to stop.

Damn it, he was falling in love with her.

To the dogs, he said, "Watch him while I go make a call."

Grimshaw perked up his ears and plopped down right in front of Vaughn. His lips rolled back to show sharp teeth and a growl poured out of his throat.

Looking love struck, Lakeisha sat behind Grimshaw.

As Ozzie strode over to the phone, he thought, *What a way to start the day.*

Then a pair of jeans hit him in the stomach and he

looked up to see Marci eyeing him. Or, more precisely, she eyed a certain part of his anatomy.

"Does my nakedness bother you, Marci?" he teased.

She muttered, "You're shameless," but her gaze remained below his navel.

He couldn't help it—he smiled. Marci Churchill was in his house. She eyed him with lust.

It really was a hell of a way to start any day.

He was beginning to think it'd be a good way to start most of his days, from now until the end of eternity.

Now that he didn't have to worry about the reporter bothering them, Ozzie looked forward to Christmas morning with a lot of anticipation.

Since Marci had come to stay with him, everything had changed. For the better. In too many ways to count, she enhanced his life. The dogs loved her, and he loved the dogs.

Dining with her was always a unique experience, because Marci never indulged in ordinary conversation. She could still make him nuts on occasion, but now he was starting to like it.

She kissed him good-bye and welcomed him home with a hug, but she didn't smother him. She was independent, but not prickly about it. She had her own interests, and he was one of them.

Making love with her was the stuff of fantasies, but sleeping with her, listening to her even breathing, holding her close, was pretty damn sweet, too. Because of his third-shift job, though, he didn't get to sleep with her as often as he'd have liked.

When it came to his house, Marci had wonderful ideas about how to remodel. When their ideas clashed, she didn't push the issue. Unlike other women he'd known, she didn't insist that her view was the right or better one. For that reason more than any other, he found himself agreeing with her more often than not.

Little by little, Marci taught him how to read various signals from the dogs. A certain look or gesture, a sudden show of excitement. When he paid attention, it wasn't so hard to figure out what the dogs felt and why.

They knew when he started to get ready for work, and they reacted to it. Lakeisha would get antsy and Grimshaw would mope. Now that Ozzie was keyed in to their moods, he took the time to reassure them each and every night, and he felt better about leaving them with Marci there to keep them happy.

He couldn't decipher their thoughts the way she did, and when it came to other animals, he was hopeless. She loved to chat with the birds and squirrels that came each day for the seed she put out. She even conversed with white-tailed deer and the occasional fox. It amused Ozzie, but he no longer felt so clueless about her talent.

He no longer doubted her.

After the holidays, she'd probably need to return to her aerobics job. That thought didn't set well with him. He'd gotten used to having her around. The dogs needed her. They all meshed.

He considered cementing their relationship in some way, but he was still cautious enough that he held back. Marci's uniqueness made her special, but it also made her unpredictable. When he used his brain, instead of his gonads, he knew it'd be wise not to rush things.

For that reason, he refrained from any and all declarations and just tried to enjoy his time with her.

The night before Christmas Eve, while Ozzie was at the station working, another storm dumped seven inches of snow, topping it with sleet. He imagined the house would look beautiful all frosted in white, glowing with the lights they'd strung up from every window and door, every bush and tree.

In another hour, his shift would end. Marci would be up waiting for him. She and the dogs would greet him at the door. After breakfast, he'd take the dogs out to play, then he and Marci would indulge in some alone time. A wonderful routine.

He could hardly wait.

Ozzie had just pulled out of the parking lot when his pager went off. A rape-and-kidnapping suspect had barricaded himself in a woman's home. Neighbors said they heard the woman's screams.

With everything he'd need for a call out already on his person or in his truck, Ozzie turned around and headed to the location. He figured it'd take him less than fifteen minutes to get there, but fifteen minutes could mean life or death to a hostage.

As SWAT, he was used to being on call and didn't even think to resent the intrusion. It was his job, and he was damn good at it. Marci faded from his mind and he went into SWAT mode.

As soon as Ozzie and the other team members arrived, a detective filled them in. Ozzie learned that the suspect had a violent past and an extensive criminal history.

"Everything I've got right now is really vague," the detective explained. "I know that we've got an adult female being held against her will. Her mouth and hands are duct taped."

Ozzie nodded as, by rote, he prepared himself.

"We believe the victim is an old girlfriend of his, but we haven't been able to confirm that yet."

In rapid order, the SWAT team evacuated all the

neighbors. Some joined a television crew outside a blockade down the street, while others made use of an enclosed unit brought in to offer a place of warmth for the residents. Even though uniformed officers kept the reporters and camera crews too far away to interfere, Ozzie detested having them around during a time of crisis. He could do nothing about it, so he ignored them.

The SWAT team concentrated on establishing contact with the suspect. The man was antagonistic, desperate, and probably pumped up on drugs. After a couple of hours, when he still refused to come out peacefully, the team formulated a new plan.

They couldn't wait any longer, not with a female hostage inside.

Most of the SWAT team spread out, taking sniper positions that gave them the cleanest shots. Then, a couple of them deliberately broke the front windows of the home, drawing the suspect's attention while Ozzie slipped in through the back. On silent feet, he crept forward. He could hear the suspect cursing, outraged over the broken windows.

And he could hear the woman crying.

Keeping his H&K .40 caliber at the ready, he edged around a wall—and came face to face with the suspect. The panicked bastard fired a shot at him, but Ozzie was already moving.

Without a single second's hesitation, Ozzie brought his forearm up and slammed it into the man's face.

The man's nose shattered and he dropped his gun while staggering backward. In a heartbeat, Ozzie had him contained. He called in the rest of the team, and the crisis was over, with no innocents injured.

All in all, a job well done.

Once the scene had been cleared, the suspect arrested, and the hostage transported to the hospital via ambulance, Ozzie started for home. Reporters tried to interview him, but he dodged them.

As usual, the adrenaline began to fade, making him bone tired. But today, he wouldn't be heading home to an empty house. He thought of Marci waiting for him, and contentment seeped in.

The snow was thick on the ground and it crunched beneath his tires as he pulled down the long drive. He parked, trod through the white stuff to the door, and stomped to clear his boots.

To his bemusement, no one stood at the door waiting.

He walked in, heard an awful racket, and located Marci seated on the family room floor with both dogs, in front of the television. Tears tracked her cheeks and the dogs were howling, which probably explained why she hadn't heard him arrive.

"What's going on?"

They all looked up at once. For two seconds, time stood still—then they rushed him. The dogs reached him first, jumping and barking and circling. Sniffling, Marci threw herself against him.

Getting worried, Ozzie caught her close. "What is it, honey? What's wrong?"

She hiccupped, and burrowed closer. "I'm sorry," she said, and her voice sounded strained and unsteady. "I know you don't want a woman who frets. I tried not to."

Her hands knotted in his coat and she pushed back to glare at him. "But let me tell you, Osbourne, it's unreasonable of you to make such demands."

He had no idea what she was talking about. As usual. When he said nothing, she tried to shake him. "We saw that awful situation on the news!" New tears welled up. "The reporters said what you did, and that you got shot at, but they didn't know anything beyond that."

"Damned reporters," he grumbled. "I'm fine."

"I see that. *Now.* But you could have been killed."

His mood lightened and he had to fight a smile. "So you were worried about me?"

"Worried, and . . ." She gulped, hugging him close again. "And so proud. You saved that woman."

Still amused at her, and touched by her concern, Ozzie ran his hands up and down her back. "It's my job, honey."

"And, thank God, you're very good at it."

She wasn't going to complain about the danger? She wouldn't ask him to quit? Ozzie had never felt so loved—until Lakeisha peed on his foot in excitement.

"Oh, hell." He jumped out of the way and poor Lakeisha lowered her head in shame.

Marci switched alliances in an instant. "Osbourne, she's sorry. It was just an accident. She's been as worried as me."

"Is that so?" More than likely, the dogs were reacting to Marci being upset, but he didn't want to correct her.

"It's okay, Lakeisha," she said to the dog. "He understands. Osbourne, tell her you understand."

"I understand." He scratched the dog's ears and she relaxed again.

Marci nudged Ozzie, saying as an aside, "Don't forget Grimshaw. We don't want him to get jealous."

Ozzie wasn't sure if it was Marci's emotional upheaval, her instruction, her understanding, or the way she catered to the animals, but in that instant, everything became crystal clear to him.

Marci wasn't like other women. She sure as hell wasn't like Ainsley. Marci didn't have a mean or manipulative bone in her entire body. She was so open with him that she showed him a side of her he'd once scorned.

Her heart was big enough to care for everyone and everything, even when it earned her derision from others. And most of all, she trusted him.

Ozzie realized that he not only trusted her, too, he loved her. Everything about her.

Before he could think to censor his thoughts, he said, "I'm proud of you, too, Marci."

"You are? But why?"

"You're gifted, and caring, and strong. Strong enough to keep helping animals despite the grief people give you."

Her eyes welled with more tears. "Thank you."

"I love you, Marci."

She froze. Dashing away the tears, she blinked at him, then nodded. "I love you, too. I have almost from the first time we met. I knew you'd be different." And to the dogs, she said, "Didn't I tell you he was different?"

Ozzie touched her chin to bring her attention back to him. "Will you move in with me for good?"

"Yes."

Her quick answer had him grinning so big, his cheeks hurt. "Will you help me remodel the house so that we both like it?"

"I'd love to."

He went for broke. Dropping to one knee and taking her hand, he asked, "Will you marry me?"

Her smile trembled, then broke into a grin that rivaled his own. "The dogs think it's a wonderful idea."

"They're obviously smart dogs." He kissed her hand. "So what do you think?"

Laughing, she straddled him, then laughed some more when the dogs started jumping on them. "I think I'm getting everything I ever wanted this Christmas."

And he was getting everything he hadn't even realized he wanted. Thank God Lucius had insisted he keep an eye on Marci, otherwise he'd still be a lonely, miserable fool.

Now all he had to do was explain to Lucius why he'd disregarded his order not to touch Marci. Maybe when he got a ring on her finger, that'd do the trick.

"You want to go shopping?"

She pressed back to look at him. "Now?"

"Yeah." He kissed her. "I have one more gift to buy you, but I'd like your input."

"What is it?"

"An engagement ring." Ozzie stood with her still wrapped around him and started for the stairs. "I want every available male to know you're mine."

She laughed. "I knew you watched them watching me."

Of course she had. There was a lot Marci knew, because she was a very special, intuitive person. And now she knew they belonged together.

What had started out as the loneliest Christmas of his life was now the very best. He hugged her tightly and said, "Thank you, Marci."

"You're very, very welcome." She kissed him, and whispered, "Merry Christmas."

Bah Humbug, Baby

Gemma Bruce

For Roddy and Laurel,
who know how to keep
Christmas all year long.

One

Marcie
Subject just left, driving east. It's a go.
Greg

Greg
Ditto at my end. Driving west. Expect rendezvous at 22
hundred hours. Keep your fingers crossed.
Marcie
PS Merry Christmas

* * *

Allison Newberry downshifted her BMW and climbed upward through the foothills of the Rockies. She pulled the windshield visor down to block out the setting sun and tried to relax. Which shouldn't be hard. They'd stopped work early for the office Christmas party. The punch, generously laced with gin, had been consumed with the efficiency that Newberry Advertising was known for.

Now she was free. And thanks to her sister's pre-Christmas snafu, she wouldn't have to spend the week among the palm trees, doing Christmas the Newberry way at her parents' condo in Palm Springs.

No rush to the mall for last-minute stocking stuffers, no questions about her single status. No nagging her to eat more. No cloying eggnog without the bourbon. No off-keyed carols in front of the electric fireplace or oohing over a perfectly hideously colored scarf and matching mittens that seemed to be her Christmas present lot in life.

She owed Marcie big time. Actually she owed her brother-in-law, Steven, cheap bastard that he was, for nixing the ski chalet Marcie had booked for the holidays. When Marcie called, Allison was more than prepared to commiserate over Steven's penury, but she hadn't expected the bonus that Marcie tearfully delivered. She'd already paid for the chalet and couldn't tell Stevie baby, so she wheedled her sister into taking it over and sending her the money.

Ordinarily, Allison couldn't think of any place she'd rather be than stuck in the Rockies for a holiday that she wouldn't enjoy—except for Palm Springs. Marcie's coup de grace cinched the deal.

"Steven and I will take the children to Mom and Dad's if you'll just go spend a little-bitty week in a ski resort. And I'll tell the parents that it was a Christmas present. Then I'll tell Mom that you're doing it to help me out."

Allison knew she was sunk as soon as Marcie started ending her sentences on that upward swing. "Ski resort," sliding up the scale. Ditto for "Christmas present." Followed by "help me out," which added an extra glissando on the last word before sliding down again.

"And she'll tell Dad and you'll be the heroine of the day and you won't have to eat microwaved turkey."

Allison said "yes." It seemed like a no-brainer. Six whole days with no deadlines, no last-minute pullouts, no fight to the finish over logos and cover copy. Just her and her laptop. She might even get some real work done.

Maybe there was a Santa Claus after all, because her week off was certainly looking up. It seemed too good to be true.

She pushed away the disturbing thought that spending the holidays solo might be considered a little depressing. If she got lonely, she could always hit the ski lodge at night; sit around the fireplace surrounded by après ski hunks. And their bunnies. Well, hell. She could bunny with the best of them as long as she didn't have to go up the mountain on that T-bar thingee.

Nope. It was perfect. And if the spirit moved her, which she doubted, she could listen to her new disco Christmas CD—a present from her office secret angel.

In keeping with the season, she'd made a dash to the mall after work yesterday, where she loaded up on fashionable winter outerwear. Hell, she'd even bought a pair of snow boots. At least they resembled snow boots. She'd actually bought them from Nordstrom's. Okay, so they were turquoise with rhinestones; they *were* lined with fur. They made a statement.

And besides, it wasn't snowing.

* * *

Lee Simonson had learned early in life not to trust his family. But he had a soft spot for his baby brother. So when Greg presented him with an early Christmas present, the only one he'd be getting from that quarter, he didn't have the heart to turn him down.

A ski chalet in the middle of nowhere, surrounded by feet of snow. He'd promised Greg he would go. He didn't promise him that he would stay. The idea of sitting out a week in the mountains, alone, except for slope jocks and ski bunnies made his blood run cold.

And he didn't relish the idea of having time to think, to remember where he'd been last Christmas. How he'd waited for Allison at the LA airport for four hours, only to have her call and say things were running behind at the office and she wouldn't get there until the next day. Only she didn't get there the next day. By the time she did arrive, Lee was long gone.

No. One night was more than enough. Then he'd drive to the Denver airport to make a connecting flight in LA that would take him to Bogotá and his next assignment.

He'd be embedded in a covert operation that was involved in taking down a big drug cartel. It was Pulitzer prize material. His passport and ticket were in his inside jacket pocket and his cameras were packed in the trunk. He was ready to rock and roll.

And he would be able to truthfully tell his brother that the chalet was lovely. The mountains were awe inspiring. That, at least, probably wouldn't be stretching the truth. He'd throw in a few details and Greg would never know the difference. And Lee wouldn't have to mope through Christmas alone, thinking about the woman who couldn't commit.

* * *

A snowflake hit the windshield. Allison narrowed her eyes.

Another splatted on the glass, then another. She turned up the defroster. A larger flake hit and blitzed out. *Ho Ho Ho,* she thought. *Take that, you winter-wonderland reject.*

Soon hundreds of snowflakes were being zapped, then turned into rivulets of water. Melt and drool, melt and drool. It was better than a video game.

But she wasn't laughing when she reached 1,800 feet and the snow turned to a curtain of blinding white. Her BMW lost traction, skid over a slick spot, and she had to let go of the wheel to keep from spinning out of control. By the time she'd straightened the car out again, she was sweating. Nobody had said anything about a damn blizzard.

The sun had disappeared. She was surrounded by black except for the flakes that rushed toward her like computer animation. And for a second she felt a rush of panic as she imagined herself covered in a snowdrift, slowing freezing to death as she rationed out the box of Godiva chocolates she'd brought for the drive.

She slid around an S-curve and saw the dim outline of a highway sign ahead. It was completely covered over and leaned at a sharp angle into a drift of snow nearly as high as the sign. She pumped the brakes and came to a stop a few feet away from it. There was no indication of the road in front of her or to either side. Just white, fluffy wet stuff. Everywhere. Her better judgment told her to just turn around and go back to the nearest hotel, but when she looked out the back window, that road had disappeared, too.

Okay. She had been in tougher spots than this. But

only in a boardroom sort of way. She was an executive out of water here.

Resigned, she shoved the door open and stepped out of the car. She sank down to her ankles, while her face was pelted with icy spikes. Shivering, she waded over to the sign. Brushed it off with her bare hand. Found the words Good Cheer with an arrow pointing to the right. But which way was right?

Honestly, this was the last time she let Marcie talk her into bailing her out of a jam. She could be sitting by the pool in Palm Springs instead of being lost in a whiteout.

Yeah, with a newspaper hiding her "you're much too thin" body and avoiding questions like, "What happened to Lee? This is his fault, isn't it?"

Better the blizzard.

"Let it snow, let it snow, let it snow." She turned back to the car, climbed inside, knocked the snow from her boots on the runner and slammed the door. She shifted into first and, guessing where the road to Good Cheer might be, she plunged ahead.

She was actually relieved when she finally drove into the darkened town. An Alpine village circa 1950. *Where the sidewalks roll up at sundown,* she thought, as she drove down a silent Main Street. Not even an all-night diner in sight. Hopefully, the ski resort would be a little more lively.

The shopping area gave way to a row of A-framed cabins, their steep roofs covered with snow, the cute little gingerbread moldings, dripping icicles. A couple of vehicles were parked by the side of the street, barely visible under the mounds of freshly fallen snow. What appeared to be an ancient paneled truck had been abandoned sideways in the middle of the street.

She could see a few lit windows but not a sign of life. A few more lights winked up the side of the hills behind the town. But no blaze of light from the ski lodge. It must be farther out from town than Marcie realized.

Just as well; she wouldn't be distracted by the nightlife here.

She skirted the truck, rolled to a stop and turned on the interior light. Read the instructions once more, then hunkered over the wheel looking for the address of her rental.

It was a two-storied chalet, set a bit away from the other cottages, but with the same gingerbread trim, a small porch and a gable over the front door.

Just too fucking cute for words.

There seemed to be a light coming from a room on the first floor. A nice touch. At least the Realtor had been on the job. The BMW hydroplaned to a stop in front of the house, next to another vehicle completely camouflaged by snow. It looked like an SUV of some kind. One of her neighbors. God, she hoped they didn't have a bunch of screeching children.

She slid the key out of the white envelope that Marcia had Fed Exed her, grabbed her laptop and her suitcase and made a dash for the front door.

She nearly missed the steps since they more closely resembled a ski slope. She tripped up them and reached the porch just as a heavy, wet glob fell from the gingerbread trim and landed inside the collar of her jacket. She banged through the storm door, managed to fit the key to the lock and practically fell inside.

She dropped her suitcase in the small, tiled entrance hall and looked around. The first floor seemed to be one main room. Ahead of her was an open wooden staircase that led up to a second floor. And she could see kitchen appliances through the open risers of the stairs. To the left was the living area. Several lamps were lit and it was toastily warm. She hung her laptop on a peg by the front door and stepped back. There was a sheep-skin jacket and scarf already hanging on the peg.

The Realtor must be waiting for her. She probably had special instructions about heat and water and stuff. Maybe even a welcome basket with food and a bottle of wine.

Or not. This was not the Four Seasons, she reminded herself. And at this point, she'd be thankful for a piece of beef jerky. She took off her coat, shook off the excess snow and stepped fully into the room.

She heard an odd crackling sound, like the pop of wood in a fireplace. Noticed the smell of a fire. There was a fireplace. She could see the brick of the chimney on the other side of a long, dark-colored couch.

From behind it, a man stood up and turned toward her, surprise etched on his face.

A face that she knew all too well. The room went out of focus. Her knees buckled. A tall, dark-haired man dressed in a black sweater and jeans. Eyes an unusual shade of gray. And they belonged to Lee Simonson. Her soulmate, her nemesis.

She should have stopped for a burger on the road. Obviously hunger was doing weird things to her mind.

She blinked. Blinked again. He was still there and it was still Lee. Down to the scowl.

"You," she said as his mouth opened and "You," echoed back at her. Then, for a long moment, neither of them spoke, or even moved. Like the freeze-frame of a gorpy movie.

He moved suddenly, stepped toward her.

A bubble of joy rose inside her. Had he planned this? Was it possible? She hadn't seen or heard from him in over a year. And their last parting had been hurtful and final.

Then he checked, staring back at her as if he'd seen a ghost—or an ax murderer. He was as surprised as she. And he wasn't happy about it.

All the anger and hurt came back to replace that one unguarded moment of joy. She somehow found her voice, stammered, "What are you doing here?"

His scowl deepened. "Don't worry," he said. "I won't be for long." He tossed the piece of wood he was holding onto the fire and strode toward the staircase.

Allison felt a sharp stab of disappointment. Just what she swore she'd never feel if they ever met again. Which she had gone to some pains to ensure would never happen. And now here she was again, feeling humiliated, rejected and stupid.

"No. Don't."

He hesitated, his foot poised on the step. He glanced back at her and for an instant she thought she saw an expression of hope flit across his face. But then it was gone, leaving only the hard, cold eyes and the stubborn set of the jaw that she knew so well.

"I mean—I'll leave. You were here first."

"Forget it." He turned and took the stairs two at a time.

He was desperate to get away from her and she could hardly blame him. She felt awful about what had happened between them and hated herself for taking the responsibility. After all, he was the one who refused to compromise. Refused to give up any of his peripatetic life to share life with her. And, of course, being Lee, he blamed her.

Anger washed over her. A reaction so tied up in their relationship—check that, their ex-relationship—that she fell into it without having to try.

She stomped after him. Because she had to tell him that she hadn't planned this. Not that he would believe her. But she went anyway. Knowing that only accusations and recriminations would follow. But, damn it, for once he wouldn't get the last word.

When she reached the bedroom, he was throwing things into a duffel bag. His camera gear was packed and stacked in a corner.

"Where are you off to this time?" She knew she sounded bitter. Well, she was, so sue her.

She saw his shoulders rise and fall as he took a deep breath. How many times had they played this scene, her expecting to spend time with him and him running off somewhere to shoot the next Pulitzer prize–winning photograph.

"Columbia . . . the country, not the university," he added as if she were some dimwit.

"I didn't think you would stoop to doing campus news," she snapped, and then bit her tongue. This was stupid. She told herself just to back out of the room and sit somewhere out of sight until he had gone. She'd planned to be alone this week, and she'd be damned before she let Lee send her into a fit of depression or see her disappointment.

She was a fool for thinking even for a moment that he had planned this. Lee would never have stooped to tricking her into spending Christmas week with him, not in a snow-covered Alpine village, where the streets were probably lit with Christmas lights and people served hot cider and sang carols . . .

He zipped up the duffel and walked past her to the door.

She stepped aside, her throat clogging with lost hope of what might have been. She knew it would never work. Hadn't they proved that a thousand times? She had really thought it was over after he stood her up the last time. All because she was two days late. It was all right for his work to come first but not for hers.

It was finished. It had taken nearly a year, but she had gotten over him. And she was sure he had gotten over her.

So why did she feel so awful?

She knew why. They were soulmates. From their very first meeting, they had shared a complete connection and an unbridled passion. It should have been perfect—It was anything but.

She heard him run down the stairs and back up again, while she stood in the doorway, immobile. He brushed against her as he came back into the room. Awareness invaded her mind and body. She held her ground. Willed away the desire to fling herself at him. To ask him to let them try once more.

He slung a camera case and tripod carrier over his shoulder, picked up the last bag and walked past her, letting the case bang into her as he did.

She followed him out to the landing. Just as he reached the front door, she called out, "I didn't have anything to do with this."

He turned slowly and looked up at her. And she was hit by déjà vu of so many partings. Almost all acrimonious.

"You don't think *I* did?"

She shook her head, suddenly unable to speak.

He grabbed his coat off the peg and picked up his gear. "We were set up. Don't worry about it. I was only staying a night anyway. I have a flight to catch. Enjoy yourself."

As if she could after this. And she was going to kill Marcie for having interfered, and then she'd go after Greg.

Lee opened the door. A blast of cold air and snow burst into the room. With the snow swirling around him, he looked like an arctic explorer.

"I don't think you'll get far in this weather."

"I can try."

"Go ahead. Be stubborn. It's what you do best. But if you slide off the side of a cliff, don't blame me."

He gave her a long, hard look, then he stepped outside and disappeared into a wall of white. The door slammed behind him.

"Good to see you, too," she called. "And Merry Christmas." Her whole body was thrumming with adrenaline. With anger. And now she was stuck in this godforsaken town, having just been left by the man she loved—had loved, she reminded herself. But she was smarter now.

She gritted her teeth and growled, though it sounded awfully close to a moan. Disgusted, she grasped the banister and cautiously climbed downstairs on shaky legs. She needed something to eat and some coffee. She ducked behind the stairs to the kitchen and flipped on the light switch, praying that the last occupants had left a tin of coffee, or even a tea bag.

She opened a cabinet. There was an unopened tin of coffee. There was also a bottle of Courvoisier and several bottles of wine lying on their sides. She opened another cabinet. Cans of soup and condiments. A loaf of bread, boxes of gourmet crackers.

The fridge was stocked, too. The milk carton had a sell date a week away. Cheese, fruit, vegetables, eggs. There was enough food here for a house party.

And then she saw the bottle of champagne.

That hurt most of all. He'd lied to her. It was obvious he'd planned to stay more than one night, and it looked like he was planning to spend it with someone else. What if she showed up, only to find him gone and Allison playing happy hostess? How embarrassing would that be?

She nixed the coffee and poured out a glass of brandy instead. Then she piled cheese and crackers onto a plate and carried them back to the living room.

The fire was smoldering. She didn't know shit about fires. And there wasn't a Duraflame in sight, only a stack of real wood in a basket off to one side and a metal box stuffed with kindling.

Big deal. How hard could it be. She started sticking pieces of kindling in what she thought might be strategic places and was surprised when flames jumped to life. She added one of the split logs, trying not to think about Lee driving the mountain road, probably too fast, like he always drove. Fishtailing around a turn and sliding out into the air. The moment of freefall before the car crashed to the bottom and ignited into a conflagration of flames.

Shit, she shouldn't have let him go. What if he got killed? She shoved another piece of wood on the fire and stood up.

Not her fault, not her fault. She sank down onto the soft cushions of the couch. She tucked her feet up and stared into the fire. Tried to feel comfortable and cozy. She reached for her brandy, slid a piece of cheese onto a cracker and shoved the whole thing into her mouth.

He'd be fine. He always was. The man had survived more scrapes than a cat. And this was just a measly mountain road, a little snow. A piece of cake.

Two

Lee waded toward his SUV. It had snowed another six inches since he'd arrived two hours before. Damn Greg and Marcie for meddling in something they didn't understand. Hell, he didn't understand it and he was living it. He stopped in dismay as he took in the white mountain that had been his Range Rover.

Cursing under his breath, he knocked snow away from the handle and wrenched open the back door. A wall of wet, heavy powder fell on his feet. He cursed out loud. He threw his gear in the back and shrugged into his jacket. He opened the driver's door. This time he had the sense to jump back as the snow cascaded to the ground.

He turned the key, jacked up the heater and flipped on the wipers. Nothing happened. Then slowly they began to scrape in a plodding arc across the windshield. As soon as a crescent appeared in front of him, he shifted the car into reverse. The wheels spun, caught and the SUV jerked back. Snow from the roof dropped over the windshield, cutting off the outside world. The wipers stopped, trapped by the weight of the snow.

Lee shoved the car into park and got out. Used his arm to clear away the latest deluge and climbed back inside. His jacket was coated with snow, his toes were numb inside his boots, his fingers were stiff, and he was pissed. Pissed at Allison, at Greg and Marcie, but mostly pissed at himself for reacting like an ass. He could be sitting in a warm chalet, drinking champagne with Allison beside him. They could be making love in front of the fireplace right now.

But instead, he was uncomfortable, rapidly becoming drenched as the snow melted and seeped into his clothes, and he had an arduous drive down the mountain ahead of him.

He started to back out. Had to rock the SUV back and forth, before it jumped over the drifts and slid into the street. He shoved the gears into drive and the car shot forward—for two seconds. Then it fishtailed wildly before straightening out again.

Water began to trickle off his hair. It caught on his eyelashes, rolled down his temples, pooled at the back of his neck. He drove down the darkened street, calling himself ten kinds of fool.

At the edge of town, the road made a sharp turn and began to serpentine down the mountain. He shifted into second gear, cut the headlights to dim. Hunkered over the steering wheel, trying to distinguish the road from the rest of the snow. But all he could see was the look on Allison's face as she stood at the top of the stairs. Her dark eyes flashing with anger where he wanted to see acceptance. Her hair wild, curling black around her face like Medusa, like a siren, like the woman he loved. He'd wanted to drop his gear and throw her to the floor, make love to her before she had a chance to say no. But she wouldn't say no. And it would be wonderful . . .

The road curved back on itself, the SUV slid sideways. Lee could feel the rear tires sinking into the soft shoulder. He held the steering wheel with both hands, struggling to keep the tires straight, fighting the urge to wipe away the moisture dripping into his eyes. The rear end of the SUV continued to sink. Lee eased his foot down on the accelerator, the rear tires caught, and the SUV wobbled onto firmer ground. As soon as he was sure he was on the road, he quickly passed a soggy sleeve across his face.

He didn't see the tree until it rose suddenly out of nowhere. The car slammed into it with a crunch of crumpling metal. Lee was propelled forward. He hit the steering wheel as the white cloud of air bag surrounded him and the world went black.

Allison paced between the fireplace and the couch. She was wearing her new plush bathrobe and was on her second brandy. She'd showered in the European-style bathroom upstairs. Which, she had not failed to notice, was stocked with an array of body oils and lotions with provocative names like Strawberry Kisses and Aphrodite's Desire. She snorted. Some little elves had been busy for their arrival. Some little elves that were going to be mincemeat before the holidays were over.

The fire was blazing merrily, the room was toasty enough to walk nude if she wanted to. Which she didn't. She wanted to be out of here. She wanted to call Marcie and ream her into the New Year, but she'd tried using her cell, to no avail. And the house phone was deader than Marley's Ghost.

With a groan, she threw herself on the couch. Tossed back the rest of the brandy and heard the front door open, then bang against the wall. He'd come back. Relief rushed through her, he was safe. She jumped up, turned to the door and screamed.

Whatever was in the doorway, it wasn't Lee. Tall as a man, but four times as wide, deformed and lumpy, encrusted in snow and ice. A monster. A yeti. Big Foot. She was going to be a holiday statistic.

The lumps fell to the floor, spraying slush out in all directions and revealing a duffel bag and . . . camera equipment. Allison's mind switched into gear, just as he toppled forward.

She rushed toward him, sliding over the last few feet of wet tiles. He'd pushed up to his hands and knees, and she came to a stop between his arms.

"Got me where you want me," he said shakily and keeled over to his side.

She dropped to her knees and turned him onto his back. His eyelashes fluttered. She loved those lashes, dark and long. She brushed his hair off his forehead, uncovering a gash that was dripping a mixture of blood and water.

"Lee, my God. You're hurt."

He groaned and tried to get up. "No shit."

"Don't move."

He kept struggling. "A little late. I just walked the length of Colorado to get here."

She grabbed his elbow and hauled him to his feet. He fell against her and leaned heavily onto her. She staggered into the kitchen and dumped him into a straight-backed chair. Raced over to the sink and pulled several paper towels off the holder.

Blood was running into his eyes and she gently wiped it away before dabbing at the cut itself.

"Ouch," he said through chattering teeth.

She dropped the paper towel and began unbuttoning his jacket. He managed to lean forward while she wrestled it down his arms and threw it onto the counter. He was just as wet underneath.

"Christ. Did you swim back?"

"Har," he said and began shaking.

Allison looked frantically around, at a loss about what to do first. She grabbed the discarded towel and stuck it on his forehead. He yelped.

"Hold that right there," she said and ran back to the entryway. She returned seconds later with an armful of dry clothes. He was smiling at her. She narrowed her eyes. His face fell to neutral.

She pushed back any suspicion that he was faking it. After all, his forehead was cut open. He might be concussed. He might even have broken bones. Internal injuries. He might be in shock. And she couldn't even call the EMTs. She dumped his clothes on the table and reached for the waist of his sweater.

He grabbed her wrists and a totally inappropriate response rocketed through her. Shit. She was doing triage here and her body was on the prowl.

She yanked at the sweater.

He held on. "What are you doing?"

"Getting you out of these wet clothes."

The sweater came off over his head.

"Ouch."

She started on the buttons of his shirt. His chest lifted and stayed there while he held his breath. She leaned into him, her fingers arrested at his throat. She swallowed and unbuttoned the next one.

He exhaled. "I can do it."

She frowned at him. He frowned at her. And they seemed to get stuck there. Just looking at each other. Her fingers on his chest. His fingers wrapped around her wrists. And she wanted to kiss him. Wanted to slip her hands inside his shirt and feel the strength of his chest, the warmth of his skin.

That brought her back. His skin wasn't warm. It felt more like the skin of a raw turkey.

She broke free of his eyes. He stood up so quickly that she had to take a step backwards to get out of the way.

He swayed. "I'll do it." He grabbed the pile of clothes off the table.

She wrestled them away and put them back on the table. "You're getting them all wet."

They both looked at the clothes. Allison drew her tongue over dry lips.

Then Lee reached for the T-shirt that was lying on top. "Turn your back."

Allison's eyes flew to his. "What?"

"Turn around so I can get dressed." He was chewing on his bottom lip, a sure sign that he was disturbed. He was clutching the T-shirt in front of him, like he was deciding whether to put it on or throw it at her.

Allison rolled her eyes. "A little late for modesty, don't you think?" But she turned away.

Lee finished unbuttoning his shirt, keeping one eye on Allison's back as she reached into the cabinet and took out a tin of coffee. He quickly replaced the shirt with the tee and sweatshirt. He turned toward the table and watching her over his shoulder, he shucked out of his jeans and underwear, grinding his teeth when he realized he'd forgotten to take off his boots. He sat down in the chair and threw the sweatpants over his lap. They didn't quite camouflage the reaction that he didn't want

Allison to see. But it was the best he could do. He leaned over to untie his boots; the laces were wet and he couldn't get them loose.

Fuck. What was he going to do? If he asked her to bring him a knife to cut them free, she would see how hard he was. She'd love that. Wouldn't she just be smug as hell, to know that even after their relationship was over, after a whole year of not seeing each other, she still made his cock leap to attention.

He reached over to the table and snagged the pair of socks and boxers. He placed them strategically over the sweatpants on his lap. "Can you hand me a knife? I can't get my laces untied."

"Hmmm?"

She looked over at him, took in his shoes and the jeans down around his ankles, and started to smile. She caught it before it became a real smile, but he saw it just the same. She reached in a drawer and handed him a huge carving knife. She stretched over and held it out at arm's length. He saw her eyes flick to his lap and away. She didn't smile this time. He took the knife and she jumped back.

Funny. Did she really think he'd use it on her? Even if she was so damn provoking, he'd rather have her lying on the rug out by the fireplace beneath his naked body. Rubbing his throbbing—he leaned over and viciously attacked the laces.

Lee was sitting on the couch, wrapped in a blanket, when Allison brought in two cups of coffee and the bottle of brandy. She handed him a cup and poured brandy into her empty glass.

He held out his free hand.

"Not a chance," she said, moving the brandy bottle out of reach. "Alcohol is a depressant."

"I'm too cold to be depressed."

"That's not what—oh, here." She shoved the bottle toward him. If he was recovered enough to bandy words, he could drink himself into a coma and she wouldn't be responsible.

He reached around the bottle and took her glass. The blanket fell from his shoulders as he leaned forward, cradling the glass in his hands.

She caught herself staring at his fingers, the memory of his touch creeping past her defenses. This was going to be a nightmare. Hell. It was already a nightmare.

They were a two-car crash test, a couple of dummies, stuck in a snowstorm in a bad commercial. Life just didn't get much better than this.

But she was already tired of fending off feelings she'd been wrestling with for years. Suddenly weary, she slid down the couch cushions until she was sitting on the floor.

The carpet was plush, just the kind of carpet for making love in front of the fire. Yeah, and probably harbored all sorts of germs and icky stuff from previous couples. She sighed. Felt Lee lean back on the arm of the couch. Caught the movement of his legs as they stretched out along the cushions.

Could swear she felt the heat of his legs only inches behind her head. She sipped coffee, stared at the fire, concentrated on the ad campaign she'd planned to work on while she was here.

She should be working on it now. All she had to do was go over to the desk and flip open her laptop. Better still, she could carry it upstairs to the bedroom and shut the door.

Something tickled her neck. She shivered. Lee's toes were playing with the strands of hair that waved around her shoulders.

She should move away. He was just toying with her.

Then his toes traced a line down her neck. Worked their way under the edge of her robe.

She remembered the champagne in the fridge and the fully stocked pantry.

"Aren't you expecting someone?"

Silence.

Her heart sank.

"Who would I be expecting?"

She turned so that he couldn't see her face and put her cup down on the floor beside her. "Someone you were planning to drink champagne with."

"I didn't bring champagne. I didn't bring any of that stuff."

"Greg and Marcie," she said.

"Had to be." He'd managed to pull back the collar of her robe and his toes slid inside. The arch of his foot rested on her shoulder, heating the skin there. His toes began to walk across her bared collarbone. And what toes they were. They were so close that if she just turned her head a fraction, she could suck one of them into her mouth.

She squeezed her thighs together and tried to think about something else. She had to stop him before they both did something they'd regret soon enough. But traitor that it was, her hand broke rank and slipped over his foot, her palm settling there. And the heat shot right up her arm and didn't stop until it hit ground zero. Her hand slid to his ankle, up the wiry leg hair until it was stopped by the elastic of his sweatpants.

She tried to pull it away before he got the wrong

idea, which would be the right idea, but he didn't need to know that. She really tried to reclaim her hand. Her hand was having none of it. Her index finger eased itself under the elastic; she felt Lee's calf muscle ripple beneath it. She came to her senses and tried to pull it back. Lee covered her hand with his.

Caught by surprise, she looked at him. He looked back. Heat, desire and a sense of inevitability pulsed between them.

He pressed her palm to his calf and held it there. She opened her mouth to protest. Nothing came out, not even her breath. His mouth was clamped shut. It didn't matter. They didn't need to talk. The front of Lee's sweatpants were talking loud enough for both of them.

He pulled her toward him.

She rose to her knees. "This is probably a stupid thing to do," she said.

"It doesn't feel stupid. We're here."

And they weren't going anywhere tonight. Why not have a final fling. Leave this time without the anger and hurt. Something broke inside her and she thought, *Well, why the hell not.* They *were* here. Couldn't get away. It was useless to try to pretend they didn't want each other. They were consenting adults. They could walk away from this none the worse for wear.

Who was she kidding.

"Ally," he said. A low whisper.

"Yes." She pulled her hand from his sweats and glided her palm up his calf.

Lee's head fell back and his eyes closed.

"Are you going to pass out?"

"Maybe. Just keep going."

She did. Both hands skimming over his thighs, feeling his reaction to her touch. She slowed down as her hands pressed higher. So slow that he grabbed her hands and led them to where they both wanted them to be.

He sighed.

She sighed and let her fingers curl around him. He pushed against them. She climbed onto the couch and straddled him. Peered down at him through a curtain of hair. Her robe gaped open above and below the tie at her waist. There was nothing but her underneath.

Lee grunted in response and he rocked beneath her. Then he reached inside the robe and cupped both her breasts in his hands.

They both groaned and Lee arched against her. She pressed him back down and sat astride him, circled her hips against him, shuddered every time the ridge of his erection hit the place that sent electricity through her.

He rubbed his palms against her breasts. Squeezed her nipples, then ran a finger across the tight tips. She rocked up and down the length of his erection, the fabric of his sweatpants setting off wave after wave of pleasure.

His fingers fumbled at the sash of her robe. It was loosely tied. He should be able to open it without the aid of the carving knife. The thought gave her such an unexpected rush that she almost laughed. He finally got it untied and slid it off her shoulders. She rose to her knees and he pulled it away and tossed it to the floor. She towered over him, spread-eagled and ready.

"I've missed you," he whispered and cupped her between her legs. He slid one finger deep inside her. Her muscles clenched around it. He pulled it out and pushed it in again, while the heel of his hand pressed against the sensitive skin at her crotch.

"You've missed me, too," he breathed, as his finger

picked up a rhythm that threatened to send her spiraling out of control.

Not that much. That's what she meant to say. But somehow, by the time it reached her mouth, it had morphed into a breathy "yes."

A second finger joined the first.

She slipped her hands past his arm and took hold of his sweatpants. He lifted his butt so she could pull them off. She pulled them down his thighs. He kicked them off. And they joined her robe on the floor.

She eased away from his fingers so she could enjoy the view.

Oh, yeah. Just as thrilling as the first time she saw it. She'd been so flashed at first sight, she'd sent up a prayer to the sex pixies for sending her such a package. She was thanking them again. A girl couldn't ask for a better Christmas present. Sure beat those handmade acrylic mittens.

He curled up and nipped her hip bone. "Don't look, if you're not going to buy."

"Hmmm," she said, though she had already made her decision several finger passes ago. She pushed him back down, scooped up his cock and shuddered as the sleek, hot skin came even more alive at her touch. She lifted it up, squeezed and pulled up the length of him. Cupped the head of his penis with her palm.

He dragged three fingers between her legs, then pushed her hand away and rubbed the tip of his penis with her juices.

"What's the cost?" she asked.

His eyes flicked. The fire reflected in them and for a heart-stopping moment Allison was afraid she'd gone too far.

"Whatever you want to pay. Or—nothing at all."

She smiled. "The price is right."

"Suck me."

Oh, yeah. She'd suck him until he begged for mercy. "Ask nicely." *And do it quickly before I lose my mind.*

"Suck me now."

"You are such a gentleman." She leaned over until her lips touched the tip of his cock. She flicked her tongue across the cleft of it, tasting herself as well as him. Lee grabbed her shoulders. His fingers dug into her flesh.

She sucked saliva into her mouth, then spread it over the head of his cock, following it with her tongue. Lee groaned and eased his grip on her shoulders.

She circled him with her tongue, then sucked him deep into her mouth. It occurred to her that if she had been the vindictive type, Lee would be in big trouble now. But she wasn't. And she would never hurt him, though she was inspired to suck a little harder and gently rake her teeth up the sensitive skin.

Lee groaned. Reached under her armpits and drew her up his body. He clamped an arm around her waist and rolled them onto the floor, she on her back and Lee braced on his hands and knees above her. He reached back onto the couch and pulled down a large throw pillow, which he pushed beneath her butt.

He spread her knees and fitted himself between them. Lifted her leg and draped it around his waist. The fire in his eyes bored into hers. He kissed her, driving his tongue past her teeth and claiming her mouth with insistent thrusts. Then, shifting his weight to one hand, he used the other to place his cock between her thighs. He didn't enter her, just teased her, manipulating himself through her folds, then sliding back to press against her opening. Promising more but withholding it, until she was tempted to shove it in herself.

Before she could move, he pushed into her, a mere inch. She captured the head of his penis with tight muscles. She pulsed around him, trying to draw him farther in. He was smiling diabolically and she could feel him start to withdraw. Quickly she reached up and tweaked his nipples. He made a guttural sound and drove hard into her.

She smiled even as the heat built unbearably inside her. He had such sensitive nipples, not a trait a girl found every day. She had him where she wanted him. And she wanted him. God help her, she wanted him.

"Not fair," he gasped and pulled out far enough to drive inside her again.

Allison didn't answer. The game was suddenly out of her control. And she bet out of his, too. It had always been that way. They hungered for each other. Always. Threatened to burn up when they came together. Swept into a vortex of passion that would eventually drown them. But she didn't care. Not now.

She met him thrust for thrust, twined her fingers in his hair. Wrapped her legs around his waist. He drove and drove, pushing her up the carpet until her head bumped the leg of the club chair. He lifted her and shifted them to the side. Rolled them back down the carpet until they were once more in front of the fire. And he kept driving into her until without warning she imploded then burst outward in a explosion of fireworks.

Lee gave three last disjointed thrusts, each punctuated by a cry wrenched from the very depths of him. Then he shuddered and collapsed on top of her. Rolled onto his back, taking her with him until she lay across him, heavy and fulfilled. And they floated, maybe slept, until Lee said lazily, "The fire is going out," and dumped her unceremoniously onto the carpet.

He stood up and put more wood on the fire. Stirred it with the poker until it was ablaze again, then turned and looked down at her.

"You have a great butt," she said.

Lee stretched, his eyes heavy-lidded, his mouth curving into a satisfied smile. "It's all—" He bit back the rest of the sentence.

And Allison wondered if he'd been about to say, "It's all yours." He'd said it enough in the past. But he hadn't really meant it. And she'd just fallen for it again.

Three

A persistent pounding yanked Lee from a deep sleep. He rolled off the bed and crouched on the floor; he blinked. A bed. A floor. He was in a cabin with Allison, in Colorado, not in a tent in the jungle in Columbia.

He stood up and looked across the crumpled comforter to where Ally's dark curls spilled across her face. She stirred and his dick responded. The pounding began again.

The door. Someone was knocking on the door. He looked around for his clothes. Remembered they were downstairs. So was his duffel.

Maybe whoever it was would go away. He waited. The knocking continued. Lee sighed and jogged down the stairs to grab his sweatpants and shirt off the floor.

"Coming," he called and hurried across the frigid tiles to the front door, hopping into his sweatpants as he went. He pulled the sweatshirt over his head and opened the front door.

He had to squint against the brightness. Snow was piled everywhere and sunlight sparkled off every surface. It turned the figure in front of him to a silhouette. Short and round and Lee thought "a bowl full of jelly," before pulling himself together and saying, "Yes?"

"Saw your car smashed into the tree out by the cross-roads. Just wanted to make sure everyone was all right." He shifted onto one fat leg, which put him in the shadow of the eave. He suddenly came into focus. A round, fat man in a red parka and Himalayan knit cap. A white beard spilled across the front of his parka and he stuck out a plump hand encased in ski gloves.

"Chris Olsen," he said as Lee automatically stuck out his hand to be shaken. "Mayor of Good Cheer for twenty-five years and owner of the Watering Hole for longer."

"Lee Simonson," said Lee, hoping he wouldn't have to invite him in.

"Well, as long as you folks are okay, I'll just leave you be. But stop by the Hole sometime and I'll buy you a round." He nodded his head once, as if it were all settled, and turned to leave.

"Is there a garage in town? Or a car rental? I need to catch a flight out of Denver this afternoon."

"There's a garage. Don't have a car rental. But it don't matter. You won't be catching any flight today or any other day this week, most likely. We got a snowplow. Cleans up the town streets good enough, but the highway's plumb covered over. Can't do a thing about it. We're not a high priority with the state highway department."

Lee looked over the mayor's shoulder to the street. A one-lane path had been carved out along the center but the plow had deposited mountains of snow to either side. Allison's car was completely buried. It would take them all day to dig out. He gritted his teeth. "What about the ski resort? They must have a snowplow."

The mayor's bushy eyebrows knit together. He shook his head and chuckled. His parka vibrated. "Ski resort. That's a good one. Besides, that SUV of yours isn't going anywhere. Might as well enjoy yourselves while you're here. 'Tis the season after all." Then, continuing to shake his head, he turned and waded through the snow back to the street, where he waved a chubby hand over his head and walked away, still chuckling and shaking his head.

Lee stared after him, the cold seeping from the tiles into the soles of his feet, while his mind heated with indignation and exasperation. If he could get his hands on Greg right now, he'd beat the living crap out of him for taking part in this travesty. His teeth began to chatter and he slammed the door against the cold.

He just stood in the foyer, taking in his camera equipment and duffel lying where he'd dropped them the night before, the clothes draped over the furniture and piled on the carpet in front of the cold grate.

He and Ally had gone at it until they were both wrung out; then they'd stumbled upstairs for rounds two and three. And, to his dismay, he wanted more. And he knew it would be a disaster.

Ally was like a drug. A total out-of-body high. An experience like none other he'd ever had. Until you started coming down. Then the results were ravaging. The fights would start, the accusations, the silences. And before he knew what was happening, she'd be walking out the door, or standing him up, or not answering her phone.

They were doomed. He'd sworn after last Christmas that he would never be caught like this again and here he was, thanks to their two meddling siblings. How had he been so gullible? How had Allison? A niggling suspicion was trying to get his attention. Probably trying to tell him that it was fate. That they were made for each other. That they were meant to be together. And maybe that was true, but they just couldn't figure out how to make it work.

They never would. Ally would never compromise, neither would he. Their work was more important than their relationship, and neither of them would ever settle for being second best.

"Who was that?" Ally stood at the top of the stairs, the comforter wrapped around her and trailing out behind her like a train.

Lee smiled in spite of himself. "The mayor of Good Cheer."

"Huh?" she asked on a yawn.

"He found my car. Wanted to make sure no one was hurt." He was moving toward the stairs. Drawn toward her. Needing to touch her. He couldn't stop himself.

Ally just pushed her hair out of her face and yawned again. Oblivious. Then she looked down at him and smiled.

Lee's desire ignited. He took the last few steps in a single bound and pulled her close, comforter and all. She cuddled into him, making purring sounds.

This was how it should be. Waking to love in the morning. No rush. No competition. Just the two of them. He held her closer. He knew it wouldn't last. He should probably be looking for a way down the mountain. He had only the mayor's word that they were snowed in. He might still be able to make the flight. But he didn't move. Just gave in to the feel of Ally warm against him.

"This is a disaster," she said.

The cold in Lee's feet shot right to his chest. "Probably," he said after swallowing the tightness in his throat.

"But it seems we're stuck here. The roads are closed. Might as well make the best of it."

"Hmmm," she said and snuggled closer.

Lee started to relax.

Then Allison pulled away and screeched, "What?"

Lee reared back, the word clanging in his ear. "Jesus, you don't have to deafen me. The mayor said the roads are closed and we won't be able to leave for several days, maybe a week."

Allison pushed him away. "I can't stay here a week. There's no Internet service. You have a plane to catch. There has to be a way out."

Lee shook his head.

"The ski resort. They must have a way down. We could ski down, if we have to."

"You've never skied in your life and, besides, there is no ski resort."

Allison's eyes widened. "You mean . . ."

"We're stranded."

"*Grrr.*"

And strangely enough, Lee began to feel better rather than worse. It was probably Allison's look of desperation that did it. Not the hard executive face she showed to the world. But the girl Lee had fallen for seven years before. And he felt a glimmer of hope. Even after all the breakups, all the reconciliations, the promise never to fall for it again, Lee fell. He scooped Allison up and pulled her against his chest.

At first she was unwieldy, all floundering arms and legs. But then she softened and sighed and fit into him like she belonged there. "Stuck in Good Cheer for Christmas. It's so . . . embarrassing."

* * *

Allison sat at the kitchen table, nursing a mug of coffee and watching the windows fog up with steam. Lee was puttering at the stove, flipping pancakes on the griddle and lifting strips of bacon out of the cast-iron frying pan with a long two-pronged fork.

It was hard not to settle into this homey scene, even though she knew it wasn't real and would shatter soon enough. Still, she felt toasty and loved and the coffee was just like she liked it: strong and black.

Lee put a platter of pancakes and bacon in front of her and she smiled up at him, though she'd warned herself not to. He smiled back and the air vibrated with contentment.

Which was also an illusion, she knew. But the pancakes were fluffy and the syrup real, and though she didn't make a habit of eating breakfast, she settled down to this one like a starving woman. She concentrated on eating, not daring to look up and take the chance of catching him looking back at her.

Illusion, she cautioned herself. Illusion. Illusion.

"Want to take a walk and check out the town?"

He'd caught her off guard and she looked at him before she could stop herself. His face was open. Anticipation danced in his eyes. He could always make the most insignificant, stupid things fun and exciting. Yeah, and he could also turn it right back on you and make you miserable, she reminded herself.

"Sure."

They pulled on coats and gloves and hats. Lee made catty remarks about her rhinestone "ski" boots but took two close-ups of them, before settling his cameras around his neck. Then he brushed the steps free of snow with the side of his boot and held her elbow as they slid their way down the crust of ice. Helped her climb over the four feet of snow piled up at the edge of the street, then lifted her down to the plowed section.

Along the other side of the street behind an identical mound of snow, Allison could see brightly colored hats and bare heads bobbing along. Occasionally, one would disappear from view, only to reappear a few seconds later. A green umbrella passed. A black-and-white spaniel clambered up the other side and slid toward the street. There was a bright red bow around his neck and a jingling brass bell. Two little heads appeared over the mound. Then two children, dressed in bright red snowsuits, scrambled over the top and chased the dog down the street.

"That doesn't look safe," said Allison. "A car would slide right into them in this ice."

Lee put his arm around her waist and pulled her into him. "There don't seem to be any cars anywhere."

Allison looked down the street. It was deserted except for pedestrians. A snowball fight was in progress half a block away, the participants sheltered behind forts carved out in the piled-up snow. Everywhere children screeched and squealed. Ahead of them, adults, bundled against the weather, passed through tracks tunneled out from the sidewalk to the street.

Lee and Allison waited for a group to pass and then walked single file to the sidewalk. Only it wasn't a sidewalk, Allison discovered, when she reached the end of the tunnel and stepped onto a wooden deck. It was more like a boardwalk, like one of those towns from the Old West.

"I hope this isn't going to be one of those places where everything is theme related," said Lee.

"You mean like the Buffalo Burger?"

"I was thinking more along the lines of 'Prospector's

Pastrami on Rye.' Look up there." He pointed to the mountains that rose straight up from behind the wooden buildings.

"What?"

"See those black squares? They're mines."

"Gold?"

Lee laughed. "Got your interest, huh?"

She gave him a shove. "I just didn't know that miners still had to crawl down in those gas-riddled shafts."

"They're probably closed up. Left over from another era." Lee took off the lens cap of his camera and as he shot, a rapid whirr filled the air. Then he turned the camera on Allison. "Smile."

Before she could protest, he clicked the picture and turned to capture two men maneuvering a trolley loaded with kegs through a narrow doorway. And then an old man walking toward them, with a snow shovel balanced on his shoulder.

Lee was certainly a cheap date, thought Allison. Everything and anything interested him. And most of what interested him was captured on film. There were quite a few shots of her somewhere in the boxes of prints on file in his Los Angeles apartment.

Unless he'd tossed them, burned them or shredded them into little pieces after the last breakup.

She stopped in front of a plate glass window. It seemed to be an old-fashioned toy-and-candy store. Licorice sticks, jaw breakers and a variety of other rot-your-teeth delights were contained in glass jars lined up on shelves along the far wall. In the window, stuffed animals and dolls vied for space with Lincoln Logs and fire engines. An electric train ran on an oval track around them. Little houses with picket fences and fake trees and stores were lined up along the rails, and everything was covered with flakes of sparkling plastic snow.

A doll, dressed like a Victorian girl with bustled skirt and her hair piled up on the top of her head, stood in one corner next to a black-iron toy stove. It was probably one of those American Girl dolls that all her nieces collected. Now there was a good setup, thought Allison. She'd kill for an account like this. Expensive, high-end toys, well made, historically accurate within reason, even a little history lesson to go with them. An ad exec's dream come true.

She'd never been a doll person herself, but she could appreciate the fine craftsmanship of this one. And she felt a pang of disappointment when the shopkeeper reached over the backdrop, lifted out the doll and carried it to the counter.

"Hey, Tiny Tim, give us a smile," said Lee in an execrable British accent. Allison rolled her eyes at him, just as he snapped a picture.

"You are such a tourist," she said and walked past him down the boardwalk.

"Yeah, I guess I am," Lee said, catching up to her. He let his camera fall to his chest and squeezed her around the shoulders. "I'm also feeling a little Ho-Ho-Ho and those turquoise boots are turning me on."

"Shh," she hissed back at him and looked around to make sure none of the citizens of Good Cheer had heard him.

Lee just stood there grinning, then started walking again. A few minutes later, they had traversed the entire two blocks of town and had come to a field of snow. At the far side, a framed building that must be the town hall or library, belched smoke from its chimney. A crew of men were digging their way toward the center of the field to where a wooden band shell nestled in the snow like a frosted gingerbread house. Garlands of pine festooned the eaves and were caught up with giant red bows.

It was perfectly hokey. Obviously the decorations were, one: real, and two: made by the local lady's club, because each bow was a different size and shape, some better than others, and every few feet, the stem of a pine bow stuck out from the rest like a fork in the road.

Quaint, thought Allison, not at all missing the perfectly designed decorations of the city.

Off to one side, a row of Christmas trees leaned against an ancient, green-paneled truck. A sign with a big ANY TREE $10 printed on it was propped up in front of one of the back tires.

They crossed the street again and began walking up the other side, back toward their bungalow. There was a tea shop, a hardware store and a store named Cal's General Merchandise.

"Let's go inside," said Lee and dragged her through the door of Cal's. "Oh, wow," he said, sounding like a kid. Three old men right out of a Norman Rockwell painting were sitting around a wood-burning stove.

Allison had to give them credit. The early-twentieth-century theme really worked. It was so Americana. So Christmas Spirit. She knew it was a gimmick. She might have even come up with something like this for one of her ad campaigns. Even so, it began to work its spell and when Lee said, "Oh, wow" for the second time, she hurried over to see what he'd found.

An array of antique lead soldiers were lined up on a shelf behind the counter. The shopkeeper, who introduced himself as Cal, was dressed in obligatory overalls and red-flannel shirt. He took a cannon down from the shelf and placed it on the counter in front of Lee.

They both gazed raptly at it. Allison rolled her eyes and moved down the counter, past boxes of Christmas decorations to where bolts of material were stacked up on a cutting board. There were ginghams, wools and something that looked suspiciously like hand-tatted lace. Not a piece of polyester in sight. She had to hand it to them, they were authentic. They must be making a fortune.

She glanced around the store; she and Lee were the only tourists there. Surely other people had been caught in the storm. They were probably out skiing. Wait. No ski resort.

Marcie must have been confused. Just like her ditsy sister, to go off half-cocked and rent a place without researching the location. They were lucky to have ended up in Christmas Village Land. They could be stuck in the wilderness without heat or electricity.

Still, all the cuteness was beginning to cloy. She'd had enough. But Lee and the proprietor were bent over the counter, engaged in what appeared to be a full-scaled battle.

Allison sighed and moved on to a freestanding wooden shelf that held an assortment of kitchen implements.

Implements was the only word she could come up with. There was a hand-turned eggbeater, a rectangular grater, butter molds and cheese wires. She picked up a metal flour sifter with a green wooden handle and looked at the cardboard price tag. Then looked at the price of the grater. They were incredibly inexpensive, hardly more than wholesale.

Tourism must be down in the Rockies. Too bad. It was a great concept. It didn't feel like a theme park on its last legs. It seemed to her that the store, the whole town, exuded longevity, and she found herself thinking that she could stay here forever.

She shook herself. Whoa. Imagine her succumbing to a marketing ploy. Maybe this week wouldn't be a waste after all. She might pick up a few finer points of product immersion while she was here.

She might also lose her heart to Lee all over again. And that would be a disaster. She didn't think she could take another breakup. It was just too damn painful.

She felt two hands come around her waist and looked over her shoulder to see Lee standing behind her.

"Feeling domestic?" he asked on a smile, then immediately released her. There was a moment of uncomfortable silence. Allison knew he had caught his mistake the moment he'd uttered the word "domestic." *That* she would never be. And that was one of the major gulfs that separated them. Lee wanted a wife to be waiting for him when he deigned to return home between adventures. He didn't get that this was the twenty-first century and women had their own lives to lead.

He reached over her to pick up an eggcup. "Look at this."

"An eggcup."

"Eggs and soldiers."

Allison sighed. She supposed it was only natural that a photojournalist would be obsessed by war. Why couldn't he be a nature photographer? Or take artistic shots of skyscrapers and subway tunnels. Then they could . . .

"My mother used to make them."

She frowned at him. "What?"

"Eggs and soldiers. Soft-boiled eggs and strips of toast that you stuck into the yolk."

Allison stared at him. He never talked about his family. She knew there was bad blood there, but he'd never volunteered any information and she'd never pressed him to talk about what was obviously a painful subject. If this is what American Redux did, she wasn't sure she was ready for it. Maybe Cal sold snowshoes. How far would they have to trek to find an IHOP and a pay phone?

Lee turned the eggcup in his hand, then put it back on the shelf. "What do you say we stop by the Watering Hole and have a coffee and Kahlua?"

"I'd say it's still morning."

"Wrong," said Lee and turned his wrist so that she could see his watch.

It was three o'clock. Jesus, they must have slept until noon. "Sounds like happy hour to me," she said and took his arm without thinking.

They stopped at the counter to say good-bye to Cal.

A gust of frigid air swept in from the back of the store.

"Close that door," said Cal.

The puppy that they'd seen earlier galloped past them, the bell around his neck jingling like crazy. He skidded to a stop before turning around and jumping at the two children who'd followed him inside.

"My holy terrors," said Cal proudly. "Jen and Jamie."

Together Jen and Jamie let out a treble, "Hi."

The dog barked, setting off another round of jingling. And Allison wondered how long it would be before somebody throttled the poor creature.

"This is Spanky. He's a puppy," said Jamie.

Lee knelt down and ruffled the dog's ears.

"All right, you two, get on home now."

The two children ran toward the front door; the puppy took off after them. The door slammed closed.

"Gotta love 'em," Cal said. "Little rascals."

Lee and Allison said good-bye and followed the children out.

Cal nodded. "Come back anytime," and he began returning the soldiers to the shelf.

A few stores down, a sandwich board stood in the middle of the sidewalk. A green hand-painted arrow pointed to double doors, and the words The Watering

Hole were spelled out in crude letters. They went inside.

The interior was dark, with unpainted wooden walls and a wooden floor covered in straw. Several men in mountain wear stood at the bar, their booted feet resting on a brass foot rail. Behind the bar, a short, round man with an improbable beard was handing out mugs of draft beer.

"There's Chris," said Lee and strode over to join the other men.

"Please don't tell me his last name is Kringle," whispered Allison, squeezing in beside him.

"Olsen," said the bartender. Allison blushed. No way he could have overheard her crack. She smiled at him, feeling foolish. "It's the beard," she said meekly.

Chris pulled at the tip. "Yeah, we're old friends." He winked at her. "And I have been known to hand out a present or two at the Christmas Eve Revels. You folks are invited. Starts with carols at the band shell and moves into the town hall on the other side of the square. Got hot cider and donuts, a pageant that the kids put on and plenty of mistletoe for you young people. And a visit from Santa, of course." He tugged at his beard. "Six o'clock. Rain, sleet or snow."

He poured out two mugs of dark, rich coffee. He didn't stock Kahlua, but he gave them a sampling of his homebrewed Christmas cordial, which at first brought tears to Allison's eyes, then went down in a smooth medley of blackberry, lime and fire.

"Mr. Olsen," said Allison when she got her breath back.

"Chris."

"Chris. My sister said there was a ski resort nearby. Was she mistaken?"

"Well, there was this fellow decided to open a lodge

for skiing. But it didn't draw much business. Most folks around here cross-country when they need to get anywhere. Went belly-up after a couple of years. No, we depend on mining mostly. Or did until a while back."

"And tourism," added Allison.

"We get our share of visitors," said Chris and winked again.

Allison smiled back at him in spite of herself. She was falling under his spell, and she had no doubt if he showed up on her roof in a red suit, she'd ask him in. Maybe even sit on his knee.

"What are you smirking about?" asked Lee.

Allison heard him through a fog of blackberry cordial. She turned her smile on him. "I'm happy." Her eyes widened. Her smile vanished and she saw it transferred to Lee. What a stupid admission. How had she let her guard down like that? And worse, how had she let herself feel something so stupid? It must be the liquor. She pushed her glass away. "Let's go."

Lee's smile widened.

She wanted to stop him right there. Tell him not to read too much into her words. She didn't mean that they should hurry home to make love, but she knew that was what he thought she meant. And she couldn't correct his misconception. Everybody in the bar had ceased their own conversations to tune into theirs.

Lee shoved his hand in his pocket.

"On the house," said Chris.

Lee thanked him and they gathered up coats and hats and put them on as they crossed toward the door. Allison could swear she heard Chris chuckling as the door closed behind them.

Four

The cold hit her hard, but instead of sobering her up, it only increased that damn rosy glow she was feeling from Chris's home brew. Lee took her hand and was striding down the walk, away from their bungalow, not toward it. So much for love in the afternoon.

When they reached Cal's, he said, "Wait here." And rushed inside.

He came back a few minutes later with two bulging paper bags. "Come on," he said and headed down the boardwalk.

She hurried after him. And her mouth fell open when he stopped before the row of Christmas trees.

She cringed. She refused to be beguiled into playing Happy Families. Even though it was *the* season.

"Hold these," said Lee and shoved the bags at her. "And don't peek," he said, as he went over to the teenage boy who was warming his hands at a barrel fire.

He and Lee walked along the row of trees while Allison watched, helpless. Finally the boy pulled one away from the truck. Lee turned to her, grinning like a kid. "How's this one?"

His enthusiasm was infectious, damn him. Allison grinned back at him. "Perfect." Perfectly ridiculous.

Lee handed over his ten dollars. The boy wrapped several loops of cord around the branches and Lee hefted it to his shoulder.

It wasn't until they had hauled the tree over the snow mound to the cottage, laughed as they tumbled down the other side, dragged it up the icy steps, slipping and sliding and falling into each other, and deposited it at a safe distance from the fireplace, that they realized they didn't have a tree stand.

"I'll think of something," said Lee, his excitement undimmed. He began rummaging in cabinets and cupboards.

It was Allison who found the funnel-shaped holder, with its three curved, supporting prongs.

Lee looked incredulous when she handed it to him. "It looks like some torture device from an old Flash Gordon movie," he said. But he set it on the floor and together they managed to balance the tree upright. Allison filled the cone with water and they stepped cautiously back and regarded it like two proud parents looking at their firstborn.

"And now," said Lee, and made a drum roll with his tongue, "the pièce de résistance." He opened the paper bags and began lifting out boxes of shiny colored glass balls, painted tin bells, a big papier-mâché star with glittered tips and a rectangle of cardboard wrapped with furry, and slightly mangy looking gold garland. He lined these up on the sofa cushions and looked to Allison for her reaction.

She could only shake her head. He was forever surprising her. Calling on a portable radio phone with machine gunfire in the background one day and making brownies the next. But, she thought with a pang of tenderness, she had never seen him so openly boyish. And she felt a little heart stab, that soon they would have to return to the fast lanes of their lives—their separate lives.

She ignored the little voice that said, "Why? Why can't it always be like this?" Because she knew it couldn't be, and though it was a bittersweet feeling, she appreciated it for being able to finally end their relationship with good memories instead of bad.

It was consolation they both deserved.

"What?" Lee asked when she suddenly ran from the room and started up the stairs. "What's wrong?"

"Nothing, just wait a sec." She came back down a minute later, holding her hands behind her back. She flipped open her lap top and inserted the disco CD. She turned up the speaker and the room was filled with the sounds of a "Frosty The Snowman" hustle.

She danced back to him and opened the box of Christmas balls, while Lee laughed and tried to grab her butt.

Soon the tree, which Allison noticed listed a little to one side, was filled with bright decorations. She was reaching up to place the last red bell on one of the higher branches, when a strand of garland was looped over her head. Lee tightened it around her shoulders and pulled her back into his chest. She let her head fall back against his shoulder. He rubbed his cheek against her hair, then moved down to nuzzle her neck.

Allison sighed and stretched her neck to give him more room. The garland drooped when Lee put his arms around her waist. She could feel his erection against her lower back. She swung her hips from side to side in rhythm with "Santa Claus Is Coming To Town," mirror-ball style. She sang, "You better watch out," and Lee released her long enough to pull her sweater over her head.

Her turtleneck came next. Lee looped the garland around her waist and unclasped her bra. "Nobody's gonna be sleeping," she extemporized along with the words of the song.

"Not if I have my way," said Lee in a low growl. The bra was flung across the floor, and Lee's hands spread across her bare breasts. Allison switched her hips from a swing to a circle and Lee groaned.

They moved together, half-dance, half-seduction. Lee pulled off his sweatshirt and tee in one movement, moving all the time. He looped the strand of garland loosely around her waist and flipped open the buttons of her jeans. She shimmied out of them, leaning over to pull off her wool socks, intentionally giving him a candid view of her ass and the dental floss thong that was her underwear.

He shucked pants and socks and eased up behind her. He slipped his fingers inside the thong and pushed it down legs. She stepped out of it and kicked it away with her toes. She was feeling absolutely giddy. Dancing naked in front of the Christmas tree. It was downright pagan. And incredibly liberating.

Another strand of garland was draped over her breasts, and Allison adjusted it so that it hid her nipples. The metallic sheen of the tinsel pieces tickled her skin and sent an electric shock deep to her groin.

Lee grasped the ends and crossed them over her back, looped them to the front again and leaned into her. Their bodies pressed together, warm skin rubbing against warm skin, Lee's dick jerking each time she rubbed against it.

The music changed and a raunchy "Must Be Santa" was replaced by "Merry Christmas, Baby." Allison spread her feet and bumped her hip against Lee's crotch. He threw the garland down her front, but instead of pushing her to the floor, he reached between her legs and pulled the two ends across her crotch, up her butt, and tied them to the strand across her back.

"Merry Christmas, Baby," Allison sang and turned to face him.

His face was flushed and he was staring at her torso like a man about to dive in. He licked his lips. Allison bumped her pelvis forward. He stepped closer. Ran his fingers over the ragged pieces of tinsel. His hands stayed an inch from her body, but she could feel the heat of him as he ruffled the pieces of foil.

She lifted her arms and gathered her hair onto the top of her head. And still she continued to sway and lift and circle her hips to the music. With a lurch toward her, Lee grasped her around the butt and lifted her up. Her legs went around his waist. Then he lowered her until his cock rested at the inviting opening between her legs.

"Guide me in," said Lee in a choked voice. She released her grip of her thighs and reached between them. She found the pulsing length of him and slid it across her crotch. Lee bit his lip and swayed on his feet. She pushed him inside her and the sway became a rock, then a thrust. The music played on, but they left its steady four-four behind, as they accelerated, faster and faster, slamming into each other with more ferocity each time.

Lee shifted her weight into one arm. He captured her breast with his free hand. Pulled it gently and rolled the nipple between two fingers. Allison felt a surge of energy and increased the thrust of her hips into his.

The garland shifted and tightened around her, tickling her skin. Then the feel of it, the smell of the fresh spruce tree, the crackle of the fire all receded until the fire between them was the only thing left. Her eyes closed, her head fell back and there was nothing in her world but the two of them, each driving the other to completion. Each thrust escalating with more force than the one before.

Lee's hand left her breast and traveled down until it found the place where they were joined together. He opened her with two fingers. Used a third to stimulate her to the point of exquisite pain. But she wasn't ready to let go. She wanted to ride him forever.

But she couldn't hold out and she fractured just as she heard Lee cry out as he came.

Allison collapsed against him and slowly slid down his body, her legs too weak to hold her anymore. Lee managed to get them to the sofa and knock the empty boxes onto the floor, before they collapsed in a heap on the soft cushions.

Lee's heart was banging against hers and they were both breathing hard. They lay there, stunned, and then Lee found her mouth and he kissed her.

Allison's eyes grew heavy. Her body floated. And she felt peaceful. At length, Lee sat up, resting on his knees between her feet, his hands resting on her knees.

He look poleaxed. His dick was still semierect and if she could do it without moving, she would have sucked him back to full erection. But he was too far away and she couldn't get her arms or legs to work.

Lee's stomach growled. The tranquility burst.

Allison pushed herself to her elbows. "You're hungry," she said, resigned. Men were always hungry after sex. She hoped that didn't equate in some way to the satisfaction they got from sex. Or lack thereof.

"Yeah, well." Lee glanced at his wristwatch, the only thing he was wearing. He jumped to his feet. "Shit."

Allison's heart sank. He must have to make a call, or try to get to the airport again or do something else that didn't involve her.

He grabbed her by her wrists and hauled her to her feet.

"It's six-fifteen," said Lee, throwing clothes toward her.

"So, it's not like we're going anywhere soon," said Allison and tried to sit down on the couch.

"The Christmas Eve Revels. They've already started." Lee yanked on boxers and jeans, uncovering Allison's thong in the process. He tossed it toward her. "Hurry up."

Allison yawned. "I think I'll just stay here."

The look Lee turned on her made her feel like the Grinch.

"Oh, all right, little boy. Maybe Santa will have everything on your list."

"I doubt it," said Lee. At least that's what Allison thought he said; it was hard to tell since he'd pulled his sweatshirt over his head as he spoke.

She unwound the garland that was looking a little worse for wear and changed into her clothes. They'd grown cold while she and Lee were playing. And she had no doubt they would be getting colder before they finished listening to carols on the green. At least the village hall would be heated. Even if they did have to sit through an interminable Christmas pageant with the audience oohing and aahing over children she and Lee wouldn't know. What were the chances of the cider being hard?

She pushed her feet into her turquoise boots, shrugged into the down parka and found her leather gloves crumpled in the pockets. Lee was dressed and looking impatient. Two cameras were hanging around his neck, a digital and his old standby, a battered Nikon, with telephoto lens.

"You're weird," said Allison and opened the front door.

The minute they stepped outside, the distant melody of "Adeste Fidelis" rose from the far side of town. They followed it to the green, which was completely filled with people. The whole area had been cleared down to the last foot of snow, probably by elves, thought Allison as she scrambled over the frozen snow. A choir stood on the band shell. The choirmaster faced the crowd and was leading them in the song, though Allison could already tell that those in back were a half-beat behind those in front. It made a funny warbling effect that was totally charming.

She and Lee threaded their way through the crowd until they found a space closer to the band shell. He flipped his camera out of the case and began taking closeups of the people around them. They didn't seem to notice. Which was good, because it was kind of a philistine sort of thing to do, with everyone full of good cheer and singing their little hearts out.

Allison caught herself humming along, and pretty soon an occasional word, forgotten for years, found its way to the surface. By the time they got to "Once in David's Royal City," her voice was ringing out with the others. And, oddly enough, Lee's camera hung at his side and his voice rose next to hers and she realized that this was the first time she had ever heard him sing.

He smiled at her and leaned over to whisper in her ear. "I didn't know you could sing."

She stared at him in the shadows made by swags of little white lights that ran overhead. He couldn't mean it. She sang all the time. Or maybe not. She tried to think back to the last time she had sung out loud, other than this afternoon to the disco Christmas CD.

She drew a blank. Couldn't come up with the last time she'd been to church or sung along with the radio or in the shower. *God, I don't sing,* she thought, panicked. At least not when she was with Lee. And he didn't sing when he was with her.

That really must say something about their relationship. Their ex-relationship. Why their relationship didn't work out.

"Humbug," she said.

Lee's mouth opened, not in song but in astonishment. Allison blushed to the roots of her hair. Or at least would have, if she ever blushed. Which she didn't.

One carol led into another, and as the night wore on, Lee stood closer, and she could feel his body warmth through their coats. She felt like they belonged, like she belonged, and she didn't know whether to feel all fuzzy inside or run screaming for the nearest helicopter.

But then they were being pulled along by the crowd toward the open doors of the village hall. Bright yellow lights shone from inside. And the smell of hot cider wafted out to them as they waited their turn to file up the steps.

They stopped just inside the door and looked around. Pine boughs and ribbons hung from the rafters. A huge tree stood to one side of the stage and rose to the ceiling. At the other side, a dilapidated upright piano was pushed against the wall.

Allison felt Lee and her being gently nudged aside, as others entered behind them. And, sure enough, there were the expected *oohs* and *aahs,* and some of them were coming from her.

Children raced past to get a closer look at the tree. Allison's throat constricted and she felt an uncomfortable urge to burst into tears. She took a deep breath and reminded herself it was all part of the setup. She had to admit it was a perfect place to bring the kiddies for Christmas. And she couldn't stop herself from glancing at Lee as a totally inappropriate thought popped into her mind. Only this one didn't have to do with sex. But what the outcome of sex might be, at the right time, with the right person. And Allison's biological clock started beating time with the "Little Drummer Boy."

Fortunately the lights flickered at that moment changing her focus. Two slender women, wearing matching calf-length wool skirts and twin sets, stepped in front of the curtain. One stood at the side of the stage while the other took her place at the piano. A hush fell over the crowd and everyone turned to face the stage.

The lights dimmed until only those shining on the apron of the stage remained lit. A few tinny notes rose from the piano and the woman onstage began to recite, "And there were shepherds . . ." The heavy black curtain parted in a series of jerks and creaks.

Sure enough, four shepherds—each three feet tall, wearing striped robes and pieces of cloth tied around their heads with twine—stood side by side. Their crooks faced in different directions. One shepherd was picking his nose. The shepherd next to him smacked his hand. A titter ran through the audience.

"And suddenly a star . . ."

On cue, a glittery cardboard star swung out above their heads. It continued to swing back and forth until it settled off to one side. The shepherds pointed at it and began to walk toward it. The bottom of the nose-picker's crook caught the third shepherd on the ankle and he tottered forward; but they all managed to stay upright until they got offstage and the Three Wise Men entered.

The Wise Men were a little older and better rehearsed and managed to follow the star without a hitch. There was a blackout onstage. And the sounds of shuffling and scraping in the dark. The piano music changed to "Away In A Manger." The lights popped on to reveal a tableau of a little Mary and Joseph, a cradle with a doll in it, and the shepherds and Wise Men kneeling around them. Allison recognized the holy family as the children they'd met at the general store, Jen and Jamie. Even their puppy was there, stretched out by the cradle, representing the lowly oxen, no doubt.

The curtain closed, reversing the series of jerks and creaks, and applause and talking broke out. Hot cider was passed around.

Then, from outside, the sound of sleigh bells. All faces turned toward the side door, which swooshed open.

"I gotta get this," said Lee and disappeared into the crowd. Allison pressed forward to see. Chris Olsen burst through the opening, ho-ho-hoing in a voice that resounded through the room. From everywhere, children squeezed past adults until they were sitting at his feet beneath the tree.

Half-dressed shepherds and Wise Men bounded through the opening in the curtain and jumped off the stage. Mary, Joseph and Spanky followed behind, and when Joseph took too long to jump, Mary gave him a shove, then jumped down after him.

Spanky ran back and forth across the stage until the pianist took pity on him and lifted him down to the floor. The puppy immediately headed for Santa, yipping and jumping at his black boots. Santa ho-hoed louder and began to pass out presents.

Allison could see Lee kneeling at Chris's side, getting closeups of the children as Santa handed them their gifts. He looked as excited as the children.

This time she couldn't stop the tears that blurred her vision. She mentally kicked herself for falling into that trap. Thinking of Lee as the Happy Daddy. Happy Daddy would probably never even be home for Christmas, would just send a card or make a quick call from Timbuktu. She surreptitiously wiped her eyes.

Hadn't he left her stranded at the LA airport, just because she was two days late? It wasn't like she did it on purpose. Everyone in her department had worked overtime that year. She'd left straight from the office and taken a cab to the airport after forty-eight hours without sleep. Drunk coffee during the entire flight and put on makeup in the airplane toilet, so she would look good when she arrived. Except that when she got there, there was only a note, left with the airline desk, saying he couldn't wait. Or wouldn't, was more like it. So, after all she had gone through, she spent Christmas alone at the Sheraton LAX. So much for a future together.

Finally the presents had all been handed out. Santa called out "Merry Christmas!" and took his leave.

Then Lee was by her side, smiling. She sniffed and turned away. The lights dimmed again. He slipped his arm around her and squeezed.

White candles with paper holders were passed to each person in the room. Two candles were lit. Those people turned to light the candle of the next two people. As each person's candle was lit they turned to light another, over and over again until the room was filled with winking light.

The pianist began to play "Silent Night." Group after group joined in singing until the carol joined the flames to fill the room.

Allison saw Chris Olsen, changed back into his overalls, slip quietly into the room and take a candle. Everywhere couples stood together, husbands and wives, parents and children, teenagers, old people, all singing like there was no tomorrow.

"Marry me."

Allison stopped singing, stopped breathing. That was Lee's voice. She must be hearing things, because she thought he said—she looked again. Lee was looking at her, horror on his face.

Holy shit. He had said what she thought he said. He'd been swept up in the spirit that was tangible around them. And now he was regretting it. Allison steeled herself and gave him what she hoped was an ironic look.

"I love people like you. A sucker for every marketing ploy. They should test Hallmark cards out on you." She immediately regretted her words. He hadn't done it on purpose to hurt her. It had just slipped out. She couldn't blame him for falling for all the Christmas feel-good stuff. She knew how it worked. It was what she did for a living. This was the kind of response she was paid to achieve. Make people buy things against their will. And these people were good. Even she was succumbing to it.

Lee turned away and began looking everywhere but at her.

Allison gritted her teeth. Now they would have to sit out the rest of the week in total discomfort. She should have pretended she hadn't heard him. But she'd been so shocked that she'd immediately started defending herself. Before he could take it back, or say he was kidding or pretend that wasn't what he'd said to begin with.

She looked up and saw Chris Olsen standing in a group across the room. Their eyes met. He shook his head. Allison lowered her eyes. It was almost as if he'd heard their conversation and was disappointed. When she looked again, he was gone.

The revelers began to leave, carrying their candles out into the night. They dispersed through the darkness, calling out, "Merry Christmas!"—their voices growing quieter, quieter, until there was no sound at all, just the flicker of tiny lights as they returned to their homes.

Lee and Allison were quite alone. Walking back to their little chalet, like two strangers.

They didn't talk, just stared at their own candles as if keeping them lit by sheer willpower. It was better than talking. Allison had no idea what to say. Better to act like nothing had happened. Give Lee the chance to breathe easy again.

When they reached the front steps, Lee blew out his candle and tossed it into the snow, then went to open the door. Allison snatched it up and slipped it into her pocket, then blew out her own candle and followed him inside.

Five

Lee rummaged in the fridge, waiting to see what Ally would do. How she would react, if she reacted at all. He wasn't hungry anymore, hadn't been for the last half hour. What had possessed him to blurt out something like "Marry me," in the midst of a crowd of strangers? Maybe he *was* possessed.

Yeah, by all that schmaltzy Christmas stuff, with the little kiddies and Santa and the cider. Jesus. What had he been thinking? She was married to her family's ad agency and he was married to his camera. It was pretty pitiful, but what were the choices? He couldn't exactly picture them living . . . where? Denver? LA? He'd never want to raise a family in LA.

Family. Who said anything about family? It was that damn Christmas pageant.

He heard her come into the kitchen, pull out a chair. And he knew if he took his head out of the fridge, she would be watching him, accusing.

"Lee."

"Hmmm," he said. What would happen if he just climbed into the fridge and waited until she left the room? Suffocate, that's what.

"It's a fridge not an oven. You can't take the easy way out."

Oh, shit, confrontation time. Only this time after the blowup there would be no place to run. Maybe Chris had a spare bedroom at his house. He grabbed a jar of mustard and stood up.

Sure enough, she had that look, the one that pinned him like a hapless beetle. He swallowed. "You want a sandwich?"

Her eyes flashed. He braced himself. But she surprised him.

"No thanks." She stood up and left the room. Leaving him holding the mustard instead of her.

She was going upstairs. He could see her feet through the open risers of the staircase. And he didn't think she was hurrying up to get ready for him. Her feet were dragging, if that was possible. Certainly moving slower than he'd ever seen her move.

He wanted to go after her, to explain. But his feet were rooted to the linoleum. And explain what? He didn't have a clue. If she would just stay and eat, things would blow over and they could get back to doing what they did best with each other.

He'd missed his chance. He heard the bedroom door open and shut—shutting him out. All because he'd blurted out that stupid marriage proposal.

Okay, so it wasn't the most romantic way of doing the thing, but it wasn't like he'd planned to say it. He ran his hand through his hair, realized he was clutching the mustard jar to him like it was his salvation. He quickly put it on the table and hurried after Allison.

He took the stairs two at a time. The bedroom door was locked. Perfect. What else could go wrong this week. This year. This lifetime.

He knocked softly on the door. "Ally?"

"Go away."

Lee sighed, counted to ten. "Al, what's going on?"

"You tell me."

"If you'll let me in, I will." No, he wouldn't. Jesus. He didn't know what was going on. They couldn't get married. They'd kill each other on their honeymoon. No, they wouldn't. They wouldn't have time to take a honeymoon. He'd have some urgent assignment, she'd have a major deal to broker. He must have been out of his mind. And yet . . .

The door opened, and Lee's nerves began knocking around with gale-force intensity. He stepped inside. Ally stepped back, then crossed the room to look out the window. Her arms crossed in front of her. Her back to him. About as off-putting as she could make it. And it hit home.

He cautioned himself to keep his temper. After all, they were going to be stuck together for God knew how long. And, besides, said a niggling voice that he hated, *You started it. Either finish it, or finish this relationship for good.*

Lee sighed. He thought he *had* finished this relationship. A year ago. Christmas, to the day. His head began to ache. The two of them were on a fucking treadmill. It was time to make a change. For better or worse.

He walked across the carpet, silently, but he could feel her shoulders tense as he came up behind her. He slipped his arms around her. No response. Okay. She was going to punish him for a while before she let him have it. He knew the drill.

But damn it. He didn't deserve this. She didn't deserve it, either. And Lee realized, for the first time, that he never thought about how she felt. Because he was always reacting to her. Maybe it was time they both learned to be more understanding and less demanding.

He tightened his arms around her, rubbed his cheek along her hair. "I meant it," he said. "Before. What I said. Why don't we get married?"

He felt a tremor go through her. Repulsed? Laughing? He took a long breath. *Stop second-guessing. Go with it.* "Look at me." He tried to turn her around, but she wouldn't budge. He slipped in front of her. Not the brightest move, since she could easily push him through the glass. He took her by the shoulders. "Look at me."

Slowly she lifted her head. But just enough so that she could see him beneath lowered lids.

"Look at me, damn it." He pushed up her chin and immediately drew back when he saw the look in her eyes. She was hurt, not angry.

Why couldn't she just have a normal reaction to a proposal? Just say I do, or I don't. It didn't take a rocket scientist.

Stop it, he warned himself again. They had to break this habit of fighting, if there was going to be any future between them.

He bent his head and kissed her lips. Lightly, gently, meaning to make the kiss an opening to some dispassionate, not argumentative, discussion. But, as always, it quickly ran out of his control. She kissed him back. Her lips and tongue shooting sparks through his bloodstream. His mind started on its own journey, not the one he'd planned.

Allison was responsive and he wanted her. Needed her. Now. He walked her backwards until they were standing at the bed.

His lips moved to her neck. "I meant it. What I said at the Revels." He kissed her jaw, trailed his tongue up to her earlobe. Followed the curve of her ear. She shuddered and pressed against him.

"I know," she said so softly that he almost missed it. She nudged his face away and licked across his mouth.

"Then what are we going to do about it?"

"This." And she pushed him down on the bed.

Allison knew he meant it. Knew he loved her. Knew she loved him. And knew it would never work. It seemed the two of them were good only at making love, not committing to it.

"And this," she said, slipping her hands beneath his sweatshirt to rub her palms along his stomach.

And who could blame them. Love was ephemeral. You couldn't bank it. You couldn't sign it. You could go to contract, but it was a contract more easily broken than the most insignificant business deal.

Lee leaned back and she explored him. She was looking for something. Wanted something. Oh, how she wanted something, and she didn't think it was just his body.

Lee pulled her up beside him and threw his leg over hers. "I—"

Allison curled into him and covered his mouth with hers. The sentence died in an umph, and segued into a groan when Allison slipped her tongue past his teeth. Lee pushed her to her back, rolled on top of her and kissed her. She felt hot and ready and reprieved.

Lee's weight was heavy on her, his cheek covered her nose as he deepened the kiss. She would have to come up for air before much longer, but she was afraid to stop kissing him because he might start talking again.

And even though she knew he meant all the things he was going to say, she also remembered that good old quote by John Dryden. It had stuck with her through graduate school and internships and business negotiations. "The road to hell is paved with good intentions."

And she didn't intend to ... She sighed as Lee pulled his mouth from hers. Straddled her and spread his fingers over her shoulders. Then, deliberately he dragged them down her front, over her breasts, the rough skin of his fingers catching on the fine wool of her sweater.

She gripped his thighs. He squeezed them tighter around her. A lock of dark hair fell over his forehead. His eyes turned smoky with desire and he looked like everything she had ever wanted, but couldn't have.

His fingers gripped her sweater and turtleneck and pulled them up her body. Pulled them over her shoulders and head, cutting off her view of him.

And when she could see him again, he wasn't looking at her but at her breasts.

"Take off your clothes. I'll be right back." He swung a leg to the floor and pushed off the bed.

"Where are you going?" Allison asked bemusedly. Her mind was befuddled by desire and her thought processes had gone the way of foreplay.

"To the bathroom. And not for a cold shower." He grinned in that way he had when nothing was bothering him. Which she saw only during sex and wondered if he ever showed it to someone else, when she wasn't around.

Better not to know. She unsnapped her jeans and pulled them off. She tossed them on a nearby chair. Sent first one sock and then the other after them. Slid her underwear down her legs, rolled it into a ball, then threw it across the room.

It was floating to the carpet when Lee returned, wearing nothing but a pulsing hard-on and carrying two bottles of body oil. He stepped over her thong and placed the bottles on the bedside table.

He shrugged. "Might as well make use of these, since Marcie and Greg went to the trouble of buying them."

"Wouldn't want to hurt their feelings," said Allison.

He reached for the one labeled Aphrodite's Desire. There was a splash of red across the white plastic and a curl of smoky blue that wrapped itself around the bottle.

"If you say 'good packaging,' you're toast." Lee yanked the comforter off the bed and straddled her, holding the bottle open above her.

"Great packaging," she answered, letting her gaze settle on his erection.

"Thank you," he said, and squeezed a pinkish oil into his palm. "Turn over."

"This isn't going to be a mutual slide fest?" she asked, but turned over onto her stomach. She heard Lee chafing his hands together to warm the oil. Then felt his hands on her back. Sliding down her spine. And she let out an involuntary sigh of pleasure.

He picked up the bottle again, ran his hands back up the way they'd come, then said, "Oh, hell." He picked up the bottle for the third time and Allison felt the trickle of oil at the base of her neck.

It was cold at first, but as he poured it down the ridge of her spine it grew warmer. And when it reached her butt, and Lee let a steady stream run between her cheeks and into her crotch, it burst into heat.

The air was permeated with the aroma of cinnamon and sex. Allison breathed it in but didn't move, just enjoyed the feeling of the oil flowing over her and mixing with her own pooling heat. Then she wiggled her hips against the sheet, letting the oil farther into her crease.

She teased herself until she was close to the edge. "Oh, God."

"Yes?" Lee dripped oil onto the back of her thighs. He shifted down her legs, poured oil onto her calves. Then he spread her legs and settled on his knees between them.

A frison of anticipation rushed through her. She lifted her butt to accommodate him.

He took her feet in his hands and began to massage them.

Allison groaned. "You're kidding, right?"

"Just lie there and relax. Did you know that massaging feet lets off a huge amount of tension?"

"I'm not tense," she said through gritted teeth. It felt incredible but instead of relaxing her, his foot massage was sending a message right to her crotch and it was getting tense as all hell.

"I think you better check your source," grunted Allison as he hit a particularly sensitive spot on the sole of her foot.

"Honey," said Lee, moving on to her calves, "you're going to be loose as a goose when this is over."

He poured more oil onto her thighs. It ran down the sides and tickled the inner flesh. Lee followed it with his fingers. She spread more for him.

But he flattened his palms on her cheeks and began kneading her glutes. "You've got a great butt," he said hoarsely.

He was driving her crazy. Another two seconds of this and she'd be writhing around like a woman possessed. "You should see what's waiting for you underneath."

"I could come just looking at your butt."

"Don't you dare."

He took the bottle from the table again. He moaned. "Oh, yeah, this is—"

Her eyes jerked open and she twisted her head so she could see what he was doing. He poured oil down his chest, catching it with his palm and rubbing it against his pecs, stopping only long enough to squeeze his nipples, and start again. His cock twitched at every touch. Slowly, he rubbed down his midsection, stuck his finger in his naval and gave her a lascivious smile.

Allison licked dry lips as his hands traveled lower. He spread the oil on his cock, over his groin, between his legs. He hissed through his teeth when his fingers cradled his balls. And all the time he was smiling at her.

"Okay, that's it," said Allison. "Don't think you're going there without me."

She tried to turn over, but he pushed her back down with his free hand. He held her butt with one hand, while he slid the other up and down his erection. The bed rocked beneath them.

Then his hand slipped between her cheeks, past her sacrum. And, finally, tortuously slow, slid home.

Allison cried out. Lee was panting behind her. "Okay, now, baby. Hold onto the headboard. I want you deep. Really deep."

She shifted to her knees, pulled herself up until she was braced on the wooden bedframe. Lee spread her knees, took a searing lick up her butt before kneeling between her legs. He leaned against her, biting her neck, her ear, her shoulder, all the while sliding his cock along her inner folds. The oil, the cinnamon and their combined arousal drove them tighter and tighter.

Then, in one quick movement he guided his dick into her. He lay against her back, not moving. One arm around her waist, the other cupping her crotch. He released and thrust. His cock impaled her. His chest slid against her back while his finger circled her front.

And Allison held onto the bed for all she was worth.

The rhythm quickened, each thrust lifting her off her knees and driving her closer to the headboard. Then he stopped moving; the hand at her waist moved to her breast. Each time he circled her nipple with one hand, he pressed the fingers of his other hand between her legs.

She was holding her breath, trying to prolong the build- up. But she was being twisted, higher and tighter. She could feel Lee trembling with the effort of not coming.

And then her head fell back against his shoulder in a silent cry. And they came undone, spiraling into darkness, out of control, crying out in guttural moans, pumping, and thrusting and shuddering until they collapsed in a heap together against the headboard.

They huddled there, spooned together. Allison still impaled on his penis. Not talking, not moving, not even pulling the sheet over them when their oil-coated bodies began to cool.

"Better than Christmas garland," whispered Lee, sounding like he might nod off any second.

"Hmmm." For once, Allison was hungry. For food, for a glass of wine and for more of this man who would be gone again before she could say Buffalo Burger.

"Baby, you can hang yourself on my tree anytime."

Taken off guard, Allison snorted. Lee's cock slipped out of her and with it a rush of warmth. The room had grown cool, something she hadn't noticed. She scooched down and reached for the sheet. She pulled it over both of them and they stretched out, their arms wrapped around each other, while Allison wondered why they could never stay happy.

He turned back to her and pushed a lock of hair from her face. He kissed her, leisurely this time, and it was all the more powerful for its ease. It was something they didn't find often. Ease. Leisure.

Illusion, she reminded herself. She sat up. "I need dinner."

"Do you want to cook or build the fire?"

She gave him a look. She could cook. What self-respecting ad executive couldn't. "I guess you failed to notice when you returned from snow surfing last night, that the fire was still going."

"I did notice and I'm impressed." He grinned at her. "You can build the fire."

She grinned back at him. "I'll cook."

Six

The pantry and fridge were stocked and Allison picked out mushrooms, onions, peppers and tomatoes. She chopped them into symmetrical shapes, each the same size, concentrating on each slice of the knife, so she wouldn't think that this could be their last meal together. She sautéed them into a ragout. She boiled water and cooked pasta. Made a salad and a vinaigrette from scratch.

Lee finished building the fire and wandered in to see what she was doing. She just kept chopping. He opened a bottle of pinot noir and set it on the counter to breathe. Then he left again.

She could hear him rummaging in his camera bag and thought with a sinking heart that he was already somewhere else. In the jungle. Or wherever. It didn't really matter. It would always be somewhere and it wouldn't be with her.

She pulled down plates and wineglasses, poured out the wine and took a healthy gulp to get started.

"Hey," said Lee from the hallway. "Wait for me."

Story of her life, thought Allison, but not with bitterness. She was too sad to be bitter. And it had never been about bitterness. It had been about fear.

She loved him. She tried not to. Didn't want to give her heart to someone who traveled all over the world, risking life and limb, in search of the ultimate photograph. She couldn't take it. Every time Lee left for another assignment, she wondered if it would be his last. If she would ever see him again.

And while she worried and wrestled with overwhelming terror, her work suffered. And when he did return and her fear finally released its grip, she had to work twice as hard to catch up. It made her brittle and unapproachable. It also gave her the edge to win. But it took its toll in other ways.

And now he was here again. Tempting her to risk everything for something she couldn't control. She reached for the second wineglass and handed it to him with trembling fingers.

He saw. Frowned and cocked his head at her. "Ally?"

She shook her head and turned back to the stove. Lifted the top off the pasta pot and burned her fingers. She dropped the top and Lee was by her side. Pulling her to the sink and holding her hand under cold water.

"I'm all right," she said. "The pasta is going to be overcooked."

"You're not all right."

No, she wasn't. She never would be as long as she let him turn her world upside down. She couldn't live with him and she couldn't stand to live without him. Her life was a cliché. And it was tearing her apart. She had to deal with it once and for all. And she dreaded it. How she wanted to say *I do*. To live happily ever after with Lee. And she could kick herself for even thinking like that. There were no happily ever afters. Life was a constant struggle, and life with Lee would be, well, it would be life with Lee when and if he was around. It was too much stress. "I can't do this."

She heard his sigh. Could feel his disappointment in her. Could feel the anger welling up inside him. She could feel his feelings like they were her own.

He pushed her away from the sink. Grabbed two potholders and poured the pasta out into the colander. Slammed the pot back onto the burner so hard that it rattled. Then he turned on her.

"I don't get you. I love you. You love me. I ask you to marry me. And you pretend like it never happened. Being around you is hell." He began dishing the pasta onto the plates. Spooned the ragout over them and placed them on the table. "Why can't you commit? Is it me? Is that it? Is there something about me that just doesn't make it for you?"

He turned toward her then, anger and hurt zeroing in on her most vulnerable place. "Just tell me and let's end it. It won't be the first time I haven't measured up to someone's expectations. Hell, I'm so used to it, I probably won't even notice if you get added to the mix."

"Stop it," she cried, not wanting to see that look of hurt in his eyes. Not wanting to be a part of whatever rejection he expected from those who should love him. "It isn't you. It's me."

"Oh, ha. Surely an ad agency barracuda could come up with something more original than that." He poured wine into his glass. Put the bottle on the counter and held it there. "Maybe it's you. Maybe you are the problem. You just can't commit. Why should I be surprised?"

"I'm committed."

"To your work."

That did it. The tears that had been hovering broke

loose. Her mouth twisted in an effort to control herself. And then everything she had felt and feared and wrestled with came pouring out. And she didn't have the strength to stop it or even temper it.

"Of course I'm committed to my work. I can trust my work. I can depend on it."

"And you can't trust or depend on me. Great. You know, Ally, I'm trustworthy and dependable. You just can't commit to me."

"Commit to you? How can I, when I never know if you're coming back? What's to commit to?" She dashed at her tears but she didn't turn away. Not this time. It was time she laid her soul bare and let him do what he would.

He was just staring at her. Dumfounded. His anger washed away in a split second, to be replaced with total confusion. "I—I always come back. You know I do."

"Not if—not if something were to happen to you."

His eyes narrowed and the color rushed from his face. He frowned, reached behind himself to pull out a chair, and slowly sank into it.

Allison ran her palms quickly over her cheeks to dry them. He looked up and she jerked them away.

"Is that what keeps you back? You're afraid I'll get killed?"

She nodded slowly, the tears starting up again.

"Nothing's going to happen to me."

"That's what all you guys say. And look how many of you haven't made it back. It only takes one bullet or one bomb or whatever."

"Jesus, Al. Why didn't you say so?"

"Because it's stupid and selfish and it's what you do."

* * *

Lee sat by the fire and listened to Ally cleaning up the dinner things. All this time he had thought it was her job that kept them apart. But it wasn't. It was his. And she was right. It was what he did, but he'd never realized before that it was fear for him that kept her from committing. Now he wondered if there was a way he could reassure her; if it was even possible for them to overcome years of miscommunication and misunderstanding.

He knew that they had spent most of that time reacting to each other rather than acting for each other. Was it too late? Had they built so many bad habits that they were doomed to failure?

He didn't believe that, not deep down inside. But he knew that he needed to get her to take the final step. It was now or never. He felt it intuitively. And if there was one thing he had come to trust over the years, it was his intuition.

But was he being selfish? He did risk his life, not all the time, but enough. He loved the thrill, the anticipation of getting the next great shot. But did he love it more than he loved Ally?

He didn't know. And if he gave it up for her, and it didn't work out, he'd be up the creek.

The kitchen was spotless, yet Ally stood at the counter, prolonging the moment before she would have to go into the living room. She looked out the window into a world so black that it could be anywhere or nowhere. She was so aware of Lee sitting just on the other side of the staircase that she could almost taste him. Wanted to taste him. Was powerless against the attraction that pulled her to him.

She was being stupid and cowardly. She'd dropped her bombshell and now she would have to confront Lee's reaction to it. They had eaten dinner without continuing the discussion about her commitment. Had also eaten without tasting much of anything. But she knew once she went out, she would be starting the course to the final parting. The roads would be cleared by tomorrow, the next day at the latest, and this time when they parted, Allison knew it would be for good.

She took a deep breath and steeled her resolve. Surely even that would be better than this awful limbo they were living in.

Lee looked up the minute she stepped into the living room. "Come here."

She did, to sit beside him, trying to soak in the sense of him, the feel of him, and wondering how empty her world would be without him.

He put his arm around her, pulled her close. But for once, they didn't drop everything and go at each other like two randy teenagers. They were at a crossroads and they both knew it.

She rested her head on his shoulder. Felt his heart beating beneath his sweatshirt. Felt every contour of him, the heat of him, the smell of him, and thought her heart would break.

They sat looking at the fire, together as they should be, and both helpless to make it happen.

When they finally went to bed, they made slow and attentive love. Each moment bringing them closer to the time when they would part for good. Allison lay awake for a long time afterward. She knew Lee was awake, too. But they didn't talk and at last she fell asleep.

It seemed like only minutes had passed when Allison felt herself being shaken. She pried her eyes open to find Lee hovered over her.

"Wha-a-t," she said on a yawn.

"It snowed again."

Was that a hint of excitement in his voice? She blinked up at him.

He was smiling. "Another foot at least."

Which meant no driving down the mountain today. She could shout for joy. She tried not to smile. Failed miserably. "You don't mind?"

He trailed his hand down her shoulder and slid it underneath the covers, cradled her breast. "Not at the moment," he said and climbed in beside her.

She shouldn't feel so relieved. Neither should he. But she turned into him, felt his erection against her hip, and thought, this is the way it's supposed to be.

Lee nibbled her ear, her neck. His hands moved down her back, setting her skin on fire. And she was ready for him, instantly, as always.

He eased her onto her back. His mouth moved to her breast, then to the other. He kissed a line down her midsection, pulling the covers with him and leaving the air to caress her wet nipples.

She lifted into his mouth. Shuddered when his tongue flicked the sensitive skin between her legs. And she gave herself up to the heat that he drew from her. He licked and sucked, teased and caressed, until she burst into flame. He pushed her knees farther apart until his tongue could push inside her, then came back to claim her again. When she began to splinter he released her, pushed his body up hers and rammed his cock into her.

She climaxed around him, called out his name as

her own name echoed in her ears. They came together, hovered for a breath-stopping eternity, then collapsed into a heap.

"Merry Christmas," said Lee. He shivered and pulled the comforter over them.

It was Christmas. They'd actually managed to make it to Christmas. Together. She snuggled against him, just as a loud, insistent knocking split the air.

Lee started. Then groaned.

"What's that?" asked Allison.

Lee rolled to his feet. "My best guess? Santa's here." He reached for his jeans, yanked them on and headed downstairs.

When he returned several minutes later, he wasn't carrying presents or good cheer. He was frowning and he looked pale and worried. He went straight to his duffel bag and began pulling out clothes.

"What's the matter? Who was it? Where are you going?"

"It was Chris. Jamie and Jen are missing. The whole town is out looking for them. Chris asked me to help."

"Jamie? Jen? Cal's kids?" Allison pushed back the comforter. "They're probably just out playing in the snow."

"No one's seen them." Lee pulled on two pairs of socks. "And with the new snowfall—" He looked at her with worried eyes. "Chris says that with all the new snow the hills are unstable, they could, they could . . . I have to go."

"I'll come, too. Just let me get dressed."

"Too dangerous. I'll let you know as soon as we find them."

The "if" he hadn't said was palpable in the air.

Allison began throwing on clothes.

"No," said Lee. "You wouldn't last two seconds out there in those rhinestone boots." And he was gone.

The hell she wouldn't.

She dressed quickly. Ran downstairs, but Lee was already gone. And so were his two cameras.

Trying not to think that Lee might actually be out there to take pictures of the rescue, she threw on her coat, hat and gloves. She shoved her feet into her rhinestone boots. They were pretty stiff already and the lovely blue color had turned to muddy gray. But they would do the job and so would she.

Seven

The day was overcast, but a weak blue patch of sky promised the sun would come out. As long as it didn't melt the snow and make things start sliding around, thought Allison, as she used Lee's footprints to climb over the mounded snow to the street. The street was covered with new snowfall and Lee was nowhere in sight.

At the far end of the street near the green, a small knot of people were gathered. She waded toward them as fast as the snow would allow, but when she was halfway there, they moved away in the opposite direction.

She would never catch up to them. She stopped in the middle of the street, looked around. It seemed like she was the only person left in town. She shaded her eyes with her hand and searched the mountains that rose behind the row of stores. Saw groups of people fanning out in all directions. She might be able to catch up to one of them if she could find a shortcut.

Then she remembered Jamie and Jen bursting

through the back door to the general store, Spanky tearing around the counter. What had they been doing out behind the store? Where had they come from? There might be a path that she could use to connect with one of the search parties. She came to the passageway to the stores. Snow had partially covered it and several chunks of packed snow had fallen from the sides. She climbed over them and stopped on the boardwalk to catch her breath. She was completely alone.

She hurried toward the general store and looked in the window. No one appeared to be inside. Cal must be out of his mind with worry. And his wife, Tracy, whom they'd met at the Revels.

She tried the door handle. The door opened and she stepped inside. The room was warm, the Franklin stove had been left unattended.

She walked straight through the store and opened the back door. And came up against a wall of white. The mountain seemed to grow straight up from the back steps. Trees stuck out of the snow like candles on a cake. Above her and to the left, she found the nearest group of searchers, slowly making their way along a ridge. They were carrying shovels, rakes, picks, anything that could be used for digging.

A gust of wind blew snow into her face. Holding her arm in front of her eyes, she jumped down into the drifts. Wasted a few precious seconds looking for a path. Found it almost directly in front of the steps, but it was nearly indiscernible from the rest of the mountain because of the drifting snow. She started up it, sinking knee-deep where the fresh powder had accumulated.

She had struggled upward for less than fifty feet when she tripped over something. She fell forward on her face. Fear closed her throat. She struggled to all fours, crawled to where something was sticking out of the snow and desperately began clawing out a hole with both hands. Nearly cried out in relief when she discovered a jagged rock just beneath the surface.

Struggled back to her feet. There was no time to lose. No one could survive out here for very long, especially not children or a small dog. She thought of Jen and Jamie bounding after their puppy, how still they stood onstage as Mary and Joseph, their delight when Santa arrived.

She was covered with snow, her eyelashes were wet with it. She wiped her face with her coat sleeve and plowed ahead. At last she came to a place where the powder was tamped down by the prints of many boots.

She followed the prints as they wound back and forth across the incline. It was hard going and after a several minutes she had to stop and catch her breath. And it seemed she had gotten no closer to the search party. She was high enough now to see other search parties in the distance, some on the mountain, some down by the road. Except for an occasional cracking sound, or a thump when a clump of snow fell from a tree limb, it was eerily silent.

Then she remembered what Chris had said about the unstable mountains. Hadn't she seen on a nature show how a yell could start an avalanche? Surely that's not what he meant when he said unstable. She looked above her, to where the mountains rose into the gray clouds and disappeared.

Those kids couldn't have gone very far. The snow would have come up to their thighs. And Spanky would have sunk right to the bottom. No, they must be someplace close.

Allison took a final deep breath and was about to start off again, when she heard a sound. She stopped and listened. Not snow falling. More like a bird? No. There it was again. A bell. The tinkling of a bell.

The bell she heard their first day as Spanky bounded over the snow to the street. She looked around. Strained to decipher from what direction it came. Silence. She waited, hardly daring to breathe.

And it came again. Off to the right, she was sure. She looked in the opposite direction to the search party that was moving farther and farther away.

She opened her mouth to yell, then stopped. No yelling. And besides it might not be Spanky. It might be a decoration from the green, carried off by the wind.

A few feet later, she found a fork in the path, and even though there were no footprints to follow, the wind had cleared some of the snow and there were places where she could get a foothold.

Here and there she saw indentions in the snow, but it was impossible to tell if they were prints or just the natural evidence of a changing landscape. Every few feet she stopped and listened. Heard another tinkle and knew she was headed in the right direction.

And suddenly there he was. A little black-and-white dog, a red ribbon around his neck, hopelessly caught in a tree branch.

He barked excitedly when he saw her.

"Shh," she ordered and plowed toward him.

He lunged for her and twisted against the branch. She grabbed him. "Hold still," she said as she worked the ribbon from the branch. As soon as he was free, he jumped up, licked her face and promptly sank into the snow.

She lifted him out and put him on firmer ground. "Find Jamie and Jen," she said in an excited whisper. "Go on, boy, take me to them."

Spanky bounded away, then stopped and looked back

at her. He was standing perilously close to the edge of a narrow ridge and Allison realized that she would have to cross it. Hugging the mountain, she gingerly followed. Something cracked above her head. A clump of snow fell right in front of her, nearly burying Spanky. He shook it off and waited for her to catch up. Then he took off again.

She was sweating inside her coat with the exertion from keeping on her feet and not tumbling over the edge of the ridge. She looked down. She had gone beyond the buildings and was looking straight down on the village green. *You're not that high up,* she consoled herself. *It's not the goddamned Alps or a glacier. Just a foothill.* Foothill, her ass, it was a straight drop to Main Street. She puffed out air. It couldn't be more than a hundred feet at most, with lots of snow at the bottom to cushion her fall, if she fell, which she was not going to let happen, because she had children to rescue.

And warning herself not to look down again, she eased along the rock.

At last she stepped out onto a platform of snow and hopefully rock beneath. Spanky had stopped and was standing at attention in front of a black opening. Not large enough to be a mine entrance. Thank God. This was more like a natural schism.

She peeked inside. Okay. More like a cave. She shuddered. If those children were alive and well, she hoped they got the spanking of a lifetime. *Please let them be alive and well.*

She leaned into the darkness. "Jamie? Jen? Are you in there?" No answer. She was afraid to call out much louder. She was psyching herself out, but she wasn't about to take any chances with an avalanche and she wasn't going to go in there unless she had to.

"Jen? Jamie?" she called a little louder.

"In here," a small voice echoed back.

Thank God. Allison looked for any searchers that she could signal. They were all really far away. She waved her arms anyway. No one seemed to notice. She took a step toward the entrance, but before she could force herself to go inside, Jen appeared out of the dark.

Her eyes were round and her face was pinched with fear. Her lips quivered. Allison dropped to her knees and the child fell into her arms.

"Where's Jamie?" Allison asked, trying to keep the panic out of her voice. Trying not to frighten Jen any more than she already was.

"I'm in here," another small voice echoed from the shaft. "I need help."

"He dropped the flashlight and it broke," said Jen, sniffing. She rubbed her sleeve across her nose. "And he hurt his foot looking for it. Stupid. Boys are so dumb."

"I am not," came the voice from the dark.

"Are, too," said Jen, starting to cry. She looked at Allison. "Aren't they?"

Allison smiled, blinking back her own tears of relief. "Yeah, they are," she whispered. "But it isn't nice to let them know we know."

"Oh," said Jen.

"Hurry," came Jamie's wavering voice.

"Come on," said Allison. But she let Jen lead the way.

Jamie was only a few feet from the entrance and the area was lit from the opening. But still Allison had to look twice before she understood what she was seeing. He was surrounded by . . . Christmas packages. Wrapped up and tied with ribbons.

She fell to her knees and started inspecting him. "Where are you hurt?"

"My foot. I can't stand up on it."

"Do you think you could hold on to my neck so I can carry you out?" How heavy could a small boy be? And it hit her with sad chagrin that she had no idea.

Jamie didn't answer. But he wrapped his arms around her and she staggered to her feet. As soon as she was standing, he wrapped his legs around her waist. He was shaking with cold and fright.

Allison held him tight. "Okay, let's blow this joint."

"Wait," said Jamie. "Don't forget the presents."

The presents, of course.

"I'll get them," said Jen, and began piling the boxes on top of each other.

"I gotta ask," said Allison. "Why do you have Christmas packages in here?"

"It's where we hide them, so nobody will peek before Christmas. We always come get them on Christmas morning and sneak them into the living room. But Jamie dropped the flashlight."

"I couldn't help it," he said. "I tripped."

"You should have let me carry it. I'm the oldest," said Jen from behind a mountain of packages.

"Maybe you should make two trips," said Allison, worried that the child couldn't see where she was going. She shifted Jamie to her hip, grabbed hold of Jen's coat and, with Spanky jumping and racing between their legs, she led them outside.

They stood huddled together on the ledge outside the mouth of the cave. Allison could see several search parties in the distance. She let go of Jen long enough to wave an arm trying to get their attention. But still no one noticed her and she began to fear that she would have to get them all down the mountain by herself.

And then a group suddenly appeared directly below them. She waved more vigorously. Hazarded one quick, "Up here."

One of them looked up, then another. Allison could have fainted with relief. Suddenly they were all looking up and pointing. And Allison heard the rumble that seemed to come from right overhead. Below her, everyone froze as the first snow rained down on her and the children.

Jen screamed. Jamie buried his head in her shoulder and Allison had just enough time to throw them all against the rocky wall before the rumble became a roar, and masses of snow fell down the mountain.

Allison pressed Jamie and Jen against the wall, shielding them with her body.

"Spanky!" cried Jamie, before his voice was drowned out as snow and ice and boulders thundered past them.

They were going to die, thought Allison. They were going to die. And in that stereotypical last moment before death, her life flashed before her. And all she saw was Lee.

Lee watched, unable to move. His camera fell from his hand and thumped against his chest, while people ran in all directions as a curtain of white unfurled toward them. Someone grabbed his arm, pushed him aside, as the world went white around him.

"No-o-o-o!" he cried and struggled against the arm that was holding him back.

On and on it came, filling up the village green. Snow and chunks of ice and broken limbs and boulders, sliding down the mountain like primordial lava. The earth shuddered and quaked. He watched, helpless. Saw Allison and the children disappear behind a mountain of white.

And then it was over, except for the crunch of settling ice. Eddies of snow filled the air. It covered Lee's face, his hair, his clothing. Slowly, he became aware of those around him. Standing at the edges of the flow, Cal and his wife, Tracy, clung to each other, shock and horror carved on their faces.

And no one moved.

Lee started toward the mountain. He didn't have a plan, he just had to get to them. To Allison.

The world shifted again and he fell back. Someone grabbed hold of him to keep him from falling. Chris.

"We have to do something," Lee stammered. "Something."

"And we will," said Chris, keeping his voice even. "As soon as everything settles and it's safe."

Lee shook his head. "Now. They'll suffocate while we're waiting until it's safe."

"Have to wait," said Chris, but Lee pushed him away and started dragging himself through the snow and detritus. He'd barely gone ten feet when he sank in up to his waist. Two men took him under the arms and pulled him out. Lee tried to fight them off. "Let go." He thrashed his arms out at them, but with his legs sinking into the snow, he had no leverage. They pulled him back to where the others stood, holding their shovels and picks, shaking their heads.

And that's when Lee gave up hope. He dropped his face to his hands. Allison was gone, they'd never get them out alive, they weren't even trying. Because they knew it was futile. It was too late. A cry escaped him, he didn't try to hold it back. He didn't care about anything, not anymore.

The roaring had stopped, but the world was black. Oh, God, they were—Allison opened her eyes. Not dead. They were alive. They must be in an air pocket. The rock overhang had saved them.

"Are you okay?" she whispered, afraid any sound or movement might set off another avalanche. She felt two little heads nod.

Spanky, who had taken shelter on Allison's feet, wiggled free.

No, thought Allison; the slightest movement might collapse their fragile shelter. Carefully, she turned her head away from the wall. And stared. Oh. My. God. She grabbed the rough stones for support.

"Lee. Lee, boy." Chris was shaking him. Lee shook his head. He couldn't watch. Couldn't witness Cal and Tracy's grief, couldn't let them see his own.

"Look up, dammit." Chris pulled his hands away. Lee looked up. The sun broke through the clouds and blinded him. He blinked, squinted, but all he could see was eye-dazzling snow.

"There," Chris whispered and pointed to something. A murmur went through the rescue party. Someone sobbed.

There was snow all around them, up the mountain, covering the place where a few minutes ago Allison had stood with two lost children. And then right at the spot where they had disappeared there was a flurry of snow. Lee could only watch with a feeling of inevitability. Another slide.

The flurry became a little tornado of white. Something black and white scrabbled over the top, barked, then sank out of sight.

Lee stared, rubbed his eyes, stared again. Nothing. He was seeing things. Then another tremor in the snow and a pair of black ears appeared at the surface. And behind him, the sunlight casting auras about them, three heads rose over the top. A whispered cheer rose about him, not loud, but heartfelt, for all its softness.

Allison waved and Lee swayed on his feet.

"Careful, son," said Chris. "We'll get them down."

Mechanically, Lee stepped forward.

"You stay here. We know what we're doing. Be patient." He signaled to Allison to stay put, and the line of men began slowly to wind their way up the mountain.

Except for Lee, who found Allison's eyes and held them.

It seemed to take days but actually took only a half hour to get them free. The avalanche had completely passed them by.

Lee watched the proceedings while standing next to Cal and Tracy. Spanky sat between them. Together they watched the men return down the mountain with Allison and the two children. Lee held his breath at every sound, every time they disappeared behind the snow. And couldn't believe it when he actually saw Allison running toward him.

She hit him with such force that he stumbled backwards.

"Al," he said. "Al." It seemed to be the only word his lips would form. Maybe because she was squeezing the breath out of him.

Allison was so relieved to actually be in Lee's arms, it took her a few minutes to realize he was shaking. "Lee?" She pulled away to look at him. "Lee," she said indignantly. "You may think this is funny, but we could have died up there." Lee shook his head. Hiccupped. Shook some more. Let go of her to wipe his eyes. Gulped in air, trying to get control of himself.

Allison grabbed him by the coat lapels and shook him. "You're hysterical."

His grin twisted suddenly and he bit his lip. "I . . . just . . . It was the relief . . . It's just—Jesus, I thought I'd lost you."

Lee pulled her close. Her chest banged against the cameras hanging around his neck.

"I hope you at least got some good shots," said Allison, nuzzling her way past the telephoto lens. "What we did on our Christmas vacation."

"Well, um . . ."

She pulled back to look at him. "Don't tell me you didn't."

"I forgot. I mean, when you disappeared behind that avalanche, catching it on film just sort of skipped my mind."

"Yeah, well, when my life flashed before me, all I saw was you." She was trying to hang tough, but her lip trembled, giving her away.

Lee rubbed his cheek across her hair. "I'm not willing to lose you for all the Pulitzers in the world."

"We're in big trouble here."

"Don't I know it."

"Well, you folks are mighty lucky," said Chris bringing up Jen and Jamie, who was clutching a shivering Spanky. Cal and Tracy walked behind them, supporting each other, watching their children with adoring smiles.

Allison pried herself away from Lee.

"We're so very grateful to you for saving these two scallywags," said Cal. Tracy nodded vigorously from behind Cal's handkerchief.

"Thank you for saving us," Jen said politely.

"But I wish you would've saved our presents, too," said Jamie.

"Jamie," warned his father.

"But now Jen and I don't have anything to give you and Ma for Christmas."

"We got all we want or need," said Cal, and sniffed. "Mighty beholden." This to Allison, who was beginning to feel embarrassed by all the attention and was uncomfortably aware of the snow melting inside her boots.

"You're welcome," she said. "But Spanky deserves the real praise. I heard his bell and when I found him, he led me to where they were." She reached out and petted him. "Oh, he must have lost his bow in the excitement."

"We'll get those presents down after breakfast," said Chris. "And Spanky's gonna get a big new bow with a bright, shiny bell. This calls for a real celebration. Everybody come on down to the Watering Hole. Pancakes and beer are on me."

Eight

Two days later, the state highway department cleared the roads leading out of Good Cheer. The Range Rover was towed down the mountain to a body shop in a larger town. Lee and Allison dug out her BMW and packed up the car. They drove to LA, and Allison spent New Year's Eve on Santa Monica pier while Lee caught the fireworks there on film.

The next morning, Allison sat at Lee's kitchen table reading the paper. Lee was in his darkroom, developing film, while his digital pictures were being downloaded into the computer.

She was thinking silly thoughts, like how maybe she should start a photo album, chronicling their days in Good Cheer, so they would have something to show their children when they asked how "you and Daddy got together." Because before Good Cheer they had not been together at all.

An hour later, Lee stepped out of the darkroom. Allison looked up expectantly. He was holding a proof in each hand. And then she saw his expression.

"What's wrong?"

Lee shook his head. "They didn't come out."

"What? Impossible." Allison stood up. "Let me see."

"Well, they came out. But—" He dropped one of the prints onto the table. Allison looked. Looked again. There was Main Street. Covered over in snow. It was daytime and it was empty.

"Where is everybody?" she asked.

"They aren't there."

"Probably all behind the snowbank."

"No. They aren't there." He dropped the second print. The inside of the village hall. The piano and Christmas tree and not one person.

"What about the others?"

Lee shook his head and motioned her to the darkroom. There were several rolls of pictures. Lee holding the Christmas tree. But no teenage boy and no truck. Allison looking in the store window. An empty sidewalk. An empty village hall. The black curtain across the stage tattered and torn, but no Nativity scene. No Spanky. No Chris Olsen.

A shiver ran across Allison's skin. "I don't get it."

Lee moved past her through the door. She followed him to the computer, waited while he clicked onto his photo gallery. More pictures of the two of them. Allison in the kitchen. The BMW covered with snow. No Spanky scrambling over the mound of snow.

"What's going on? Is there something wrong with your cameras?"

Lee snorted. "Like in some twilight zone, that only allows me to take pictures of you and me? *Do-do-do-do.* They weren't there."

"What do you mean? Who wasn't there?"

"Chris. Cal. The dog. The kids." He pushed his fingers through his hair. "Only you and me."

"I'm calling Marcie." Allison rummaged in her bag for her cell phone. It was a good thing she had speed dial because her fingers were shaking too badly to have punched in more than one number.

Marcie answered on the second ring, with a meek, "Hi?"

"Marcie, did you rent a ski chalet in Good Cheer?"

"What's with you? Of course I did. You sound funny. Didn't things work out?"

"But you never planned on spending Christmas there, did you?"

"W-e-e-e-l-l." Marcie's voice slid up the scale.

"Just answer yes or no."

"Okay. Okay. But don't get upset."

"Just tell me," said Allison beginning to pace.

"Calm down," said Lee beside her.

"Calm down," said Marcie over the line. "Actually, Greg and I planned it. For you both to go there. We were sure if you two could just get together for a few days without all the outside garbage getting in the way, you'd figure out how much you love each other."

"And you stocked it with food and wine and things."

"We had it delivered."

"You didn't spike the brandy with anything weird, did you?"

"What are you talking about? Where's Lee? Are you really mad?"

If she only knew, thought Allison, even as she sighed with partial relief. At least she and Lee hadn't been mutually hallucinating. "I'm with Lee and we're not mad, at least not at you."

"Well, don't be mad at each other or at Greg, either. He was only trying to help."

Allison could tell that her sister was close to tears.

"Marcie, it's all right. Actually, it was a good thing to do. But just tell me. Where did you find this chalet?"

"Greg read about it in one of his magazines. Here. I have a copy of the ad somewhere." The sound of rummaging. "Here it is."

Weekly rentals for Christmas. Perfect for those who need a break from the harried season.

"We talked to a really nice real estate agent who arranged everything."

"Do you have this agent's name?"

"Sure. It was Chris something. Why? Didn't you like it?"

"We loved it. Had a wonderful time."

"Really? Or are you being sarcastic? "

"No. Really." Allison looked over to Lee, who was frowning at the computer. Then it hit her. "Chris?"

Lee looked up. She widened her eyes at him.

"What was his last name?"

"I'm thinking."

"Could it by any chance be Olsen?"

"Hey, yeah, that was it. Did you meet him?"

"Yeah, we met him, nice guy."

Lee was motioning her over to the computer.

"Hey, I just called to say thanks. I have to go." Allison hung up. "Guess what? Chris Olsen was the real estate agent. See? Nothing weird."

Lee just crooked his finger at her. She came to stand behind him, looked over his shoulder at the computer screen. It was a newspaper clipping with the headline "Mining Town Becomes a Ghost Town." Allison's stomach dropped, and she leaned closer.

The town of Good Cheer, the last bastion of shaft mining in the Colorado Rockies, closed for good on Wednesday. Chris Olsen, mayor and owner of the local bar and grill, was the last to leave. Asked what he would do next, Mr. Olsen said, "I've been mayor of Good Cheer for twenty-five years and owner of the Watering Hole for longer. There's still plenty that I want to do. No need to worry about the good people of Good Cheer. We're just taking our Good Cheer elsewhere."

"There," said Allison. "I told you things were not looking good for Good Cheer. Something must have gone wrong with your film."

"Allison," said Lee in a strained voice. "Look at the date."

Allison scanned the top of the page. *Mid Rockies Gazette,* was printed in the center, and in the top corner: December 23, 1952. She stared. "This is a joke, right?"

Lee shook his head. "This is stranger than fiction."

"Shit." Allison's knees went weak. She swayed and Lee caught her around the waist and settled her onto his lap. "Greg," she said. "A trick."

Lee shook his head.

"So what does it mean?"

"It means we're taking a six-hour ride to Good Cheer."

They drove, stopping only to get gas and once to grab a bite to eat. They arrived midafternoon. The roads were cleared all the way up the mountain and into Good Cheer. Lee parked the BMW at the edge of town.

"See," said Allison. "We're not crazy. There's the village green where we sang carols." They both stared out the front window at the village green and the carpet of snow that covered it. Several feet had drifted up the sides of a sagging band shell. There were no pine swags, no red ribbons. Not one person in sight.

Slowly they got out of the car and, holding hands, walked down the middle of the street to the town. It was deserted. Snow covered the sidewalk. Here and there a roof had caved in under the weight of snow. There was no glass in the windows of the toy shop, only dark, empty space inside. The general store was completely boarded over.

Lee tried the door. But a rusted padlock held it in place.

The doors of the Watering Hole sagged on rusted hinges. A shutter lay half buried in the snow. Another banged against the clapboards each time a breeze ran past.

Lee's hand tightened around Allison's, and they squeezed through the opening.

It took a while for Allison's eyes to adjust to the darkness. When they did, she could make out shadows of chairs turned upside down on tables. Several had fallen over and lay on the floor. She stepped on a rotted floorboard and was saved from falling only by Lee grabbing the back of her coat.

Carefully, wordlessly, they made their way back to the street. Allison blinked against the sudden brilliance. Lee rubbed his eyes with both hands.

They walked on until they came to their chalet. There was a hollowed-out space where the BMW had been parked. There were still footprints leading up the stairs to the porch. They climbed up and tried the door. It was locked. They'd left the key on the kitchen table as instructed. Lee crunched over the rime of ice on the porch and peered into the window. Allison came up beside him and put both hands to the glass to look inside.

It was just as they had left it. The couch, the club chair. Too bad she couldn't see into the kitchen, because if the key was there . . .

"Wait a minute." Allison slipped her way back across the porch and down the steps. She ran to the side of the house and called to Lee.

"It's here. Our Christmas tree." Their ten-dollar Christmas tree lay on its side in the snow, just where they'd left it.

Lee took a deep breath. "At least we were really here."

"Of course we were here."

"So where is everybody else?"

Allison looked at him. He looked at her.

"Hallucination?"

Lee shook his head.

"Group hysteria?"

Lee shook his head. "I don't know what it was, but let's get out of here."

They backed away.

Allison took a last fond look back at the chalet. "Well, it can't be, couldn't be, impossible that it was . . ."

"That it was just us?"

"It can't be."

They walked back to the car looking right and left, looking for someone, anyone, to explain what this was about.

"Fantasy Island," said Allison halfway down the street.

"What? Where?"

"It was a TV show when we were kids. Don't you remember? People would pay to come to this island to live out their fantasies. Remember? There was a dwarf and Ricardo Montalban."

"And who paid for our version of this fantasy? It would cost a fortune."

Allison sighed. "Not Marcie. She has to account to the husband for every penny."

"And not Greg. New-age medicine doesn't exactly pay 'fantasy' wages."

They fell silent again and stopped only when they came to the mountain of snow that had been the avalanche.

"At least this really happened," said Allison with a shudder.

Lee put his arm around her and they stood looking up to the black shelf of rock that had saved Allison and Jen and Jamie.

She glanced at him as he frowned up at the mountain. When they'd left the apartment, he'd thrown his digital camera onto the backseat. He'd even stuck it in his pocket when they first got out of the car. But he hadn't taken one picture. Hadn't even reached for it.

"Come on," she said. "Let's go."

Without a word, he turned her around and they climbed down to the street. Near the bottom, Allison stopped.

Lee held her tighter. "Careful." He took her firmly by the elbow and moved her on.

"Wait, there's something caught on my boot." She reached down. Sure enough something had snagged on the rhinestones. She pulled it off. A soggy red ribbon with a giant brass bell.

"It's Spanky's collar. They were here and we aren't crazy."

"Only about you," said Lee. And kissed her.

Then he took her arm and they walked back to the car, to their lives, to their future. And the only sound was the crunch of their boots on the ice-covered snow and the muffled tinkle of the bell that Allison held tightly in her hand.

"Lee?"

"Hmmm?"

"Someone went to a lot of trouble to get us here."

They walked on.

"Lee?"

"Hmmm."

"You know that offer you made when we were here?"

Lee hesitated. "Yeah."

"Is it still on the table?"

Now he stopped and turned toward her. Her heart did a little flip-flop.

"Yeah. It is."

"In that case . . ." Allison gripped Spanky's ribbon and looked up to the man she loved. "I do."

Lee took her in his arms and they hugged each other, alone in a ghost town in the middle of nowhere. And Allison could swear she heard Chris chuckle, wherever he was.

By Firelight

Janice Maynard

For Anna and Chris:
God bless and keep you as you celebrate
your second anniversary.
May your marriage always be as bright
and beautiful as your Christmas wedding.

One

The Irish setter dozing on the rag rug in front of the hearth lifted her head and whined. Grant looked up from his book. The shrieking of the wind was nothing new. The weather had worsened progressively during the past two hours, and the gusts of blowing snow buffeting the small cabin were increasingly loud. The howling storm wasn't entirely unprecedented for late December in central Virginia, and on his sky-high mountaintop the inches of white stuff were piling up fast.

But the dog had slept through most of it. Why was she uneasy now? She growled low in her throat, rising and lumbering toward the door. Her age and accompanying arthritis made her slow. The dog sniffed the door.

He stood and followed her. "What is it, girl?" Automatically he checked for the rifle standing to the left of the doorframe, just out of sight of any intruders. He enjoyed his self-imposed isolation, but he wasn't immune to its dangers.

The dog barked, a sharp, quick sound filled with knowledge denied to the inferior hearing of humans.

Grant felt the hair rise on the back of his neck as his pulse picked up. What was out there? A bear? A bobcat? Either was a possibility.

Something hit the door, and the dog went wild, scratching and pawing at the sturdy oak. Grant hesitated for a split second, and then a sound, almost surely human, made the decision for him. He unlocked the door and jerked it open, jumping back in surprise when a bundle of snow-covered cloth tumbled in and literally landed on his feet.

The next few minutes were chaotic. The dog jumped and barked at the lump on the floor while Grant struggled to close the door against the force of the wind. When he finally managed that and quieted the frantic dog, the resulting silence resonated with unanswered questions. He knelt cautiously and put a hand on what he now could see was a person's shoulder. Gently, he turned him/her over.

He sucked in a shocked breath. His visitor was definitely a woman, but for one heart-stopping second he thought she might be dead. Carefully, he edged the hood back from her face, brushing aside the layers of caked snow and ice. Her hair, once freed, was a reddish-gold, lighter at the back of her head where it was still dry.

Her skin was so white and her lips so blue, she looked like the ice princess he remembered from a childhood fairy tale. He stripped away her sodden gloves and felt for a pulse, sighing shakily when he found one. But it was by no means steady.

He removed her damp outer garments, including her pants that were wet to the knee, then raced to a hall closet and retrieved a heavy wool blanket. Scooping her up in his arms, he carried her closer to the fireplace and snagged a couple of sofa cushions to make her a nest. The dog curled up beside their unexpected guest, offering her own warmth as well.

He tugged off the woman's shoes, grimacing when he saw they were cloth sneakers rather than boots. The socks were wet through, so he tossed them aside and began rubbing his charge's delicate feet. She was slender all over, including a pair of spectacular legs, which he'd been hard-pressed not to notice as he wrapped her up. Nor did he spend an inordinate amount of time admiring the lacy pink panties that were now safely hidden.

When it seemed as if the blood was finally flowing back into her extremities, he checked her pulse once again and grunted with satisfaction. It felt markedly stronger.

Without warning, her eyes opened.

He released her wrist, feeling strangely guilty. He watched her warily.

One hand gripped the blanket, pulling it toward her chin. Her eyes were amber, an unusual color a few shades lighter than his dog's soft coat. Her lips moved but no sound emerged.

Grant leaned closer, smiling to reassure her. "You're okay. I'm Grant Monroe. This is my cabin."

Her free hand reached out and grabbed his arm, her slender fingers gripping him so tightly her nails left crescent-shaped marks on his skin. Her voice was a hoarse whisper. "My bag. Please get my bag."

He frowned. Surely she didn't expect him to go out in the storm for a few personal possessions.

She must have seen his instinctive refusal. Her eyes welled with tears. "Please. It's important."

He wasn't immune to such naked entreaty. He tucked her arm beneath the blanket and rose to his feet. "Okay. But don't move. You need to stay by the fire until you thaw out." Her eyes drifted shut, and he didn't know if she heard him or not. Her skin was regaining a bit of color, but she still looked infinitely fragile.

He dressed quickly in his coat and snow boots and wrapped a heavy scarf around his head. He had a high-powered flashlight that should give him enough illumination, despite the gathering gloom of dusk. When he opened the door, a swirl of snow entered the room, and he exited quickly, unwilling to sacrifice any of the cabin's precious heat. The cold and wind took his breath away.

He brushed flakes from his eyes and stumbled down the steps, shining a beam of light in front of him. Her small footprints were still visible, but just barely. The heavy snow was filling them rapidly. He followed the narrow indentations, stopping now and again to make sure he was on the right track. About thirty yards from the cabin he found what he was looking for.

A large, black backpack lay in the snow, its bulky outline softened by a thin blanket of white. He picked it up by one strap and cursed as he realized how heavy it was. That slip of a female had been carrying this? Impossible.

He trudged back to the house, pausing on the porch to stomp his feet and brush the worst of the snow from his clothing. Inside, the dog barked a greeting but didn't move from her post. She seemed to understand the gravity of the situation. Grant dumped the pack in a chair and knelt beside the dozing woman. When he touched her cheek, her eyes flew open. "Did you find it?"

He motioned across the room. "It's over there." The relief in her eyes made him glad he'd done as she asked.

He detoured to the bedroom and rummaged in a

drawer for the heaviest socks he could find. When he returned and put them on her feet, she barely moved. He brushed his thumb across her cheekbone. "I'm going to heat up some soup and hot chocolate. Won't take but a minute."

Maddy peeked from beneath her eyelashes and watched as he left the room. Her pulse beat with rapid jerks that had as much to do with her rescuer's almost-overpowering presence as it did with her recent ordeal. He was a huge man, broad through the chest and shoulders, and tall enough to tower over her even if she was standing.

But the kindness in his deep blue eyes and the gentle touch of his hands erased any qualms she might have felt about her safety.

In hindsight, entering a strange man's cabin in the middle of nowhere was not the smartest move she'd ever made, but at the time her options had been limited. Even if Grant Monroe had been a card-carrying member of an antigovernment survivalist militia group, she would probably have kissed his feet and thanked him for bringing her in out of the cold. Seeing the light in his window had literally saved her life.

There had been a brief half hour when she faced the very real possibility that she was going to die. The knowledge had been sobering. She hadn't been scared, not really, but she remembered feeling a searing regret that she was going to exit this earth without ever experiencing the kind of love the poets wrote about.

She snorted, causing the dog to lift her head and whine. "Sorry, girl." Maddy stroked the canine's silky ears and blinked back a rush of tears. Love. Hah! Judging by her parents' recent antics, love was a myth, a pretty illusion invented to dress up the sex drives of men and the emotional needs of women.

Her own brief experiences with male relationships were nothing to write home about. After three abortive tries at the love/sex dance, she had given up on men, and when her own physical needs demanded attention, she found release with a phallic toy and a couple of AA batteries.

Sex was messy, and love . . . if it existed . . . was impossible to control. Who needed the aggravation? Her self-imposed celibacy suited her just fine—at least until she came face-to-face with death and then was rescued by a man who made her rethink the virtues of plastic.

She pulled the blanket more closely around her shoulders and stared into the fire, mesmerized by the pop and crackle of the dancing flames. The heat was so delicious she wanted to purr. She understood now why primitive man worshipped fire. It was life-giving.

Her eyelids were heavy, but she blinked drowsily, determined to stay awake. She surveyed the room with interest, noting the large leather chairs and sofa as well as the brightly colored rag rug partially covering the hardwood floors. Some kind of antler chandelier hung overhead, casting a warm circle of light. A coffee table, littered with books and magazines, occupied the center of the room. The bottom shelf of the table held an assortment of childhood games—Chutes and Ladders, Candy Land, Monopoly. To the left of the fireplace, in the corner, stood a brightly decorated Christmas tree.

Seeing the tree made her heart squeeze with a now-familiar ache. She'd done her best to forget that today was December twenty-second. And she was a bit surprised to find that a single man living alone had gone to the trouble of putting up a tree. Well . . . She assumed he was single. But that might be wishful thinking. As far as she could see, there were no signs of anyone else occupying the cabin.

Which brought her to the picture. Over the mantel hung a large oil painting, probably four feet wide and at least two feet high. The subject was a nude woman, reclining on a patchwork quilt in a field of daisies. Her hair was black, her skin olive. She had a lush, sensual beauty that riveted the viewer. Her breasts were full, and the curve of her hip was nothing like the stick-thin Hollywood version of beauty. The picture was striking, the artist's vision pure and full of joy.

Maddy wondered who the woman was and if Grant knew her or had simply purchased a beautiful picture.

She got to her feet, swaying as her head swam and the room spun dizzily. She sucked in several deep breaths and concentrated on not throwing up. Her hands and feet tingled painfully. She took a tentative step toward the kitchen, stumbling slightly in the overlarge socks. The blanket made a modest, if cumbersome, skirt.

She paused in the doorway and studied her surroundings. The cabin might be rustic, but it was far from primitive. The appliances were top of the line, brushed aluminum with black trim. The walls were rough wood, the windows covered with simple muslin curtains, edged in hunter green.

A rectangular oak table with bench seats was set with navy and green plaid placemats and plain ivory dishes. A loaf of bread, still steaming, rested in the center of the table. Her stomach clenched with sudden, fierce hunger.

She steadied the blanket with one hand and swept her hair away from her face. "Can I help?"

He looked up, his expression etched with sharp concern. "Sit down," he barked. "You look like you're going to pass out."

She didn't argue. He supported her elbow as she took the few steps toward the bench and slid in awkwardly, hampered by the blanket. Fatigue threatened to overtake her, but hunger won out, barely.

Grant was torn between concern and amusement. She looked like a lost child. He handed her a mug of hot chocolate and watched as she sipped it cautiously. Her hands trembled and dark smudges beneath her eyes emphasized her exhaustion.

He turned back to the stove, making his voice deliberately casual. "My brother-in-law is a police chief in a D.C. precinct. You can call him and he'll vouch for me. If it would make you feel safer."

When she remained silent, he kept talking, keeping his voice matter of fact. "You know my name. How about returning the favor? I promise I'm not an ax murderer. My worst sins are leaving the cap off the toothpaste tube and occasionally washing my whites and my darks together."

Her eyes were large and expressive, and he hadn't missed the wariness hidden in their depths nor her defensive posture.

She responded to his teasing with a faint smile. Her voice was soft but clear. "I'm Madison. Madison Tierney. Most people call me Maddy."

He ladled vegetable soup into two bowls and carried them to the table. Before sitting down, he grabbed a beer from the fridge for himself. He settled across from her and smiled. "So . . . Miss Maddy Tierney. Want to tell me why you were wandering alone in the woods in a snowstorm?"

Her cheeks flushed under his steady regard. She took another sip of her chocolate, bending her head and allowing a riot of ginger-red curls to obscure her delicate profile. "No."

He chuckled, charmed by her obstinate honesty. "Don't you think I deserve an explanation?" He leaned forward and tucked her hair behind her ear, his fingers brushing her neck for a brief second.

She flinched and he removed his hand. He took a spoonful of soup and watched as she did the same. She ate with ladylike manners, but the fact that she was starving couldn't be missed.

He allowed her to eat in peace for several minutes, while he cut hunks of bread for each of them and buttered them. In no time she had emptied her bowl.

He reached for it. "More?"

She shook her head. "No. I'm fine. It was delicious."

He carried the dishes to the sink and returned to the table, determined to crack her silence. She cradled the mug of hot chocolate between her palms, her expression pensive.

He sighed. "You might as well tell me. We're going to be snowed in for several days."

Her head jerked up, her face shocked. "Several days?"

He frowned. "Did you really not check a weather forecast before you set out? The snow won't end until morning. The temperature is supposed to drop tonight. We'll be lucky if the power stays on."

Her mouth drooped. "Well, that's just peachy."

He realized that his masculine pride was a bit piqued. He knew at least a handful of women who wouldn't consider being snowed in with him such a bad thing. Clearly Maddy was not of the same mind.

He ground his teeth together. "Spill it, Maddy. What was so important that you risked your life? You *do* know you nearly died."

She glared at him. "Of course I know that. Despite evidence to the contrary, I'm not stupid. I'll admit I made a few bad choices."

He snorted. "That's the understatement of the century."

She nibbled a piece of bread, her eyes shooting sparks at him. "Why do men have to be so damned judgmental?"

He handed her another piece of bread as she finished off the first. Then he stood and paced. "Why do women have to be so suicidally impulsive?" He wasn't shouting, but it was close.

They each stopped dead, staring sheepishly at one another. Her lips twitched. "Nothing like a little hidden baggage to spice up a meal."

He sat down again, groaning and dropping his head in his hands. "Hell, I'm sorry. Can we start over?"

She sighed. "You're right. You do deserve an explanation. But I don't know where to start."

"Anywhere will do. I promise not to be judgmental."

She grinned. "Don't be so rash. You haven't heard my story yet."

Grant felt a funny little jerk in the vicinity of his heart. Rested, and with a bit of food in her stomach, Maddy Tierney was regaining her spunk. The lively intelligence in her eyes and the gamine charm of her quick, expressive gestures delighted him. She was feminine and soft and yet clearly not a pushover. Her face, unadorned by makeup, radiated health and youth. He guessed her to be in her midtwenties.

He poured her some more hot chocolate, adding a handful of miniature marshmallows, and opened a second beer. "I'm all ears."

She wrinkled her nose. "It started out innocently enough. My friend Mimi is a schoolteacher. Most of her family is out in California, and this year she couldn't afford to make the trip home for the holidays. Another friend, Daphne, just got divorced, and her family is the

'I told you so' kind, so she didn't *want* to go home for the holidays. The three of us agreed to spend Christmas together, and we decided it would be fun to walk part of the Appalachian Trail. We thought we might stay in one or two shelters, but when it was practical, we would walk off the trail and stay in a town. The first night out the shelter had mice. At the second night's shelter a group of rowdy Boy Scouts kept us awake."

"No offense, Maddy, but you don't strike me as the hiker/outdoors type. You weren't even wearing boots."

"There's a reason for that. I *was* wearing boots to begin with. But they got pretty muddy the first day and I didn't want to get my sleeping bag dirty. I set them just outside the shelter that night, and some animal dragged them off."

"Ah."

"It's the truth. I didn't know that would happen. I had tennis shoes in my pack as a backup. I hadn't intended on wearing them."

"So where are your friends?"

She scooped out a gooey marshmallow with her fingertip and sucked it. Grant's breathing quickened. Hell, he'd had too much alone time, apparently. He cleared his throat and forced himself to look at something other than Maddy Tierney's little pink tongue.

She was still speaking. "The novelty wore off pretty quickly. My friends decided they wanted to go home. Mimi came down with a cold and was feeling crappy, and Daphne's mom called on her cell phone and gave her the big guilt trip. They both left this morning to head down the mountain and rent a car."

He frowned. "They sound like fair-weather friends to me. A woman hiking alone is an easy target. They shouldn't have abandoned you."

She bristled. "They're the best friends in the world.

We spoke with a family group who was hiking at the same pace we were, and made sure they would be at the next shelter so I wouldn't be alone tonight."

"But you never actually made it to the shelter."

She shrugged. "The weather was a wildcard."

"Why didn't you leave with your friends?"

Her face closed up, shutting him out. Her chin jutted. "I wasn't ready to go back."

He tapped his fingers on the table. Something didn't add up. But he could wait. The snowstorm had brought him an unexpected Christmas gift, and he was prepared to unwrap it a bit at a time.

He stood up. "Let's sit by the fire." With the stove turned off the kitchen was getting chilly. She didn't move immediately, and he raised an eyebrow. "Do I need to carry you?"

She lifted her chin, her cute little nose in the air. "Of course not." She got to her feet, clutching the blanket like a lifeline, and made her way to the sofa.

Despite a strong urge to join her there, he stationed himself away from temptation in an armchair on the other side of the coffee table. She was flustered, he could tell. Her cheeks were bright red, and she was avoiding his gaze, her fingers picking restlessly at the fringe on the blanket.

Now that the immediate danger was past, he allowed himself to enjoy the novelty of having a woman in his rural retreat. He propped his feet on the coffee table, leaning back and lacing his fingers behind his head. "So why weren't you ready to go back? Isn't the week of Christmas kind of an odd time to be away from home? Do you need to call family and let them know you're okay?"

She bent her head. "No," she sighed, her teeth mutilating her bottom lip. "Not necessary. But I'll call

Daphne and Mimi later and let them know where I am. They'll be freaking out when they hear the weather report."

For a brief moment her expression revealed a bleakness that bothered him. Was it his mention of family? Unable to keep his distance, he went to her and scooted down on the sofa, sitting close but not quite touching. "I'm sorry," he muttered. "I'm being too nosy, and you've had a rough day."

She scrubbed a hand over her face. "I'm perfectly fine."

He smiled. "I believe you. You're tough, I can tell."

"Don't patronize me," she snapped. "Collapsing on your doorstep was an anomaly. I can take care of myself."

He held up his hands. "I was being serious. Not everyone would have survived getting lost in the woods in a snowstorm. My cabin is at least a quarter mile off the AT. I'm not sure how you managed to find it."

"I saw a light through the trees. I decided it was my only hope. I kept walking and walking, and every time I wanted to quit, I forced myself to focus on the light. It sounds a little overdramatic, I know—"

"I'm glad I was here."

"What do you mean?"

"I only arrived yesterday."

They sat in silence for long seconds, each realizing how close she had come to death. Maddy sniffed, and he reached in his pocket for a handkerchief. "Here."

"Thanks." She blew her nose. "You want to know what I thought about when it got really bad?" Her voice was so soft, he had to strain to listen.

"Tell me," he urged, his tone equally low.

"I hated it that I was going to die without ever having been in love."

Her bald statement hung in the air between them. Grant cleared his throat, at a loss for words. What could you say to a pronouncement like that?

She went on, apparently unconcerned with his silence. "Of course, that's assuming there's any such thing as love."

He cocked his head, surprised by the depth of cynicism in her voice. If he'd been a betting man, he would have pegged her as a dyed-in-the-wool romantic. He took one of her hands, playing with her fingers. "You don't really mean that."

She half-turned, her expression defiant. "Have *you* ever been in love?"

He opened his mouth and then shut it. Damn, she had him there. "No," he said reluctantly. "Not really."

She shrugged. "I rest my case."

He twisted a braided gold ring on her right hand. "How does a woman your age not believe in love?"

She pulled her hand out of his grasp, tucking it beneath a fold in the blanket. "Six months ago I would have told you my parents were a shining example of love for the long haul—"

"But . . . ?"

She bent her head, her hair obscuring her face. He was beginning to think that little move was intentional.

He reached for a stack of mail on the table and pulled a rubber band from a magazine. Without asking for permission, he gathered her long, thick hair at the nape of her neck and secured it. He tipped up her chin. "But?"

Her chin trembled just the tiniest bit. "After thirty-five years of marriage they decided they don't have anything in common."

He winced.

She went on, her eyes dark and sad. "The divorce was

final at Thanksgiving. They each decided they needed to *find* themselves. Daddy is on safari in Kenya, and Mother is cruising the South Pacific."

Grant had a sudden real urge to find the elder Tierneys and knock their heads together for not having more compassion than to leave their daughter at Christmas, especially when she was still adjusting to their newly dissolved marriage. He probed carefully. "Brothers and sisters?"

"I'm an only child," she said simply. "I have aunts and uncles and cousins, and they've all invited me for the holidays, but I told them I would be traveling."

Now he understood. She was enacting the adult equivalent of running away from home. "So that's why you let your friends leave without you today. You didn't want to go home."

She opened her mouth to speak, and then clearly changed her mind.

"Maddy? Was that it?"

"Not exactly," she muttered. She looked at the fireplace. "Don't we need more wood?"

Maddy watched her host as he carefully stacked three new logs on the fire and poked it until the flames were once again licking greedily up toward the flue. His squatting position pulled his faded jeans taut over a truly noteworthy butt. His shoulders threatened to split the seams of his soft flannel shirt. She had enjoyed sitting cozily with him on the sofa, way too much, if she was honest with herself. He exuded the kind of dependability and caring that made a woman feel protected.

A man as stunningly masculine and virile as Grant Monroe was probably tired of women throwing themselves at him. It would be terribly selfish of Maddy to use his kindness as an excuse to insinuate herself into his affections. On the other hand, nearly dying tended to change a woman's perspective. Carpe diem and all that. From now on she would reach out and grab the opportunities life sent her way . . . And Grant Monroe was the most delicious *opportunity* she'd met in a long, long time.

As he moved around the room, she watched him surreptitiously. He was surprisingly graceful for his size. She wondered if he was big everywhere, and then she had to choke back a giggle as she realized the direction her wayward thoughts were taking.

He must have sensed her amusement, because he turned around and raised an eyebrow. His hair was dark, and she could see the shadow of late-day stubble. "Am I entertaining you?" he asked with a gentle smile.

Her nipples tightened, and her breathing was shallow. His smile was lethal. She licked her lips. "I was just thinking about something that happened on the trail the other day. It had nothing to do with you."

His knowing glance made her squirm, but he went back to his task. He disappeared for a few minutes and came back with coat hangers and marshmallows. He held up the bag. "Want some?"

She nodded. "Sure. But I don't think I can manage this blanket and cook at the same time."

He glanced at the clock on the mantel. "I threw your clothes in the dryer. They're probably done by now."

He headed back toward the kitchen and returned minutes later, triumphantly bearing her pants. "The shoes are still damp."

She took the jeans from him. "Turn around."

He put his hands on his hips, ignoring her demand. "Spoilsport. Surely you know I got an eyeful earlier."

She looked down her nose at him. "That was different. That was a *medical* situation. You were saving my life."

His teasing smile faded. "Those long legs of yours nearly stopped my heart. You're beautiful, Maddy."

The simple sincerity in his voice caught her off guard. One minute they were exchanging banter, the next he was looking at her like a prospective lover. She stood mute, not knowing how to respond. The air grew thick and heavy. She focused on his lips, full and firm. Eminently kissable. What would he do if she launched herself into his arms?

A log popped and hissed, sending a shower of sparks up the chimney. It broke the strange spell holding them hostage. He turned back to the fire, his shoulders stiff. "I won't peek," he said gruffly.

She dropped the blanket and wriggled into her jeans. They were toasty warm from the dryer. She relinquished the blanket reluctantly. It had afforded a certain amount of protection.

She picked up one of the coat hangers and speared a duo of plump marshmallows. Grant already had one toasting deep within the fire. When he extracted it, it was a deep golden brown. He blew on it and then held out his hand. "Open your mouth."

She obeyed like a spineless puppet. The sweet, gooey sugar melted on her tongue.

Grant's finger seemed trapped somehow between her lips, and he flushed as her teeth grazed it when she sucked the last of the residue from his skin. She managed to swallow without choking. His chest rose and fell rapidly. Her own breathing was jerky.

"Delicious," she said, shivering as he traced her bottom teeth with his fingertip.

"Damn." His sudden exclamation shocked her until

she followed the direction of his gaze. The marshmallows she held over the fire were an unrecognizable black glob. Grant took the coat hanger from her hand and raked the burning mess off onto a log. He glanced at her wryly. "I take it you weren't a Girl Scout."

"Hey," she said, frowning. "That wasn't my fault. You distracted me."

"*I* distracted *you?*"

She nodded vigorously. "You're the one who was feeding me. I can't help it if I got sidetracked."

He stared at her mouth, making her stomach quiver with nerves and something else much more dangerous. "Your lip is sticky," he muttered, leaning forward.

She froze, afraid to respond. He moved slowly, closing the gap between them. When his lips brushed hers they both sighed. It was sweet and delicious and scary as hell. Her heart was pounding and her legs trembled.

"You taste better than the marshmallows," he muttered. He stepped back and turned on a lamp, flooding the room with additional light.

She walked to the sofa on unsteady feet, unsure if she was disappointed or glad that he had called a halt. The man was a stranger. Despite the confidences she had shared with him, he had offered nothing of his own background.

She watched moodily as he put on his snow gear and took the dog out. The silence in the cabin when they left seemed overpowering. She wandered down the hall and found a bathroom. After taking care of her most urgent need, she glanced in the mirror and winced. She looked like a cat dragged through a bush backward. She washed her face and found a comb in a drawer. She took down her hair, straightened it as best she could, and then resecured it with the rubber band. Listening carefully for Grant's return, she rummaged in a small zippered pocket of her pack and found some flavored gloss. It wasn't nearly as yummy as the marshmallows, but it put a faint shine of color on her lips. After a quick call to reassure Daphne and Mimi, she returned to the living room.

When Grant and the dog entered some minutes later, she was sitting on the sofa reading the latest *National Geographic*. She looked up as they came in, feigning an expression of mild interest. "How is it out there?"

Grant looked at her like she was demented. "It's snowing," he said, irritation in his voice. "What did you think?"

"You don't have to be so grumpy. *I* didn't make it snow. By the way, what's the dog's name?"

"Van Gogh."

"But isn't the dog—"

"A female? Yes. But the dog doesn't know who Van Gogh is, and I happen to like the name." He said it as though daring her to challenge him. She wasn't about to go there. His mood had turned surly.

He poured food and water in the dog's dish, then settled in a chair across from her, his jaw clenched with determination. "No more stalling, Maddy. If your parents weren't the reason, I want to know why you didn't go back with your friends."

She gnawed her lower lip, not wanting to reveal all her secrets, but sure he would spot a prevarication. Oh, what the hell . . . She tossed the magazine on the table. "I needed to figure out how to murder someone on the AT and dispose of the body."

Two

Grant's jaw dropped. He felt it hit his chest. He was locked in his own cabin with a psychotic killer. And she looked so normal. Sweat broke out on his forehead. He walked casually toward the door. He wasn't sure he could actually shoot a woman, but the rifle might dissuade her from causing him bodily harm . . . if he was lucky.

His pretty little wacko burst out laughing. "Oh, Lord, Grant, if you could see your face." She was grinning from ear to ear, and he wondered if hysteria often preceded cold-blooded murder.

He took a step closer to the rifle, resting his shoulder casually against the door. "What do you mean?" he asked, wincing at the crack in his voice.

She left the couch and approached him. His pulse quickened, and not in a good way.

She put her hands on her hips, a move that thrust her small but shapely breasts against the thin fabric of her burgundy turtleneck. "You can relax," she said, still grinning. "I'm not really going to murder anybody."

He shifted uneasily from one foot to another. Wasn't that what the killer said right before you got whacked?

She put a hand on his arm and, to his shame, he flinched. She rolled her eyes. "Open my backpack, Grant. Tell me what you see."

He eyed her warily. "Okay." If the murder weapon was in there, perhaps he could dispose of it quickly. He opened the bag, ready to encounter a knife, a gun . . . perhaps a vial of poison. His hands closed on a slim, rectangular object. He pulled it out and stared at it blankly. A laptop. It was a laptop.

She started laughing again. "I write murder mysteries, Grant."

Understanding dawned, and he felt his face flush with embarrassment. Had he really thought, even for a second, that this delicate little woman was capable of murder? He looked up, seeing the amusement on her face. Amusement at his expense. "Ha, ha . . . You got me," he said, tucking the computer back in its hiding place. Now he understood why she'd asked him to make a foray into the storm to retrieve her bag.

He tugged her ponytail. "You did that on purpose."

She shrugged, unrepentant. "You were badgering me for information. I simply told you the truth."

"Brat," he muttered. "I ought to put you over my knee." He said the words lightly, jokingly, but the care-less comment took on a life of its own. Maddy's eyes widened and he watched in fascination as her nipples thrust against her sweater. The room was quite warm.

He tried to swallow, his throat suddenly parched. "A writer, huh. Tell me about that."

She ignored his inane attempt at conversation. Her hands crept up to his shoulders. Her head tipped back, her golden eyes filled with purpose. She stepped closer, and her soft breasts teased his chest. "Are you interested in having sex with me, Grant Monroe?"

His eyes narrowed. *Yes, hell yes.* His cock jumped to attention. Grant ignored his importunate body part and reminded himself he was an honorable man. He removed her hands and checked her forehead. "You've had quite an ordeal, Maddy. Don't make any rash decisions. You need to rest."

"I can't believe this. Several million sex-starved men in Virginia and I find the only one with scruples. Unbelievable." She frowned. "And I'm not delirious, darn it. Surely you've been propositioned before."

His lips quirked. "You don't strike me as the kind of woman who goes in for casual sex. Is this about almost dying?"

She ground her teeth. "No, dammit. I said I hadn't been in *love,* not that I haven't had sex. I've had sex . . . lots of sex . . . great sex."

He grinned and remained silent.

She threw up her hands. "How hard is this to understand? You're here. I'm here. We can't leave. Why not enjoy it?" She paused, clearly struck by an unpleasant notion. "You're not a priest, are you?"

He chuckled, shoving his hands in his pockets. "I'm not a priest."

"Believe me, Grant, I feel fine—well, maybe a little tired, but that's to be expected."

He shook his head, unsure if he was trying to convince her or himself. "You're off balance from coming so close to . . . well, you know." He couldn't say it out loud again. The thought of Maddy lying dead in a snowdrift made him feel sick.

Her expression cleared. "If you think this is about that whole dying-without-love thing, you can rest easy.

I'm not asking you to be my soulmate. This is about sex
. . . two adults enjoying carnal pleasure."

She said that last part with a defiant toss of her head.
He grinned, pretty damn sure this intriguing woman
was not really so cavalier about sex. Despite her question that tested his self-control to the limit, he couldn't
help but believe this was not her usual style.

He doggedly changed the subject. "I want to hear
about Maddy the novelist."

Her smile told him he wasn't off the hook, not by a
long shot. "What do you want to know?"

"The usual. How did you get started? When did you
know you wanted to be a writer?"

She perched on the arm of the sofa. "I always knew I
wanted to write. My great uncle was a fairly well-known
mystery writer in the sixties. By the time I was a preteen
he wasn't publishing much anymore, but he would let
me read all of his books. Pretty inappropriate for a
twelve-year-old, let me tell you. But I devoured them. I
majored in journalism in college, but after a stint as a
reporter during my senior year, I realized I wasn't cut
out for *just the facts, ma'am*. I was lucky. I won a couple
of fiction competitions. And one of my professors had a
relative who was an editor. He got my first manuscript
read, and the rest is history." She cocked her head.
"*Now* can we discuss sex?"

He glanced at his watch, refusing to be drawn in
again. "It's late, Maddy. You need sleep. We'll talk about
this tomorrow. I'll bunk down in here and you can have
my bed."

"No way." Her response was adamant.

He raised his eyebrows. Was she really going to offer
to share his bed? His noble intentions would carry him
only so far.

She waved a hand. "You're huge. I'll be fine on the sofa. No arguments." Her outthrust jaw defied him.

He shrugged. "Fine. I'll get some bedding."

A half hour later she was tucked in a nest of blankets with the lights turned out. He added more wood to the fire and replaced the screen. "I'll tend to it during the night," he said. "We can't afford to let it go out in case we lose power."

He couldn't read her face. The firelight cast heavy shadows, and she had pulled the covers up to her chin. He stood, irresolute, reluctant to walk away from her. "Are you comfortable?" he asked, his voice husky with the effort not to say all those other, less-appropriate things that were buzzing in his brain.

Her nod was barely visible. "Yes."

He approached the couch, his feet at odds with his brain. He sat on the edge of the coffee table. "How do you feel?"

"Fine." Her voice was sulky.

He leaned forward and stroked her cheek. Her skin was soft and smooth. He wanted her with a driving urgency that had nothing to do with her artless invitation and everything to do with the warmth she had brought into his home. And he hadn't even realized he was cold. Such sudden emotion was suspect. He wasn't in the habit of jumping into relationships, sexual or otherwise.

But Maddy touched him deeply, made him yearn for things he had given up on a long time ago. He slipped to his knees and knelt over her. "Can I kiss you good night?" he whispered.

Her eyes were dark and mysterious. "I think that was pretty much included in my earlier blanket offer." Humor laced her unsteady response.

He felt his pulse jump and gallop. Part of him—most of him—was still ready to take what was offered and consequences be damned. He brushed her lips. "I'm glad I found you."

Her tongue peeked out to meet his. "Technically, I found you," she muttered. She moaned as he moved down to nibble the underside of her jaw.

He didn't stop her when she shoved the heavy blankets aside. "I'm hot," she complained.

"Hell, me, too," he groaned as his hands slipped under her shirt and skated north. His palms closed over warm, plump feminine curves. He started to shake.

She arched her back, murmuring incoherent pleas and demands. He pushed her top out of the way and sucked one of her nipples deep into his mouth. Her response was electric. She jerked and cried out as an orgasm ripped through her body.

He laid his head on her shoulder and stroked her hair as she quieted.

Her voice when she spoke was a tiny thread of sound. "Well, that was embarrassing. I guess we know now who's the sex-starved one."

"Not embarrassing, Maddy. Amazing. Do you have any idea how much I want you?"

She turned on her side and raised up on her elbow. "Then why?" she asked, her cat's eyes gleaming with confusion.

He toyed with a curl that had escaped the rubber band and lay tumbled against her creamy breast. "We have several days. Let's get to know each other. Then, if you're still of the same mind . . . well . . ."

"You'll jump my bones?" she asked hopefully.

He shook his head. "You really are a brat, aren't you? Go to sleep, honey. We'll see what tomorrow brings."

* * *

Maddy lay awake for a long time, watching the dancing flames. It should have felt strange to be here in unfamiliar surroundings. But instead it felt safe, warm. Here in Grant's cozy cabin she could ignore the shambles her personal life had become. With her parents acting like children and her last boyfriend a distant memory, facing the holidays had been more than she could bear.

Now fate and Mother Nature had given her a reprieve, and she intended to make the most of it. Grant Monroe was kind and gentle and so sexy he made her ache. He was also apparently unattached. Her brazen invitation had shocked her as much as it had Grant. But she didn't regret it. Who could blame her for stealing this little slice of heaven? She closed her eyes and sighed. Van Gogh lay on top of her feet, the dog's weight and warmth a comforting presence. For the moment, one simple, wonderful moment, life was perfect.

Grant slept fitfully, waking every hour or so to tend the fire and to check on his charge. She slept deeply, the lines of exhaustion still etched on her face. He sent up a prayer of gratitude for her safety. She said he had saved her life, but she really had saved her own. Only her dogged courage had given her the strength to make it as far as she had. She could so easily have died.

He touched her occasionally, just to reassure himself that she was real. He came to the cabin seeking answers. And Maddy dropped into his lap. What did it mean? He wasn't much of a believer in fate, but life was funny sometimes. He'd known Maddy less than a day, but already she had a hold on his heart. Maybe because of the dramatic way they met. Maybe because she was the kind of woman he had been looking for, deep in some unacknowledged part of his psyche.

He snorted. Holy hell. He'd need a shrink if this kept up. He brushed a butterfly kiss across her lips, careful not to wake her. Whatever the reason, Maddy was his . . . at least for the next few days. What was that old saying? If you saved a life it belonged to you? He would gladly take credit for rescuing her if it meant she was tied to him in some way. He might not have all the answers yet, but he would soon.

And in the meantime, he would do his best not to take advantage of her vulnerability. She was hurting from her parents' divorce, feeling lost and alone, and on top of that, she had survived a dangerous ordeal that could have ended her life. She was off balance, emotionally overwrought. Only the lowest kind of worm would agree to her artless invitation. Heck, by morning she would probably have changed her mind. He wondered why that thought didn't give him the least bit of satisfaction.

Sometime before dawn the storm finally blew itself out, leaving twenty-two inches of pristine, powdery white snow. He took Van Gogh out early, using the back door, so Maddy could sleep on.

By nine-thirty he was getting a little worried. He shook her shoulder. "Maddy, honey . . . You about ready to wake up? I've got bacon and eggs and pancakes almost done."

Her face scrunched up and she pulled the blankets completely over her head. "Go away."

He grinned. Clearly his houseguest wasn't a morning

person. "That's not what you said last night." He chuckled, sliding his hand beneath the mound of covers to tickle her belly.

She yelped and uttered a word that was not at all ladylike. "I'm liking you less and less, Monroe."

He waved a steaming cup of coffee near the bump that was her head. "Hot coffee, no waiting."

She struggled to a sitting position, her hair a riot of auburn corkscrews. "Give it to me."

He surrendered the mug without protest and watched amazed as she drained the contents in short order. "What? You have an asbestos-lined mouth?"

She flopped against the back of the sofa, nodding. "I don't do mornings very well. Caffeine's my salvation."

"I'll make a note of that."

Suddenly she remembered to be shy with him. Her face went beet red and she flapped her hands at him. "Get lost. Scram. I look a fright."

He threw the bedding to one side and scooped her into his lap, nuzzling the top of her head. "You're rumpled," he corrected. "It's a good look on you."

He tipped her backward over his arm and found her mouth. She tasted like coffee and cream and sweet, warm woman. He explored her mouth with his tongue, sliding one hand beneath her to trace her spine. His cock stiffened immediately, and he knew the exact moment she realized it.

She froze, panting slightly, her eyes cloudy. "You're hard," she muttered.

He nodded ruefully. "You seem to have that effect on me." She wiggled her bottom and he groaned. "Easy, baby."

She nipped his bottom lip. "Can I touch you?" she asked, her voice and face entirely serious.

"What about breakfast?" he asked weakly, struggling to survive.

She was already wriggling around to gain access to his now-constricting jeans. "It's overrated."

She lowered his zipper and every ounce of blood in his body rushed to his groin. Her small, talented hands slid past his boxers with startling ease. When her fingers closed around his aching cock, he shivered. She stroked him gently, murmuring words he was too far gone to understand.

When he managed once to open his eyes, he saw her staring raptly at his genitals, her eyes big and her lips wet where she had licked them. Such unabashed admiration did wonders for a man's ego.

He groaned, barely remembering his resolve. "Enough, little witch. It's time to eat."

She scraped a fingernail down his shaft. "I'm ready if you are."

He jerked her hand out of his pants. "I'm going to the kitchen," he said through clenched teeth. "I expect you to join me there in three minutes or less."

Maddy sighed as she made a trip down the hall to the bathroom. Just her luck. She finally decided to spice up her sex life, and she picked a man bent on protecting her from herself. It was just too depressing. But as she glanced in the mirror, she couldn't help smiling at her reflection.

Look at her. Out of control hair, no makeup, pale skin, negligible curves . . . and Grant Monroe wanted her. True, he hadn't done anything about it yet, but a man's body didn't lie. That impressive erection was because of her.

She washed up rapidly, pausing long enough to use a little of her lip gloss. Some war paint never hurt. When she entered the kitchen, Grant was at the stove, his posture unnaturally rigid.

Guilt pinched her. She really needed to back off. She didn't mind making the first move with a guy, but she had invaded Grant's home, and they were both trapped for the duration. He might even have a significant other tucked away somewhere. That thought made her stomach churn.

She had to know. "Do you have a girlfriend?" She blurted it out with an appalling lack of finesse.

He turned around, holding a plate of pancakes and eggs. His brows were drawn together in a frown. "No, of course not. Did you really think I'd be fooling around with you if I were otherwise committed?"

She shrugged. "Men do."

"Well, not this man." He set down the plate with a thunk and returned for the bacon. "If that's the kind of men you've been going out with, it's no wonder you're a little cynical about love."

"You said yourself that you've never been in love."

His face got a funny look. "That doesn't mean I haven't been with women I respected and admired."

"Oh." She fell silent, suddenly envisioning a stream of beautiful, sexy women entertaining Grant Monroe. They probably all had big boobs . . . like the one in the picture. Her confidence slipped a notch.

He joined her at the table and they ate mostly in silence. At one point she leaned down to give Van Gogh a chunk of pancake, and she groaned as her muscles protested from the abuse she'd given them the day before.

Grant's eyes sharpened. "What's wrong?"

"I'm sore, that's all."

"There's ibuprofen in the cabinet to the left of the stove."

She wrinkled her nose. "I thought you might offer to give me a massage. Strictly medicinal, of course."

He carried their dishes to the sink. "I'm not falling for that. My mother warned me about women like you."

She grinned, enjoying his dry humor. "Your loss."

He glanced out the window. The sun was out and the snow was so bright it hurt to look at it. "I need to chop some wood. Can you entertain yourself for awhile?"

"I think I can manage. I might alphabetize your spices."

"Won't take long. I think it's pretty much salt, cinnamon and pepper."

"Spoken like a typical bachelor."

When Grant started chopping wood, he realized he was smiling. Maddy's sass and wit made him laugh. She had bounced back incredibly quickly from a bad experience. Her sexuality was an innate part of her personality, and he admitted to himself that he wouldn't be able to resist her for long, nor did he want to. Any man of his acquaintance would jump at the chance to have a few days of uncomplicated sex with a fascinating woman.

But he found himself wanting to prove to her that love did exist. Which was really pretty damn funny since he had no personal knowledge of such emotion. Maddy was the kind of woman who deserved to be loved. She was smart and strong and full of life. If she hadn't found love, it wasn't her fault. The men in her orbit must be idiots, or at the very least blind.

The back door opened and his heartbeat jumped, but it was only Van Gogh lumbering out to see him. Maddy must have taken pity on the dog's whining. Van Gogh loved to be outside. But the deep snow was giving her problems.

Grant used his arm to clear the drifts off the top of the picnic table and gently lifted the dog so she could bask in the sun. The temperature was in the midtwenties, but there was no wind, and the sun felt remarkably warm.

He returned to splitting logs, relishing the strain on his muscles and the sheer physical labor. In forty-five minutes he had more than enough wood, but he kept working. He was sweating now, so he shrugged out of his heavy coat. His plan was to make himself tired enough to forget how horny he was.

He and Maddy might end up in bed, but he wanted to make sure she was recovered, both physically and emotionally, from her frightening experience . . . And in all fairness, he needed time to explain his own situation. He had a few secrets of his own to confess.

When he returned to the house, everything was quiet. He found Maddy in the living room, but she never even looked up when he entered. She was sitting cross-legged in one of the big armchairs, working on her laptop. He made a fair amount of noise, carrying in wood and adding logs to the fire, but her eyes remained glued to the small computer screen.

She had a pencil tucked behind her ear, and a couple of notebooks lay scattered on the coffee table. He sat down across from her and glanced at his watch. It was exactly thirty-two minutes before she stopped typing and realized he was there.

He grinned as she visibly shook off whatever world she had been in and returned to the here and now. He cocked his head. "I take it things are going well?"

She nodded, her eyes gleaming with excitement. "I worked out the whole murder scenario while I was walking yesterday. I found a steep part of the trail over a deep ravine where I could conceivably shove a body off and have it disappear. I had already researched how and where to give a fatal knife wound between the ribs. So it's all coming together."

"How many books have you published?"

"Three so far. This will be my fourth."

His eyes widened. "Wow. You're pretty young to have done so well."

Her lips quirked. "How old do you think I am?"

He shrugged uneasily. Discussing a woman's age was never a smart thing to do. "I don't know . . . twenty-four . . . twenty-five?"

She laughed. "I'm thirty-one, but thanks."

He studied her face carefully. No way would anyone believe that. Although now that he thought about it, she did have a certain confidence about her that came only with experience. He sighed theatrically. "I'm relieved. At least now when we make love, I won't have to worry about cradle robbing."

She flushed bright red, her expression rattled.

He grinned devilishly. "What? It's okay for you to proposition me, but I can't make my intentions known?"

She licked her lips. "You surprised me, that's all." She shut down the computer. "We need to talk."

Uh-oh . . . Those four words never preceded anything good. He shifted uneasily in his chair. "Okay. What about?"

She pinned him with a don't-give-me-any-crap stare. "Who's the woman in the picture?"

Shit. He'd hoped to work up to this gradually. He smiled weakly. "My ex-wife, Jillian."

* * *

To say Maddy was shocked was like saying George Clooney was kind of cute. She finally found her voice. "You've been married?"

"A long time ago."

"And you keep her picture over your mantel?" Her voice ended on a squeak, and she tried to regain her composure. Sick disappointment filled her stomach. If he cared enough to look at that gorgeous woman every day, then Maddy was out of luck. She could never hope to compete with the voluptuous beauty.

Grant was frowning. "I keep the *picture*," he said with careful emphasis. "The subject is merely incidental."

She glared at him. "Do I look like I was born yesterday?"

His lips firmed, but he didn't respond to her snide comment. "Look at it up close, Maddy."

She stood and crossed to the fireplace. The picture was breathtaking from any angle, the colors and strokes filled with energy and emotion. She glanced at the signature in the bottom right-hand corner: G. Monroe.

She spun around to find him watching her carefully, a rueful smile on his face. She looked at the painting again. "*You* painted this?"

He nodded slowly.

"But it's brilliant . . . museum quality."

A hint of red tinged his cheekbones and she realized she had embarrassed him. She lifted her hand to touch the rough wooden frame, its simplicity a perfect foil for the setting. "I don't know what to say, Grant."

He joined her at the mantel. "I'm glad you like it. But I want you to know that Jillian is nothing more than a slightly nostalgic memory from my past." He touched her cheek. "I'll tell you everything you want to know, but it will be a lot more pleasant with you in my lap." He tugged on her arm, pulling her toward the sofa.

Maddy allowed herself to be persuaded, eager to hear what he had to say, yet uneasy as well. When she was snuggled in his embrace, he began kissing her . . . first her lips, then her throat and then sliding down her collarbone. She arched her neck, feeling her need for conversation wither and die. She shoved a hand against his chest. "Talk," she whispered, her breathing constricted. "You promised."

He cupped her breast, making her whimper. "Are you sure?"

His gentle tug on her nipple nearly made her cave. She ached to feel his hands on her bare skin. "I'm sure," she said, trembling and hot. Lord help her when he finally decided to make love to her in earnest.

He eased back, allowing her to sit up. She tried to shift away, but he pulled her close. "No distance," he muttered.

They sat, twined in each other's arms while their breathing steadied. Maddy probed, unsure if he would volunteer anything on his own. "Tell me about your marriage."

He sighed. "I'm thirty-five years old. It all seems like so long ago."

"I'd like to hear about it," she said softly.

"She was my girlfriend in college. Right before we graduated she told me she was pregnant. I did the honorable thing and married her."

"But she wasn't?"

"Nope."

"Did she lie on purpose?"

"Yeah. She admitted it later. I was angry and she was remorseful. We tried to put it behind us. We had been friends for a long time, and we did have physical attraction going for us."

"But you didn't love her."

"No," he said quietly. "Not really."

"So when did you divorce?"

"I ended up working as an investment broker. Turns out I was pretty good at it. I made other people and myself a pile of money. But one day it started to bore me. The thrill of winning was gone, and I told Jillian I wanted to see if I could paint."

"Did you have any artistic background?"

"I took art classes in high school . . . wanted to major in it at college, but my dad was pretty skewed in his thinking. He thought all artists were flaming homosexuals. So I played football and baseball, and I went to college with his money and I majored in business."

"Then what happened?"

"When I quit the firm, Jillian and I split. She hadn't signed on to be the wife of a reclusive artist. She liked the trappings of my job and the endless flow of money. She was angry. That was when it ended, eight years ago. I have three galleries in Virginia and one in D.C. I've done okay."

"Has it been everything you thought it would be?"

"Yes and no. I've been unsettled lately, wondering if I should go back to my old job part time—not for the money, but for the challenge. Apparently I have this whole left brain/right brain split, and I'm needing to feed the other side for awhile. Or maybe I'm just getting stale."

"Was that why you came up here? To think?"

"Yep." He squeezed her. "And look what I got instead."

She choked out a laugh when he hit a ticklish spot

between her ribs. "I resent the implication that you can't think with me around," she said primly.

"Oh, you make me think," he said, sliding his hand between her thighs. "But it's mostly with my cock and not with my brain."

The pressure of his finger on the center seam of her jeans made her crazy. "Is this foreplay or torture?" she asked, panting slightly as she twisted to get a better angle. He seemed to be getting way too much enjoyment out of making her beg.

His teeth raked the shell of her ear, sending shivers down her spine. "I was thinking of it as foreplay, but torture could be fun, too."

She had a sudden flash of being tied up and at his mercy, and she groaned.

He shifted their bodies until she was flat on her back and he was half on top of her. The heavy ridge of his erection pressed her hip. He found her mouth, no teasing this time. His tongue thrust deep, mimicking the ultimate goal.

She felt herself melting in a million different ways. Nothing had ever felt this good. Nothing ever would.

He nuzzled the sensitive skin beneath her ear, his breath hot, his whisper unsteady. "There's only one thing I want almost as much as I want to make love to you," he said, his large body trembling.

"What?" she cried softly. "What?"

He pulled back just enough for their eyes to meet, hers cloudy and unfocused, his hot and determined. "I want to paint you . . . in the nude."

Three

Her face blanched, and her involuntary glance at the painting over the mantel was telling. She squinched up her nose. "I don't know, Grant. I'm not really model material."

His chest was tight with a feeling that was as unfamiliar as it was scary. He cupped her cheek. "You're beautiful, Maddy." He saw in her eyes that she wasn't convinced.

Her fists were clenched, and he realized suddenly that he had upset her. His heart squeezed. "Sweetheart, you're the prettiest thing I've ever seen. You're a knockout, honest to God."

Her scowl was underlaid with an entirely unexpected vulnerability. "You haven't even seen me with all my clothes off."

He chuckled. "I've seen a lot . . . and I've groped the rest."

Her lips twitched. "Does that smooth, romantic banter get you hordes of women?"

"I'm devoted to my work," he said piously, pressing

his hand to his heart, happy to play the fool if it would bring back her smile.

She sighed deeply, her chest rising and falling in an entirely distracting way. "Are you serious? Really?"

He kissed her eyelids, her nose, her perfect lips. "I'd consider it an honor," he said huskily.

Her eyes softened, and he saw arousal begin to build again. His own had never waned. He wrestled with his libido and won, but it was a close call. Good things come to those who wait, he reminded himself ruefully. And the snow wasn't going anywhere. At least not yet.

He stood up, his cock crying out in protest. "Let's see about rustling up some lunch," he said, his voice tight, his balls aching. Being a hero was a hell of a thankless job.

Maddy learned a lot about Grant that afternoon. Not so much the facts of his checkered past, but the essence of him as a man. His competitive nature rivaled hers. Over a cut-throat game of Scrabble, they squabbled happily.

Grant groused about having only one-point letters and finally put down l-i-t. "Three points," he grumbled.

Maddy looked at her tiles and grinned. It was early in the game, and the board was wide open. She picked up five of her pieces and arranged them carefully in front of and behind his word.

He blinked and stared. His voice sounded strangled. "Clitoris?" he asked, outrage building in every syllable.

She gave him her most serious expression. "It's a body part," she explained slowly. "The source of feminine pleasure."

"I know what it is," he snapped. "I wasn't aware we were allowed to use pornographic vocabulary."

"It's entirely legal." She drew five replacement letters.

Grant played. P-e-n. "Five points," he said, his jaw tight.

She looked at her letters and widened her eyes dramatically. "Wow. What are the chances I'd draw another *I* and an *S*?" She placed them carefully. "Penis. That's a male . . ."

He leaned back in his chair, his eyes gleaming with something entirely dangerous. "You seem to have sex on the brain, Ms. Tierney," he said, drumming his fingers on the table.

She folded her hands in her lap. "Not at all. I merely minored in anatomy in college. Although, being an artist and all, you probably should know this stuff. Particularly if you're going to paint naked people."

"They're called nudes," he snarled.

It got nasty after that . . .

He played "oat." She made it throat. He played "it." She made it "tit." Finally her luck ran out. He played "church" on a double word. Nobody could make a sex word out of church. Plus, it got him a whole lot of points. She sighed and laid down the entirely ordinary "duck."

Grant studied her last play, his expression shuttered. He leaned forward and casually flipped her *D* to the floor, replacing it with an *F*. Then he sat back and smiled.

She ignored his blatant disrespect for the rules and pointed out the obvious. "That's slang," she said. "Take it back."

He rolled up his sleeves, baring muscular forearms. "And yet you played 'tit,' " he reminded her mildly.

"That's not slang."

"It sure as hell is," he stuttered.

She raised an eyebrow. "Are you challenging me? The dictionary is right there on the shelf."

He stared at her intently for long seconds, daring her to back down. She just smiled.

Muttering under his breath, he retrieved the oversized dictionary and started flipping pages.

She got up and leaned over his shoulder. "It should be the third one down," she said helpfully.

He made it to the *TI*s and started running his finger down the page, his brow creased in concentration. She wondered if he even noticed that her breast was pressing his shoulder.

He made a little sound and she grinned to herself. "Why don't you read it out loud, Grant?" She licked his ear.

He jerked and cursed, nearly dropping the dictionary. He read the words slowly, incredulity in his voice. "A small worn-out horse, a nag."

She bit his earlobe. "Never play Scrabble with a writer," she whispered. "I'm sure you have many other talents."

He moved so fast, she didn't have time to react. He got to his feet, backing her toward the wall. It was a blatant attempt to use his physical size to intimidate her, and she should have been indignant. Instead, she felt a burgeoning excitement. His face was calm, but his eyes twinkled.

She swallowed. "You can't bully me."

He raised an eyebrow. "Is that what I'm doing?"

One more step, and her shoulder blades met resistance. She flattened her spine against the wall, her breathing jerky. "Sore losers are pathetic."

He cupped her butt and lifted her off the ground. Instinctively, her hands grabbed for his shoulders. Her legs wrapped around his waist. Their groans mingled as their bodies strained toward each other.

He leaned his forehead against hers, his hands kneading her ass. "I think you cheated. I demand a re-match."

She wiggled, close to begging. His erection tormented her even through layers of cloth. And judging by the rapid rise and fall of his chest as he struggled to breathe, Grant was interested in playing a much more intimate game than Scrabble.

"I don't like waiting," she whispered, her voice agitated. In her books the characters always did exactly what she told them. At least most of the time. Grant's obstinacy, especially in the face of his undeniable arousal, frustrated her. And she *hated* being frustrated.

He heaved a sigh and released her, letting her legs slide to the ground. "Have you ever had sex with a man you've known less than twenty-four hours?"

His blunt question made her wince. It was hard to *carpe diem* when the man in question was determined to be reasonable. "No," she muttered.

His smile was strained. "I am absolutely committed to being the man you spend Christmas with, but I don't want to be the guy you regret the morning after."

She could see the struggle on his face, the determination to make sure she knew her own mind . . . And in that instant, she fell a little bit in love with him.

They went their separate ways after lunch, Maddy to her writing, and Grant to try and dig out his Jeep. He breathed in the bitter cold air, and wished the weather had the power to affect his dick. He wondered how long a man could have an erection before his cock exploded.

Maddy was an almost irresistible temptation, but he meant what he said to her. She might not realize it yet, but he had every intention of exploring a relationship with her beyond this cabin. Previously nebulous thoughts and dreams were beginning to solidify. Family. Permanence. Home.

He looked at Maddy and saw a world of possibilities.

He used his hands and a small piece of plywood to scrape the thick snow from the vehicle. The cabin boasted neither a garage nor a carport, an omission he was rethinking. Of course, since he mostly used the cabin in the summertime, the issue had never really been critical.

He started the engine and let it run for a few minutes. What if Maddy had required real medical attention? What if he had needed to get her down the mountain? The narrow gravel road he had negotiated with ease two days ago was invisible, no sign of its boundaries remaining. Even if he could have forced the Jeep through the deep snow, he would likely have run off the road and gotten stuck. Thank God it hadn't come to that.

When he was satisfied that the battery and gas line were operational, he turned the engine off, and wondered what he could do next—other than returning to the house. That wasn't an option.

If he had to stay outside until his balls froze, he would do it. He picked up an ax and headed into the woods.

Maddy held the curtains aside, peering anxiously across the unbroken expanse of snow. The sight that caught her eye made her laugh. A snowman? Grant had made a snowman? And not just any snowman. This particular example was a work of art. Impulsively, she slipped on her dry tennis shoes and put on her coat.

Standing on the porch, she shielded her eyes against the glare of the sun. Facing west, the setting rays were blinding as they reflected off the snow.

She went back inside and retrieved a small disposable camera from her bag. When her world returned to normal, she wanted to have a few memories to hold on to. As she snapped a couple of pictures, Grant startled her, appearing unannounced from behind the cabin carrying a burlap sack.

"You shouldn't be out here in this cold."

She turned to greet him, unable to suppress a smile of happiness. "I love your version of Frosty. Do you have a scarf and a hat we can use?"

He grinned. "Probably. I would have asked for your help, but I don't want to risk you getting sick."

"I'm healthy as a horse." Nonchalantly, she scooped a handful of snow from the porch rail and pressed it into a snowball. When he wasn't looking, she fired it at him, hitting the back of his head with gratifying precision. "Intramural champ. Softball. UVA, junior year," she called out.

A shiver snaked down her spine when he turned around, fire in his eyes. He scraped the wet glob from the back of his neck, cursing when part of her projectile slid beneath his collar. Her nervous giggle was entirely involuntary.

He cupped his hands in the snow, rising with an impressive icy orb in his hand. "Baseball captain. Virginia Tech. Three years running." He caught her off guard, lobbing the ammunition while he was still speaking. When she turned to get away, it splatted on the side of her head, stinging her cheekbone.

His face changed in an instant, remorse sending him empty-handed toward where she stood. It was the perfect opportunity. She fired twice in rapid succession. "Back off, Monroe. This is war."

Both of her shots hit the mark. He retreated rapidly, covered in snow. "You'll pay for that," he warned, beginning to build an arsenal.

"I'm so scared," she whimpered, hitting the front of his coat over his heart. "The big bad man might hurt me."

They fought in earnest, neither giving any quarter. Her best and most entertaining shot hit directly between his legs. His face went slack with surprise, before he winced in discomfort. He grinned up at her, rubbing his crotch. "You might keep in mind that damaging the equipment could impact your plans for the weekend."

She laughed and pelted him again, prudently avoiding the zone below the belt. "Thanks for the reminder."

Unfortunately, her battle position was inherently flawed. While Grant had the entire expanse of snow-covered ground to mine for ammunition, Maddy had quickly cleared the porch, steps and rail. Her base was wiped clean and her opponent was just getting started.

She backed toward the door. Grant made chicken noises. She stopped, her pride at stake. "I'm out of snow," she pointed out.

He hit her shoulder with a *thwack*. "Should have thought of that earlier." Then he fired with both hands at once.

Snow coated her hair and dripped into her eyes. She glared at him. "This is entirely outside the Geneva Convention."

He shrugged. "Never been to Switzerland, myself."

The next snowball hit between her breasts. Desperate times called for desperate measures. She peeled off her coat, her sweater and her bra in quick succession.

Her skin was hot and damp from exertion. The cold air slammed into her chest, stealing her breath and furling her nipples into tightly peaked buds.

But any momentary discomfort was well worth it. Her attacker stood frozen, seemingly stunned, his mouth opened but mute, his eyes glazed. She walked down the four steps into the yard, sinking in snow up to her knees. She lifted her chin. "Open your coat."

He seemed befuddled, but he cooperated, dropping the snowballs he still held. When he had unzipped his heavy parka, she waved a hand, scarcely noticing the cold. "Unbutton your shirt."

He complied, more rapidly this time, revealing the golden brown skin of his chest. Her breath hitched in her throat. "Lie down on your back."

He crouched and fell backward, letting his hood cushion his head. She lifted her knees and struggled toward him, her eyes locked on his. She straddled his hips and leaned forward, pressing her freezing breasts to the warm, hair-roughened planes of his torso.

He started to embrace her, but she pushed his arms back. "Make me a snow angel." He held his arms stiff, moving them up and down as she asked. She smiled sweetly. "Now you can hold me."

Grant slipped his arms from his coat, then snuggled her close, his flannel shirtsleeves rubbing over serious amounts of gooseflesh. He nuzzled her neck. "You're certifiably crazy. You know that, right?" He arranged her legs on top of his, so no part of her body was touching the snow. "And just so you know, your dirty tactics would never hold up in military court."

She licked his collarbone. "Are you complaining?"

"Hell, no." He slid his hands beneath the waistband of her jeans. The feel of her tits on his chest was making him light-headed, but one of them had to exhibit some sense. "Come on, Mata Hari. I'm taking you in."

"For questioning?" she asked demurely, sucking his bottom lip, and then nibbling on it.

He held her head in his hands to steady her, and drove his tongue into her mouth, perilously close to losing control. Only the knowledge that she was half-nude in twenty-degree weather kept him from taking her in the snow. He kissed her wildly, roughly, shaking with a level of arousal he had never experienced.

Finally, with one last thread of self-control, he tucked her head to his chest and held her tightly, his breathing jerky. "This is insane."

She licked his nipple. "I like insane . . . I haven't been insane enough in my life." He blinked his eyes against the red haze obscuring his vision. He could have his cock inside her in sixty seconds flat, if she cooperated. But then he felt her shiver, and his brain was back in control.

"Up, woman." He rolled them both to their feet, practically lifting her through the snow and depositing her on the steps. As she was picking up her discarded clothing, he salvaged the burlap bag he'd dropped earlier.

Inside, he stared at her, shaking his head. "Now, *all* your clothes are wet and dirty."

She rummaged in her pack, triumphantly holding up a scrap of red nylon. "One last pair of clean undies," she announced with glee.

He swallowed, consigning her tiny underwear to hell and back. He sent her to the bathroom. "Strip off. I'll find you something . . . if I'm lucky."

He returned with one of his flannel shirts and some gray, fleece-lined sweatpants. He knocked on the bathroom door. "Hand me your stuff."

Her slender arm appeared, thrusting a pile of wet clothes into his hand. In exchange, he passed in her new wardrobe. When she came out a few minutes later, he smothered a grin. She had tried to roll up the shirt-sleeves, but they were already drooping. She was holding up the voluminous pants with her hand, and the green woolen socks on her feet clashed horribly with the turquoise shirt.

"I look like a hobo," she groused.

"Good," he said fervently. "Now maybe we can get through dinner."

They worked amicably, side by side, fixing chili and store-bought sourdough bread. Fortunately, Grant had brought more than enough food, so there was no chance they'd go hungry. While they were washing up afterward, Maddy noticed the bag he'd dropped by the back door. "What's that?" she asked curiously.

He smiled sheepishly. "Mistletoe."

She laughed. "You really thought we needed mistletoe?"

He poured the leftover chili in a container and stuck it in the fridge. "It's traditional. It's seasonal. It's ambiance."

She just shook her head. "Okay, Martha Stewart. If you say so."

While Grant began to set up his easel and paints, Maddy began having serious second thoughts. It was one thing to flash a guy during a snowball fight. It was another thing entirely to sprawl out buck-naked on a sofa and let him stare at you for a couple of hours. Her eyes returned again and again to the painting over the mantel. Grant's ex-wife made a stunning model, her lush sensuality a perfect subject for any painter. Maddy, on the other hand... Well... She certainly wasn't Rubenesque. The great artists of that era would have passed her by without a glance. As her feelings of unease mounted, Grant, in contrast, seemed remarkably comfortable. He added log after log to the fire, until the room began to feel like a sauna.

When he began to sweat, he stripped off his shirt and kicked off his boots and socks. No fair, Maddy wailed inwardly. How was a woman supposed to show good sense in the face of such blatant provocation? Half-dressed, he seemed even larger, more powerful. Sleek muscles in his arms and back glistened with a sheen of perspiration.

Her throat went dry.

She wandered around the room, keeping her distance. "Be careful you don't start a chimney fire," she warned weakly.

He smiled absently, intent on positioning his workspace. "I'm making it warm in here. You'll be nude for a couple of hours, and we can't have you getting cold."

Cold? She was burning up.

She nibbled her lower lip. "Do you mind if I take a shower first?"

He looked up, his brow creased in concentration. "Hmmm? Oh, sure, whatever you want."

She escaped to the bathroom. She washed her hair during a twenty-minute shower and would have lingered longer, but the water began to run cold. Shutting off the faucet and stepping out, she towel-dried her hair, shivering despite the wall heater. She found a hairdryer underneath the sink and, after combing out her tangled tresses, began blow-drying her unruly mane a section at a time.

Grant positioned a swath of fern-green cloth over the sofa. Velvet was a bit cliché, but the color would be spectacular with Maddy's hair. He was making his preparations on autopilot, one-half of his mind on familiar routines, the other centered down the hall where Maddy was so obviously hiding out.

He admitted reluctantly that he had no right to pressure her into posing for him, but he wanted it badly—badly enough to ignore his gentlemanly side. He could soothe her nerves. He would be blasé if it killed him.

But first he had to pry her out of the bathroom. He went down the hall and knocked on the door. The dryer stopped. "Open up, Maddy . . . if you're decent—or even if you're not," he added with dry honesty.

She eased the open door a crack. "I'm not finished with my hair."

He could see she was dressed, so he shoved the door wider. "Come into my bedroom. I'll help you."

Her eyes blinked, her expression wary. "I can do it," she insisted.

He tugged on her hand. "It'll be more fun this way."

He coaxed his unwilling model a few more steps down the hall and into his bedroom. He watched, amused, as she catalogued its contents.

She wrinkled her nose. "Kind of bare, isn't it?"

He tried to look at the furnishings through her eyes. The cabin was strictly a vacation home. He'd spent the majority of his money outfitting the kitchen and living room. Since he only slept in the bedroom, and since he never brought women here, he'd figured throwing a quilt on the bed and a rug on the floor was enough.

He brushed her cheek. "You could have a go at it," he said softly. "You know . . . Give it a woman's touch."

Her face closed up. "It's fine, Grant. I didn't mean to criticize."

He sighed inwardly. She was a prickly creature. He tugged her toward the bed, positioning her between his legs and leaning his back against the plain pine headboard. "Give me your comb."

She handed it over reluctantly, her back poker straight. He worked carefully, allowing the silky strands to curl around his fingers. By the time he finished, only a bit of dampness remained. He buried his face in the back of her neck, smelling his shampoo and her feminine scent. "I love your hair," he said huskily. "It's like holding sunshine in my hands."

A bit of the starch left her spine, enough that he was able to pull her against his chest. Her butt pressed firmly into his groin. He was rapidly losing interest in painting her. He cleared his throat, resting his hands loosely beneath her breasts. He hated not being able to see her face. "You can't put it off forever, sweetheart."

She huffed. "Sure I can. How would you like to be naked as a jaybird and have me stare at you for two hours?"

His cock stirred urgently beneath her. She wriggled her butt just the tiniest bit. His hands trembled. "If it was *you* looking at me, Maddy, I'd find it damned appealing."

He cupped her breasts deliberately, rubbing his thumbs over her nipples. He felt the ripple that went through her body.

She answered him with her usual sass, but the rasp in

her voice gave her away. "You're only saying that because you know I can barely draw a stick man."

He slid his hands down the soft curve of her belly, delving into her heated warmth. Slick moisture welcomed him. Her head lolled on his shoulder, her eyes tightly closed. He opened her with one finger. "Maybe I can take the edge off your nervousness," he said, sliding over her most sensitive, swollen spot with a delicate but firm touch.

He felt her quiver, and a rush of testosterone-laden, caveman satisfaction gripped him. Maddy Tierney was *his* woman. He refused to think about any other man who might have seen her like this. Fate had brought them together. She had come to him through the storm, and he would not let her escape him now.

He stroked her urgently, taking cues from her moans and sighs. She was beautiful in her abandon, the flush on her cheekbones and the arch of her neck sheer poetry. But flowery words were her expertise. His job was to capture her fragile loveliness on canvas.

He slid three fingers inside her without warning and felt her vaginal muscles grip him as she crested, her voice caught in her throat, her hands gripping his forearms. Long moments passed before he removed his hand slowly, hugging her to ward off the possibility of escape. If she looked at him now, with invitation in her eyes, he was a goner.

Suddenly, he couldn't bear to be in this room and not fuck her. Shaking, almost sick with hunger, he rolled away from her and muttered some inane excuse before exiting the room and, moments later, the house.

Maddy heard the front door slam and lay stunned, her body still humming with the aftermath of incredible pleasure. The level of sexual heat between the two of them could light up a small city. All he had to do was touch her and she spun out of control. It was as frightening as it was miraculous. Such intense feeling had to burn itself out eventually, and then what? He had a life outside this cabin, as did she. They each had jobs, families, obligations.

Questions swirled unanswered in her head, but the one that occupied her most was: when? When would Grant make love to her? Fully. In every way. Not knowing was driving her crazy, and if her recent aberrant behaviors were any sign, she didn't have far to go.

She tiptoed back down the hallway, listening intently. The cabin was silent, empty. It was dark outside, and Grant's shirt and shoes were still on the floor. The idiot man had gone outside half-dressed. She opened the door six inches or so, shivering when the gleeful wind found an opportunity to invade.

She peered into the darkness. "Grant . . . Are you out there?"

His voice came from the end of the porch, closer than she had expected. "Go away, Maddy."

She retreated momentarily and gathered up his shirt, socks and boots. She tossed them to where she thought he was standing, feeling slightly foolish. "What are you doing out there?" she whispered.

His reply was laden with sarcasm. "Having a smoke. Beat it."

"But you don't smoke . . . do you?"

"How would you know? You met me yesterday."

Ah, that was the problem. They were back to the same old issue, both of them distrusting the wild, almost violent nature of their physical response to one another. Too much, too strong, too fast.

How was he standing the cold? The night was bitter. She shifted from one foot to the other.

His voice was sharper this time, commanding. "Shut the door, Maddy, or suffer the consequences."

She scuttled into the kitchen, her heart pounding. But she was smiling. Grant Monroe was more man than she had ever hoped to find. She rummaged through the cabinets. She would enjoy making him her one and only culinary masterpiece, a banana cream pie but, given the limited ingredients at hand, it would have to be microwave popcorn.

She heated milk and filled a couple of mugs with chocolate mix. He would be cold when he came in—or maybe not, she thought, grinning smugly. She put two bowls of popcorn and the hot chocolate on a plain wooden tray, adding two paper towels at the last minute in lieu of napkins.

When she pushed open the kitchen door, the living room was still empty. She set the tray on the coffee table and curled up in an armchair, avoiding the velvet-decked sofa. She glanced at the clock. He'd been outside twenty-five minutes. She shifted into a more comfortable position.

Fifteen minutes later her smile had faded, and the hot chocolate had cooled. This was ridiculous. She stood up, ready to drag him in by his hair, if necessary.

The door swung open suddenly, causing the fire to shoot up the chimney with bright, dancing flames. Grant filled the doorframe, his jet-black hair tousled from the wind, his cheekbones red with cold. He did not look happy.

Her pseudosmile faded and she took a step backward. "Grant?"

He shut the door and folded his arms across his impressive chest, pinning her with a dark-eyed stare. If tough, no-nonsense masculinity had a poster boy, Grant was it.

She tried a conciliatory smile, but it melted into uncertainty.

He flipped off the lights, plunging the room into firelit intimacy. "Take off your clothes, Maddy."

Four

She froze. Her heart started pounding. Now? He was going to make love to her now?

Grant ignored her and went to the fire, adding more logs and poking the coals until he had achieved the original level of intense heat. Once again, he ripped off his shirt and shoes and kicked them aside. He turned to look at her. "It's getting late. Undress, please."

Despite the polite words, it was a command.

"I thought artists needed a well-lit studio."

"I want to paint you by firelight." The words were a promise, a verbal caress. His voice was deep, whiskey smooth.

She hesitated still. "I made popcorn and hot chocolate."

"I'm not hungry."

"We could do this tomorrow," she said, grasping any opportunity to postpone the inevitable.

"I have other plans for tomorrow."

His meaning was clear. She flushed from her collarbone to her hairline, and it wasn't from the fire's wicked heat. She licked her lips, her mouth and throat as dry as the Sahara. "Will you turn around, please?"

"No." His response was unequivocal. Buried beneath his impassive expression was a dare. He expected her to be confident and daring. She wasn't sure she had it in her.

She slipped off the floppy clown socks one at a time and dropped the bulky sweatpants. The turquoise flannel shirt covered her respectably, but her legs and feet were now bare.

A muscle in his granite jaw flexed, but otherwise his face didn't change. "Keep going."

Which would be easier? Panties first or the top? Deciding that the long shirttails provided the most protection, she reached under and dragged her underwear down her legs.

He was waiting patiently, but she stalled, shaking with nerves. He had seen her breasts only hours before. Why was it so difficult now? Perhaps because he was staring at her with all the hungry intensity of a young cowboy eyeing his first hooker. Not that Grant would ever have been forced to pay for a prostitute. He would have been the kind of Western hero who got the preacher's daughter *and* the brothel owner *and* every other woman in town.

She unbuttoned the shirt, her fingers clumsy and chilled, despite the room's toasty temperature. When the fabric hung free, she managed to look at him. His chest rose and fell with his breathing, and his hands were clenched at his sides. She shrugged her shoulders and the shirt slipped to the floor.

His muttered imprecation was audible in the quiet room, but his next words were calm. "Lie down."

She sat awkwardly, tucking her legs protectively to her chest.

He frowned. "Turn partway on your side. Let your back rest against the back of the sofa."

She did as he asked, refusing to look at him. She sensed his approach, and her breasts tightened in anticipation. He tucked a small throw pillow beneath her head, and winnowed his fingers in her hair, spreading it in careful disarray. His actions were matter of fact, impersonal.

He lifted one leg so her knee was bent, and positioned her arm loosely balanced on her hip. She jerked when she felt his touch between her legs. He fluffed the curls there, combing them with his fingers. Moisture gathered in the secret folds of her body, and hunger began to build.

He tucked her other hand under her cheek, a position that gave him a clear view of her breasts. Without warning he bent and suckled her nipples, one after the other. "Don't move," he said.

His mouth tugging at the tips of her breasts sent an agonizing wave of need crashing though her body. She moaned, desperate to pull him inside her. She grasped his arm.

He moved away, his voice unsteady. "We're ready to begin. Get comfortable. Let your body conform to the sofa."

She tried to find a place inside her head where she could exist without being so terribly aware of Grant's presence. She slowed her breathing, consciously relaxing each muscle, closing her eyes and drifting on a daydream . . .

Grant mixed a swirl of paint and saw his hand shake. He wasn't entirely sure he could follow through with this and not go stark raving mad. He was being ripped apart by opposing forces. The artist in him exulted in the chance to create a painting that would be perhaps the best he had ever done. The man, uninterested in such high-flown ambition, wrestled with primitive lust.

Keeping one in check while allowing the other to thrive was a challenge that required his utmost concentration. He looked at his subject, trying to view her nonsexually. Her pale skin took on a golden sheen in the flickering firelight. The red highlights in her hair caught the fire's glow, and the planes and curves of her body reminded him of a medieval canvas he'd once seen at the National Gallery, its ancient beauty still mesmerizing.

He steadied his hand and began to paint.

Maddy was dreaming. She lay curled on a blanket beside a gurgling creek. It was spring, and wildflowers bloomed in profusion. Across the water on the other shore, a horse pawed the ground restlessly, its silent male rider eyeing her intently, his hand resting on the hilt of a sword.

She lifted a hand to wave, but the rider turned the horse suddenly. The animal's front legs reared in the air. She tried to call out, to tell the man to wait, but it was too late. Horse and master disappeared into the distance.

Her heart sank. She had missed her chance, and somehow she knew in her heart the silent rider would not return. Sad, bereft, she closed her eyes and wept.

Grant glanced at his watch and cursed in stunned disbelief. It was almost midnight. He looked at Maddy, with the man's eyes this time, and saw the steady, gentle evidence of her breathing.

His lips twisted in wry self-mockery. The artist had won out over the man, but only once, for this one night. Never again.

He carried the damp canvas to his bedroom, facing it toward the wall. No one viewed his unfinished work. It was a long-standing rule. He returned to the living room and added more wood to the fire, then covered Maddy with the sheets and blankets from the night before. It was late, and she was still tired from her ordeal, though she would never admit it. Only a selfish bastard would wake her.

Maddy roused sometime during the night, and several things happened at once. She felt an urgent need to go to the bathroom. She realized she was naked. And she saw the empty easel and knew that she was alone.

She slipped on the flannel shirt, tiptoeing stealthily down the hall to the bathroom. That accomplished, she ventured a few steps farther to pause at the open doorway to Grant's bedroom. He was snoring softly, his face turned away from her. Enough illumination from the moonlit snow outside sneaked in around the curtains and enabled her to see that his big, long body was nude.

His bedroom was far cooler than the living room, but he seemed impervious to the chill. She debated climbing into bed with him. She had never actually tried to seduce a sleeping man, but knowing the mechanics of the male species, it surely wouldn't be too hard, no pun intended.

She calculated quickly. They'd known each other thirty-six hours as of this moment. Would that meet with his approval? She shifted from one foot to another, her toes curling on the cold, hardwood floor.

Oh, poop. She was a big, sniveling coward. She'd wait

for daylight to launch her offensive, and if Grant Monroe still resisted . . . Well, then it was his loss.

Grant listened to her soft footsteps fade away and, with a whoosh, released the breath he'd been holding. His heart pounded and his cock was hard. Tomorrow was Christmas Eve, and he was pretty damned sure Santa had promised him just what he'd always wanted.

December twenty-fourth dawned with brilliant sunshine but no sign of warming temperatures. Grant listened to a weather forecast on the radio and heard the promise of a quick thaw on Christmas Day. His jaw twisted in dismay. He didn't want this little idyll to come to an end, particularly not when things were about to get very interesting. The deep snow was his ally.

After a mostly silent breakfast, rife with heated looks and snatched glances, Maddy holed up in the living room with her laptop. She typed furiously, barely lifting her head other than to occasionally pet Van Gogh and scratch the ecstatic dog behind her floppy ears.

Grant hovered on the edge of being jealous of the dog. That would be the last straw.

He paced restlessly from one room to the next, unable to settle on any one activity. He had more than enough wood for two blizzards, and the front porch was swept clean of snow, thanks to yesterday's snowball fight.

He retrieved a staple gun from the toolbox in his Jeep and began hanging sprigs of mistletoe from every available doorway. He wasn't averse to helping Santa out. The old guy was pretty busy, after all.

The air in the cabin was thick with the childhood excitement of the day before Christmas, but the treats in store were entirely adult in nature. Grant wanted to have a gift for Maddy, but he was too selfish to part with the painting. It was his. He brought out his sketchpad and decided to do a drawing of Maddy and Van Gogh.

Maddy was nearing the end of her book, and the words seemed to be flowing from her fingertips onto the page. Maybe sexual frustration was good for creativity, she mused, not completely able to block out Grant's disturbing presence. He seemed restless, and if he was feeling a tenth of what she was, she knew why.

When he wasn't paying attention, she scribbled lines on a notepad, trying to write a poem worthy of a Christmas present for her host. The words seemed stilted, maudlin. And she despaired of capturing her feelings on paper. What did she feel for Grant Monroe, anyway? She could write an X-rated verse, but she accepted, with no small amount of trepidation, that she felt something deep and significant . . . something new and exciting.

Was it real? Could it be trusted? That was the sixty-four-thousand-dollar question.

They ate the last of the chili for lunch, cleaned up the kitchen and played another game of Scrabble. It was a completely civilized experience. No suggestive words, no cutthroat competition, no heated challenges. It was boring as hell.

The afternoon dragged on, neither willing to bring their unspoken plans out into the open. Finally, Grant proposed finishing the picture.

Maddy frowned. "The light won't be the same."

He shrugged. "I'll make do."

She pondered the ramifications of stripping in broad daylight. If she was going to do this, there at least had to be a payoff. She faced him, ready to pick a fight if necessary, her hands propped on her hips.

He raised his eyebrows. "What, Maddy? Spit it out."

"How do you feel about having sex with someone you've known forty-eight hours?"

Heat flashed in his eyes but was quickly hidden. He smiled lazily. "I suppose I could make an exception for you, if it's that important."

She lifted her chin. "It's no big deal. But our options are rather limited. You don't even have cable."

His lips twitched. "I'm sorry I've been such a lackluster host. I'll try to do better."

"That's more like it," she muttered. Without any ceremony, she stripped down to her bare skin and sprawled on the sofa. She had the satisfaction of seeing his eyes bulge and his jaw sag.

After a few long seconds, he removed his hungry stare from her body and went to get the canvas. He returned, holding it carefully, so she couldn't sneak a peek. His cheekbones were streaked with color, and he walked slowly, as though in pain. When he had positioned the canvas on the easel, he brought the radio and plugged it in near the fireplace. After several spins of the dial, he found a station with less static than most, and Bing began singing about a white Christmas.

Van Gogh ambled over to the sofa and rested her chin beside Maddy's arm, begging to be touched. Maddy lavished her attention on the dog, though she was aware of Grant's every move. As he prepared his brushes, she decided it was as good a time as any to get the rest of the answers she'd been waiting for. "So, tell me, Grant. Why are *you* spending Christmas alone?"

He paused for a split second and then continued what he was doing. "I'm not," he said simply. "I'm spending it with you."

"You know what I mean. Why aren't you with family?"

He sighed. "My parents passed away in the last five years. They had me when they were well up in years. I was the unexpected baby. My two older sisters live in the D.C. area. I would normally spend Christmas with them but, like I told you, I was restless. I needed to think. About my old career, about painting, about whether or not my life was what I wanted it to be. And to tell you the truth, it's a little difficult sometimes to be around all that happy-family stuff knowing I had a chance at marriage and blew it."

His blunt honesty stunned her. "I don't think the end of the marriage was your fault."

He shrugged. "I wasn't willing to compromise at the time."

"Maybe you weren't supposed to. You were following your dream."

His lips twisted. "Dreams are cold company when you want a woman in your bed at night."

"You can't tell me there hasn't been an ample supply of women parading through your bedroom."

"Fewer than you think. And I'm not talking about having *a* woman. I'm talking about *the* woman. The once-in-a-lifetime, other-half-of-me, mother-of-my-children woman."

"That's a tall order."

"You don't think it could happen?"

"I'm not sure. I used to."

He began painting, his brow furrowed in concentration as he glanced from her to the canvas to her and back again. "How do you feel about Santa Claus and the Easter Bunny?"

"I wonder why we lie to our children. Maybe the whole 'happily ever after' thing is a lie, too." She heard the cynicism in her voice and winced. Was she asking him to convince her otherwise?

He worked in silence for several minutes. Finally he looked up. His dark gaze tracked over her body, male appreciation assessing her femininity and letting her know he liked what he saw. Her skin warmed, his admiration almost physical. She willed him to forget the damned picture, but he didn't move.

She felt the velvet beneath her, smelled the slightly acrid tang of wood smoke in the air. The radio's melodies evoked memories of Christmases past, happy Christmases. In the corner, the small, unassuming Christmas tree blinked and twinkled brightly. Suddenly, fiercely, she wanted to believe. True love. Forever. The Easter Bunny and Santa Claus. She wanted it all.

But believing was so hard, so scary. It demanded everything. And if you reached for the star at the top of the tree and missed, it was a long hard fall.

Not for the first time, Grant seemed to see inside her head, recognizing her yearning, her fear. His smile was gentle, filled with warmth and affection and something else that made her shake. He sighed softly. "Happiness isn't a lie or a myth. Christmas is about magic and miracles, Maddy. Your coming here was a miracle. What I feel for you is magic."

He laid down the brush he was holding and stepped back, his eyes sober as they looked at the picture. "Want to take a look?"

She dressed rapidly, glad she was once again wearing her own clothes. Did she really want to see herself as he saw her? She approached warily, expecting to be slightly embarrassed. After all, she hated looking at herself in dressing room mirrors. This would probably be infinitely worse. He stepped to one side, allowing her to view the canvas full on.

A sharp, quick gasp escaped her throat, and she twisted her hands together, almost needing to touch the wet paint. It was beautiful, amazing. The colors glowed, and the sensuality of her own image stared back at her.

She looked up at him. "I don't know what to say."

"Do you like it?"

"That's much too tame a word," she whispered. "It's . . . I don't know . . . It's more than I expected."

He seemed pleased by her response, although she felt inadequate to express what the painting made her feel. Humbled. That was part of it, and awed—awed that a man could be so gifted.

He stepped up onto the stone hearth and lifted the heavy painting of Jillian off the wall. Gently, careful not to smudge the wet paint, he rested the unframed canvas on the exposed nails. Maddy's heart turned over in her chest. As a grand gesture, it was a doozy.

Then he took her in his arms, his firm lips finding her softer ones in a long, lazy, exploratory kiss. He was a heck of a good kisser. They were both breathing hard when he released her.

He cupped her cheeks in his hands. "When we were growing up, we always got to open one present after dinner on Christmas Eve."

She looked at him, mute, confused.

He traced her lips with his fingertip. "I want you to be my Christmas Eve present, Maddy . . . more than I've ever wanted anything in my life."

She shivered. "Yes," she said simply. "Me, too."

And so they set about preparing the cabin for that most magical night of the year, December twenty-fourth. Maddy was light-headed with excitement and anticipation and plain, old-fashioned horniness. While she raided the fridge and kitchen cabinets for anything that could remotely be considered festive cuisine, Grant was busy transforming the living room into what he called, with a leering grin, the *love nest*. His cheerfulness was contagious.

The table was pushed to one side, ready to bear their holiday repast, and the sofa cushions were commandeered along with several blankets to make a cozy bed in front of the fire. The Christmas tree, lifted to a spot of importance atop an end table, shone down on it all.

Grant brought in extra wood, enough to last through the night, he told her with a chuckle, laughing when she blushed. Maddy found the last of the mistletoe and tied it in little bunches to the prongs of the antler chandelier overhead.

All in all, they created a pretty darned good holiday ambiance, Maddy decided, frowning as Grant put a small, newspaper-wrapped present under the tree. "What's that?" she asked.

"Just a little something for tomorrow."

When he wasn't looking, she rolled the poem she'd written for him into a skinny cylinder and tied it with a red twist tie from the bread package. She tucked it in a branch of the tree.

Sadly, Grant's bachelor staples left much to be desired. Maddy wanted to make cookies or at least a pie, but she had to settle for sprinkling cinnamon into a pot of boiling water. Her strategy worked, and soon the air was fragrant with the aroma of fresh-baked goodies, pseudogoodies . . . but what the heck. It worked.

Grant opened a bottle of wine to accompany their frozen pizza rolls and packaged tossed salad. He grimaced. "I'll make it up to you when we get off this mountain," he promised. "Prime rib . . . lobster . . . my treat."

*   *   *

He watched Maddy eat, her small white teeth sinking into gooey tomato and cheese. His cock was in permanent erection mode, and had been since this morning. He'd given a damned good impression all day long of being a relaxed, congenial guy, but inside was a pathetic, sex-starved male, ready to beg if necessary.

Maddy had jumped into the Christmas preparations with enthusiasm, and he had a clear vision of spending future Decembers with her under different circumstances . . . watching hokey holiday movies, their legs intertwined beneath a plaid wool blanket. Missing the end of the picture when their need for each other won out. Shopping for Barbies and dump trucks and Cocker Spaniel puppies.

His throat grew tight. He wanted desperately to lay it all on the line for her, but he sensed she was still skittish, still not ready to admit what he knew in every fiber of his being to be true. Against all odds, they had found each other . . . And he loved her. It was that simple.

They cleared away the meal debris and Maddy suggested Scrabble. Her voice was a tad higher than usual, betraying her unease. He pulled her down into the newly made nest of cushions and leaned over her, stroking her hair. "Are you scared of me?" he asked, not entirely kidding.

That drew a small smile. "Of course not."

"Then why do I get the feeling you're stalling?"

Rosy color blossomed on her cheeks. She couldn't quite meet his eyes. "I'm not . . . not exactly."

He kissed her forehead. "Want to talk about it?"

She nibbled her lower lip, a crinkle between her eyebrows deepening. "This is all pretty intimidating," she admitted, her voice almost inaudible.

"You're intimidated by Christmas?" he asked, playing dumb.

She punched his shoulder. "Very funny. It's hard . . ."

Grant laughed. "Damned straight." He pressed her hand to the front of his jeans, and she jumped as though she'd touched a hot iron.

Outrage, mixed with embarrassment and feminine curiosity, danced across her expressive features. "I'm being serious here," she wailed. "We've spent two damned days building up to this. What if we've created a big, romantic fantasy and it amounts to nothing?"

He curled a strand of her hair around his finger, watching fascinated as it clung to his skin. "Are you afraid I'll disappoint you?"

Her chest rose and fell in a heavy sigh. "No. The sex will be great. At least I think so," she added with wry honesty.

He chuckled. "Then, what?"

She searched his eyes, hers big and dark gold, filled with doubts and fears and dreams. "I want this to be more than sex," she admitted, her voice husky. "I need to know that this matters. It's crazy . . . We just met. I don't even know your middle name. But that's my Christmas wish, Grant. That's what I want."

He traced the contours of her face with a shaky hand, his heart expanding like the Grinch's at the end of the story. "Tyler," he said softly. "My middle name is Tyler." He kissed her slowly, tentatively, pretty certain the words wouldn't come out right, but determined to show her with his body.

He lifted her and removed her turtleneck. Her pretty breasts were small and round and her raspberry-hued nipples begged for his touch. He played with them gently, pulling and tugging until they puckered into tight buds. Maddy's eyes were closed, her breathing rough and unsteady.

He tugged her to her feet and divested her of shoes,

socks, jeans and panties in short order. A less-hungry man might have stretched out the disrobing, but he was beyond such patience. He stripped off his own clothes, leaving only his navy boxers between him and her. He needed some flimsy help to keep from mounting her like a horny adolescent.

He slid her up onto a pillow so that her upper body was at an incline. He gripped her thighs and tugged them apart, revealing a narrow fluff of curly golden hair. His breath lodged in his throat. The delicate folds of soft, hidden flesh were glistening with the evidence of her arousal.

He lowered his head and used his whole tongue to stroke her. She tasted sweeter than any holiday treat. She cried out and bucked, but he held her down, thrusting his tongue inside her and using his finger where it mattered most to drive her higher and higher. Her orgasm, when it came, was powerful and beautiful to watch, her slender body quivering with pleasure.

He trembled, burying his face in her belly and holding her tightly until the last tremors faded away.

And then he started again.

Maddy was not prepared for a lover like Grant Monroe. He was insatiable, as though starving for the taste of her. He flipped her to her stomach and rubbed his cock up and down her spine, finally lodging it between her buttocks and stroking lightly back and forth against her damp skin.

He lifted her onto her knees, and she felt his hand part her, enter her, first one finger, then two and finally three. She was extremely sensitive, tender from her earlier orgasm. He knew exactly where to touch. He brushed her clitoris, and she came again, this time with his fingers deep inside her.

When she caught her breath, she rolled to her back, struggling to gain some kind of control. He sat back on his haunches, facing her, his long, thick penis rearing proudly against his abdomen. His eyes were hooded, glittering with intense emotion. His hands rested on his thighs. A pulse jumped at the base of his throat, and his broad shoulders were rigid.

She came up on her knees and pressed against him, breast to chest. Her hand slid between them to cup his balls, and a heavy shudder wracked his frame. "God, Maddy," he ground out in an agonized voice.

She expanded her field of exploration, kissing him as she gripped his cock. Her tongue entered his mouth while her thumb toyed with the wetness at the eye of his eager shaft. He was trembling like a sailor in the throes of malaria.

She knelt to take him in her mouth, and he thrust her away almost roughly. "Next time," he choked out. "I can't bear it."

His sudden movement tumbled her to her back again, and he was between her thighs before she could catch her breath. He reached for a condom, but she stopped him. "I'm on the pill . . . it's okay." He nodded tersely and lifted her legs to his shoulders, the blunt head of his cock pressing urgently to find entry. The position made her feel painfully vulnerable.

On his face she saw the violent struggle to hold back, and she arched her back, taunting him. "Don't be gentle, dammit," she cried, craving him with a need that was frightening. "I won't break."

He surged forward in one heavy thrust, burying himself deep in her vagina, probing and stretching and filling her almost unbearably. He paused to let her adjust to his size, his great chest heaving with his labored breathing.

Their eyes met, his slightly unfocused, hers filled with shock. Ripples of feeling clenched and clawed deep in her core. She squeezed him with inner muscles, exulting when her subtle motion made him groan. "Do it," she challenged. "Take what you want. Let it go."

He held perfectly still for maybe three seconds, and then with a moan of surrender, he began rocking in and out of her, withdrawing almost completely before surging deeper still, the cords in his neck standing out in relief and his clenched teeth bared.

He rode her hard, giving no mercy, his massive body held above hers, driving pistonlike toward a goal they each craved. Maddy loved it, loved him. He surrounded her, filled her. His scent filled her head. Her hands gripped his sweat-slicked shoulders as she felt her third orgasm rising inexorably. "Now, Grant, now," she pleaded, her leg muscles aching.

He halted long enough to look in her eyes, his own filled with something that looked suspiciously like love. Quivering, his muscled arms keeping his weight from crushing her, he pressed a quick kiss on her throat. And then he shouted as his own climax roared over him and he came, deep inside her.

Five

Grant slumped on top of her, barely able to keep from crushing her beneath his weight. Every bone and muscle in his body had been vaporized, destroyed. He hadn't known such pure physical pleasure existed.

He felt euphoric, ready to spout poetry, prepared to slay ferocious dragons for his lady-love.

His amazing lady-love squirmed, her voice breathless. "Air, Grant. I need air."

He rolled to one side, muttering an apology as he nuzzled her breast and watched, fascinated, as the nipple tightened.

She laughed, her face bright with happiness, her eyes soft and sated. "I might need a little time before round two."

They lay curled together, touching, stroking. In the background, Grandma got run over by a reindeer and silver bells began to chime. Grant lifted himself on one elbow. "Now?" he asked hopefully. He slid a thigh between her legs and began licking her rib cage.

She shoved his face away, laughing. "I'm ticklish," she complained. "Behave, Mr. Monroe."

He excused himself for long enough to clean up and tend to the fire, before returning to her side. When he slid between the covers, his bare feet touching hers, she squealed. "You're freezing."

"Then warm me up," he replied, rolling her on top of him.

She wriggled down the length of his body like an erotic gymnast, stopping when her mouth found his cock. Already semierect, he went from zero to sixty within seconds of feeling her mouth swallow his length.

She was enthusiastic, and she was talented. He wasted half a minute on jealousy, wondering whom she'd practiced on, before his mind shut down. Her teeth scraped the underside of his shaft, and his brain went fuzzy. His cock screamed for release, but his brain wanted to be inside Maddy when he came.

With surprise on his side, he twisted and turned and entered her from behind. It was a tight fit from this angle, each of them breathing heavily as they found their rhythm. He grasped her hips, loving the supple, firm feel of her butt. He grabbed a handful of her hair so he could see the side of her face. "Is this okay?" She was awfully silent, except for those little pants that were driving him crazy.

She wiggled her fanny, making him see stars. He reached beneath her and captured a breast, teasing the nipple. Maddy moaned.

He asked a second time. "Honey, do you like this?"

He leaned forward so he could reach underneath and stroke her directly. She cried out, her inner muscles squeezing him as she came, stealing the last of his control. He surged inside her warmth again and again, his question forgotten as he succumbed to the inevitable.

Minutes later, maybe hours, he pulled her, spoon fashion, against his chest and tucked the covers around them both.

When the gray light of dawn seeped into the cabin, Maddy stirred and yawned. Her cheeks heated as memories of the night before came out of nowhere, making her thighs clench. That was all real? As a dream, it would have merited an X-rating. Grant had wakened her three times during the night, each time his body hot and hard as he spread her legs and entered her.

Her curious fingers slid to his abdomen and skated lower. The man could give lessons to the Energizer Bunny. She contemplated her swollen and sore flesh and weighed it against the hunger that simmered unabated deep in her gut. No contest. She straddled him and gently lowered herself on his rigid length.

Each time she told herself the newness would wear off, that this coupling thing would become old hat. It hadn't happened yet, but she was more than ready to keep testing her theory. She winced as she took him an inch deeper. Soaking in a hot bath might be a good idea.

He woke up a split second before she grounded herself on his morning erection. He blinked rapidly, his long, dark lashes and mussed hair making him look adorably sweet and vulnerable. He growled deep in his throat, and she scratched those last two adjectives. It was like waking a hungry lion.

"I hope you don't mind," she said, breathing heavily as she rotated her hips. "I started without you."

He grunted. "So I see." His powerful arms quivered as he lifted her by the waist and settled her on his mouth. Before she had a chance to miss his cock, he was tonguing her roughly, his thumbs parting her so he could reach her aching nerve endings. She came slowly, a rolling, cresting wave of pleasure that left her weak and spent. He showed no mercy.

He laid her carefully on her back and entered her while the last tremors of her release were still rippling. He was gentle this time, almost lethargic. His movements were so slow, she wanted to scream with frustration.

He bent his head, whispering urgent words, his breath tickling her ear. "Come for me, honey . . . one more time."

"I can't," she wailed, petulant. "I'm exhausted."

Another careful withdrawal and penetration. The achingly lazy movements rubbed her intimately. She shivered, wild with conflicting needs. "I've had enough," she said. "I can't stand this."

He went perfectly still, his arms rigid, his dark eyes filled with guilt. "God, Maddy. I'm sorry."

He tried to leave her and she grasped his hips wildly, leaving red scratches. She bit his shoulder. "Ride me hard. Don't make me wait."

His compliance made them both a little crazy.

In the aftermath, the room was quiet, quiet enough to hear the steady drip, drip, drip of melting snow.

Maddy felt . . . Well, she wasn't sure what she felt. She was afraid to look at Grant. Her behavior made her wince. When she stood up, he didn't stop her. She went to the bathroom to shower and change, ruefully donning the same old clothes, but glad at least to have the other pair of undies she had washed and left to dry on the towel bar. She brushed her hair and pulled it back into a ponytail with the same old rubber band. Until now she had never realized how much she took her nice wardrobe and her many toiletries for granted.

She heard the phone ring, the unfamiliar sound jarring in the cozy little cabin. Curious, she hovered in the living room, listening as Grant answered and his deep voice filled with warmth and affection.

The person on the other end was clearly someone of importance. She pushed back a curtain and gazed bleakly at the melting snow. The thermometer on the porch measured forty-five degrees. The thaw had arrived with a vengeance. She wanted to cry and scream and bawl like a baby. She and Grant needed more time. They hadn't even begun to—

Well, that was the kicker. They had begun something, she just wasn't sure what it was. As he was making his good-byes, she casually entered the kitchen, as though she hadn't been avidly straining to hear his every word.

"That was my sister, Beth," he said, his eyes alight with happiness. "The rug rats are missing me. They want me to drive up for a late dinner tonight."

Her heart thudded as it hit the floor. Her numb lips twisted in a smile. "You should go. My apartment's in Charlottesville. You could drop me there if you don't mind."

His smile faded. "What's this?" he asked, his words laced with tender concern. "You look like you're about to cry."

"Christmas is for family, Grant. You need to get there as quickly as you can." She smiled, but it was an effort.

He held her shoulders. "I want you to come with me."

She shook her head violently. "It wouldn't be right. Your family wants to spend time with *you*, not a stranger you met three days ago."

Temper flashed in his eyes, taking her by surprise. "Don't do this, Maddy," he ground out, his teeth clenched.

She shrugged, the ache in her chest threatening to consume her. "The magic is over, Grant. The snow is melting. We both knew we would have to go back eventually. You can't shut out the world forever."

Grant listened, incredulous, as his nebulous dreams turned to ashes. She had cut him loose so fast he was having trouble making sense of it all. He tried one last time. "Then we'll both stay here. That was my original plan, anyway. The family will understand."

She shook her head a second time, and now the regret in her eyes was no longer veiled. "Christmas is for families," she whispered, her voice thick with emotion. "You're lucky to have people who love you so much. Go to them. They need you. It's important."

She walked out of the kitchen. He stood there for long moments, his arms hanging at his sides. Old Santa Claus was a mean son of a bitch—to give a present and then snatch it away. If he found the fat old guy in a dark alley, he'd beat the stuffing out of him.

Anger swept in, masking the dull pain. He wouldn't beg. It took two people to make a relationship, and he didn't need a woman who couldn't even last through the first tough spot. He flashed back for a moment to an image of Maddy sprawled by the fire, her lips curved in a smile of invitation. His throat closed up, and he swallowed hard. How had this soured so quickly?

* * *

They didn't speak after that. Since Maddy had very little of her own to clean up, she finished zipping her backpack and then began tidying the rest of the cabin. There were blankets to fold, dishes to wash and dirty laundry to be bundled into a garbage bag. She found Grant's cooler on the back porch and unloaded the few remaining perishables from the fridge. The other food she tucked in a cardboard box.

She had no idea what to do about the Christmas tree, but she unplugged the lights and, as an afterthought, retrieved the poem she'd tucked in the branches. Somehow she doubted that Grant would appreciate it now. He was so angry with her, but she knew in her heart she was right. He needed to be with his family. And as for his impulsive invitation . . . Well, it was tempting. But imagining the questions about their relationship made her cringe. Three days? They would think Grant had lost his mind. And they might be right.

He was busy draining the pipes and stacking all the firewood he had cut onto the porch. By noon the temperature had climbed to the lower fifties. He finally came inside, and when she looked at him inquiringly, he handed her the small package that had been under the tree. "Merry Christmas," he said, his eyes shuttered.

She opened it, her mouth curving in a smile when she saw what it was. With a few pencil strokes, Grant had captured Van Gogh's mournful eyes and the dog's delight at being in Maddy's lap. She looked up to thank him, but he had disappeared again. She bit her lip and sighed. Feeling an unutterable sadness, she tucked the small drawing inside a book in her pack for safekeeping.

They left shortly after, having exchanged no more than a dozen words since morning. Van Gogh slumbered in the backseat.

The winding gravel road leading down the mountain was slightly dangerous but not impassable. The only real trouble spots were places in the shade where not as much snow had melted. Maddy thought a couple of times that the Jeep might get stuck, but in each instance, Grant wrestled with the wheel until they were moving forward again. At the base of the mountain, the gravel surface gave way to pavement, and soon the little two-lane road led to the interstate.

It took just over two hours to get to Charlottesville. When they reached the outskirts of the city, Grant slowed and asked for directions, his voice gruff. When they pulled up in front of her apartment complex, Maddy grabbed her bag and prepared to jump out. She was more than ready to escape the awkward silence.

Grant stopped her, keeping the doors locked. "Not so fast. I'm coming upstairs with you."

She opened her mouth to protest, but the glare on his face silenced her. At the door she had to fumble deep in her pack to find the house key. As they went inside, stale air made her wrinkle her nose.

She dropped her backpack on a chair and faced Grant, her stomach churning with nerves. "Thanks for rescuing me," she said, forcing a lightness into her voice she didn't feel.

He ignored her glib comment. Slowly, he gave himself a tour of her small apartment, pausing to pick up a photograph here and there, a CD, a knickknack. She trailed after him. He wandered down the hall and found her bedroom. After a cursory look inside, he moved on to her office.

He stayed longer there, examining her bookshelves, flipping through a reference book, checking out her computer. He studied a framed photo on the wall. It had been taken when she'd rafted down the Colorado with a group of friends.

He finally spoke. "You don't *look* like a coward."

"What do you mean?" she asked, stung by his not-so-veiled insult.

He shrugged. "It's pretty clear to me that you're afraid of what's happening between us."

She couldn't think of an answer to that.

He went on. "Just because it hasn't happened in a traditional way doesn't automatically make it suspect. We could have met at a church social, dated for six months and still ended up where we are right now."

"And where is that?" she whispered.

He shoved his hands in his pockets, smiling wryly. "Well, that's the problem, honey. I'm beginning to think you're in a different place than I am."

Her heart began to pound. "What does that mean?"

His smile was lopsided. "I'm in love with you. I should have told you last night, but I didn't think you were ready to hear it."

There was a buzzing in her ears and her fingers were tingling. This would be a bad time to faint. She licked her lips. "Can you say that again?"

His smile deepened and his eyes warmed. "I'm in love with you. The real McCoy. Hearts, flowers, till death do us part."

She stuttered, torn between joy and suspicion. "But you said you'd never been in love."

"That's how I know. You've made me feel something brand new. It's hit me dead between the eyes. No doubts, no second-guessing. I'm sure, Maddy. But clearly, you're not."

"What if it's not real?" she asked, voicing her deepest fear.

Tenderness etched his features. "I don't think you're really worried that it's not real. I think you want me to tell you whether this will last."

She flushed, her emotions raw. "So, can you?" she demanded.

He shook his head. "Sorry, honey, I can't. I don't know your parents, and I don't know why they gave up on something they'd spent a lifetime building. But I know that I can't ever imagine not needing you in my life. I've had the imitation, and it wasn't very good. With you . . . Well, I look at you and I see forever."

A single tear trickled down her cheek. "It would kill me if we start this and it doesn't work."

"And why is that?" he probed gently, still keeping his distance.

Her chin wobbled. "Because I love you, too."

The look on his face when she said the words humbled her. He looked like a man who'd been given the keys to heaven.

They met in the center of the room, their arms locked around each other, their hearts pounding in unison. It was the first time they had touched since leaving the cabin. He kissed her forehead, her nose, her eyes. And all the while he whispered nonsensical love words . . . silly, wonderful, comforting words.

When tenderness gave way to heat, he scooped her into his arms and carried her to the bedroom. "You'll be late," she fretted.

"Shh," he muttered, folding back the covers and lowering her onto the bed before stretching out beside her.

He undressed her slowly, as though he was anticipating a long-awaited Christmas present. Given their activity the night before, their hunger should have been less intense, less urgent. But it wasn't so. Their need simmered in the air, trembling and hushed, waiting to be assuaged.

Clothing disappeared as if by magic, and when he lifted her to sit astride him, her eyelids fluttered shut.

He slid into her slick passage with a groan. "Open your eyes, sweetheart. Look at us." She obeyed, drugged with pleasure. Where their bodies joined, he used his thumb to stroke her. She watched his thick, hard flesh enter and leave and enter again. She started to tremble, the erotic sight etched on her brain.

He pulled her down for a rough kiss, pressing her breasts against his chest. The new angle put pressure, delicious, tantalizing pressure on a very sensitive spot. She felt her orgasm hovering just offstage and tried to shove it back. She didn't want this to end . . . not yet.

She rose again and stared at his face, her breathing ragged. His eyes were half-closed, his face rigid with concentration. She pressed her fingers to his lips, caressing them.

His eyes flew open, his pupils dilated. "What, angel? You okay?"

She smiled at him, the joy in her heart expanding in ever-widening circles. It was magic. It was a miracle. It was love. She laughed out loud. "Let's go home for Christmas."

He clenched her hips and drove upward, nearly unseating her. She barely heard his hoarse shout of completion. Her own release crashed over her, leaving her spent, exhausted and at peace.

After that, it was a race to the finish. Grant showered while Maddy threw some things into an overnight bag. He retrieved a pair of nice slacks and a dress shirt from the Jeep while Maddy debated fretfully between a simple black jersey dress with pearls and a green pantsuit. Grant voted for the dress. "Wear it without panties," he suggested, laughing at her look of horror.

He tweaked her chin. "I'm warning you, hon. Don't expect me to keep my hands off you just because we're at my sister's house."

Maddy escaped into the bathroom, locking him out. Her nerves were jangled as it was, and teasing about sex when she was about to meet his family wasn't helping, not at all.

They fed and walked Van Gogh and less than an hour later they were on the road. They pulled up in Georgetown at seven o'clock on the dot. The attractive Federal-style brick home with black shutters sat amidst a lawn of melting snow, the façade's many windows each filled with a single white candle. The wreath on the door was enormous.

Maddy smoothed her dress, her fingers icy. Grant gripped her hand. "Relax, sweetheart. They're nice people, I swear."

Grant's sister Beth opened the door. Her eyes widened when she spotted Maddy, but before she could do more than utter a cheerful greeting, half a dozen children from toddlers to preteens clustered around Grant and Van Gogh, clamoring for attention. Grant kissed and hugged them all, and in the melee Maddy was squeezed to the sidelines.

She didn't mind. Watching Grant with his nieces and nephews made her heart turn over in her chest. They clearly adored him and, judging by the wide smile on his face, the sentiments were mutual. His dark slacks and crisp white shirt, accented with a whimsical Santa tie, made him look stunningly attractive. The fact that he had the dress clothes with him made her wonder if he'd intended all along to give himself the option of coming to D.C. today.

Fortunately, he didn't leave her stranded for long. Beth was making a move in her direction just about the time Grant eased away from the pack and tucked Maddy against his side.

Beth's curious grin demanded an explanation. She held out her hand. "Hi. I'm Beth Parker, Grant's older sister."

Grant waited for the women to shake hands and then kissed his sister's cheek. "Merry Christmas, Sis. This is Maddy Tierney."

Beth wasn't about to be denied the details. "And . . ."

He laughed. "And I invited her to spend Christmas with us."

Maddy felt herself blushing, but Beth's intent regard was kind. "Come on in and see the others. We're about ready to eat."

The house was filled with warmth and Christmas cheer. In the large living room, carpeted in a lush moss green, the remnants of wrapping paper and bows were evidence of a frenzied gift exchange. Maddy met the other sister, Laura, the two brothers-in-law Pete and Edmund and each of the kids. Everyone was starving so, after introductions, they moved en masse to the formal dining room. The children were allowed to sit at the massive table along with everyone else, and Maddy was impressed to see that the same china and silver was set for them as for the adults.

Grant squeezed her hand under the table as he passed her the sweet potatoes. "So, what do you think?"

She scooped out a generous serving. "I think I was right. You *are* lucky. You have a wonderful family."

"They like you, too."

"How can you tell?" she asked, nibbling a piece of turkey.

He chuckled. "They let you sit at the big table."

"Very funny."

Grant eyed the Norman Rockwell scene with a smile of satisfaction. He knew this wasn't a fake family picture. Sure, there were fights from time to time, marital discord, children acting out . . . But through it all, there was love.

Watching Maddy in the midst of this Christmas celebration made him want to seal the deal. She was beautiful and naturally charming, and his family loved her. How could they not?

During the dessert course, he stood up and clinked his glass, snagging everyone's attention. He rested his hand on Maddy's shoulder. "I want you all to be the first to know . . . Maddy and I are getting married."

Noise exploded around the table, a mix of exclamations and cheers and laughter.

Beth glanced at Maddy, sensing her stillness. "Is this true, Maddy, or is my baby brother trying to stage one of his end runs to get you to say yes?"

Grant tugged Maddy to her feet, sliding his arms around her waist. All eyes were fixed on them and, predictably, Maddy was blushing. "Well, honey, tell them. Are you really going to marry me?"

Her slow smile loosened the knot in his gut. She went up on tiptoe and kissed him. "Yes, Grant. I believe I am."

By nine the kids were drooping and getting cranky, worn-out by a long day of Christmas excitement. Laura and her crew made their good-byes and headed home to their house, only a couple of miles away.

Grant cornered Beth. "Maddy and I are going to slip on over to a hotel."

Beth wouldn't have any of it. "Don't be ridiculous," she said. "The guestroom upstairs is all ready for you— you know . . . the one with the king size bed." Her smirk was teasing but kind.

Her laughter followed them as they headed up to bed, but Grant noticed that Maddy didn't seem the least bit embarrassed. Her head nestled trustingly on his shoulder, and her small hand was tucked in his.

The bedroom was fairly large and beautifully furnished. His sister had exquisite taste and the means to indulge it. Maddy sat on the end of the bed and ran a hand over the elegant cream damask bedspread. She wrinkled her nose. "Maybe we shouldn't have sex while we're here. I'm afraid we might . . . stain something."

The look on her face made him shout with laughter. He scooted her out of the way and removed the spread, folding it into a bundle and tucking it in the closet. "I don't want to hear any more of that," he said, pulling her close for a quick kiss. Her soft lips fired his imagination, among other things, and he backed her toward the crisp white sheets. "I'll be careful," he muttered, ready to promise her anything.

But she resisted, and he groaned. Surely she was kidding. He smiled tightly, his groin aching. "You can't be serious."

She looked puzzled, and then it was her turn to laugh. "I was teasing about not having sex, you big dope . . . But I want to give you your Christmas present. Go sit over there."

"Sex in a chair—sounds good to me," he said, waggling his eyebrows suggestively.

She rolled her eyes. "Your present is not sex, at least not yet," she amended, giving him hope for the immediate future. "Now, go sit."

He obeyed reluctantly, sprawling in a big overstuffed armchair and kicking off his shoes. Maddy went to her purse and opened it, taking out something small enough to fit in her hand. Her hair glowed like a flame against the black of her dress. She'd left it down, confined only by two small, pearl-studded antique hairpins.

Looking at her made him ache.

He swallowed hard. "I shouldn't have sprung the marriage thing on you like that," he said, suddenly remorseful.

Her gaze was unusually serious. "No, you shouldn't have. What if I'd had to say no?"

He shifted restlessly. "I wasn't going to entertain that option."

Her lips twisted into a wry smile. "You weren't kidding about liking to win, were you?"

His face sobered. "I'm sorry."

"Apology accepted." She came to sit at his feet. "I wrote something for you yesterday before we made love the first time. I don't want you looking at me while I read it. You'll make me nervous."

"Okay. If that's what you want."

She rested her back against the base of the chair, her head near his knees. He tangled his fingers in her soft, silky hair, sighing as he felt the warmth of her body. This was gift enough for any man.

She opened what appeared to be a scrap of paper and began to read, her voice soft and low.

In snow and ice and cold I came to you. You warmed
me through . . .

By firelight.
We laughed and played, our burdens set aside. I
loved your dog . . .
By firelight.
We chanced to share our hopes and dreams and
fears. You were so kind . . .
By firelight.
You captured naked truth with paint and brush. You
saw my soul . . .
By firelight.
And then when words and canvas weren't enough,
you came to me . . .
By firelight.
Whate'er the days ahead may send our way, my heart
is yours . . .
By firelight.

Maddy folded the paper with shaking hands and stared at her lap. He hadn't moved as she read. She couldn't even hear him breathing. He slid to the floor and wrapped her in a crushing hug, cradling her in his lap. She realized he was trembling, and she pulled back, shocked to see his eyes wet with tears. She used her fingertip to gather one that clung to his lower lashes.

"Grant? Say something."

He covered her face with rough, hungry kisses, his hands almost bruising. She could feel his thunderous heartbeat.

He finally spoke, his voice rough as broken glass. "God, Maddy." He rested his forehead against hers. "I don't know what I did to deserve you, but I'll spend the rest of my life making you happy. I swear."

"So you liked it?" she asked, more anxious than when she'd submitted her first manuscript.

He cupped her face in his hands. "It's so perfect it

deserves to be published," he said simply. "But I'm not sure I'm that unselfish."

She lifted her lips to his. "I didn't write it for anyone else," she whispered. "Only for you."

She pulled away suddenly and glanced at her watch. "Quick," she said, her lovely amber eyes alight with happiness. "It's five till midnight. I want to give you the rest of your Christmas present."

She stood up and reached behind her back to lower her zipper. The dress dropped to the floor and Grant forgot to breathe. She wore sheer black stockings and a lacy black garter belt . . . with no panties. He scooted forward until his lips were brushing the tops of her hose.

"You've been a naughty girl," he muttered . . . "And Santa's very, very appreciative." His tongue found her secret, moist flesh and began to stroke, his hands gripping her smooth thighs.

Maddy clenched her hands in his hair and closed her eyes, letting the Christmas magic begin.

Here's an excerpt of Lori Foster's
"The Christmas Present,"
one of the sexy holiday stories in
I'M YOUR SANTA.
Available now from Brava!

With each step he took, Levi pondered what to say to Beth. She needed to understand that she'd disappointed him.

Infuriated him.

Befuddled him and inflamed him.

In order to get a handle on things, he had to get a handle on her. He had to convince Beth to admit to her feelings.

He needed time and space to accomplish that.

Thanks to Ben's directions, Levi carried her through the kitchen toward the back storage unit, where interruptions were less likely to occur.

The moment he reached the dark private area, Levi paused. Time to give Beth a piece of his mind. Time to be firm, to insist that she stop denying the truth.

Time to set her straight.

But then he looked at her and he forgot about his important intentions. He forgot everything because of his need for this one particular woman.

God, she took him apart without even trying.

Among the shelves of pots and pans, canned goods and bags of foodstuff, Levi slowly lowered Beth to her feet.

He couldn't seem to do more than stare at her.

Worse, she stared back, all big dark eyes, damp lips, and barely banked desire. Denial might come from her mouth, but the truth was there in her expression.

When she let out a shuddering little breath, Levi lost the battle, the war . . . he lost his heart all over again.

Crushing her close, he freed all the restraints he'd imposed while she was his best friend's fiancée. He gave free rein to his need to consume her. Physically. Emotionally. Forever and always.

Moving his hands over her, absorbing the feel of her, he tucked her closer still and took her mouth. How could he have forgotten how perfectly she tasted? How delicious she smelled and how indescribable it felt to hold her?

Even after their long weekend together, he hadn't been sated. He'd never be sated.

Levi knew if he lived to be a hundred and ten, he'd still be madly in love with Beth Monroe.

The fates had done him in the moment he'd first met her. She smiled and his world lit up. She laughed and he felt like Zeus, mythical and powerful. She talked about marrying Brandon and the pain was more than anything he'd ever experienced in his twenty-nine years.

Helpless, that's what he'd been.

So helpless that it ate at him day and night.

Then, by being unfaithful, Brandon had proven that he didn't really love Beth after all—and all bets were off.

When Beth came to him that night, hurt and angry,

and looking to him for help, Levi threw caution to the wind and gave her all she requested, and all she didn't know to ask for.

He gave her everything he could, and prayed she'd recognize it for the deep unshakable love he offered, not just a sexual fling meant for retaliation.

But . . . she hadn't.

She'd been too shaken by her own free response, a response she gave every time he touched her.

A response she gave right now.

They thumped into the wall, and Levi recovered from his tortured memories, brought back to the here and now.

He had Beth.

She wanted him.

ALL SHE WANTS FOR CHRISTMAS IS . . .

If Amber Taylor doesn't find a way home for Christmas, her mother is definitely going to disown her. Unfortunately, there's no way she can afford to buy a plane ticket on her paltry salary. Luckily the universe obviously has her back. Why else would a single, drop-dead gorgeous actor suddenly show up on her doorstep and offer to drive her cross-country for the holidays?

A HAPPILY EVER AFTER . . .

Hunky Scott Cardoza was everything Amber desired in a boyfriend—except that he definitely had heartbreaker written all over him, which is why Amber promised herself that their road trip was going to be anything but romantic. Yet being cooped up in a tiny car for three days with the man of her dreams was turning out to be quite a challenge. Good thing rules were meant to be broken . . .

"Alan again offers readers a story filled with humor and heart."
—*Romantic Times*

Please turn the page for an exciting sneak peek at Theresa Alan's THE DANGERS OF MISTLETOE now on sale at bookstores everywhere!

Twenty-eight days before Christmas

The night began with a simple philosophical question—
is it possible to eat yourself into a cheese popcorn
coma?—and ended with reindeer-print boxer shorts
draped over the lamp and a total stranger passed out
and coiled up like a conch shell on my couch.

When I got home from work, I found a package waiting for me in the entranceway of my brownstone walk-
up apartment building. It was a present from Aunt Lu.
Every year around Thanksgiving she sent a giant vat of
popcorn in a decorative tin. In theory this was a nice
gesture, but as a single woman who had no self-discipline
whatsoever, this was actually a very dangerous gift.
Brimming with excitement (I loved presents! Even ones
that would make my thighs bloat up like the cheeks of a
chipmunk at a nut convention!), I took my booty, raced
up the rickety green stairs to my apartment, tore off my
many layers of winter outerwear, and opened the box to

Theresa Alan

reveal a tin that was bisected with a sheet of spongy cardboard to separate the two flavors: cheese and caramel. I sat on the couch, turned on the television, and began shoveling cheese popcorn down my throat from my popcorn trough. The first few bites were ecstasy—the decidedly unwholesome neon-orange cheese powder melted on my tongue in a manner that was thoroughly delightful. Soon, however, I was no longer actually tasting anything; I was merely shoveling food down my throat as if my snack was a timed event and the buzzer would go off at any moment. I was riding a giddy wave of excess and loving it. At some point I realized my stomach was rumbling and I felt slightly ill but there was more cheese popcorn to consume and I was powerless to stop myself from bringing yet another bite to my mouth. It was only when my doorbell zapped that I put a lid on the tin, dashed to the sink to wash off the radioactive orange powder from my fingertips, and temporarily concluded my popcorn orgy. I peeked out the window to see my girlfriend Chrissie standing on the steps below with an entourage of cute guys.

Wasn't it every single girl's fantasy to have cute guys simply show up at her doorstep? It was up there with winning the lottery without having to buy a ticket. And the crazy thing was, it was something I fantasized about a lot. Every time I got home from work, I would have a small flutter of hope that my life might have changed while I was gone—I'd have a message from a new client who would end up becoming my husband or I'd get a steady gig at a salon so I didn't have to make money exclusively with clients I found on my own. Or maybe there would be a message from that guy I met at the coffee house last week and suddenly I wouldn't be a romanceless, sexless schmuck anymore. Or I'd come home to a letter with a giant check in it from some mysterious tax rebate or something. The fact that none of these things ever happened did nothing to diminish my hope that something exciting was just around the corner. And look, here I was, with a bevy of cute guys suddenly on my doorstep.

I took stock of my appearance: I was wearing my hair back in a ponytail, which was somewhat unfortunate. It could look cute in a ponytail, but lots of guys told me my hair was my best asset—it was long, wavy, and butterscotch-colored—so I usually wore it free when trying to impress. But if I pulled it out of the elastic band now there would be an unfortunate telltale crimp, so the ponytail stayed. Other than that I didn't look too awful except for the bright orange powder glittering across my chest. I quickly brushed it off and bounded down the stairs to open the door. (My building was too old for fancy advancements like being able to buzz friends inside.)

"Hi," I said.

"Merry fucking Christmas," Chrissie said cheerfully. She held aloft a fifth of spiced rum. I sensed danger.

"What are you doing here?" I asked.

"Are you going to let us in? It's freezing out here."

"Oh. Sure. Come in. Um, my place isn't clean since I wasn't expecting . . ."

"Your apartment is never clean. Never fear. We won't judge you."

I stood back and let my guests in. "I'm Scott," said a good-looking guy in a baseball cap and navy blue Patagonia ski jacket. With his dark hair and caramel skin he looked like Kelly Ripa's husband what's-his-face who used to be on *All My Children*.

"Yo. I'm Vince," said another dark-haired guy.

"Brian," the blond guy said.

No one said anything for a moment. I was trying too

hard not to look at Scott again in any obvious or carnivorous way. Finally I realized they were waiting for me in the arctic cold. "Oh . . . I'm Amber. Amber Taylor. Follow me."

"We brought rum for the eggnog," Chrissie said as she charged up the stairs. Chrissie's long strawberry-blonde hair curled in Shirley Temple corkscrews. I imagined that when her hair was wet it must have reached her ankles. She had *tons* of it. She often attempted to push at least part of it out of her face with a headband or a network of barrettes, but tonight she wore it loose and it bounced as she walked.

When everyone was in my microscopic apartment, Chrissie began rooting through my cabinets for a pitcher to whip up a deadly concoction of eggnog and rum.

I went to massage therapy school with Chrissie. Being a massage therapist is my twenty-eighth "career." I've also been a sushi deliverer, the personal assistant to an eccentric writer, and, of course, cliché of clichés, an unemployed actress. I came to New York to pursue acting, but I couldn't even get parts in unpaid theater roles let alone roles in movies or on TV. As much as I enjoyed rejection and poverty, when the office I was temping at offered me a full-time position in event planning, I pretty much gave up on acting and took it. I'm not a detail-oriented person, and event planning is all about detail, but I managed to do all right on the job for almost two frazzling years. Amazingly, I only messed up at work a few times, and my getting fired wasn't about my mistakes: half the company got the ax due to a severe budget shortage. Still, when I got laid off I felt like I'd gotten a divorce—betrayed and hurt. It was worse than breaking up with a boyfriend. I'd worked so damn hard for the company, and my reward for my sixty-hour weeks was getting canned without a dime in severance pay and no place to go. I packed all my things into a box and walked out of the office feeling like I'd been cheated on. After reeling from being let go, I simply couldn't bring myself to get another job doing the same thing. Anyway, being an event planner had never felt like a calling.

I needed a job that made me feel like I was making a difference. That's why I went to school to be a massage therapist. If a person was in pain, it affected every other part of his or her life. In this field I could help people feel better physically and spiritually. I enjoyed being a massage therapist, but since I was just starting out, the money wasn't exactly rolling in. Plus, I was still paying off my student loans from getting a bachelor's degree in theater (*What* was I thinking? A degree in button making would have been more lucrative), culinary school (which I sort of flunked out of due to the fact that cooking school teaches you not only how to cook, but how to calculate how much food to buy and how to run a successful restaurant—no one told me there would be math involved in cooking school!), and massage school. Despite the fact that I gave the federal government a hefty chunk of my monthly salary, I was on the you-will-die-well-before-you-can-pay-off-your-student-loans payment plan. Though I wasn't making much money, at least I knew that as my own boss, I could never get fired again.

As Vince, Scott, and Brian made themselves comfortable in my living room, I said, "Um, so how do you guys know Chrissie?"

"We met atta bar," Vince said, shrugging not just with his shoulders but with the entire length of his arms, his palms facing up, as if to say, *You know how it goes.* "Brian and Scott, these are my guys."

I nodded just as the phone rang.

"Excuse me for just one sec," I said, walking only a few feet into what passed as my bedroom. "Hello?"

"Tell me you have your ticket." It was my sister, Emily.

"I haven't *exactly* bought my ticket yet."

"Christmas is a month away. You should have bought your tickets weeks ago. Prices are going to go through the roof."

Emily, of course, *would* have had *her* tickets back in July even with a wedding to plan and a house to buy. "Well, you know, sometimes if you wait you can get those last-minute bargains."

"What are you going to do if you don't get a last-minute bargain?"

I exhaled at the same moment Chrissie thrust a cup of eggnog in my hand. The girl was a tornado—an unstoppable force of nature.

I mouthed the word "thanks" to Chrissie. Aloud I said, "Emily, don't you think it's a little silly to spend hundreds of dollars so we can see each other for just a couple of days?" I took a sip of the spiked eggnog, which could better be described as rum with a splash of eggnog. It nearly singed the hair off my head it was so high octane.

"Of course. It's ludicrous. Christmas is ridiculous in every way. But if you don't come, Mom will kill you."

I moaned. Emily was right. "You're right. I'll never hear the end of it."

"Never."

"But I just saw all of you at your wedding in August."

I had no money in my savings account whatsoever, and I had abused my credit cards so badly I couldn't even charge a ticket to Denver. Why had I ever left home to move to New York? Everything was so much harder out here. My rent on this five-hundred-square-foot hovel nearly bankrupted me while Emily just moved into her first home. Her place was three times the size of mine, yet she paid two hundred dollars less on her mortgage payment each month than I did on my rent.

"We're your loving family. It's not like we can see each other only once a year. And let me reiterate my main point, which is that you'll never hear the end of it from Mom if you don't come home for Christmas. You know she's psychotic about the importance of this holiday. She will torment you every day for the rest of your life if you don't come."

"She will, she will." My mother really could be a broken record at times. When I lost my job in event planning, she would call day after day and tell me to get a real job. I'd think, *Mom, I get it. I'd like to find a real job, too.* Then, three minutes later she would say the same thing in a different way. Something like, "You know, you could work in an office and wear pretty suits. Wouldn't that be nice?" *Yes, Mom, if only I could find a job I'd love to wear pretty suits.*

I huffed into the phone. It was so unjust to be thirty-two and still letting my mother tell me what to do. "Why is she so weird about it? We're not religious. We're not traditional. I don't get it."

"I don't know why, but the point is that she'll make your life a living hell if you don't get out here. Even if you make it to every Christmas for the next thirty years, Mom will be pestering you about how you broke her heart because you didn't make it to the first Christmas I'm hosting in my life."

"You're right. You're right." I took another sip of my eggnog-flavored rum. I loved my mother, but she could be such a pain. Still, making her happy made my life so much easier. How the hell was I going to miraculously come up with the money for a plane ticket? Maybe I could sell some of my organs off. Did I really *need* two lungs?

"Plus," Emily continued, "Mom said she's going to make some big announcement."

I paused. "What kind of announcement?"

"I don't know."

"What do you think it could be?"

"I don't have a clue."

"You think she and Mork are getting a divorce?" ("Mork" was our nickname for our mother's husband, Jesse Moss. He looked just like Robin Williams in his Mork days, with straggly longish hair. That, combined with his obsession with suspenders, had caused us to call him Mork ever since Mom began dating him way back when Emily was twelve and I was ten. How were we to know Mom was actually going to marry the guy? Mom didn't know about our secret nickname for him. We loved him, but secretly we were happy he was her second husband and not our dad because we both preferred having the surname Taylor rather than Moss.)

Emily made a noise that roughly equated to, "I don't know."

"Well, she's too young to retire and anyway she loves her job," I continued. "Maybe she's secretly gay. Maybe we're really adopted. I know! We're secretly wildly wealthy and Mom and Dad hid the money from us when we were growing up because they didn't want to spoil us but now we're going to come into our inheritance!"

"Yeah, right. Anyway, don't you want to see Luke's and my new house?"

"Why won't she tell us the secret early?"

"Because she wants us all there in person."

"We're going to become wealthy, I just know it. I bet

she's won the lottery and is buying a boat and going sailing around the world and taking us with her!"

Emily sighed in exasperation. "Just get your ass out here."

"Fine." I sniffed. "I'll keep checking Priceline and hope for a miracle."

"Why don't you just ask Mom for the money?"

"Because I can't bear to have her lecture me on how it's time that I got a husband and a 'real' job. I'd thought that with you getting hitched she would lay off, but no, it's only made her even more determined to get me married off. She acts like I'm beating men away. I'm *trying* to find someone."

Mom did sort of have a point: the truth was, I got asked out a lot. I was the queen of the first dates. The problem wasn't that the guys didn't like me but that I didn't like them. There was never that spark I longed for. It was nice having men take me out to expensive dinners and shower me with gifts, but I wanted to find a guy who made me light up when I saw that he'd left a message on my voice mail or sent me an e-mail. Usually I cringed when I got a call from a guy because I knew I'd have to give him that "I'm not into you" speech.

"If I don't find the right guy soon, my eggs will have rotted away and I'll never have kids. But I can't just marry the first sperm-carrying male who crosses my path."

"Since when have you been all hot and bothered to start having kids?"

"It's the holidays. They make me think about what my life is going to be like twenty years from now if I never get married and have kids. Mom will be dead and I'll be all alone for the holidays."

"You'd always be included in my Christmas."

"It's not the same. I'd be the pathetic spinster tagalong. It's too depressing. The other day, I saw a commercial for *The War of the Worlds*. It's a movie about Earth getting attacked by aliens, and when we're under attack, all the families come out of their houses and hug each other while watching the battle rage. Don't you see, Emily? If we get attacked by aliens, I won't have any family to hug and console. You and Mom are all the way in Colorado. I'll be all alone."

"Amber, if we get attacked by aliens, you'll have bigger things to worry about than whether you'll have family to hug while the planet is being destroyed in a blaze of alien fire. Anyway, you get asked out on dates all the time. You either turn them down flat out or only give them a few dates before you give them the ax. How are you going to find someone if you don't give anyone a chance?"

"If you don't feel it, you don't feel it."

"This has everything to do with your fear of commitment. This is just like you flitting from job to job."

I groaned. "I told you, I couldn't get work as an actress, I got laid off from being an event planner, and the other jobs were just too mind-numbing for words. You sound just like Mom."

I could picture Emily clearly. She would be wearing freshly washed pajamas—actual pajamas rather than a tank top and sweats like normal people—her straight honey-brown hair would be perfectly neat in a sleek bob that cradled her face. Her nails would be short and neat and trim, and her skin would be flawless as always because a zit would never dare try to break out on her face because Emily simply didn't tolerate disorder.

"I'm sorry if I sound like Mom, but it would behoove you to think of her wrath if you don't get your ass out here."

My stomach rumbled irritably and I felt a sharp pain. I moaned and clutched my unhappy gut.

"Spending time with your family won't be that bad," Emily protested.

"No, that's not it. I got my yearly tin of popcorn from Aunt Lu and I devoured like half the cheese popcorn in a single sitting. You think popcorn is some light and healthy treat, but I've looked at the nutritional information on the bags of cheese popcorn at grocery stores, and the stuff has a jillion calories and is loaded with fat. Yet I'm utterly powerless to resist."

"I know. I could eat the entire thing of caramel popcorn in a single sitting. When I got the tin in the mail, I refused to open it. I'm waiting for my office holiday party and I'm going to give it away to the person I'm the secret Santa for."

"Wow. What willpower. If you were here, I'd gladly give you all my caramel popcorn."

"If you came out here for Christmas I'd give you all the cheese popcorn."

"No. The last thing on this earth I need is more. Thanks anyway."

I really did want to figure out a way to get home. I was dying to see Emily and Luke's new place, and I always liked hanging out with Emily and Mom. Plus, now that Emily was a stepmother, I had a stepniece and stepnephew I couldn't get enough of.

"I assume you're not going to Dad's this year for Christmas, either?" Emily asked.

Since our parents were divorced, we always had two different Christmases. I usually missed the one with Dad because he was understanding about the difficulty of me flying to California the weekend before Christmas and then flying to Colorado the next weekend. (Mom always got the actual holiday; Dad got the weekend before, mostly because he understood that the important thing was to be with your family, not the exact calendar day you did it.) Also, I'd never been particularly close to Dad. He always worked a lot when Emily and I were young and now that I was an adult, we just didn't have much to talk about. He didn't get my world and I didn't get his. It wasn't that we didn't get along, but our relationship was formal and distantly polite.

"Nope. Dad even offered to pay for my ticket, but I told him I can't afford the time off from work."

"Then you definitely need to come out here."

"I know. I miss you."

"Oh, by the way, don't forget to send Luke a card. It's his birthday next week."

"Of course I won't forget." I *had* forgotten; thank goodness she'd reminded me.

"What was that sound?"

"I have some friends over."

"Ahh. I'll let you go, then. I love you. But promise me you'll be here for Christmas. I had to suffer through Thanksgiving with Mom and Mork and Luke's mother all by myself. I can't bear to be on my own for another holiday."

"I'll do my best. I love you."

"I love you, too."

After hanging up the phone, I rejoined my guests in the living room. I sat on the floor because Vince and Chrissie were on the couch. Brian and Scott sat on the two chairs from my microscopic kitchen table. I owned very little furniture as I couldn't afford it and didn't have room for it anyway. The television was propped on two cement blocks covered in a batik blanket. That was all the furniture I had except for the mattress in my coffin-sized bedroom and a small used dresser for clothes.

My place was messy and cluttered, but I blamed that on the matchbox size of the place.

"How do you two know each other?" Scott asked Chrissie and me. He sat with his legs parted with his hands on his blue-jeaned legs. He had an easy confidence about him.

"We went to massage therapy school together," I said.

"So you're a message therapist, too, huh?"

"Yep."

"Do you give happy endings? Chrissie claims she doesn't," Scott said.

Immediately, my jaw involuntarily clenched and I felt a wave of irritation. If you were going to make a living as a massage therapist, you had to be ready for some guys to think you were little more than a prostitute. A "happy ending" was something that apparently enough female massage therapists offered their male clients that some men came to look forward to them. I'd only had to deal with a few men with hard-ons and unrealistic expectations, but the stereotype of massage therapist as prostitute irritated me to no end.

"No," I snapped.

"There's no reason to get defensive," Scott said. "I just think a massage is incomplete if you ignore that area. It would certainly help a guy relax."

"He can go relax that part of his body anytime on his own. Did you ever notice how you can't tickle yourself and you can't really massage yourself, but on that area of your body, things work just fine when you're solo?" I took a defiant swig of my eggnog-rum and nearly stripped the lining of my esophagus—it was like drinking Drano.

"It's better if somebody else does it, though," Scott insisted.

I glared at him. Unfortunately, he was so good-looking, I found it difficult to maintain my righteous indignation. Plus, I realized I was allowing myself to become irritated. *Nobody makes you angry; only you allow yourself to become angry.* How many times had I read that in one of my eight zillion self-help books? Reading these books was all part of my plan to become a better human being who was at peace with humankind and in a perpetual Zen state of mind and all that kind of shit.

As I looked at Scott and tried to calm myself, I realized he looked familiar.

"Scott, have you and I met before?"

"Scott was in that Verizon commercial," Chrissie said. "Do you remember it? It was the one where . . ."

"Oh, yeah, I remember you! I know the commercial you're talking about," I said excitedly.

Scott's face flushed. "The residuals helped me pay my rent for the last few years."

"That's so cool. I feel honored to have a semifamous actor in my apartment."

He shrugged. "It's been a while since I've gotten any work."

"Still, it's great that you got the part. I tried to be an actress and failed miserably. You must be so proud."

"He's being modest," Chrissie insisted. "He was in a couple movies, too. Have you ever heard of *Red Rose?*"

"Uh, no. Sorry."

"Don't worry about it. It was in the theater for like, ten minutes." He shrugged.

"You were in a movie. That's awesome," I said, genuinely impressed.

I was distracted by Chrissie's shriek as Vince pulled her onto his lap and thrust his tongue so far down her throat he could probably taste whatever she'd had for dinner swirling around in her stomach.

This was Chrissie: making out while I was stuck staring at two strange men and feeling decidedly awkward. I glanced at Scott again. Scott was so comfortable in his skin, so confident. I really wanted not to like him. He had that sort of alpha-male arrogance about him that successful businessmen, college athletes, and men who have always had power seemed to have. But I found that Scott's sureness of himself was strangely intoxicating.

"Ah, so Brian, what do you do?" I asked, trying to ignore the porno audition taking place on my couch.

"This and that."

I cleared my throat. This was going to be harder than I thought. "Uh-huh. Are you from New York originally?"

"No."

"How long have you been here?"

"A while."

I nodded, then stood. "Why don't I get us some more drinks?"

"I'll help." Scott followed me to the kitchen. "I hope I didn't offend you with my comment. I was just kidding."

"No, not at all." I became very busy mixing the rum and eggnog.

"That's a really cool necklace." Scott gently caressed my pendant; the pads of his fingers grazed my collarbone. The heat from his touch shot through my body; I shivered involuntarily.

"It's a goddess symbol."

"Are you a goddess worshipper or something?"

"Not really, not exactly anyway, no, uh-uh." My tongue was stuck on some channel of stupidity. "I just believe there is a power that women have, and when I'm going through tough times, I can tap into that energy. Does that sound New Agey and weird?"

"No. I get that. I believe that everything gives off energy. You know, vibrations that can be either negative or positive. It's like how electrons bounce from person to person, from this counter to you, from the counter to the glass. If you give off positive energy, you attract it."

"Doesn't positive attract negative?"

"Maybe, but I like my way better."

I smiled. "I do, too." I was slightly taken aback to hear his theory. He was classically handsome, and I tended to think that guys who were that attractive didn't think about much more than getting drunk and laid. Plus, I liked his idea. It was the what-goes-around-comes-around philosophy, and I personally believed that if you did good things, good things would happen to you.

He returned my smile. I nearly whimpered with longing.

When we returned to the others, Chrissie finally came out of her lip-lock with Vince. "You know what this party needs? Music!" she said.

I surveyed my CDs. In recent years, most of what I'd added to my music collection were compilations of chanting by yogi masters and meditation gurus. All I can say is thank goodness I had crappy taste in music during my misspent youth (which, granted, was only a few years ago), and I had some suitably pop-sounding party-mix CDs.

The next few hours involved a great deal more rum and conversation on topics I suspect were less than high-brow.

When I woke in the morning, I found myself on the floor in the living room with carpet lint up my nose. Brian was curled up naked on my couch, and a pair of red boxer shorts with smiling reindeer was draped over my lamp.

Why oh why was Brian naked? I bolted upright and did a quick status check—I appeared to have all my clothes on. Of course, clothes could always be put back on, so that didn't necessarily mean I was safe. Please,

please tell me I didn't sleep with Brian the Monosyllabic Wonderboy.

Further reconnaissance revealed Chrissie and Vince in various states of undress on my bed, as if my bedroom karma wasn't—pardon the expression—already screwed enough.

Scott, I noticed, was nowhere to be found.

I looked around for telltale condom shrapnel or worse, a used condom lying like a smooshed sea snail in a sad and gooey heap. There was no sign of condom detritus, which meant either I was in the clear or in worse trouble than I thought.

"Chrissie!" I hissed in a whisper. "Chrissie!"

She lifted her head and cracked open one eyelid about a nanometer. "Huh?"

I waved frantically to indicate I wanted her to come over to me. Wrapping the sheet around her, she staggered over. Her hair looked like Medusa's might have if Medusa had just been shocked by a bolt of lightning.

"Why is there a naked man on my couch?"

Chrissie's gaze followed the direction my finger was urgently pointing.

"Brian? Brian's just one of those guys who goes a little crazy once you get a few drinks in him. He started singing 'Rudolf the Red-Nosed Reindeer' and doing a striptease."

"I didn't mess around with him, did I?"

"He passed out not long after the striptease."

"Thank God."

Chrissie woke up the guys and told them it was time to get going. After my houseguests sheepishly dressed and departed, I straightened up a little.

If only the disaster that was my checking account could be cleaned up so quickly. I was afraid, however, that it wasn't going to be quite that easy.

All mystery author Maggie Kelly wants for Christmas is to snuggle under the mistletoe with her fictional Regency Era creation who's miraculously come to life. Too bad someone has something a bit more sinister in mind for Maggie this holiday season . . .

She hasn't always been nice . . .

Maggie is still marveling at the fact that the drop-dead gorgeous Regency hero of her novels—Alexander Blake, the Viscount Saint Just—has miraculously come to life and is shacking up in her twenty-first-century apartment. Unfortunately, the handsome rake is demanding more than a few heart-melting kisses under the mistletoe. For one thing, he's hell-bent on being her protector, even though Maggie's made it quite clear she's no helpless damsel in distress. For another, he's made himself quite comfortable—in her bed. (Not that she's complaining . . .)

But she's definitely *never* been this naughty . . .

What is troubling Maggie, though, is that ever since Alex turned up, she's developed this nasty habit of tripping over dead bodies. And when she receives an overnight package with a not-so-merry present, it's obvious she's become the next victim to be crossed off some homicidal maniac's list. At least Alex is finally feeling useful. Now if only he'd stop talking about making her his bride and continuing the family name . . .

"Maggie's wit and Saint Just's antics will raise the holiday spirits of Michaels's fans."
Publishers Weekly

Please turn the page for an exciting sneak peek at Kasey Michaels's HIGH HEELS AND HOLIDAYS now on sale at bookstores everywhere!

Saint Just stood just inside the small wire cage at the very back of the basement of the Manhattan condo building, a scented handkerchief to his nostrils as he looked at the tightly tied green plastic garbage bag lying on the cement floor.

"Grateful as I am, Socks, that you are cognizant of the strictures as laid down by all of the many crime-scene investigation programs on television, I do believe you might have safely disposed of the body. Unless, of course," he added facetiously, turning to his friend Argyle Jackson, doorman of said condo building, "it was your thought that I might wish to perform an autopsy?"

Socks held his hands cupped over his nose and mouth as he shuffled in place, clearly wishing himself anywhere but where he was at the moment. "Hey, Alex, when I called you in England you told me to not touch anything. I'd already opened the box, so I just tossed everything in that bag and brought it down here until you got home. You never said to throw away the body."

"Were there identifying marks with which we could trace the thing, Socks? Scars? Distinctive tattoos? A wooden leg, perhaps?"

Socks shook his head. "Okay, okay, I get the point, Alex. It was a rat. Just like every other rat in Manhattan, except that this one was dead."

"Then you could have safely disposed of the thing, and I apologize most profusely for not being more explicit. Now, before we open it, could you tell me what else is in the bag? And remind me, please, of the particulars of the delivery of the package. I was rather involved with other matters when last we spoke."

"You really want to do this now?" Socks asked, taking another step backward. "You just got home from the airport a couple of minutes ago. Some trip, too, from what Sterling told me before he headed upstairs to see Henry. Isn't that something, Alex? Give one of them a white fur coat and he's a pet, like Henry. Make another one ugly and he's just another damn rat. Would that be discrimination, you think? Sterling said you solved more murders while you were in England, huh? You sure have all the luck."

"We will discuss all of that later, Socks, if you don't mind, as I'm anxious to begin my investigation. According to you, there has been a threat on Maggie's life. I don't believe there is anything to be gained by delay, do you? Besides, Maggie is busy upstairs, undoubtedly cudgeling her brain for reasons to put off unpacking for at least a week, and won't notice that I'm gone."

"Okay, but do I have to be here?"

"To tell me what I've just asked you to tell me, yes, you do," Saint Just said, manfully lowering the handkerchief, because he'd just remembered reading that allowing your olfactory senses to be inundated by the sickening smell of decomposing flesh was the best way to shut down those senses, rendering himself at least temporarily immune to the stench. Of course, the shutting down part took several minutes, and he only hoped the rather pitiful chicken salad sandwich he'd had on the plane had already been fully digested.

"All right," Socks said, still speaking through his cupped hands, "but I'm going to have to take my uniform to the cleaners again, and I just paid twenty bucks for the first time, when I opened the package. Mrs. Loomis said I smelled like a three-week-old gefilte fish, and threatened to report me to management."

"Remind me to give you forty dollars when we get back upstairs," Saint Just said, breathing as slowly as possible through his nose. Socks might be happy with a newly cleaned uniform, but Saint Just had already mentally consigned every stitch he wore to the dustbin. Which was a pity, for the black cashmere sweater was one of his favorites. Ah, the sacrifices he made for his Maggie.

Socks appeared slightly mollified by the offer to pay for cleaning his uniform. "Okay, Alex, thanks. So the mail came, and there was this package for Maggie, see? Came right through the mail, an overnight delivery package, so you tell me how careful Homeland Security is, huh? Run that sucker through an X-ray machine and, bam, little rat skeleton. Little rat head, little rat teeth. I'm asking you, who could miss that?"

Saint Just continued to eye the garbage bag. "Another topic for some other time, fascinating though it is, Socks. Continue, please."

"I put the package under my desk, like I always do with packages, but when I got to work the next day I noticed the smell. I wasn't sure where it was coming from at first—I always have five or six packages under there— but then Maggie's package started to leak, you know? That's when I opened it, and then I called you."

"So it was a standard overnight packaging?"

"Oh, yeah. Damn. Either one- or two-day delivery—I forget which. Sorry, Alex. But you'll see it—one of those red, white, and blue boxes with an eagle on it, you know? I do remember that it was postmarked here, in Manhattan. Anyway, I opened it and out came two more things— a clear plastic bag and another package. I think the bag had been filled with dry ice—to keep the rat cold, you know?—but that was pretty much gone. And the other bag was *really* leaking. And really reeking. I brought everything down here before I opened it, and out came the rat." He moved his hands from his mouth and nose, to hold them on either side of his face and make up-and-down motions with his fingers. "Whiskers. Those long, pointy front teeth. Definitely a rat. And then the note."

"Ah, yes, and now it becomes interesting. But you didn't keep the note separate, did you?" Saint Just asked, pulling on a pair of thin latex gloves he'd purchased at a drugstore some weeks earlier, when his own interest in television shows showcasing crime-scene investigation had been piqued. Preparedness was half the battle in crime solving, he believed. Brilliance was the other half, exemplary powers of deduction. His forte.

"It was already all wet, Alex," Socks protested, his hands over his nose and mouth once again. "You're just lucky I didn't just call the cops, or at least Steve Wendell. But then I figured you'd kill me if I did that, so I used my master key to get into Mr. O'Hara's storage locker and used his grabber to pick up everything—you ever see one of those, Alex? They're really cool. Old people use them to reach things on high shelves. When Mr. O'Hara broke his hip and couldn't reach stuff he had me go buy one for him, so I knew where it was, since Mr. O'Hara's been just fine this past year or more. Married again and everything, and by the looks of Mrs.

O'Hara, if he didn't know how to use his hips she'd find someone else who could, you know what I mean?"

While Socks was giving his informational talk on grabbers and . . . well, grabbers, Saint Just had been undoing the twist tie on the bag. Once opened, the smell, which had been unpleasant, became nearly unbearable. Still, Saint Just persevered, using a small flashlight to peer inside at the contents.

If there had been a return address on the box, the decomposing rat had made reading it impossible, and any address would most probably be bogus at any rate. Saint Just was luckier, however, with the note, as it had landed on top of the box and was relatively undamaged. Calling upon what he believed had to be awesome untouched powers he hadn't known he possessed, Saint Just reached into the bag and snared the note, then quickly replaced the twist tie and retreated with more haste than decorum from the storage cage.

"You're not going to throw that away?" Socks asked, or perhaps pleaded. "What am I supposed to do with it?"

"As having the rat bronzed or stuffed and mounted is probably out of the question, I suggest the Dumpster in the alley," Saint Just said, holding onto the note by the edges as he stood beneath one of the bare lightbulbs that hung from the ceiling. "Computer generated, I would say, which narrows down the suspects to all but about three people in the entire country. I imagine that, even in its present sorry state, there exists some way to extract fingerprints if there are any, but we'll leave that for now, shall we? More important, and more ominous, is the note itself."

Socks had commandeered Mr. O'Hara's grabber yet again and was busy inserting the foul-smelling green garbage bag inside a second, larger green garbage bag. "So you can still read it?"

"Yes, indeed. *Roses are red, violets are blue. This rat is dead, and you could be yourself.* How very charming. I believe we can rule out Will Shakespeare, Socks."

"Yeah, yeah, yeah. Are we done here? We can turn over all this stuff to Lieutenant Wendell now that you've seen it, right?"

"I think not, Socks," Saint Just said, slipping the note into a clear food storage bag he'd brought down to the cellar for just that purpose. Detecting had become more sophisticated since the Regency, but Saint Just considered himself nothing if not adaptable. "I'd rather Maggie not know about this, at least for the moment."

"She'll murder you," Socks said, shaking his head as the two of them headed back through the maze that was the basement of any building of any age in Manhattan, heading for the stairs.

"Yes. I'm shaking in my shoes at the prospect of her righteous anger, Socks. But let's think about this, shall we? A dead rat and some execrable poetry. All the makings of a one-off prank, don't you think? A disgruntled reader, most likely. As Maggie is wont to say, everyone's a critic. This particular critic simply had access to a dead rat. Now that he's vented his spleen, said what he had to say, that should be the end of it."

"And if it isn't?"

Saint Just stripped off the thin gloves and tossed them in a nearby empty bucket that didn't seem to have a purpose, so he gave it one: waste can. "If it isn't, we'll know soon enough. In any event, we will all—you, Sterling, and myself—stay very close to Maggie for the next three weeks, until she and Sterling and myself adjourn to New Jersey to celebrate Christmas with her family. If there are no more rats, and nothing untoward occurs, we can then probably safely conclude that this particular rat had no siblings."

"She's still going to murder you," Socks said, grinning. "Maggie doesn't like secrets. Hey, you didn't say—did you see how the guy signed the note?"

"No, I didn't." Saint Just stopped beneath yet another bare bulb and held up the note inside its plastic covering. "I don't see . . . oh, there it is. N . . . e . . . *Nevus*? What in bloody blazes is that supposed to mean? Nevus? A nevus is a—"

"A mole," Socks said brightly. "I looked it up. A bit of skin pigmentation or birthmark."

Saint Just tucked the plastic bag back into his pants pocket. "And you still think we should take any of this seriously, Socks?"

"No, I suppose not. Anyone who'd call himself a nevus has got to be a little crazy."

Saint Just stopped, turned around, looked at Socks. "Well, thank you, my friend. Now, for the first time, I do believe I'm a trifle worried. Yes, we'll all stay very close to Maggie, won't we?"

"And you'll talk to the lieutenant? You know, like without telling Maggie?"

"Possibly. Although I doubt there would be much of anything he could do unless the threat becomes more specific. I'll think on it, Socks."

"I saw him the other night," Socks offered carefully as they continued their way through the rabbit warren, Saint Just pausing only to pick up his sword cane, which he'd retrieved from his condo and brought downstairs with him. He felt naked without his sword cane, which was Maggie's fault, because that's how she'd made him.

"You saw the *left*-tenant? And why does that sound so ominous, Socks?"

"Well, he wasn't alone."

One corner of Saint Just's mouth curved upward.

"Really, Mr. Jackson. Feel free to expand on that most intriguing statement, if you please?"

Socks looked to his left and right, as if expecting Maggie to be hiding behind one of the stacks of boxes. "I'm not one to gossip. . . ."

"No. Definitely not, Socks. You are the soul of discretion and I commend you for that. Indeed, I am in awe of your powers of circumspection. And now that we have that out of the way—please go on."

The doorman grinned. "A blonde, and hanging on his arm like she couldn't navigate without him, you know? They were coming up out of the subway just as my friend and I were going down. We looked at each other, and then pretended we didn't see each other—you know how it is. But, man, did he look guilty. Do you think Maggie will be upset?"

"Only if she believes it wasn't her idea that she and the *left*-tenant stop seeing each other as anything but friends."

"You want to run that one by me one more time, Dr. Phil?"

Saint Just smiled. "Please, don't attempt to compare me with a rank amateur. It's simple enough, Socks. If Maggie stopped seeing Wendell as a beau, which I do believe she has already decided to do, that would be fine with her, as she's already realized that she thinks of him as a good friend, but no more. But for him to stop seeking her attention in favor of some other female before she can make that clear to him, let him down gently, as I believe it's called? No, then she'll decide she's just managed to allow what could have been the man of her maidenly dreams slip through her fingers. It's all in the timing, my friend, so we will not mention that you saw Wendell with another woman."

Socks shook his head. "Women. It's times like these that make me so glad I'm gay."

Saint Just chuckled, then frowned as he lifted a finger to his mouth, warning Socks to silence. "Someone's approaching."

A few moments later Maggie popped her head around the corner of a pillar, holding a shovel in what some might consider a threatening manner. She sighed, and put down the shovel, the look in her green eyes daring him to mention the makeshift weapon against Things That Go Bump in the Cellars. "Alex? I thought I heard someone talking. What are you doing down here?"

"Maggie, my dear," Saint Just said smoothly, inclining his head in acknowledgment of her presence. "One could reasonably ask the same of you. I was assisting Socks here with something he had to carry downstairs for Mr. O'Hara. You?"

"You carried something down here? Performed manual labor? Why can't I get a mental picture of that?" Maggie said, turning back the way she'd come, Saint Just and Socks exchanging "whew!" glances before they followed her. "But I'm glad you're here. I was upstairs, just sort of looking for something to do."

"Something such as unpacking your suitcases?"

"Yeah, right. My favorite thing," Maggie said, stopping in front of one of the many wire storage cages that lined the walls. "Anyway, I was looking around, and I suddenly realized that it's December, and we're not going to be here for Christmas unless we have a blizzard and they close the New Jersey Turnpike—which has never happened, even though I've prayed for it every year. I usually put up my Christmas decorations over the Thanksgiving weekend, so I can enjoy them longer, but we went straight to England from Jersey this year and now the condo looks naked, you know? So . . . who's going to help me get all of these boxes upstairs?"

Saint Just peered through the wire of the cage, at the

stack of boxes that seemed to be three deep and reach to the rafters. "Your holiday decorations are in those boxes? *All* of those boxes?"

"Yes, most of them anyway. And you love manual labor, right, Alex?"

Socks shrugged. "I'll go get the dolly, and we can use the freight elevator."

"Thank you, Socks," Maggie said as she slipped a key into the lock that hung on the door, then stepped inside the storage area. "My mother hates Christmas, you know. The Grouch Who Stole Christmas, every damn year," she told Saint Just, who was still mentally counting boxes.

"So, naturally, you adore the holiday to the top of your bent, correct?"

Maggie's grin was deliciously wicked. "You know me so well. Oh, Alex, you're going to love New York during the holidays. The tree at Rockefeller Center, the office party drunks ice skating nearby, the department store windows. Barneys is always so *out there*. Oh, that reminds me. I've got to get to Bloomie's for a cinnamon broom. I get one there every year—it's a tradition. I *love* the smell of cinnamon. And cookies. We're going to make *lots* of cookies."

She lifted up two fairly flat cardboard boxes and handed them to Saint Just. "You see, I've just decided something. Bernie's already got next year's hardcover in-house, so I'm just not going to worry about writing again until after the new year. You've been here for months now, Alex, you and Sterling, and I've never really shown you New York. So that's what we're going to do." She added a third cardboard box to the two Saint Just was holding. "Right after we decorate the living crap out of my condo. Come on, Alex, *smile*. It's Christmas!"